FREE CHOCOLATE

Latina culinary arts student Bo Benitez becomes a fugitive when she's caught stealing a priceless cacao pod from a heavily defended plantation. In the far future, chocolate is Earth's sole valuable export, and it must be kept safe from a hungry galaxy.

Now she's on the run, she quickly realises that she's a link that could lead to Earth's tasty treasure – a fact not lost on both her supposedly devoted (and supposedly human!) boyfriend and a creepy reptilian cop.

But when Bo sneaks onto an unmarked starship things rapidly go from bad to worse, for the vessel belongs to a species famed throughout the galaxy for eating stowaways. Fleeing across the spacelanes, surrounded by dangerous yet unnervingly hunky aliens, Bo starts to realise that the threat to Earth might be far more immense than she first thought...

"You had me at monkey robots."

ARIANNE "TEX" THOMPSON, AUTHOR OF THE
CHILDREN OF THE DROUGHT TRILOGY

AMBER ROYER

Free Chocolate

ANGRY
ROBOT

ANGRY ROBOT
An imprint of Watkins Media Ltd

20 Fletcher Gate,
Nottingham,
NG1 2FZ
UK

angryrobotbooks.com
twitter.com/angryrobotbooks
All because the lady loves

An Angry Robot paperback original 2018

Cover by Minchen Chen
Set in Meridien and Infinity by Argh! Nottingham

Distributed in the United States by Penguin Random House, Inc., New York.

Angry Robot and the Angry Robot icon are registered trademarks of Watkins Media Ltd.

ISBN 978 0 85766 750 2
Ebook ISBN 978 0 85766 751 9

Printed in the United States of America

9 8 7 6 5 4 3 2 1

To Jake, world's most awesome husband,
alpha reader and cheerleader.
You are the best!

Mario Benitez wiped the sweat from his face with his sleeve and watched the girl fall three floors. She looked so much like his oldest daughter Bo had at that age, baby-round face, huge dark eyes – only this child's eyes had gone wide with fear as she plummeted silently. She screamed as she hit the safety gel that kept her entrails from being splatted all over the sidewalk. The flames hadn't reached this room yet, though they would soon. Mario took off one glove and reached into the pocket of his heat-retardant suit for a proper handkerchief to wipe the salt out of his eyes before he lowered the faceplate, which he had lifted to reassure the girl when she'd been horrified by his bug-like appearance. His fingers encountered a softening mass of foil-wrapped chocolate. Damn.

He'd meant to put everything he'd found relating to that altered bar in his locker, but the call had come in and he'd never had a moment alone. He lowered the faceplate. No more life signs registered on the screen.

"Where do you think you're going?"

Mario didn't recognize the rough American voice, nor the figure he saw as he turned, encased as it was in a dove-gray, heat-retardant suit identical to his own. The man's faceplate glittered gold with reflected firelight from the hallway.

"Out. We're done here." Mario banged his palm against the

edge of the visor to make it refresh. Nada. Still no life signs. He should be alone.

"You don't really think you got out of the lab clean with those samples?" The guy reached behind his back and drew a small pistol, the design of which Mario had never seen. Something small fell out of the guy's pocket and rolled toward Mario's boot.

Mario swallowed, his throat raw from the smoke he'd already inhaled. Out of the corner of his eye, he could see the safety gel in place below the window. He might be small, but he was still encumbered by fifty pounds of firefighting gear. He'd never make a clean leap through the open sash before the guy shot him. The floor crackled as fire reached through near the corner. Dying didn't terrify him the way it once had, but failing in his mission, that made his stomach hurt. Still, all he had was his gear, and he'd dropped his axe out in the hall because the girl had been scared. He wasn't even close enough to blast the guy with foam.

The man took a step towards him, holding the gun carelessly in one hand. A few more steps, and he'd be in range. "Doesn't Benitez mean beautiful in Spanish?"

Mario blinked. "You're thinking bonito. I'm not getting out of here, no?"

"No. I'm sorry, but you should have considered this possibility when you became a thief."

The guy sounded rational, calm, while Mario's heart was trying to beat its way out of his chest. Maybe he was a little more scared than he'd been prepared to admit. Nobody wants to die. "So chocolate is this important? That you would kill to keep its secrets?"

"It's a shame that you won't get to say goodbye to your son, or those three bonito – that's how you say it, right? – daughters of yours."

Mario dodged toward the window, ready to jump after all,

but he felt a sting in the back of his arm as a dart pierced his suit, dousing his system with a drug that brought him to his knees mere inches from the sill. His heart filled with terror for his little girls, whom he could no longer protect. "Please," he managed, through doughy lips. "Por favor. Mi familia knows nada about chocolate except how to eat it." He fell over, fully aware but unable to move as the man removed the dart then searched his pockets and took the vials of green and yellow liquid, but left the chocolate on the floor, where it had already started to leak from its wrapper.

"Don't worry. Your family will be taken care of better than if you had lived. We wouldn't want to give anyone reason to look into your death. That drug will disappear from your system well before the fire cools, so though you are a traitor to your world, you get to die a hero. Is that irony or just coincidence? I never can figure that out." The man looked down at him, waiting for an answer. "Sorry. I forgot you can't speak anymore."

Mario wanted to protest that he wasn't a traitor, just a seeker of truth, a real buen hombre, but he was having enough trouble just breathing. He never meant to become a firefighter. He'd taken the job to get close enough to investigate HGB. As the man disappeared from his field of vision, Mario could already feel the heat of the floor building painfully in his ungloved hand, contrasting with the relative cool of the suit. Waiting for smoke inhalation to kill him while he roasted alive was going to take a long time, time filled with regret. He was leaving his wife, his vida, to raise four children alone. The chocolate started to bubble and then burn, the acrid smell even more unpleasant because it was supposed to have been something sweet.

CHAPTER ONE

Our waiter comes back, one tentacle wrapped around a barrel-style cheese grater. His black jacket looks almost comical, what with the dozen armholes, and the dark spots on his face that remind me of pimples. He hasn't got much of a neck, more an inward curve between his jaw and his chest. I sorta know this guy, who's a year behind me in culinary school. Last year, I interned at this same restaurant. He burbles something I can't quite comprender, then gestures toward our salads.

"No, thank you," I say in Lark. I wish he spoke one of the languages I understand, so he could crack a joke and relieve my nervousness. I'm on a double date with mi mamá, and we're meeting each other's respective boyfriends. Since she's a celebrity, we rated a back wall table with a floor to ceiling view of the beach, and a skylight meant for watching this planet's double sunset, which has just started.

There are still smudges on the window, where one of the Pops had rappelled down and peered in at us, taking holo until one of the restaurant's staff had gone up on the roof and cut the cable. The guy had gone sliding down the glass. He'd been OK, though, despite a fourteen foot fall. He hadn't been human, of course, but Mamá's famous enough that that holo will sell on the MegaGalactica channels, as well as Earth feeds.

Mamá beams at me and elbows her date. "See, Frank. I told you my Bodacious is brilliant." Of course she's impressed that I can speak Lark. She rarely leaves Brazil, let alone Earth. "Her other major is galactic linguistics. That is important in an interspecies kitchen, no?"

"Call me Bo. Por favor." I refrain from rolling my eyes at my own name as I spear a quizllen fruit onto my fork. I love these bite-size teal pear-shapes. Imagine a strawberry took a bath in honey then got all tied up in a rainbow. This salad is full of them, along with hand-carved zarroxes shaped to look like tiny peony blossoms. Gracias a Dios I don't have to make those anymore.

"Bonito Benitez." Frank rolls the words around in his mouth, affecting just the slightest hint of a Spanish accent. It should be bonita, and I'm still trying to decide whether to be enchanted or offended when he drops it and says earnestly, "Your father used to call you that. He told me bonito means beautiful, but he never mentioned what Benitez meant."

"It means blessed," Brill says, sliding my hand into his and giving it a squeeze. "And you're right, Bo is both beautiful and blessed."

Startled by Frank's revelation, I barely register the compliment. "You knew my father?" I turn to Mamá. "Mire usted?"

"Yes, really." Mamá puts a hand on the table and pats the cloth. "Frank and Big Mario worked together. Frank looked me up on the latest anniversary of your father's death, just to make sure I was doing OK. Qué bonito detalle!" She smiles over at him, showing him she really thinks he is that thoughtful. She has a beautiful smile, with straight white teeth and almost no lines to mar her generous mouth. I look a lot like she did at my age, with the same high cheekbones and slightly hooked nose. If I age half as well, I'll be contenta. "I made him stay and taste the flan I was testing for the Chocolate Festival marathon feed, and we started talking. What could be more bittersweet, pero romantic, no?"

No. I don't know what it is, but I don't like Frank. Something about him feels off.

"Tell Bo about Minerva." She turns towards me. "That is Frank's granddaughter."

"She's a great kid–"

I tune Frank out. Our waiter, whose name I still can't recall, is also handling the table next to ours, where a lady sits with three niños in high chairs. They look like triplets, all with the same protruding noseless faces and side-set eyes, their flat cheeks brilliant spots of red contrasting the bands of orange and blue crossing above and below their rubbery lips. He places solar system sundaes in front of each of the children. En serio. The most impressive desserts for sale anywhere on this planet are being wasted on toddlers whose palettes probably haven't developed past frozen pizza, no? One of the niños pops the sphere in his bowl with the back of a spoon, activating the nanite-induced dance that breaks the ice cream into individual balls that change colors and float up to form a spinning replica of the Larksis system, complete with a swirl of chocolate syrup for the asteroid belt and gold candy sprinkles clustering together for the suns. It's the most fabuloso chocolate sauce I ever tasted – and Chef won't divulge his secret, not even to students. I was planning to surprise Mamá with one of those, but now… no importa. *Never mind.*

Frank shakes his head. "Enough about me. I have questions for this young man." He points his fork at Brill. Near the front of the restaurant, a plate crashes to the floor, adding a jolt to his words.

Brill tilts his head, signaling he's listening, and at the same time showing off his chiseled jaw. Mi strawberry-blond hermoso from the planet Krom usually goes for tight T-shirts and black leather, but tonight he's wearing a starched white shirt and a tie with yellow birds all over it. The thick silver proximity band that ties him to his starship is visible at the cuff on his left wrist, but I don't think that could come off unless he cut it. I feel muy tingly inside. He's trying so hard to make a good first impression on mi mamá and her whatever-you-call Frank.

Frank's brow wrinkles, and his brown eyes sharpen hawk-like when he asks Brill, "Can a Krom lie?"

I half choke on that quizllen. "Mamá! Por favor!" Angling a stern look her way, I grab tighter onto Brill's hand. I was right not to like Frank. I drop my voice and switch to Krom, which I've learned pretty well. After all, I've been inspired. "Hanstral," *I'm sorry*, "about my mother's life choices."

Mamá's voice cajoles me inside my head, via the connection we've left open on the sublingual. *Ya basta, mija. Frank is just a little more blunt than the rest of us, no?* She's lived in Brazil since I was seventeen, but she still favors Spanish over Portuguese. So do I, to be honest. But whatever the language, I still don't appreciate her telling me to calm down.

Frank puts his fork on the table. "Now Bo, I'm not implying anything about your date. It's an honest question. I worked with a Krom when I did an exchange program. The iris changes occurred specifically according to her emotion at a given moment. I was curious, but I never got the nerve to ask. So how about it, Brill? Can you fake those feelings, or are people always going to know what you are thinking?"

Those patterns are as important to Krom non-verbal communication as body language – and just as telling. Brill's eyes right now are bright blue, tinged toward violet, showing he's happy and a little amused as he says, "That's a good question, Mr Sawyer. Not many humans are that observant." He leans forward and drops his voice, as though he's sharing a particularly juicy secret. "We can lie, but it takes practice. The part of our brain that shunts chemicals to the iris is buried deep in the subconscious. You concentrate on an old memory until you believe that the memory – the lie – is more important than the present. Much the same way humans lie, I believe."

I flex my larynx, adding nuance to my words as they flow from my neural patch to Mamá's. *Why's this guy so obsessed with lying? Dios mío, for all we know, Frank could just be another gold-digger after your dinero. Papá never would have called me bonito instead of bonita.*

She disconnects the sublingual, dismissing me with a mere thought. Mamá leans in closer, suddenly interested in hearing about Krom life, even though I've spent the past ten months trying unsuccessfully to tell her about the guy I'm dating. "So what happens if the subconscious is not working, mijo?"

"Like if I got knocked out or had a lobotomy?" Brill gives Mamá a wicked grin. "Then my irises would go clear and you'd see the burnt orange blood veins behind them."

I had always assumed those eyes proved Brill meant it when he said, oh, for instance, *Te amo*, meaning *I love you.*

I mean, I've seen Brill be less than truthful before, like when he had claimed not to remember seeing those niños who had put the dinkball through the Governor's window. Pero even then, his irises had turned purple, and then an embarrassed pink hue had crept in, though of course, the Governor's aide hadn't recognized it for what it was: Brill's neon-bright tell. Or so I thought.

What he's talking about now sounds muy diferente.

I finally manage to squeak, "So can *you* lie?"

"Not very well, Babe," he says without hesitation. Those blue irises dance through forest tones on their way towards the golden hue of our first kiss.

I smile and crinkle my nose at him as giddy sun-kissed love-bubbles dance in my heart.

Our waiter reaches over us and re-foams all our near-empty glasses at once. The foam dissolves into sparkling fruit-infused water.

Frank takes a sip. "The other thing that's always puzzled

me about Krom culture is how you claim honor by taking commodities from other people's planets. I mean, with us, it was Earth's first First Contact. Didn't that seem a little cowardly?"

My jaw clenches, and I have to relax my hands to keep them from doing the same thing. I don't look at Brill. Even from the Krom point of view, our first contact was botched. We weren't even supposed to know about it, let alone let it destroy us. Pero, it's not like it's mi vida's fault. He wasn't even *born* then.

Brill had told me a version of the story one night, when we were sitting on the hood of his rentacar, hand in hand, looking up at the stars towards his home world, the same night I had opened my eyes from kissing him and seen the first hints of gold in his gaze. The setting had been perfect for romance, with just a nip of fall in the air and the rushing waves of the Azlutian Ocean beating in the background like Larksis's heartbeat.

He told it like this. Once upon a time, before humans ever dreamed of traveling to the stars, when they crossed the world in sailing ships and felt like their globe was as immense as any galaxy, the people in the Arabian Peninsula had coffee. And while they were willing to part with bags of coffee for significant amounts of dinero, they always boiled the beans first, so they wouldn't grow. Men from Europe didn't want to pay such high prices, so in 1616, Dutchmen stole a few beans, making off with them well before they had been boiled. The Dutch shared their spoil with the French, but the climate in both countries was wrong, and the plants didn't do well.

Enter Gabriel Mathieu de Clieu, a Frenchman bound for Martinique, which had the right climate. When his government refused to give him clippings to found a plantation, he stole a pequeño coffee tree. Aboard ship, someone tried to steal the plant from him, and the precious green thing was torn apart. Pero, it survived. The ship was threatened by pirates, then bashed about in a storm, then stuck in becalmed seas. The journey took so long their fresh agua started running out. De Clieu kept the plant alive by giving it half his scanty water ration.

He was rewarded with a bountiful coffee plantation, pero coffee was too important for him to be able to keep it to himself. The Brazilians sent Francisco de Melo Palheta to French Guiana to settle a border dispute, where he managed to attract the governor's wife. At his going-away party, she presented him with a magnífico bouquet of flowers – and as a bonus, a few coffee seedlings hidden in the greenery. And so it continued, until coffee was being grown the world over, with ninety percent of the plants being direct descendants of De Clieu's stolen one. He is remembered not as a thief, pero as the man who gave coffee to the world.

By the time the Krom arrived on Earth, you could buy coffee seedlings on the Internet. After visiting a little café on the University of Iowa campus and falling in love with the stuff, that's exactly what one of them did. They catalogued it, cloned it and propagated it. And then somebody else bought it from them. So, now, the best Kona coffee in the galaxy is grown on one of the moons of Mardgar, almost ten thousand light years from Earth.

The Krom also took samples of sugar and tea and vanilla, and everything else they could catalog. But they messed up when it came to chocolate. Cocoa beans come from the cacao tree. Pero, working with limited knowledge of English, and in a hurry because of the riots that poofbanged as soon as they were discovered, the Krom First Contact party accidentally got their hands on a coca plant instead. That plant died in transit. Otherwise, they'd have imported a major drug problem.

Needless to say, Earth media didn't report it quite that way. Later, when they finally understood what had happened, our FeedCasters painted the entire Krom race as cowards and galactathieves. Pero, that's an unfair generalization. I've seen Brill be brave, seen him help people.

Whereas Frank, if he really was in the same company of firefighters as Papá, must have fled the weakening structure of the Yucatan HGB high rise the night the furnace blew, when there were still life signs inside. Talk about a coward. I call Mamá to say as much.

Qué? She sounds exasperated. I recognize the dangerous look in her eyes.

Uh oh. *Nada, Mamá.*

She hangs up on me. I try to call her back, but she's shut down her system.

Brill smiles at Mamá, pero it lacks his usual warmth. "Have you been watching the news? The colony called Farder was destroyed a few days ago, and the colonists massacred. Rumor is they'd discovered a plant people had started calling the fountain of youth. If it existed, it's gone now. They destroyed it, rather than share."

That may seem muy random, and nada to smile about, pero he's drawing a parallel between Farder and Earth, with our refusal to let anyone else have unfermented cacao beans. We'll let toda la galaxia – *the entire galaxy* – have chocolate, even cocoa nibs, as long as we keep control over how and where those products are produced. We keep the source for ourselves.

The criticism's not lost on Frank, who starts into a blustery defense of Earth's economy. Get him this passionate in front of a reporter, and an unexpected question could make him totally crashbang. That would be fun to set up, I realize I'm smiling. Mamá seems to know exactly what I'm thinking.

"Pardon, mi amor," she interrupts Frank, "but I need to powder my nose. I have a feeling Bo does too."

She grabs my arm. Her hands are strong from years of kneading bread dough, and her fake nails bite into my skin. I'm regretting the sleeveless burgundy dress I'm wearing as she drags me to the bathroom. My favorite chunky white earrings swing against my neck from the momentum.

As we walk past the other tables, I hear a guy say, "Is that Lavonda Benitez?"

Not Lavonda and Bo. No y no. Not anymore. I've been here, shadowpopped out on a backwater planet, long enough that the Pops have more or less forgotten me. And with them, the public.

"Mamá Lavonda!" a girl at that table calls, and she and the guy both wave.

Mamá gives them a smile and blows them a kiss. Without letting me go. Or stopping walking. I'm sure she'll sign autographs for them later – when she's not angry at me anymore.

Once we're inside the restroom, Mamá snaps, "Do not try to scare Frank off by putting him in front of the media, just because you do not like him. You say nada about him to the feeds, negativo or not. Comprendes?"

Heat rushes into my chest. "Mamá, I only tell the celebarazzi things like how unfair it is that the chocolatiers have to work an extra hour and a half without pay to cover the cost of the new planetary security system."

"I told you to stop those FeedCasts too, mija. Be careful what you say about the corporation that puts food in our mouths. They are not this evil conspiracy thing you keep making them out to be."

I arch an eyebrow. "Are you so sure about that?"

Mamá's FeedCasts – her entire career – have been sponsored by HGB, the monster corporation that sprouted in the wake of the First Contact War. While everyone else was trying to take over the chocolate belt by force, a group of choc-centric companies – primarily Hershey, Godiva and Bissinger, with a few marketing and management firms and a handful of botanists and independent chocolatiers thrown in – banded together. They quietly made proprietary trade agreements with other planets, at the same time selling stock to both chocolate producing and chocolate processing nations. Now, HGB is something more than a corporation, something less than a government, pero with an equal three seats on the Global Earth Court, which was set up to mirror the Galactic Court.

En breve, HGB is the face Earth presents to the galaxy, which makes it the most powerful organization on the planet, with private security forces that rival any army. At the same time, though, it needs people like Mamá because without global popular opinion, those that weren't invited to invest would jump at the chance to overthrow their control of chocolate.

Mamá rolls her eyes, though I have said none of this out loud. "This boy that you are with, he is filling your cabeza with his people's nonsense."

My face flushes unattractively in the mirror. "Do you not like Brill just because he's an alien?"

"I am trying to like this one. At least you have got your own man this time."

My breath catches. She's really bringing that up again, after all this time. "How many times do I have to tell you I didn't kiss your fiancé, OK? Hugo attacked me in the garden that night."

"And how many times do I have to tell you that I believe you?" She sighs. "The only boy you have ever been loyal to was that soccer player. I think he broke something inside you when he broke your heart. You will never be happy until you learn to stop running away when a relationship gets hard, no?"

For a second I can't speak. Or hear over the rushing sound in my ears. That soccer player, as she calls him, left me a long time ago, yet I can still recall every curve of his face. It's not fair of her to poke at so painful a memory. Finally I manage, "Unlike you? You've been engaged three times in the last five years."

She looks away. My barb landed just like I meant it to, pero I immediately want to stuff the words back into my mouth. She's been through a lot, too. Her voice softens. "Big Mario always was your hero, and losing him so young had to–"

"He was everyone's hero, Mamá. They saved twenty-nine people." The bureau determined later that HGB's negligence caused that fire. They'd installed a replacement furnace that couldn't handle the building's capacity, against the express wishes of the repairman involved. I sigh. "An HGB starwrangler approached me today after class. They want to make me the new spokesperson for a line of princess-themed chocolate bars. Something about Papá being able to trace his ancestry all the way back to Montezuma, and me being perfect for the role of the rightful Princesa de Cacao."

Mamá claps her hands in that little fluttering way she does when she's excited, the pain I'd just caused forgotten. "Fantástica, mija!"

"No, Mamá. It's insulting." I don't mention that the offer was more of a threat – stop the protest holos, or I get recalled to Earth. They could do it, too. Their influence over the Global Court – more weight than their three seats really should merit – means they could get my student visa cancelled without me even being able to file a protest. Resist, and they also threatened Mamá's feeds could get cut. They wouldn't really do that to her, though. She's too popular.

Still, I hate how she is always trying to get me back into show business. I travel halfway across the galaxy to live life away from the sleazarazzi, and she still doesn't get it. "Papá was no more gene-tied to Montezuma than Brill is to–"

"I cannot understand why you throw away every opportunity life hands you." She crumples the paper towel.

I adjust the straps on my dress and tilt my arm to the mirror. Mamá's nails have left bright red marks. "Then just be happy for me and Brill. That's an opportunity too, no?"

She breaks out a spare tube of lipstick, gesturing between me and the mirror. I could use a fresh coat, and I left my purse at the table. At least the unattractive flush in my cheeks is starting to fade. While I'm applying the deep pink shade, Mamá studies me. One of her eyebrows arches upwards. "Will you go out there and act interested in Frank's family?"

"No lo sé." *I don't know.* "Will you be nice to Brill?"

She puts a hand over mine and squeezes. "Just promise me you will be careful, mija."

I follow her out of the restroom, back toward our table. Brill and Frank's near identical hunched shoulders both look angry as they use their napkins to sop up a wine spill that has spread across the middle of the thick white tablecloth. I wish I could see their expressions instead of the back of their heads.

"Most Krom I've met wouldn't look twice at a human girl. What do you see in her?" Frank balls up his napkin and sets it at the edge of the table.

I put a hand on Mamá's arm, halting her. I desesperadamente want to hear this.

"I'm not most Krom." Brill growls out the words. "She thinks differently than I do, has such big dreams for so short a life. She... you know what? I don't have to justify love."

Frank turns his head, sees Mamá, smiles. "No, you don't."

Brill winces when he realizes I must have heard him. His eyes are still a muddy ginger, and that angry color takes a while to fade.

I set the empty bottle of Chateau Pandozale upright by the pile of wet napkins. "Now that's a waste."

"Tell me about it." Brill leaves his napkin on top of the spill. He smiles up at me, then casts a meaningful look at my mother. Looking back at me, he asks in Krom, "Reverae daiy?" *Are you OK?*

I slide into my chair. I reply half in English, "I'm fine, mi vida."

Frank stands and pulls out the chair for Mamá. I didn't think anybody did that anymore. "Bo, you must have dropped this on the way to the bathroom." He picks up a handheld phone and gives it to me.

Brill's irises darken back toward orange. "Bo doesn't carry a handheld. She's got a sublingual." Brill, of course, doesn't have any communication implants.

Oye! I hate watching guys fight. I hold up the device. "You're both right. Mira," *look*, "I borrowed my roommate's phone to holo some lectures for her from the class she missed this morning."

The handheld vibrates. I glance down at the screen. I had it in my purse for most of the day, and at some point it must have started silently going loco. My roommate's got seventy-four messages. I really need to get this thing back to her, but we've been not-quite crossing paths all day.

The waiter appears with our entrees each balanced in a different tentacle. He hesitates, like he's regretting the timing, but then smiles as much as his beaky face allows and places the plates on the table.

Brill draws in a long breath, far longer than a human could, closing his eyes. When he opens them again, the blue irises are clear and light, pure happiness. "That smells delicious."

"Sí, mi vida." I sample a bite of the catch of the day, which has been cooked in a lemony grez bud and wine sauce. The orange-tinged filet, flaky, almost buttery, practically melts against my tongue. I close my own eyes as I chew. Magnificísimo. I've been planning Mamá's visit for weeks, and the food part, at least, is going perfectly. Well, except for the upstaged sundaes.

The table starts to shake. Mamá lets out a little squeak.

I open my eyes and reach for my wine glass, downing the rest of it in one gulp. No use wasting any more Pandozale. "Don't worry, Mamá, we get tremors here todo el tiempo."

Seriously, *all the time*. Dust starts to fall from the ceiling. Around us, other diners use their napkins to shield plates of everything from fractal-shaped imported whole roast Romanesco broccoli to simple blissbean stew. There's hardly a lull in the conversation until a klaxon starts ringing outside. At nearby tables, heads turn toward the sound. I take another bite of my fish, no longer tasting the magnificent layers of flavor.

"Everything OK, Babe?" Brill looks up at the ceiling an instant before a tile falls onto the table next to ours, baring the plaster between the two skylights. One of those triplets starts crying, then it's all of them. Frank scoots his chair over and slides a protective arm around Mamá.

I try to still the panic bubbling through me, to remind myself that the situation's still not that serious, but I've never had to evacuate before, nunca. My hand that's holding my fork is shaking. I put the utensil down on the table. "Ay, that's the emergency signal. We need to get down to the beach, away from the buildings, pronto."

Frank's eyes go wide. "Isn't that dangerous? What if the quake causes a tsunami?"

I shake my head. "That can't happen here. Something to do with the planet's structure and the gravitational pull from all the moons." At least that's what I've been told.

Frank nods, just once. Mamá folds her napkin neatly at her place before she stands up, pero we're not going anywhere yet. We're stuck on the other side of a crowded restaurant, near where the hill drops away, backed up against a window that doesn't open – and other diners are already crowding the exit. Brill swirls a klavvigit in cocktail sauce as though the plate isn't jumping around. He pops it into his mouth as he stands up, scanning the room for another way out.

Our waiter is helping that family, pulling all three niños out of their highchairs simultaneously and depositing them into a busboy's cart. An enorme tremor hits, and he punches a few arm-tentacle "fists" onto the floor to balance the four thicker stabilizer limbs ineffectively suctioned against the carpet. The mother squeaks and wrenches the cart out of his grasp, rushing away from the windows. The jittering gets rougher and she trips. Brill still finds time to get another klavvigit into his mouth before he races over and catches her. After all, a Krom in a hurry looks like a blur. One of the kids lets out a wail and jumps off the cart, then ducks under a table, wrapping both arms around one of the table legs and half the cloth. Brill sets the lady back onto her feet then crawls under the cloth to retrieve the niño.

I cast a panicked glance out at the beach. We all need to get out there, to safety. Pero how? There's nowhere to go. The window glass quivers. Ay, no! I back away, cold terror knifing through my chest. Frank whips the cloth off our table, scattering silverware and klavvigit scampi. He wraps the fabric around Mamá and me, putting his body between us and the window.

The window shatters. My skin prickles in sick anticipation. I hold my breath, staring at the wine stain on the cloth, tensing against Frank's inevitable cry of pain. I may not like him, but I still don't want him hurt.

But it never comes. Instead, Frank laughs as he hugs us together through the cloth. "It's confettiglass."

A hysterical giggle rises in my throat. Claro está! *Of course.* In an area this prone to earthquakes, they're bound to take precautions in their construction, pero Frank didn't know that when he'd put himself between Mamá and danger. Tension starts draining out of my shoulders. Maybe he does have a few things in common with Papá, after all.

I struggle out of the white expanse, though everything's still shaking. The waiter moves over, using all twelve arm tentacles to pull away the cloth. He's burbling again, urgently, as he drops part of the cloth to the floor, using the freed tentacles to gesture to the front of the restaurant. He wants us to get in line to leave. I nod my understanding. As he pulls me to my feet, the skylight above us shatters, showering us with more confettiglass. Mamá screams. I look up. My heart freezes, and my shaky legs refuse to move. A segment of the frame is falling, the metal's edge thin and sharp, as the plaster around it gives way. Frank leaps toward me, pushing me out of the way. We crash together to the floor, and something heavy hits my hip.

"Ay!" I try to stifle the cry of pain, pero whatever he's got in his jacket pocket, it's going to leave a bruise.

The waiter's burbling turns into a brief screech as he dodges backwards, away from the danger, even as the frame from the next skylight falls apart, the four pieces dancing downwards like sushi knives, one segment separating the waiter's bow tie and collar, along with part of his neck, from the crisp white shirt beneath, another severing three flailing tentacles. The last two segments fall harmlessly to the carpet. Thick yellow fluid sprays the air as the guy collapses.

My chest goes so cold, I can't breathe. Finally gasping in air, I scramble to my feet and rush toward him, pero Frank grabs me around the waist, turning me around so I won't see the worst of it. I try to push his hand away. My throat has closed up in a gran lump. It's hard to force words out. "We have to help him. Por favor."

Brill climbs out from under the table, managing to pull the wailing niño off his neck and hand it back to its mother. He rushes too fast to follow over to the fallen waiter. When he gets around to the guy's bow tie, he sucks air through his teeth, but his eyes don't change. He doesn't even flinch. "It's too late." Mi vida bows, gives the corpse a closed-fist salute. "He got a family to safety and was trying to help us too. It's a noble death."

Qué? How can he be so calm? The guy got killed, right in front of us. I'm about to hyperventilate, and he's just standing there.

Frank finally releases me. "Your Krom is right."

Has everybody gone loco today? Brill wraps an arm around my shoulders, leading me away from the body. I'm trembling, and my legs feel weak even as adrenaline douses my system. Mi vida's the only thing holding me up.

I look back at those severed tentacles, lying like so much calamari on the floor. Sorrow thickens my throat, leaves my stomach leaden. "I can't even remember his name."

"It's going to be OK. You can grieve once we're safe. I'll help you, I promise." Brill squeezes me close, then he lets go and leans through the shattered window. "The wall slopes out. We have to get out of here before this whole place collapses."

I look back at the crowd at the door, including the mamá trying to block her niños' view of our sad little circle. Something must be preventing their exit. I kick off my pumps, focus on moving forward instead of curling into a sobbing ball of mess. "That would certainly be faster."

Mamá casts a distressed look at her high heels.

"Don't worry, Lavonda." Franks holds out his hands. "I can piggyback you down."

"Oh, Frank." She touches his arm. "De veras? Are you sure?"

Frank pulls her around behind him. "Just keep your arms on my shoulders instead of around my neck, and we'll be fine."

I look back at the body, almost expecting it to move, like death was all just a gran mistake. It doesn't. It's not like we can bring it with us, but I still hesitate. This feels wrong. How can we leave the guy sprawled like that?

Pero, we do. Brill jumps out the window, landing lightly on the sidewalk. I, on the other hand, have to climb down fourteen feet. Halfway into the descent, my handbag escapes from under my arm. As it hits the pavement, the phone pops out. The case cracks off before the handheld even bounces to a halt. I'd told Kayla to go with the stronger one, but she'd said it looked ugly. Claro está, now, I'll be the one who will have to replace the whole device. I hope those messages weren't urgent.

Brill examines the phone then pockets it. He meets me as I reach the ground, putting his hands around my waist to lift me across the pavement onto the sand. He leans in, almost like he's going to kiss me, and whispers into my ear, "Careful, Babe. I found a bug in the phone case."

"Qué?" I suck in a shocked breath, but Brill puts a finger to my lips.

Frank handled that phone, but what possible motivation could he have for bugging me? Why would anybody bug me? I'm barely a second-rate celeb. Pero then again, it's not my phone. Maybe somebody's stalking Kayla. Either way, it can't be bueno.

Frank gets his feet on the ground and puts Mamá down. Then he bends to retrieve my bag. He hesitates, then picks up a small white silicon circle from the pavement. "What's this?"

"You put it in the phone case. Right, su?" Brill's eyes have turned violet, and his voice seems equally amused as he addresses Frank informally as *su*, which is basically *man* or *dude*. He really looks like he thinks it's funny how bad Frank must be at planting bugs. A chill goes through me. Mi vida lied about being a bad liar.

"I did no such thing." Frank places the circle back on the ground and asks Mamá for one of her shoes. When she hands one over, he smashes the circle with the spiked heel.

"You boys and your machismo." Mamá's trying to be playful, but her voice shakes. She kicks off her other shoe, and the four of us make our way onto the beach, following a stream of people towards the stretch of land where couples sometimes go after dark to watch the stars or the phosphorescent fish in their tidal pools. Even though neither of the suns have completely set, someone has built a fire out of driftwood.

One of my teachers, a native Larksissian, waves all four of his hands at me. In Lark he tells me, "Not to worry, Bo. I've never heard of anybody dying from one of our little shake-ups. The buildings are strong, and all that. Just enjoy the party!"

"Party?" I repeat in English. I'm feeling the opposite of partyish. Somebody did just die, though my brain is having trouble accepting the reality of it. Somebody whose name I can't remember. How could I explain that to a teacher I respect? Besides, he looks so contento. Let somebody else ruin his day.

"What did he say?" Frank asks, obviously not understanding Lark.

Ahead of us, levitating trays are floating through the crowd. Another tremor hits. Still, people pluck appetizers and plastic cups off the levs, laughing as they try to get the food into their mouths despite the shaking ground, even as they have to lift their feet to keep from sinking into the beach. "He said don't worry, and enjoy the party."

"Can't. I have to find someone official to whom I can report the death. You guys stay here." Frank's being responsible so the rest of us can push the horror away, process it as we're able. I feel ashamed at how badly I'd misjudged him.

"This looks like my kind of people!" Mamá drops the high heels and runs across the sand. She processes things mainly through denial.

"Mamá! Over here!" It's a group of her fans. I'm pretty sure it's the tour that came from Earth just because they heard she'd be here. It's not the first time. When your whole planet's economy centers around something edible, foodies are more popular than rock stars. She's never done anything other than cooking feeds, but she's in everybody's kitchens, making them feel like part of one gran Earth-centric family – while at the same time assuring them that the rest of the galaxy is seeing Earth in a positive light. It used to be weird to hear random people calling her Mamá, but you get used to it.

CHAPTER TWO

I climb the steps to my dorm and scan myself in with my thumbprint. The damage isn't so bad here, just a few new cracks running up the otherwise smooth gray walls. Our building's RA, Chestla, stands in the lobby, re-programming the signs to show an ad for a dorm party after the gran event tomorrow where Mamá's getting an honorary degree. A broom leans up against the red sofa in the middle of the room, angled over a pile of plaster crumbs and broken ceramics. The sofa's velvety fabric looks like somebody sifted baking soda over it. Whatever else jounced out of place, Chestla's already put right, except for a lone cookbook, which lays splayed open on the tile, pages mushed. Claro está, it's one of Mamá's, her face smiling up at me from the back cover. I pick it up and straighten out the creases as best I can, then I put it on the long wooden coffee table next to Chestla's stack of math puzzle books.

"Hi, Bo!" Chestla smiles at me, which always makes piel de gallina – *chicken skin* – pucker my arms. Chestla's from Evevron, where her people are the top predators. The canine teeth I can only describe as fangs, plus the vertical-slit pupils set into reflective green irises, contrast with her pert nose, freckled cheeks and cheerleaderish "Go-Dorm" personality. Her honey-blonde hair, thick and wavy, hangs a bit past shoulder length. She's got purple glitter-polish on her claws... er, nails.

She bounds over to me. I freeze. It's not exactly voluntary.

"Hola, Chestla!" I work my lips into a smile. She addressed me in Lark, pero she's trying to learn a few words of her charges' native languages, so she's always bugging me to speak Spanish.

"Could you remind Kayla that visitors all have to be out by ten?" She looks down at her hands, stretching her fingers. "When I do it, there's too much noise."

Qué? Kayla rarely has company. Now I'm curious.

"No hay problema." I've witnessed more than one guy running screaming down the hall after catching sight of Chestla, and I don't particularly want to see that again tonight, not when I need a hot shower and un poco alone time with *Love Hurts*, my favorite flufferiffic soap opera – a guilty pleasure Brill knows nada about.

I try not to watch holos with Kayla, either, because she always puts her frío feet up on the couch, and if they touch me I wind up freezing, covered with all the couch blankets, while somehow, by the end of the feed, Kayla's fine. And half the time she's reading a novel and not paying attention anyway.

Chestla turns away. My muscles relax, just un poco. I feel sorry for her. She tries muy hard to be everybody's friend. I wonder how she got the RA job in the first place. Aren't they supposed to choose someone motherly that you feel comfortable bringing problems to? Maybe the HR guy thought if he didn't hire her, she might eat him.

I climb five flights of stairs because I'm afraid to get into the elevator, even though it looks like it's working. Claro, what if there are aftershocks? I stare down at the hand-woven runner rugs that line each flight, trying to find context in the complicated patterns for what just happened.

Once I reach my floor, my heels click too loudly on the slate tile as I walk down the empty hallway. Each step echoing through me, thickening my throat, bringing heat to the back of my eyes. I'm still picturing the side of the restaurant where our table had been. It's surreal how that part of the structure had slid down the hill, spilling metal and wood onto the sand, not long after we had made it to the beach. No one else had died. Everybody said it was a freak accident, that I shouldn't blame myself, that there hadn't been a quake this bad in thirty years. Still, if Mwooh, better known as Noodles, hadn't stopped to help me, he'd probably be alive right now. What am I supposed to do with that? Qué? Qué? Qué?

I swipe my thumb at the door. When it opens, Kayla's sitting with her back to me. Two mugs are on the round mahogany-like table, on either side of a mostly-eaten pie. Kayla would never feed Brill or his friends, nunca, so the second mug must be for someone else. I hesitate, not wanting to interrupt a date.

Only, Kayla's crying.

Kayla's brother comes out of the kitchen carrying our coffee pot, already half-empty. He makes eye contact with me as he refills her mug. Stephen's like a male version of my roommate, with the same blue-undertoned light beige skin, wide set eyes and curly dark hair, though his has been cropped so short you can only see the curliness on top. His eyes are red-rimmed, like he's been crying too.

Kayla looks up at me, then she dissolves into tears again. I rush over and give her a hug. She must have known Noodles better than I would have thought. I try to think of something comforting to say. "It's hard to lose an amigo. Was he in one of your classes?"

She blinks, momentarily shocked from her sobs. "Who?"

My arms around Kayla suddenly feel stiff and awkward. "Noodles?" Obviamente. Who else would I be talking about?

She just looks at me like I'm speaking another language – and not one of the eight she knows.

Stephen waves me into the kitchen, through the open area that connects that space to the living/dining area. He puts the coffee pot back onto the burner. One of the cabinets has come open, spilling spice containers all over the speckled granite countertop behind him. The flour container's wound up in the sink. He gives me a sickly smile. "It's been too long, Bo."

He doesn't mean it. We dated that one time, for a couple of weeks, right up until he met the girl that would become his ex-wife. Even though he took a gig on this side of the galaxy to be close to his twin after his marriage broke up, he only visits here when he knows I'm going to be gone.

I fake-smile, playing along. "Sí. It has."

I eye the table. That pie had been a full double-crust masterpiece when I'd left, but it has now been subtracted to a single piece. The math doesn't add up. According to Kayla, Stephen's wife used to keep him on a strict diet. He looks like he's still following it. Plus, Kayla always wants to split a piece of dessert with me, instead of eating all of it herself.

I point accusingly at the pie plate. "What happened here, chico?" I try to keep my voice too low for Kayla to hear. "That's not even chocolate."

"There's been an accident," Kayla wails. Ay! She heard me anyway. She breaks into a series of snuffling noises. A ball of dread sits like raw dough rising in my stomach. Whatever she's going to say next, I don't want to hear it.

Stephen pats her shoulder, then lets her go. "Our grandparents were on a SeniorLeisure tour, headed out towards Proxima Centauri. Their transport vessel was blown up."

"Qué?" I'm too dazed to process this.

Stephen runs both hands across his face. "I'm not up to going through it all again. If you want the details, they're all over the feeds." He picks up his mug and stares down into the coffee's darkness. "I just came here to tell Kayla in person, and to escort her to the funeral. We couldn't reach her on her handheld."

"Oh, Kayla, lo siento." I really am sorry. She's always been close to her family, and she looks broken. There's more pain arcing through me for her right now than I had felt for Mwooh, even when I'd been looking at his corpse. Or maybe it's just that this new ache is sitting on top of that one, compounding it. "Are you sure it was their vessel?" I realize as soon as the words are out of my mouth how estúpidas they sound. Stephen wouldn't have come all this way from the mines on Larksis 2 if he hadn't verified the manifest.

Kayla pushes her chair back from the table. "I need to take a shower."

After she has gone, Stephen sits down in her spot. "We already talked to the school. They're going to let her make up the work when she gets back as an accelerated crunch semester. I was hoping you'd be good enough to record notes for her."

"Sí, of course." I'll replace Kayla's broken phone while she's gone, and present the new one full of homework holos. Feeling better now that I have a useful plan, I pour myself a cup of coffee. This is going to be a long night. "How long will she be away?"

"A couple of months." He pulls the pie plate to him, picking up a few crumbs on his fingertip. He looks at them, like he's going to eat them. Then, changing his mind, he drops the crumbs back onto the plate and pushes it away again.

Crunchmester indeed. That will only leave a couple of weeks until the end of the regular semester here at school. Though Kayla's younger than me, we started at the same time, which means that after this one we both have one semester left until graduation. "It's a long trip home, no?"

I haven't been back to Earth since I left for school.

"They're going to delay the funeral until we get there. Kayla was close to her grandmother."

"I know." I look at the closed baño door, wondering how long she's going to be in there. "Will you be OK if I watch the holo? Before she comes back, right?"

He closes his eyes and sighs. "I'll go downstairs. She said some of her clothes are in a dryer in the laundry room."

When he says the word *downstairs*, I remember Chestla, and

the ten o'clock curfew. Ay no! I groan. "Have you met the RA?"

Stephen opens his eyes. "Who?"

"The Resident Assistant. She told me to remind Kayla that visitors have to be out of the building by ten." I check the clock on the wall behind our sleek hunter green sofa. It's already five after. "If you talk to her about it, maybe she'll make an exception." I wonder what his oh-so-recent ex-wife would think about him staying under the same roof with his oh-so-brief ex-girlfriend. "Or maybe she can get you into one of the guest houses."

The clock's the only thing that's still where it belongs on that wall. Kayla's collection of antique Jell-O molds lies scattered. The oversized bunch of grapes and the one shaped like an arched fish are on the sofa, the rest of the delicate copper pieces on the floor. De ordinario, she would have freaked at the thought of one of them getting dented, but today, nobody's even bothered to pick them up. Stephen and I take a few moments re-hanging them on their little brass nails before he heads downstairs. We don't talk. It's awkward. After I deactivate the lock so he can get back in, I turn on the householo and direct it onto the dining table. It isn't hard to find a FeedCaster talking about the accident.

"...on its way to Wilomia fired upon and destroyed a tourist vessel headed for the same destination. The tour, which left the Greegarrngy Refueling Depot at 0200 this morning, was apparently suffering from a communications glitch."

The holo switches to a skinny black guy with dark circles under his eyes. A floating banner labels him Kaliel Johansson, pilot of the HGB vessel *Nibs Delight*. He's only been recorded from the waist up, so he looks like he's growing out of the pie on the table. Kaliel blinks a couple of times. It sounds like the projection has been clipped out of a longer holo. "And they were flying in my radar blind, which is a classic pirate maneuver. I attempted to contact them three times, requesting vessel identification. There was no response."

As Kaliel speaks, a poll appears by the side of his head, with moving bars representing how many FeedCast users think he is *TriggerHappy!* versus how many would label him a *Hero of Earth*. Right now, the bar for *TriggerHappy!* shades in at about seventy percent. I decline the holo's request that I vote.

He continues, "My screens flashed, and the ship registered that I had been hit."

A voice from somewhere at the edge of the holo asks, "What did that turn out to be?"

Kaliel's voice shakes. "A piece of space junk. When they looked at the impact marks on the *Nibs*, the accident reconstruction scientists said I probably hit an old fuel cylinder, but I believed I'd been fired upon by a vessel that had been following a parallel course for several hours and would not communicate. So I returned fire."

The FeedCaster poofbangs back into the middle of the screen, obliterating Kaliel and his contrite, quavering chin. She smiles, her heavily made-up eyes horror-happy as she says, "Despite the outcry from the families of the seventy-two senior citizens, HGB predicts that Johansson will be exonerated. He has been assigned to duties at one of the Triumvirate's many factories, as his superiors feel he may be suffering from post-traumatic stress that would make it unsafe for him to continue flying."

I spill my coffee trying to set the mug onto the flat surface. *Estás jugando conmigo! You've got to be kidding me.* That space jockey scuttlepunched a transport full of grandmothers, and he didn't even get fired? No wonder Kayla's a wreck. Even I feel like I have the right to be outraged. Noodles' face flashes in my mind, somehow making it more personal. The two accidents are tangling together in my head, even as the coffee spreads across the table, threatening to drip over the edge.

My sublingual rings.

Hola? I'm expecting it to be Brill, or maybe Mamá. After all, it's getting late, and I have a private unlisted number.

Miss Benitez? a chirpy voice beams directly inside my skull. It's obvious that the woman attached to the voice doesn't even know me.

Sí. I feel the little hairs on the nape of my neck rising.

I'm with FeedCast JustCuzYurParanoid. We're an independent, operating from an undisclosed location offplanet. We specialize in conspiracies – and in keeping our sources anonymous. I just got through examining the ship's manifest for that tour vessel that exploded, and I noticed that your roommate had family members aboard. Do you honestly believe that becoming the face of chocolate will prevent war, or are you being forced to participate in yet another HGB coverup of one of its mistakes? Or was Johannsson acting alone, like the group of assassins who killed Archduke Ferdinand and started World War I?

I know nada about me becoming anything, and I don't give quotes to reporters. I hang up on her, as the implications hit home. This isn't just about Kayla's grief.

One ship, jangleblasted in the depths of space, might not seem that important, no? But when you put it in context, it's horrifying. One of HGB's own estúpidamente taking lives could be seen as undisputable evidence of incompetence. Which could weaken their offplanet trade agreements. Which, when there are already rumors of a coalition ready to start a Second First Contact War, could be just the spark needed to send Earth into a massive fireworks display all over again.

The FeedCaster keeps talking as I grab a towel and swipe it through her feet.

Stephen opens the door, holding a laundry basket I've never seen before. His complexion has gone the color of goat cheese. Ay, no! I forgot to warn him about the Chestla Effect.

I shut off the householo, just as the image changes to a ship in space taken from the point of view of the *Nibs Delight*. Piel de gallina rises on my arms. They were going to show it blow up. I look over at Stephen, checking to make sure he didn't see that.

I force a smile. "Don't worry. Underneath the claws, Chestla's just a big sweetie."

He blinks, still otherwise motionless in the doorway. "When you talk to her, do all your nerves stand on end and you have a nearly uncontrollable urge to pee?"

"Not exactly." I toss my coffee-saturated towel into the sink. "Pero, close. I think we all experience the prey instinct in our own special way, no? Did she say you could stay?"

"She asked me out." Stephen sounds like he's accusing me of something. Slowly, he pries his hand off the doorjamb. He walks stiffly across the room and sets the laundry basket down on the table. I recognize some of Kayla's clothes. "She kept saying how sorry she was for my loss, and would it make me feel better if we went somewhere and got a cup of coffee and talked."

I grab a fork and attack the pie. "That sounds like she was just trying to be nice. You really think she was asking you for a date?"

"When I told her Kayla and I are leaving tomorrow, she suggested dinner when we get back. She even gave me her number." Stephen fumbles in his pocket and pulls out a slip of hot pink paper. In bright green glitter ink, there's Chestla's name and number. She's made little smiley faces out of the *e* and the *a*.

That makes me smile for real. "Maybe you should call her. She might not be so intimidating over the phone." Stephen's not a bad guy. After what happened, he's definitely not for me, pero I want him to be happy. "I think since everybody is so scared of her, she gets un poco lonely."

Stephen makes a noncommittal grumbly noise. The shower turns off, and a few minutes later, Kayla emerges wearing her fluffiest pink pajamas. She's got her hair wrapped in a towel. Though her eyes are still red and puffy, she looks a lot better. "You're not going to do it anymore, right?"

"Qué? Do what?" I spear another bite of pie with my fork and pop it into my mouth.

"You're not going to represent HGB in those holomercials. Not after… this."

"I already told them no – nada, nunca, absolutely no way."

"Not according to what I saw." Stephen activates the holo, quickly switching it to a blank holding screen after fragments of shuttle explode across the table. When he gets the feed archive he wants, he pulls a holo from *FeedCast OfficialHGB*. A trim brunette starts talking in Portuguese about how I'm coming home to be their Princesa.

I had entered into a blanket contract with HGB back when I was a teenager, when I appeared for two seasons on *Mamá Cooks at Home*. While it wasn't exclusive, it did say they could cast me at will for ten years. It was un poco loco that I'd signed it without having anyone look over it, pero I'd never imagined they'd enforce the future work option clause as a form of blackmail. It won't be just a public retraction of the protest feeds. They need me to say that while my roommate's loss is unfortunate, the Triumvirate is doing the best it can to give Earth a decent place in the galaxy. And if I don't, it's possible they *will* yank Mamá's feeds.

An insistent tapping comes from the window. We're pretty high up. Maybe it's a bird. I cross the room to look. I make out mi vida's face pale against the surrounding shadows. I blink in confusion.

"Brill?"

He mimes with one hand that I should unlock the window.

I slide open the sash. "What are you doing out there?"

"I'm trying to get you to let me in." He's clinging to a climbing rope that ends with something dark shot into the building's roof. He swings closer, grabbing onto the sill. He winces, like the sudden stop jolted his arm.

I can't think of anything to say. I finally come out with a

lame, "That had better not leave a hole." Though today, I could probably blame the damage on the quake.

"Sorry, Babe. If it does, I'll fix it." His face has gone chalky in a way that's muy alarmante. "Can we just talk about it once I'm not stuck out in the open? I'm way too vulnerable out here."

"Don't do it." Kayla gestures with her coffee cup. "Maybe Krom can't come in unless they're invited."

I give her a withering look, then feel guilty for not being more supportive. Then I decide that no, despite her loss, she doesn't have to be *that* way about mi hermoso. I love my roommate like a sister, but empathy's not exactly her special dish. I turn back to Brill. "You know you're always welcome here."

As he climbs inside, I can see that his irises have gone solid black. I can't even differentiate the pupil. He tugs at the rope, and it comes free. The grappling hook on the end folds up like a reversed umbrella. Where'd he even get that thing?

"Thanks, Babe." He starts coiling up the rope. "But what have I ever done to you, Kayla Baker?"

"Nothing." Kayla looks down at her coffee.

Kayla's from Iowa, which is where the Krom First Contact party had initially landed, and she takes the invasion of her state very personally, even though it happened a couple of decades before she was born. She's usually not muy vocal about it, just does her best to avoid Brill, makes civil conversation with him when she has to. I don't think Brill has ever realized how much she dislikes him.

"No, really. I want to know." Brill drops the rope on the side table, then makes his way over to Kayla, pulling out a chair and sitting down opposite her. His irises slowly fade into a still-worried gray.

"To me specifically? Nothing." Kayla puts down her mug and looks Brill straight on. "But I don't like the way you talk about

Earth, and I don't like the nightmares Bo has sometimes after she's been out with you, and honestly, I can't stand spiders."

"Shtesh." *Geesh*. Brill blinks, lilac curiosity tinting the gray. "I'm not a fan of spiders either, but what's that got to do with anything?"

"Kayla, don't," Stephen says.

She ignores the warning tone in his voice. "That's ironic, given what they found after first contact, when our scientists took one of you guys apart."

"Kayla! Por favor!" I can't believe I'm yelling at her when she's just been crying, but that's mean. She's talking about Krom book lungs, which are a lot like what Earth arachnids have that allow them to survive on minimal oxygen. There are a few other physiological similarities between Krom and spiders, in the heart and the nervous system, enough to fuel the panic that followed first contact, but from the outside, Krom guys look just like Earth guys. Most people don't even remember the comparison, so it's not surprising it didn't immediately occur to Brill.

He gives her a thin smile. "You wonder why I'm not more enthusiastic about Earth, su? If one of your people landed on Krom and was killed in a mob riot, we'd have taken his body home, or at least given him a decent burial, not made him the subject of an alien autopsy feed to be replayed on a loop for a decade." Brill crosses his arms over his chest, and as he moves he winces again. Did he sprain something? "I grew up with that guy's nephew. His family never did get his remains back."

If it hadn't been for *that guy* – or rather the space phone in his pocket – the whole first contact thing might have blown over. I mean, sí, we knew suddenly that *we are not alone* and all of that, but what were we going to do about it? Our tech wasn't anywhere near what we needed to go star-hopping to look for other civilizations. But with that phone, we could at least call out. And the Krom were answering our questions. Not that they were coming back to give us a tour of the galaxy.

By 2073 – a year after first contact – Earth's telcom whizzbang-gurus had modeled Krom tech to speedbuild a network of satellites and scopes, with which they managed to get the attention of a Galactic Inspector – a star-hopping cop answerable only to the Galactic Courts – who was passing through the area in pursuit of an escaped convict. He captured his quarry and then returned, giving Earth the contact information for his superiors, along with a map of known planets. That would have been the end of it, except that the crew at Cape Canaveral gave the Galactacop a Harry and David gift basket, including chocolate covered blueberries. Within weeks, the Inspector's friends showed up, eager to buy more.

"What are you thinking about, Babe?"

I guess I zoned out. Brill shifts and orange blood smears from the sleeve of his black jacket onto his wrist. I look closer. There's a long, thin gash in the leather.

Sucking in air through my teeth, I gesture toward the injury. "Qué pasó? What happened?"

Brill looks down at his arm. "It's just a scratch. Somebody took a shot at me while I was getting back into my ship. It was dark, and he was shooting from sniper range, but..."

"Pero what?" Dios mío, I hate it when he trails off like that. Especially when his words are so upsetting. Nobody I know has ever been shot before, no?

He hesitates. "I'd almost swear it was Frank."

My chest goes cold. "Mamá's new boyfriend Frank?" The one I've decided I'm going to make myself like? My brain itches to call Mamá and make sure she's OK. But I need to clarify what he means by *almost*.

Brill shrugs, then grimaces as his arm moves. That's worse than a scratch. "Like I said, it was dark. But if I hadn't dropped my key fob, I wouldn't be here talking to you right now."

"Somebody really *shot* you?" Kayla squeaks. She turns to me. "I told you this guy's dangerous. If you keep hanging out with him, somebody might start shooting at you, too."

"Ga. This has nothing to do with Bo." Yet from the worried look he gives me, I'm not so sure. "When you carry high-value cargos, these things happen."

Kayla crosses her arms over her chest. "Not to me. This school is supposed to be a beach resort, not a war zone. Then you show up with a gunshot wound, wanting to hang out like everything's normal."

His eyes go an embarrassed apricot shade. "Speaking of that. I think the shooter's still watching my ship, which means I have nowhere to bunk. Can I stay here tonight?"

Kayla's staring at me. Mi vida's injured and needs my help. I can't say no, choose her over him, even after the big deal she's just made.

I glance over at Stephen. Esto no puede estar pasando. *This cannot be happening.* Kayla and I share the suite's single, tiny bedroom. After we go to bed, my boyfriend and one of my exes are going to be left alone to compare notes about me. And I never told mi vida that I'd gone out with my roommate's brother. The lump of dread in my stomach is turning acidy. I shrug. "Stephen's got pedírselo primero," basically *dibs*, "on the couch."

Brill takes off his jacket. "The floor's fine with me."

"Not until after I get that cleaned up." I nod towards his sleeve, ripped where the bullet skated through, soaked with iron-rich burnt-orange Krom blood. I pull him into the bathroom and make him sit on the toilet while I dig around in a drawer for antiseptic and bandages.

"I'm still worried about what you said about Frank. What possible reason could a firefighter have for shooting you?"

He pulls away from me, looking down at his injury. "I don't know. But I plan on finding out. If he is dangerous, we don't want him to know we suspect him. So don't tell your mom."

Fear zings through my heart. "Isn't she in danger?"

"I don't think so. Ga. He seems genuinely fond of her." He makes a face. "He was openly hostile to me."

It's all frou-frou in here, with a pink glitter-infused toilet seat, a ruffled shower curtain, and about a dozen heart-shaped candles. The deal had been Kayla got to decorate the bathroom, so I got to do the bedroom. I find the bandages, an enorme box in assorted sizes. They're pink, too, with a gran lip print in the center of each one. "Lo siento about what Kayla said. Her abuelos died in that accident that's all over the feeds. She's angry at the universe today."

"I get that." Brill strips off his shirt then uses the clean part of it to wipe away some of the blood so I can take a closer look at the wound. "And I can see her logic. Sort of. To Kayla, I'm responsible for her grandparents' death because if First Contact hadn't happened, none of the other stuff would either. I didn't realize they were aboard. I'm sorry I pushed her into talking."

He must have seen the news before he'd gotten into trouble. Pero, if he'd seen the ads about me, he would have said something, no?

"It's not just the accident that has her all emotirated. HGB is trying to get me involucrado in their media spin-wash." I soak one of the cotton rounds I use for removing eye makeup with hydrogen peroxide and start swabbing blood off Brill's arm. "You know how Povika once said that sometimes you have to do wrong things for the right reasons?"

"You read the *Codex of the Beneficent Ideals*." His voice sounds like what I'm doing hurts, but he looks happy. Krom are still raised to want to be heroes, to sweep through the worlds, bettering those worlds as they go. He'd given me a print copy of the book he lives by.

"I got through part of it. You know I speak Krom better than I read it." I throw the round in the garbage and wet a new one.

Brill hadn't recommended the cheeselation into Universal. Apparently, they got all the nuances wrong. "I think by making me their spokesperson, HGB has handed me what I need to get justice. When–"

Brill's eyes go wide, and superhumanly fast, he clamps a hand over my mouth. He lets go, then takes a device out of his pocket and runs it along all the walls. He's looking for bugs.

The diodes on the top of the box don't light up. Satisfied with whatever he doesn't see, he nods for me to continue.

I speak more softly. "When they take me in to do the filming, I'll be inside headquarters. I can get you enough cacao samples to break the monopoly." My heart has accelerated over what I've just proposed. We are, after all, talking about corporate theft – and treason. On a global scale, punishable in the Global Court.

It is just as unthinkable for an Earthling to take cacao trees – or viable cacao beans – offplanet as it would have been for anyone in the Arabian Peninsula to casually hand out coffee seedlings back in the 1700s. And aliens aren't allowed to set foot on Earth. After humans started trading chocolate bars for spaceship parts, it didn't take long for us to realize we were outmatched – in the fragility of our bodies, in technological advances and in military might – by a good portion of the known species in the galaxy.

This feartastic feeling reflected outward, as Earth legally closed its borders in 2077, filing all the proper paperwork with the Galactic Court – but also transported its entire stockpile of nuclear weapons onto a ring of space stations, pointing outwards. Which was bueno, really, because, later that year, the planet descended into the First Contact War. Claro está, the name is ironic, since there weren't any aliens involved, just scared humans fighting to control the source of chocolate. We'd come close to turning Earth into another Farder, close to destroying chocolate altogether, even without an outside threat. Close to destroying ourselves with new biological poisons meant to control where and how cacao could grow. The war was swift and brutal, but unlike what everyone had predicted for World War III, not a single nuke was dropped – in part because it would have made the land everyone was fighting over – a narrow band twenty degrees north and south of the Equator – completely unusable.

And now, we're about to give it another go, unless someone takes what everyone's fighting over out of the equation. I know it sounds loco, a human finishing the work the Krom started, basically becoming a participant in their First Contact, but if the monopoly shatters, then Earth can regain balance.

"Are you sure, Babe? Once we set this in motion, it won't be easy turning back. I don't want to see you get hurt." He flinches as I press the antiseptic-soaked cotton against the line the bullet carved out of him. "Eventually somebody is going to spill the cocoa beans so to speak. It doesn't have to be you."

"By then it may be too late. Mi abuelita still talks about the raids and the familias who died for like trying to hide cacao trees in their basements. It was one of the bloodiest times in human history, even before they brought back the guillotine and public executions." I make a sympathetic face as I slap on one of the largest bandages. It barely covers the injury.

"Ga. You don't know that the accident with the *Nibs* will lead to war." His face looks troubled. When he compared Earth and Farder, I don't think he wanted to be right.

I turn his chin so he has to look up at me. "This is what you've been asking me to do, in a roundabout way for months, right?"

He smiles, his eyes pure gold. "Only because you're smart enough to keep one step ahead of them, pretty enough to keep them distracted–"

"Human enough to be allowed on the planet."

"There is that." He squeezes my hand. "Only, now that

you've become so precious to me, I'm not sure I want to let you be the one to take the risk."

"I'm volunteering, mi vida. I'm in the perfecta position to do this."

"I should have known my Bodacious Babe wouldn't just stand back and watch things happen." He stands up and pulls me to him, kissing me.

Bésame mucho, mi vida. Lighten my heart with life and love. I kiss him back, enjoying the perfect way our mouths fit together, appreciating the strength in his shoulders as he holds me against him. By human standards I'm tall, fine-featured and well proportioned. But to a Krom? No lo sé, not for sure. I hate Frank for putting doubt in my heart. I break the kiss then run my hands through Brill's hair.

"I've got to keep you safe, Babe." He touches my cheek. "As soon as we turn the lights out tonight, I'll do a discreet search to see if anyone is monitoring your suite."

"Shouldn't you get out of here? Offplanet maybe?"

"Not if you're serious about breaking the monopoly. We both have to act like everything is absolutely normal, no matter what. I don't think we've ever discussed freeing chocolate anywhere except on the beach, so you should be safe."

"What about you?" I cast a meaningful look at his injury.

"I can take care of myself. It's not like it's the first time I've been shot."

CHAPTER THREE

By the time I make it back to the dorm after class the next day, roughly two dozen vloggers and FeedCasters are standing on the steps. I'd heard they had come, looking to interview Kayla. I guess the school ran out of stalling tactics and just outright denied them their press conference, and now they're looking for other sources of information. There's not any real celebarazzi here, not yet. The big names in the Earth press wouldn't be hanging out this far on the other side of the galaxy.

One of the Pops spots me. "We'll pay for an exclusive, Princesa!"

No y no y no. I can feel my body tensing, my hands trying to curl into fists. It's useless to answer, and anything I say about how heartless they are will be taken out of context, so I put my hands over my face and run the gauntlet through the shouted chatterclash. Chestla closes the door behind me and stares out through the glass. The reporters melt away.

When I get off the elevator on 6, my heart is still racing, part Chestla Effect, part anger at the Pops. I hear voices inside my suite. My breath catches, and my hand's un poco shaky as I hesitate with my fingers on the doorknob, trying to make out words. Brill is supposed to be hiding out in there from whoever shot him. Somebody laughs, so I guess it is one of his amigos visiting. Relieved, I scan my thumb and open the door.

The relief evaporates when I see Brill and Frank sitting on either end of the sofa, both leaning toward the empty cushion between them, playing that Krom card game Brill likes. I never can catch the rules, no matter how often he shows me, but Frank seems to be doing bien. It's hard to tell for sure, since they're not using the counters that keep track between hands.

Brill's wearing one of Stephen's nerd-slogan T-shirts. Mi hermoso's bigger than Kayla's brother, so the blue fabric stretches across his chest and biceps tightly enough to look painted on, and the bandage on his arm shows as an outline. Él está caliente. So hot. His eyes are a shade away from matching his shirt, which should mean clear sailing, even though he's been alone with the man he believes tried to murder him last night. I give him a questioning glance, but it's Frank that looks up.

"Brill and I were just discussing how fortunate your mother and I were to arrive in one piece carrying that much chocolate for the school."

I shoot Brill a look. He transports foodstuffs – both legal and gray market – into deep space, bringing needed supplies to isolated colonies and delicacies to rich metropolises. Ay! Please tell me that he did *not* offer Frank any cheap chocolate.

Brill smiles back, but his lips look tense. "Your mom probably wouldn't want you to know how close of a call it was."

Frank tells me anyway. "Some spacejacker blockaded the route with EMP mines." Frank looks straight at mi vida. "They wanted our cargo, but they didn't want to fight us for it. Pirates and black market traders, they're both cowards."

Brill examines his cards thoughtfully. He's not a pirate, but I suspect he buys stock sometimes from people who are – after all, the distinction between the gray market and the black is a fine one, no? Does Frank know about Brill's work? Is that why he's here? A cold sensation builds in my chest, though there's no tangible threat in the room, aside from that bruise on my hip from the heavy metal object that had been in Frank's pocket when he'd pushed me, which I've decided must have been a gun. Finally mi vida plays a card and says, "Some pirates are worse than others. Revwal?" *Right?*

There's this awkward silence, then Frank says, "I was supposed to meet Lavonda an hour ago for lunch, but she never showed, so I came by here." He catches the cards in the stack nearest him before they can fall into the crevice between the cushions. Good thing, too, because I never clean in there. Who knows what he'd find.

"Mamá should be here soon." She usually runs late, so I hadn't worried about rushing back for our planned mother-daughter afternoon. But lunch with Frank? Had mi mamá double-booked herself? That isn't like her at all, nunca. More likely, she planned for me to go to lunch with her and her boyfriend, and wanted to spring it last minute.

I hear gurgling coming from the kitchen. I look over the bar and see the coffee pot just finishing brewing. I smile, hoping it doesn't look *too* fake. "Perfect timing, chicos."

I move into the kitchen and pull out a mug.

"Let me grab me and Frank a cup." Brill flattens his stack of cards and starts to place them face down on the sofa, but then he changes his mind and sticks them in his pocket.

Frank laughs. "Do I worry you that much, son?"

"You have no idea." Brill says it like he's teasing, but I can tell he's not. His eyes never waver from their not-a-care-in-the-world blue as he walks into the kitchen, not until he's reaching into the cabinet for the sugar. Then his irises fade to charcoal. He closes his eyes, massages his temples, then gives me a look that pretty much says, *You would not believe how much concentration that takes.*

I lean in close and whisper, "Why did you let Frank in? He shot you, no?"

Brill whispers back, so softly I can hardly hear him, "I didn't *let* him do anything. He bypassed your lock and opened the door.

Surprised me with my head in the fridge looking for something to eat. He said the door was unlocked, but it wasn't. Still, he's been friendly enough, and he's had ample opportunity to finish me off, if that's what he came here to do. Maybe I was wrong."

Finish me off. En serio? He just said that in a contemplative tone, like it doesn't much bother him, but now I can hear my own heartbeat pounding in my ears.

"Maybe." I try to shake away the image of Brill dead, lying half inside the fridge. It didn't happen. It won't happen. I take a deep breath, deliberately slow my breathing. I'm just spooked because of Noodles.

"It'll be OK, Babe." He moves back a bit, hands me a mug.

"So what is that?" I gesture at his face, at the black irises. "I thought when Krom start fibbing, your eyes go violet then neon pink. I've seen Gavin's do the same thing, no?" Gavin is one of Brill's best friends, and he fibs. A lot.

He looks embarrassed, but his eyes only lighten to a deep gray. "That's what happens naturally, wal, if we're consciously thinking about lying but not concentrating enough to stop it showing. But that's different from trying to cover an emotion from someone who can read irises by using a different emotion."

"Are you two talking about me in there?" Frank stands up and comes into the kitchen. He opens the fridge and takes out the leche. We all prepare our coffee and take it back into the living area. The guys finish their card game, and I pretend to be excited when Brill wins.

Frank stands. "If Bo and Lavonda have plans, I guess that leaves us guys on our own. I'm starved. Want to hit the fish and chips stand out in the quad? Then I'd love to take a look at the inside of your ship."

Brill looks over at me, and for just a moment his irises flash to terrified black before recovering the blue. "I'm sure the girls would be happier if we stayed here, then took them somewhere nice for lunch. I can treat this time."

Brill never has spare money for nice lunches that don't somehow wind up including business. Nunca. He must really be scared. I'm beginning to see the false color shift for what it is – a protection more than a lie. I've done the same thing myself, pasting on a smile when I'd rather cry, straightening my posture when I'm terrified. How can I fault him for trying harder to keep his privacy, when he wears his every thought literally on his face?

"Oh, don't be absurd. Come on." Frank's already heading for the door.

Brill leans in, like he's giving me a kiss on the cheek, but really, he's whispering in my ear. "If I disappear, tell the Inspectors to go looking for that su."

My heart lurches. Tranquila, Bo, tranquila. I don't want him to go. But a normal girlfriend wouldn't have a problem with two guys going out to have lunch. Still... I kiss mi hermoso on the lips un poco longer than parental-figure-present propriety strictly allows. A little breathless, I say, "Stay safe."

He presses a note into my hand. I follow them into the hall, and once they've disappeared into the elevator, I read it. *I found a couple HoloLink bugs in your kitchen and living room. They're still in place. Good thing we had that little discussion last night in the land of pink ruffles.*

Chicken skin rises on my arms at the thought of cameras watching me pad to the coffee pot in my pajama top and underwear. Qué vergüenza! *How embarrassing.* "Dios mío!"

I have to act normal. I go back into the suite and pull out my double boiler and run agua into the bottom piece, trying not to think about those hidden cameras. I need to focus on something constructive. I also need to start making cake. I promised Mamá something spectacular for her banquet. Not to mention that it's a grade.

I dump the coffee grounds in the trash, and find myself just standing there, staring at the mess. It always comes back to coffee, no? There's a holo from that loco era before the borders closed. This vlogger had made a deal with one of the Galactic Inspectors to take her on a tour of the galaxy. The vlogger would holo all the heroic moments of the Inspector capturing bad guys, while at the same time introducing Earth to far-flung locations nobody could afford to visit, since Earth money was still considered iffy.

This popular HoloCast streamed new episodes weekly for about a year and a half, making both vlogger and Galactacop richer than they ever could have imagined, while back home, Earthlings were building the spaceport to welcome trade, and riding out the Bringolda Famine. Pero, one CastClip stands out. The holo is panning the street in a suburban-looking area on some random backwater planet, when our intrepid vlogger spots a green logo and English writing on the awning in front of a store. Inside the circular logo, there's a whale, spouting water that turns into a crown of stars. The words on either side say *StarTrucks Coffee*. Underneath, it's translated in the local script, phonetically.

The vlogger's hand appears in the bottom of the holofield. "Scrag," she says. "What is that?"

"You want some coffee?" Scrag's voice has a soft hiss to it, even with letters that aren't s-es. He's off camera, standing behind her. "I imagine you must be missing home."

"But what is this doing here?" She turns toward him, and Scrag stands there blinking, adjusting his black leather jacket, snout wrinkled in confusion.

"Quick, ain't it? Well, it never takes long. When Krom take something, they clone it and ship it across the galaxy. Immediately." His lips pull back from his sharp teeth. "The Krom contacted my world, too, back in the day. But they don't take anything you need to live, or enough of a resource to keep you from producing more. You get over it."

"Contacted?" the vlogger says. "I mean, there was a riot, and we ran them off. It's not exactly like they're keeping in touch."

Scrag's snout falls open in shock. "You still have no idea what happened, do you? Girlie, your planet's been mugged."

She follows him into the coffee shop, still casting. Scrag explains why they're there. There's subtitles in the holo as he asks the tentacled barista, "Can you give me a list of all the products you have imported from the new Sol sourcing?"

"Sure." The barista does something to a thin translucent screen, then holds up a scrolling list that looks like an order form. The holo's overlaid the English translation off to the side. Sugar. Vanilla. Oranges. Pears. Beef. En serio. They got cows on board that spaceship. And pigs. And horses. The list goes on for what feels like forever the first time you watch the holo.

And after a long silence, the vlogger asks, "So did the Krom sell you this logo, too?"

And the barista laughs. "Krom don't trade in culture." She holds up cups in half a dozen tentacles, running other tentacles proudly across the green circles. "I looked it up myself. Your Starbucks took the name from Starbuck, a character in *Moby Dick*. I love literature, so I put the whale in the center of the sphere."

"You've read *Moby Dick*?" the vlogger asks.

The barista shakes her head and most of her tentacles. "There's no jeeblkrez translation. But I read a summary."

Even then, with that list, nobody realized chocolate wasn't on it.

Still wondering what life must have felt like then, I put chocolate into the top of the double boiler and place the whole thing on the gas range. I find myself staring at the flame as I stir the melting chunks, thinking about Papá. If he were here, would he think my plan's heroic? I think he would. *Eso espero. I hope so.*

That doesn't help the minor freak-out happening inside me. Where are those cameras? I keep glancing around, then making myself stop. My shoulders are starting to ache from the tension that is building in them, no matter how often I remind myself to relax them.

I've just dropped in the piece of tempered chocolate that will encourage the molten stuff in the pot to form the appropriate crystalline structure and turned off the burner when Mamá breezes in.

"Sorry I am late, mija. I got caught up in a meeting. The admissions committee wants to offer a scholarship in my name. Where's Frank?"

I was right. She expected him to be here. I'm emotirated about the set-up, even inside the freak-out, but I keep stirring the chocolate, one eye on the thermometer. Otherwise, I'll have to start over. "You just missed him. They went to look at Brill's ship."

"They should have waited for us. I would have liked to see that, no?" Mamá washes her hands, cook's habit even though she probably isn't planning to help.

It's sweet that she cares what Brill drives, and hence what he does, but I don't let that derail my frustration, which is only heightened by my worry for mi vida. If she'd been here on time, we could have all gone to eat together. Brill would be safe right now. "You were over an hour late. That matters in some parts of the worlds, no? Frank's the punctual type, Mamá."

The chocolate hits the right temperature, so I start dipping quizllens.

Without even acknowledging I have a point, Mamá changes the subject. "That cat woman downstairs is doing a really good job keeping away the paparazzi. A ella me gusta." *I like her.* "Do you think I could hire her for my staff?"

Trust mi mamá not to be intimidated, even by an alpha predator. That finally breaks me into a smile as I hand her an hour-old martini. "You should ask her, but por favor don't ever call her a cat, like she has fur on her face instead of freckles.

She comes from a proud warrior race, and most of the worlds find it presumptuous when humans compare alien species with non-sentient Earth animals."

"We are just trying to make sense of the galaxy, put it in terms we can understand. Es tan malo?" *Is that so bad?* She takes a long gulp of the drink. "Are you not having one?"

"You know I don't like martinis." Whoever's bugging me probably already knows I'm more of a red wine connoisseur, though I have been known to imbibe a few Glowing Pink Kisses when Kayla and I get our friends together for girls' night. Or even margaritas, if the bar we like has imported any limes. Next time we go, I should invite Chestla. Then I remember. I accepted HGB's job offer this morning, so that I can get into the facility. I'm going back to Earth in a few days. There won't be any more girls' nights – and Kayla's never going to speak to me again, ever. Nunca.

Mamá sinks back onto the sofa and plucks an olive out of her martini. I started mixing them for her when I was sixteen, in those numb weeks after Papá died. We'd held each other up then, gotten so close. I think that's when Mario started resenting me, even before it all crashbanged.

I'll admit, I hadn't been completely innocent in the meltdown between me and Mamá, me and the Pops, me and my life. I went too far, trying to parlay that tiny role on *Dead Men Don't Tell* into a career that rivaled Mamá's. But I didn't sell out the way those buzzbashing malcasts said I did, romancing both an actor and a director at the same time to win influence. I have more self-respect than that, no? But Mamá didn't believe me. No one did.

And the rest of it? The truly loco things they say I did on my way to career mediacide? Pure faked holonique.

I miss being able to tell Mamá absolutely todo. Good thing Brill warned me the suite's bugged, or I might have spilled my suspicions about Frank the minute she walked in, even though he'd told me not to. She sucks on the olive. "Mija, you have chocolate in your hair."

"Sí, Mamá." I force myself not to bring my hands to my head to try and fix the problem. It's not like the cameras are rolling for her show. Though they are rolling for somebody. I look down at my clasped hands to keep from searching for the little lenses. "I was dipping fruit when you walked in."

"Hablando de chocolate..." Mamá reaches into the pocket of her blazer. "I have something for you."

She hands me what looks like a single-serving chocolate bar, wrapped in silver and sheathed in yellow paper, labeled like one of HGB's kiddie bars. Once I take the paper off, the thing inside, which has identical markings, proves to be a fully-functional handheld.

I flip it over. It's adorable. "Where did you find this?"

"I saw it in one of the gift shops while waiting for the flight. I got one for you, and one for Frank's Minerva, and I put her number in yours before I gave it to her at the spaceport. I hope you will call her, maybe get to know her a little bit. Por favor."

"Of course, Mamá." I slip the handheld into my pocket. "Más tarde." *Later.* Once I've figured out if Frank is safe enough to even belong in Mamá's life. I almost ask if she knows he carries a gun – pero I've not actually seen it. What if I accuse him, and it turns out somebody else shot Brill? I move back into the kitchen and start dipping fruit again, laying each dipped quizllen carefully onto the waxed paper. Over the bar, I call, "What's Minerva like?"

I'm facing the cabinets when she says, "Hola! I am Bo's Mamá. Who are you?"

As an answer to my question, that makes no sense. Who is she talking to? I turn, and find one of the women who'd been waiting for me on the front steps standing by my sofa. A wild tangle of curly dark hair accents her well-formed Hispanic features. She says, "Me llaman Meredith Vasquez."

"Reporter," I tell Mamá. I shield my face, turning back to the cabinets. Most feeds won't show holos of the back of your head. I switch to the language Meredith seems most comfortable in, saying, "Cómo has entrado?" *How did you get in here?*

Meredith points to the sill behind her, saying in Spanish, "You live only six floors up, and you think it is safe to leave a window open?"

This isn't the weirdest thing I've ever seen a FeedCaster do to get to Mamá, so it's not completely alarmante. Pero, what is it with people these days and windows? I must have forgotten to close that one after Brill came in last night. This part of Larksis 9 has such perfect weather, it'd be easy not to notice. But even if I left it open, that doesn't give her the right to invade my privacy. Something about the determined angle of her chin tells me that she isn't going to leave just because I ask nicely.

I ring the RA desk on my sublingual. Chestla answers almost immediately. *Hola!*

Can you come up here, like right now, por favor?

She hangs up without asking any questions.

"What do you want?" Mamá's voice sounds muffled, like she's talking through the cloth of her jacket. She probably is.

I can hear that Meredith has moved around to the open entryway to the kitchen. "Where's your roommate, Bo?"

"You're too late to get your graveside interview." The anger building in my chest bleeds through into my voice. "We took her to the spaceport this morning. She's already left for Earth."

Mamá lets out an unhappy breath. "As you can see, Bo hates publicity. Leave her be, and I will give you an interview on any topic you want, no?"

"I'm not here as a reporter. It's more complicated than that." Something about Meredith's tone makes me turn around. She pulls out a tiny vapgun from her pocket. "Look, hands where I can see them, chicas. You two are both coming with me."

"Mamá." Cold flipflops through my stomach. "She's got a gun."

Mamá lowers the jacket she's been holding over her face. "Are you kidnapping us?" She looks almost happy that she's been included. "You are, aren't you? What are you hoping HGB will give you in return?"

"Just un poco chocolate is all. A couple of tiny trees so that we can return cacao to the unwalled rainforests it's been stripped from. After the interviews I've done – no comprendes... those broken people... their need for justicia."

She's completely insane. Even Mamá, who's a much bigger celeb than me, isn't that important. HGB would let us die before they'd hand over the genetic source for their monopoly. I doubt they'd even trade cacao to get back their own CEO. "This is a joke, right?"

In response, Meredith takes aim and vaporizes one of the quizllen fruits, leaving behind the strong scent of ozone. She hits a second one, which takes part of the granite countertop with it. Vapguns are unpredictable in determining the edges of objects, which is always used to comic effect in the telenovela I favor. In real life, it's terrifying.

"Does it look like I'm laughing?"

That sounds like such a cliché, I can't help but roll my eyes, even though my clenched stomach and pounding heart are taking her seriously.

The door slides open, and Chestla rushes into the room, a plunger in one hand and a Taser in the other. I hadn't mentioned the nature of my emergency, so she'd come prepared for anything. Meredith whirls around and points the weapon at her.

Chestla narrows her eyes and says, in Lark, "And what exactly do you think you're doing?"

I flinch back against the counter, then freeze instinctively.

Meredith squeaks and fires without aiming, the random

shot vaporizing my entire refrigerator – all except the cord, which flops once, arcing a few sparks along its ragged live edge – before she drops the gun in terror of Chestla's bared teeth.

Never looking away from Chestla, Meredith bends slowly towards the weapon. I try to force myself to move, telling my leaden limbs that my RA's feartastic predatory gaze is not directed at me. I can't do it. No y no. I close my eyes, pretend Chestla's not there. It's a little better. I force my arm to extend, to move past the crater in the counter to grab a handful of quizllen fruit. I open my eyes just enough to see Meredith. I peg her in the back with a wet, sticky glob of fruit and liquid chocolate.

"Oye!" She flinches away as I throw another and then another. It's hard to see with my eyes slitted, but she's distracted enough that Mamá manages to get her jacket over Meredith's cabeza and kick away the vapgun.

Chestla grabs Meredith and pushes her into a chair, holding the Taser near her neck. She brings her face muy close to the reporter's, slit-iris eyes intense. "Why are you doing this?"

Meredith screams, a bloodcurdling, terrified sound. She overbalances the chair and it falls backwards. She tucks the fall into a roll and bounds up, running straight for the window. She jumps. Six floors.

I rush over just in time to see a jetpack unfolding itself out of the neck of her shirt. Instead of falling, she's flying. Qué acaba de ocurrir? Or in other words, what the heck? Since when do personal jetpacks exist?

"Who was that woman?" Chestla lowers the plunger, making a swish gesture that seems habitual. If she were in a kung-fu movie, I'd call it cleaning the sword.

I watch the rocket haze dissipate into the air. "She's just a HoloCaster for one of the news feeds. It sounds like she got caught up in a story and started taking sides."

"Qué?" Mamá doesn't speak Lark. I translate what we've

just said into Spanish. Mamá shakes her head. "I had heard there's a new tougher breed of paparazzi, but this is loco."

"That thing is military grade tech." Chestla, who has apparently picked up enough Spanish to understand Mamá, if not enough to reply in kind, points with the plunger at the vapgun still lying on the floor. "It will get off twelve shots before you have to refield, and weighs half as much as the standard ones. Whoever she works for, they're well-funded. That doesn't sound like any of the communications companies on my planet. What about on Earth?"

I translate, shocked. Chestla's not sounding much like a cheerful-at-all-costs RA. I know nada about her pre-Larksis past, but apparently it included memorizing weapons schematics. She's right though. Whoever's pulling Meredith's strings is dangerous. I hate to speculate, though, because of the bugs. The bug-er could be the same person who shot Brill, and Meredith still needs to get off of this planet.

Mamá tosses her jacket over the vapgun, like she doesn't want to look at it. "The only feeds with that much money are the official HGB line, and feeds HGB supports. The independents survive on ads or donations. Half the time, they're just one person with a message, funding everything themselves."

Chestla closes my window and locks it. "Do you want me to notify campus police?"

"No policía." Mamá casts a critical eye at the crumbs the guys left on the sofa. "The vulturazzi are all over this place. We do not want any more attention."

Dazed, I sit carefully on the sofa, so as not to get chocolate on it. I use the chocoholo to find more information on Meredith, sending the audio into my sublingual. I'm expecting her cast to be an off-Earth redirect, but it's from HoloCast Venezuela. HoloCasts are done using open-sourced software, without the vetting – or support – FeedCasters get. She's not major celebarazzi – casters who are famous in their own right – but she's produced tons of CastClips.

I pull up her oldest Cast, dated eight years ago – June 12, 2116. I set the holo so minúsculo, to shield it from any other prying bugs, that she looks like I'm holding her in the palm of my hand between my body and the couch. Meredith is sitting in an uncomfortable-looking modern art bucket chair, with a corgi on her lap. She was probably a teenager at the time this was recorded. She waves at the camera. "Hola everybody! We're back from the honeymoon, so I decided, new name, new life, new account. In case you're new too, this is Botas." She waves one of the corgi's paws, and it looks like the dog's wearing white boots on its front feet. "And sí, we did take him with us to Angel Falls. I'm the happiest I've ever been, despite, well, you know. It's not every day you get to marry your best friend. Did I ever tell you chicos Domingo told me he was going to marry me when we were six years old?" She holds up her hand, flashing a hunormous diamond. "Gracias, Theresa, for the bachelorette party. Realmente arrojaste la casa por la ventana!" *You really threw the house through the window!* It must have been quite a party.

She hadn't had that ring on just now. Had the relationship soured? I do a quick search and pop up something cryptically titled *The Death of True Love*. Meredith looks horrible – the date's from early 2121, but ay, she looks like she's aged ten years instead of five. Her eyes are both bloodshot and dark circled, somehow empty. She's unhealthily thin, with bruises on her collarbones, and her complexion is splotchy. She's sitting in the same chair. She coughs wetly and grimaces at the camera. "People keep asking me what really happened out here. I'm tired of talking about it, so after this, I'm just going to refer all questions to this CastClip, OK?" She closes her eyes, then nods, psyching herself up. "HGB still treats the rainforest with Pure275 once a month, to prevent cacao from popping up in the wild. You don't really think about it, right? It's just the way it's always been, since I was born at least. You go inside, stay out of the crop dusters' way on the fourth of every month. It's inconvenient, but you deal."

She points, and the ring slips off her bone-thin finger. She picks it up, jams it back on. "But all the leftovers from that process have to go somewhere, right? Correcto. They're saying it's our fault, that construction on the new mall broke up the area where they had *safely*," she says that word so bitterly, "disposed of the empty containers, that we leeched it into our own agua supply. I just watched half the town die – this horrible wasting poisoned muerte – and they're telling us that it was our own fault. That it was an accident." The dog wanders into the holo, whining, puts a paw on its mistress's leg. "Domingo's death was not an accident. My parents' deaths were not an accident. Theresa, and Bianca and Trill. This is the direct result of nearly half a century of neglect and abuse by HGB. They won the war, and we're the spoils."

I have a vague memory of an industrial accident in Venezuela a couple of years ago. Of course it made the news. Claro está, it was minimized, nada like this horror of Meredith's skull-like face. It's amazing that, now, only three years later, you can't tell she was ever sick.

She dips her cabeza and looks up, emotion smoldering in her eyes. "Next year marks the fortieth anniversary of the treaties that ended the First Contact War, that gave away our land in the name of peace with aliens that hadn't even threatened us. We gave in to fear. A half century of fear is enough."

The whole time she's been speaking, comments have been unspooling along the side of the image. One of them catches my attention, from CyberFighter321. *I agree with what you're saying. 40 years is too long. I can tell you all about the underhanded tactics HGB used to win the war. I'll give you an exclusive interview. We should meet.*

My sublingual rings. It's Tawny, the HGB starwrangler I

talked to this morning. I flinch and shut down the feed.

Are you OK, Bo? She could only know about what just happened if HGB's the one bugging me. She doesn't even pretend not to. *Our facial ident didn't get anything clear enough to identify your attacker. And we only caught part of the audio. What did she say when your mother asked her name?*

My stomach goes cold. *No lo sé. I don't know.* I'm not sure why I lie, only that I'm scared. I'm already planning my own action against HGB, so it almost feels like Meredith's a kindred spirit, even though what she just did was reckless and endangered our lives.

That's too bad. Tawny sighs in my head. *You'll be safe soon. I've got your travel arrangements set, though you'll be publicly listed on a different shuttle, in case there's another assassination attempt. Call me if you see anything else suspicious. We'd hate to lose our new Princesa*

My heart lurches. Assassination? Oi! I still can't see how I'm important enough to anybody to be worth bugging, let alone killing. Pero, Tawny's serious. And Meredith's plan could well have ended in our deaths. What have I gotten myself into? I need to talk to Brill.

Chestla's doing something to her phone. "Stay here, both of you. I need to check outside." The power goes out, leaving us all in shadow as she yanks the cord, the only evidence that my refrigerator just poofed away. She reaches down to pick up the vapgun. "And stay away from the windows."

I rub at my temples, trying to forestall the headache that's forming. This will be only the second time in my life I've not turned in a homework assignment, pero I don't care anymore. I'd had barely four hours sleep before helping get Kayla and Stephen down to the spaceport this morning. I'm about ten ticks past exhausted, totally slypered. I really want a shower and a nap in the unbugged portions of my suite – just as soon as I know Brill's safe. I call him to find out if he's on his way back. I'm terrified he won't answer, but he's there in my head, bubblechattering almost immediately. *Hey, Babe, I was just about to call you.*

En serio? I'm trying to think how to phrase what just happened, when he starts talking in a rush.

Look, Bo. He rarely calls me Bo, usually Babe or Bodacious, though I've tried to get him to give up the latter. *Frank wants to go fishing. We're going down to Pier 17 – write that down – past the Hullet Marina. I told him we don't have much time, but he's insistent.*

Brill keeps me on the phone for as long as he can, but he's using a handleld, not a sublingual so he doesn't have enough privacy to talk about potential assassins, either his or mine. Eventually, he has to get out of Frank's car, so he lets me go. Just before he hangs up, he tells me he loves me. In Spanish.

I'm still slypered. But there's no way I could sleep.

To distract myself, I find a quiet bug-free spot, where I can watch more of Meredith's feed. It's probably not bueno for my jangled nerves, but I want to see her interview with CyberFighter321.

In the holo, they're walking through an anonymous section of rainforest. His face is fuzzed out, but he's taller than her, overshadowing her in a muscle-bound masculine way, and his brown hands are spotted from the sun. A scar runs across the right one, from the base of his pinkie finger almost to his wrist.

The way she's looking at him, he could well become her rebound hermoso after the death of her husband. The corgi jump-runs along at her heels. "You promised to tell me about the war. But there's no way you're old enough to have been there."

"I'm older than you." Which sounds like a reproof of the way she's cow-eyed over him. He reaches out to touch a vanilla orchid, the vine of it wrapped around a nearby tree. His voice has been altered, too. "Mi padre died three months before the war was over – three weeks before I was born into a world of turmoil and fear. Nobody expected HGB to keep control of the plantations for very long. I spent my childhood drilling over what to do when the next war over cacao broke out. But it never did."

"Drilling?" Meredith's eyes are wide, and Botas whines, picking up on his mistress's nervousness. "With guns?"

"Does that bother you?" He plucks the orchid from the vine and holds it out to her. "Many of us arc still waiting for HGB to make a mistake tan grande that we can topple them, by whatever means necessary."

Meredith looks uneasy to find herself alone with this man in such an isolated area. Her fingers are trembling as she takes the flower. But she makes a valiant effort to get the interview back on track. "Was your father there when the war started?"

"Sí. First Contact could have represented an opportunity for farmers like him, to sell their product directly for astronomical profits. So a small group of cacao growers announced plans to start a cooperative plantation on another planet, splitting genetic stock and profits with the Nitarri. They were massacred at the spaceport. My father and two others escaped. HGB didn't even exist at that point, so nobody knew who to blame, and the whole thing toppled into war." CyberFighter321 reaches into his pocket, and Meredith freezes, but what he pulls out is a phone. "I have the holo my dad took that day."

It fills the field, with that weird distortion of 2D footage being shown in holo form. That first galactourist spaceport was in Switzerland, since so many interstellar chocofans had landed there already looking for Swiss chocolate. Which means chocogrowers from Venezuela would have already traveled halfway across the world with their transplant stock, though in a matter of hours, rather than the torturous extended journey De Clieu took.

The building is all arches and rounded glass, and an open plaza with shopping areas three stories high on either side. Mostly, the people making their way down the hallway laden with shopping bags are human, but there are a few strangely-formed faces rounding out the throng.

By the time CyberDad started filming, things had already gone horribly wrong. There's screaming and blood as men attempt to flee through the crowded spaceport while CyberDad pivots and jerks inside the makeshift shelter he's found inside a pile of luggage, trying to locate the threat.

When CyberFighter321 shuts down the holo, Meredith stumbles away from him, bends over like she might be ill. He moves over to her, rubs her back. "It won't always be like this, niña. Someday we will find peace."

It makes sense now, what Meredith was trying to do. If HGB would give up viable cacao now, while their power and reputation is in flux, it could well prevent global civil war. But giving it to someone like CyberFighter321 – even if he owns part of the de-nuded rainforest the cacao was stolen from – that isn't the answer. No y no. Every dystopian movie I've ever seen has taught me it'd just be a shift of power, which wouldn't really free chocolate. Or save us from ourselves.

CHAPTER FOUR

The suns have dipped toward the horizon, and Brill's still not back. I call him, but it goes straight to voicemail. My stomach floods with unease. Brill never ignores my calls. A poco bit numbly, I change into the black-on-white outfit all the students are supposed to wear tonight. I redo my makeup, then call him again. Nada. The unease builds, tickling its way up my spine. I realize with a sinking dread that I don't have any of Brill's friends' phone numbers. I wander back into the living area.

Mamá's made more coffee. "Why are you so tense, mija?"

I shake my head, stare down into the dark liquid. "How old is Frank, Mamá?"

"A little older than me. Por qué?"

I wonder if he's old enough to have cared about news when the vlogger who'd teamed up with Inspector Scrag had stumbled into the Embassy on Plektar a month after discovering StarTrucks, and announced, while casting live, "My planet's been mugged."

To her credit, the tentacled lady behind the desk – no gene-ties to the barista in the previous CastClip – doesn't even flinch, just says, "Oh? Do you care to explain what happened?"

The vlogger, whose face you never see, tries to explain what happened, laying out all the evidence she has collected. I'm pretty sure the camera is in her eye.

The tentacled ambassador listens patiently, nods along. Then she sighs. "I'm sorry, but there's nothing illegal about a Krom First Contact. They don't actually steal anything. They pay fair market value for whatever they take, and they never deprive anyone of the source of a commodity. From their point of view, they're actually providing a service."

The vlogger lets out an outraged squeak. "What about tax evasion? Or working illegally? At least one of them was working for a university. They couldn't have done that without breaking the law."

The tentacles shrug again. "I can file a complaint for you, but they'll just pay the fines, and send their people to serve the jail time. And they'll issue an apology for not understanding local laws. They're obnoxiously polite about it."

The vlogger slams a paper cup with the StarTrucks logo onto the desk with an empty, hollow sound. "Coffee was ours! What are we supposed to do now?"

The lady rests a row of tentacles on the desk. "If they had taken your people captive, or tried to colonize your planet, then you'd have a case. They didn't abduct any sentient species, did they? There was once a botched Krom First Contact where they accidentally took members of a secondary sentient species on a planet with great biodiversity. Of course, those members were returned unharmed as soon as a complaint was lodged."

"I don't care about other contacts! What can I do about mine?"

"I understand your frustration. It's something like waking up in a bathtub missing both your..." she consults a virtual dictionary, "kidneys. It is unpleasant and there will be scars, but eventually the organs grow back and you move on."

"Kidneys don't grow back!"

The ambassador blinks. "Are you sure?" Then she raises the row of tentacles in a shruggy gesture. "There are a few protections you can gain from future contacts from species less gentlemanly than the Krom, if your planet registers with the Galactic Court. You can set laws to regulate your borders, and entering illegally becomes itself a punishable crime, according to the laws you set on your soil. That process usually takes years, but I could expedite it for you, if I felt incentivized." She rubs the tentacle ends together in pairs. Because the gesture for and-this-is-the-point-where-you-give-me-a-bribe really is universal.

"But I just told you, Earth money is worthless."

All the tentacles shake no again. "There are already some parts of the galaxy where Snickers bars are being used as currency. I'm not opposed to dealing in that medium."

"Why?" The vlogger sounds incredulous. "Why would candy bars be worth more than cash?"

"Because, my dear, the Krom missed chocolate."

The vlogger exits the Embassy, grumbling, making empty threats. Pero, she was still missing the point. That holo changed everything.

Threats. Frank hadn't actually threatened Brill, but he may well have lived most of his life with that same underlying frustrangeration. And now he's alone with a Krom. My Krom. And I can't explain to Mamá why I'm so worried. So when she asks again, I lie and say, "De nada."

When we're ready to go across campus to the banquet hall, Chestla takes us personally down the elevator. When she's gotten out and far enough away, I make my way from the elevator car. I blink, as my brain adjusts to what I'm seeing. Right in the middle of the lobby, there's the Larksissian equivalent of a golf cart, which has been converted into a closed vehicle with the use of panels of lavender fabric that looks suspiciously like bed sheets.

Chestla pulls back one of the panels. "Get in."

I look at Mamá. She shrugs, then steps forward. "Gracias, Chestla."

The front is still open so Chestla can see to drive. I can sort-of see from my spot in the back. Chestla punches the button that opens the door automatically, and we shoot out onto the landing, scattering paparazzi as we go. We jounce down the steps this vehicle was never designed to take. I hold on as best I can, but I nearly go flying out the back.

"Princesa!" some guy calls as my face pokes, upside down, through the edge of the sheet. "An interview por favor!"

He's chasing us, despite limping on the ankle he twisted while leaping out of our way.

I get myself settled back in the vehicle, which is going faster than any golf cart has a right to.

Chestla doesn't slow down the whole way to the hall, but when we get there she's not on the guest list, so they won't let her in. She eyes the security guy, and he stares straight back with a directness that earns him a nod of approval. She smiles at me, and I manage not to run away, despite the prey instinct, despite my frazzled nerves.

"You guys call me when you're ready to go back." She turns away and we go inside the building, with its sea-green floor and crisp white walls. The nautical pattern on the chair fabric always reminds me of an oversized beach house. Each of the round tables seats ten. Since I'm sitting with Mamá, the other seats at ours are taken by faculty in starched white chef coats – except for the empty chair on the other side of her. Frank's chair. My stomach clenches. Why isn't he here? Why isn't Brill answering his phone?

One of my favorite teachers is trying to talk to me, pero I missed most of what she's said. I try to fake my way back into the conversation, then suddenly everyone at the table's talking, and it doesn't matter so much that I'm not keeping up. Looking at the faces of people who have taught me so much, I feel a pang of loss. There are so many ways my trip home could end with me dead or in prison without ever making it back to

Larksis 9. I fit in here, with the beach and the amazing sunrises and the whole rhythm of the place. I could even imagine staying on, becoming a profesora at the school.

Frank slides into the seat next to Mamá. He smiles and touches her cheek. A cold terrolting quiver runs through my stomach. I've got absolutamente no proof he's a threat. I have to swallow my accusations and greet the man I hope didn't just murder mi hermoso. I use my sublingual to call Brill one more time, but he's still not answering.

Blegart-pau, the teacher who spoke to me yesterday, moves to the raised podium at the front of the room. The part of his name beyond the hyphen is an honorific signifying his master chef status. Pau literally means blade, and he is really good with his knives. Once he's gotten everybody's attention, he bows his head, his four hands resting on the corners of the podium. "For those of you who have not heard, we lost a student yesterday." He looks up, straight at me, and my heart jolts. Ay! I'm not sure if he's accusing me of withholding information, or just sharing grief with someone he knows was there. "Many of you knew Mwooh better than I did, but I'm the school's designated singer for when there's no family present." He pronounces *Mwooh* something like the sound of a wet finger rubbing the rim of a crystal glass. "I'm sure most of you have never heard a Larksissian dirge before. It's our way of celebrating the beauty of a life we have shared, and by all accounts Mwooh's life was worthy."

Blegart sings unaccompanied. It's a happy song, with a fast tempo and tripping, trilling words, and many in the audience are smiling, a few softly singing along, even while tears fill their eyes. I don't feel it. I hardly knew the guy, and there's a vasto ball of fear blocking any sense of celebration.

What actually sounds like a dirge is the march one of the other teachers has chosen to open the ceremony that follows. The first strains of music fill the room. The dessert parade is about to start. I'm supposed to march in at the head of the line. Mamá squeezes my arm reassuringly just before I slide out of my chair. I take my place, trying to figure out what to do with my hands, since I'm the only one not holding a platter or tray or cake plate. Tawny, the HGB starwrangler who'd called my dorm, walks in carrying a chocolate cake topped with what looks suspiciously like choco-dipped quizllen fruit. She has pixie-short brown hair, ice blue eyes, and a single shell necklace dangling against a tan so dark she's got to have at least some Hawaiian blood. She's heading straight toward me.

"I brought you your dessert." She gives me a confidential wink. "And just in time, too."

I pull her away from the line. "No, no y no. I don't cheat."

"Of course not, Bo." She thrusts the cake at me. It looks off balance, about to fall out of her hands, so I take it. "We at HGB understand you've been through a trying time. After the accident in your kitchen, we jumped in to help."

"Pero nobody asked you to." I almost drop the cake myself, trying to give it back to her.

Tawny crosses her arms over her chest. A trapezoid-cut jraghite glows softly on the ring finger of her right hand. "We take care of our own. You know that."

Actualmente, I know no such thing – just look at Papá – and I start to say so, but the music gets louder. Tawny pats me on the back and pushes me into the line.

I march out, cabeza held high, even though the twenty-nine people marching behind me realize I didn't make this dessert. As I walk past the long table, which has been marked with numbered cards, mi amiga Wakiji, who is in line behind me, whispers, "I thought you said you didn't finish your cake."

"I didn't." I place the cake down over the card marked with the number one.

She places a greenish cheesecake down on the number two and surreptitiously reaches out with her long thin fingers to brush the edge of my cake, which is how she smells – not the right word but it is as close as I've got – things. "So, what, that much chocolate deliciousness just fell from the sky?"

"Sí, something like that." I move away from the table, a sick feeling in my gut. Tawny's watching me closely. I've agreed to go back to Earth, to be la Princesa de Cacao. It's weird enough suddenly finding myself mediaceptable again. How am I supposed to act normal, knowing the danger I'm in if she suspects my real intentions? Though, they can't execute you just for thinking about committing a crime – at least not publicly – so whatever happens at this point, I'm not facing the guillotine yet.

This all could have been so different. Once Earth traded for the parts to create a galactaship engine they speedbuilt that first star-hopper – and the galactourist-friendly spaceport that went with it. It was March 2076, and that first day the spaceport opened to a couple dozen out-of-area visitors, who barely filled up the Ferris wheel. It was mostly Earthlings who gathered for that afternoon's launch, watching their fellow humans walk towards the ship to undertake a shiny new mission: to visit an alien world. There wasn't anything deeper to it. The two pilots and their twenty-eight passengers were Earth's first outgoing galactourists, trading their cargo of artisanal confections for the wonders of the galaxy.

There's a muy famous recording from that day, of Martin and Green preparing to become héroes. They're strapped into the pilot and copilot seats, and they have no idea they're already being holoed. This bumpclip virafizzed faster than the FeedCast of the official speech they gave after.

Martin says, "We should say something important as we're leaving atmo."

Green's busy picking his nose. "Like what?"

Martin sighs at him and fluffs her hair. "I don't know. But this is the day where Earth comes together in peace to explore the galaxy. We're about to blast off into a *Star Trek* future. What would they say on the show?"

Green wipes his finger on his pants. "We can't use somebody else's catchphrase. Besides, this isn't science fiction anymore. It's real. We're going to meet another civilization."

Martin hesitates. "I know. It's an open spaceport we're heading for, but I still worry. Do you think they're going to be happy to see us when we get there? I mean, we don't have any real reason for going."

"They might." Green holds up that same finger. "We are after all a super-cool species. If you have tentacles or paws, you can't do this." He starts snapping his fingers and beatboxing.

Martin rolls her eyes. "You are aware that three-fourths of the sentient species in the galaxy have hands?"

Green continues his performance, incorporating the words, "Then maybe… we can teach them… to be cool."

That kind of optimism didn't last, for so many reasons. Mainly because it's hard to look cool when you won't let anybody visit in return. And once the borders closed, the spaceport in Switzerland shut down and re-opened as a virtual reality park for kids. It had been in operation for one year and three months. Good thing Green didn't live to see that, no?

He never even made it home. Green was bitten by one of the creatures he'd bought as a zoological specimen and died during the return trip from an untreatable infection – which could have been treated, if he'd still been close to the animal's native planet, by doctors who routinely handled such injuries. Knowing that before you watch them at takeoff always takes a lot of whoomph out of the holo.

My thoughts return to the present as we all return to our seats, and some first-year students start to serve the appetizers.

We eat, though I'm so sick with worry I couldn't tell you what I'm putting into my mouth. More of my teachers speak. After the entrees have been served and half devoured, Mamá takes the podium. She surveys the audience. "I admit I am intimidated by all of you, muchachos. After all, I learned to cook by watching mi mamá y mi abuelita. But do not think me being given a degree today in any way diminishes all the hard work that happens at this school."

She's speaking mostly English, one of the school's official languages, but she's flanked by two interpreters, each translating into handheld devices.

Frank leans back. His jacket flops weirdly, and I think I see the outline of that gun. There's a dark smear of something – which could be chocolate or sauce from the roast, but could just as easily be drying blood – on the outside of his wrist. My stomach fills with ice, and my chest aches as I stare at it. I'm terrified of what he might have done. Pero why would he have done it? Qué? There's no way anyone could have known about our plans to steal cacao at the time when mi vida got shot. I didn't even know yet myself. So what could Frank possibly have against Brill, who isn't important on either his world or mine? Unless Frank's some sort of pirate hunter, but that's a stretch.

People around me start applauding, Frank loudest of all, and I hurry to join in. Mamá's speech is over. I hope she doesn't ask how it went. She usually wants details, and I'm not sure I can talk to Frank without freaking out. Everyone starts heading for the dessert buffet, so I blend with the crowd and snag a handful of cookies, then I edge my way to the door.

I get a message from Kayla, who's obviously trying to distract herself on the long flight back to Earth. *Remember how I said Gavin's been choosing the worst examples of Earth literature to get a good impression of us? Please forward him this file, which is 100 awesome Earth novels, all translated into Universal for his convenience. Tell him I'm not speaking to him again until he has read them all. The jerk.*

I'm pretty sure that last bit's a reference to Gavin, not her signing off. Pero I'm amazed she cared enough what a Krom thinks to have written this at all. Maybe this is her strategy to never have to talk to him again, period.

There's a ring of paparazzi waiting for Mamá – and me. There was a time I thought I'd be happy if that ever happened again. At least they're being kept far enough away from the building that they can't see me clearly from here. I'm about to call Chestla and ask for safe passage back to my dorm, when Brill says, "Hey, Babe."

He's leaning against a stone railing, casually, like he hasn't tied me all up in knots inside over the past several hours. He pushes away from the rail as he asks, "Did you have fun?"

I rush up and wrap my arms around him, not caring if the Pops are getting holo. He winces and makes a soft unhappy noise as I press too hard against his injured arm. I let go. "Gracias a Dios! You're OK! I was so worried. I kept trying and trying to call."

He pulls his phone out of his pocket and frowns at the blank screen. He pushes a couple of buttons, but nada happens. "That's weird."

I slide my hands into his. "Can we walk down to the beach?"

"If we can keep the reporters from following us, ga."

I study the outline of his jaw. He's gorgeous, like something chiseled from marble. A héroe genuine. I'm still trying to comprender what that means, to me and to him.

He's never participated in a First Contact, and I've never gotten alcafuzzed enough to ask why. Maybe he was sick in his early twenties, when he was supposed to have taken his Voyage of Discovery. Or maybe he'd decided not to go for reasons of his own. If he had had the chance, would he have done the same thing to some other planet that the generation before him did to mine? Sometimes, traders get asked to help a group of Voyagers when there's a difficult cultural situation and that trader knows the area. Would he go, if asked? And if he did, would I be able to handle witnessing it? I'm not sure.

I comprendo the logic of what his people do, even agree with it on a philosophical level. Without this loco fight over chocolate, my people could have gone interstellar naturally, when whizzbang development or trade allowed. But thinking of First Contact happening to other specific people – without their understanding or consent – still makes me uncomfortable.

There had been some talk of going to war with Krom after Earth achieved the tech to start building starships en masse. The idea was to force reparations, since there was no recourse through the Galactic Court. But maybe it meant something that it was StarTrucks that tipped us off. In *Moby Dick*, Starbuck is Ahab's first mate (and sí, Starbucks took the name for him, a traveler of the world, just like coffee beans). And he's the one who points out to his captain the foolishness of revenge.

In this case, part of it was that the Krom simply don't fight back. Nunca. They disable weapons and use force fields to deflect invading ships, and if anything does get through, they arrest it and pay to have it transported back where it came from – even if some of their people are killed in the process.

And so, instead of wasting lives and more resources on a war we probably wouldn't win anyway, we turned our frustrangeration and conflict inwards and tore ourselves apart. That wasn't really the Krom's fault. Pero, just like Starbuck, who dies when Ahab causes the whole ship to sink because he can't find a way to move past his demencia, we gutted our society, became obsessed with looking outward for threats – and for our future.

Those who could afford it left the planet to explore the galaxy. And like everyone said, we started to move on. Krom never did give us anything in reparation for our pain. Nada. We stopped expecting them to.

Pero, we did get something in exchange for our innocence, from one of the Galactic Inspectors. The cop landed in

Switzerland, in those first heady days when chocolate was the galactourist souvenir of choice, before the borders closed. He didn't even know that the offender he'd picked up had been carrying a pet in her pocket – a female bringolda, which is something like a scaled hamster with the ability to refract light in a way that makes it close to invisible. One brood is all it takes to import a new invasive species. This one ate half the wheat in Europe before scientists found a way to make the pests visible enough to exterminate down to a manageable population. And if there's any lesson in all of this, it's that these interactions do push whizbang innovation, especially in the areas outside the chocolate belt, where people have had to re-evaluate their relevance to Earth.

Just like I'd re-evaluated my own relevance by leaving. My career – my life – was never going to recover mediaceptability after the chain of scandal that had crashbombed it. I belong here on Larksis, away from the Pops, which is why it is so unfair that they've followed me here. And so hard that I've had to accept the offer to step in front of the cameras again.

Brill unzips his jacket, and I hide my face inside the leather as he hurries us past the Pops, half carrying me, moving us faster than they can keep up. And for some reason, they don't try to chase us, even after he releases me and we run, hand in hand down towards the beach.

I look back. Chestla has melted out of the shadows created by the trees that fringe campus. Even though she's standing there alone, no one tries to pass her.

The rhythm of the waves will calm me, like a metronome for my heartbeat. It's always worked that way, since I was a child living in Chetumal, just north of the border where Mexico meets Belize, before Papá started taking jobs that had us moving around so much. I walked the whole beach near my house the day after Papá died, all those salt tears just for me.

Now we make our way down to the little seaside park where

a few granite boulders decorate a roped off swimming area. I pick up a fist-sized green seashell. Despite the chilly air, Brill and I sit together on one of the rocks, which is almost like a chair because of the taller rock behind it. I lean into his warmth, examining the lace-work frills where the shell opens. Dark and light banding circles the rounded part. As many times as I have been on this beach, I've not seen one like it. It will make an excellent addition to my collection. I have at least one shell from every beach I've ever been on, even the ones that prohibit removing them. If you look at it that way, I guess I've been a thief since childhood.

Brill takes the shell. His eyes are developing a similar tinge of green. "I found a buyer for the cocoa beans."

"Qué? Buyer?" The blood in my veins tries to turn the same temperature as the ocean – just a little too cold to swim in.

"What did you think we were going to do? Just hand them to random people on the street?"

I take my seashell back from him. "I'm not tonta. I just thought that when you free something, it's supposed to be a good deed, right? Taking from the rich to give to the poor. Parecido a Robin Hood."

"Even Robin Hood had to eat."

That stops me. I suppose he did. A wave crashes. "So how much dinero are we talking about?"

"A couple of million Krom units, for each viable bean."

My mouth gapes open. That's a lot more in dollars. Another wave pounds the sand. I feel like I am being washed around inside it, alongside all those flecks of gold.

We sit in silence until finally Brill says, "I don't think Frank shot me."

I can't hide my surprise – or my relief. Mamá needs somebody safe. "How are you sure?"

"Because he's a nice guy, once he gets the blunt questions out of his system. Because we really did go fishing, which made me feel tonto myself for being paranoid, and I didn't find any bombs or bugs on my ship after he left to go to the banquet I didn't rate an invite to."

I feel heat coming into my cheeks. "It was one of those things where nobody got to bring a date, except the guest of honor." I put a hand on Brill's arm.

He fake-pouts. "You didn't even bring me anything."

"I did so. Mira!" I reach into my pocket and pull out a napkin, which I've wrapped around the stack of cookies.

He fake-pouts some more. "I already had cookies at your dorm apartment."

"What did you expect me to bring, loco boy? The kagga fish would have dripped out of my pocket."

He takes the cookies and bites into one. "Haza. But I'm eating these against my better judgment. Next time, think about my fragile heart."

I lean in and kiss Brill. His lips taste like chocolate and sea salt. When we break the kiss, I am un poco breathless. "Tell me that this is all going to work out OK."

Brill puts his uninjured arm around me. "Wal. Everything is going to be OK, Babe. Do you think I'd ever let anything happen to you?"

I lean into him. "Te amo."

He squeezes me closer. "I love you too, Babe."

Together, we lean back against the taller rock. Earth only has one sunset. I'm going to make a point of admiring Larksis's double one tonight, for what may be the last time.

Brill pulls a clear box about twice the size of a deck of cards out of his pocket. The bottom has a layer inside of something gray. I lean in closer, trying to get a better look at the grid of little chambers inside. "Yesterday, this was a standard-issue seed viability box. They use them for planet colonization. Some seeds have to be planted right after they are harvested if you want them to grow. Cacao beans remain viable for two weeks, maybe three tops." Brill opens the box and pulls out one of the chambers. "With the standard issue, you put a seed in here and as long as the light turns green, you can go from three weeks viability to three months. Litoll?"

"Sí, very cool." Even though the clear chamber doesn't look like much more than just a plain plastic box. "And now that it's been altered?"

Brill's eyes dance toward a blissful blue. "Now we're talking three years."

"Vaya!" *Wow.* "So what am I supposed to do with it?"

"Maui is HGB's world headquarters, so that's where most of their research and quality testing happens. I'm already lining up the codes you'll need to get into the lab. All you need to do is get a pod from the quality-check bin. Likely, it will have already been counted, so no one will even notice it's missing, as long as you dispose of the pulp and the husk." He shifts, grimacing slightly and repositioning his injured arm. "But here's the genius part. That lab goes through a ton of supplies. So what you do is find a case of regular viability boxes, and you put the filled one in the middle of it and seal it back up. Mark it return to sender – defective – with a special label I'm having made, and drop it into the outgoing mail. That'll send it to a dummy address, and even if something does go wrong, they'll never be able to connect that address to you. Then it just sits there until your contract is up and you can take it offplanet when you–"

A red dot appears on his forehead, brilliant even in contrast to the setting sun.

"Ay no!" I lurch forward, pushing Brill off the boulder about a millisecond before a piece explodes out of it. He grabs the whizzbang viability box and ducks around the other side.

I freeze, my heartbeat pounding in my ears. Where did that shot even come from? It had to be the ocean. There's a boat out there, but it seems impossibly far away. And it can't be Frank, unless that boat's blazebanging fast.

"Come on, Babe! We've got to get to cover!" He's moving low, toward the dunes that separate the park from campus.

Something pockmarks the sand, not far from Brill's boot.

I scream, but that gets me moving. I realize Brill's slowed down, so I can keep up.

A couple more bullets hit the sand. The shooter's definitely targeting Brill, not me. "You're right," he shouts. "Wal. I should get offplanet."

I race for the dunes, but I keep looking back, expecting a bullet to hit one of us at any moment. I'm close to hyperventilating. I've never been shot at before. I register dimly that Kayla's going to give me one muy grande I-told-you-so over this.

CHAPTER FIVE

Brill kisses me goodbye and leaves the planet before I've even stopped trembling. And the taste of his kiss hasn't even faded when several HGB employees show up to get me to safety too.

I'm excited when they take me to board a super-express flight, that should make it back to Earth in eighteen days, instead of the standard twenty-eight to thirty. The pops are lined up next to it, taking photos of me. It's an Earthling-only vessel, which means it will land directly on Earth. I've flown with them before, and the food is excellent. If I have to go back to Earth, at least I'll go in luxury.

None of the other passengers have come aboard yet. The HGB escorts take me up to the bridge, where I get to shake hands with the three members of the crew.

I tell the Captain, "Gracias por taking me back to Earth."

She gives one of my escourts a sharp look. "Didn't you tell her this was the decoy vessel?"

My heart sinks. By the time I realize how attached I'd gotten to flying in that pretty ship, I've been shunted into a piece of luggage and out the baggage chute, out of view of the pops.

I'm already off Larksis by the time I get unzipped out of the oversized suitcase they stuck me in, and realize they've booked me a tiny room on a ginormous HGB cargo hauler, with no ability to contact the outside worlds. I mean, en serio? How can a spaceship be a no call zone?

I didn't even get a chance to tell mi Mamá adiós. Long space voyages leave me restless in the best of circumstances. You can only burn off so much energy in the gym, and unlike both Kayla and Brill, I'm not an avid reader, nunca. And this one's utilitarian, so it's not like there are on-board entertainment options.

Nobody tries to stop me from exploring the ship, but the cargo bay is locked, which is extraño enough, but why would a milk run truck need a crew of four? There's something in there that two of the crew keep going in to tend to, and at one point they come out arguing about it.

One of them says, "It's for the CEO himself. If you let the temperature go too low and it dies, what do you think will happen?"

And the other replies, "It's not my fault. Who knew a bunch of goo could be that sensitive?"

Ordinarily, I wouldn't be able to hold back my curiosity, but what I'm about to do is already so dangerous – the last thing I need is to get caught snooping. I do my best to stay busy, mainly by feeding new words into my sublingual to help with the linguistics exams I'm supposed to take when I get back to school – if I get back in time – and by people watching. The amount of drama that can take place in three weeks between a crew of four people becomes highly amusing. But with my nerves growing day by day over everything that could crashbomb aquí, I'm ready to burst out the door and suck in lungfuls of real atmo. Twenty-seven days after launch, I finally reach Earth. Before I'm done appreciating being on the ground, they shuffle me straight into a helicopter. The lone pilot looks bored.

Now that I'm away from the ship, my phone goes nuts with several hundred missed calls and notifications. Mamá has sent a dozen questions asking about the decoy shuttle – which no one seems to have footage of. It should have landed in Maui a week ago, and that makes me nervous.

I realize I've been looking at my phone for a good half hour, and we're still in the air. That doesn't feel right. I lean forward, squinting to make out the coast through the low clouds, unease growing in my stomach with each new detail that emerges.

It's hard to think over the *koo-koo-koo-koo* of the helicopter blades, but I've been to HGB headquarters enough times to realize that wherever we're headed, it's not Maui. The right kind of mountains counterpoint the tall buildings, sí, pero the coastline doesn't curve the way an island should. I never should have fallen asleep aboard this tonta thing last night. We could be anywhere now, no?

The chopper turns, and when the clouds clear, there, off to the left, stands the statue of Christ the Redeemer holding out his benevolent stone hands in welcome. My heart sinks toward my stomach and I groan, though I don't even hear the sound. Dios mío, they've brought me home all right, not just to Earth, but to the place where we moved when Mamá got famous, where they'd recorded her first official FeedCasts, where I had to remember to speak Portuguese instead of Spanish.

"We're lost, right?" I try to sound like I'm teasing, but the pilot doesn't even crack a smile.

He hands a glowing tablet over his shoulder. "That's the manifest. HGB Branch Facility, just inland from Rio."

"Isn't that just fantástica?" I can't help sounding sarcastic. Brill had prepped me to get into the secure areas of a building roughly seven and a half thousand miles away. I lean forward and force myself to breathe slowly as I activate my sublingual, using the encryption prefix mi vida taught me. He answers immediately, as though he was sitting with his handheld, waiting for my call.

I'm in Brazil, Brill. I'm gripping the pilot's tablet so hard I fear I might crack it.

Why? He sounds confused. *That's a roundabout way to Hawaii.*
I'm not going to Hawaii, loco boy. They're sending me to Rio. He

doesn't reply in the time it takes to fly around the high rises on the south side of the city, which pushes even farther than I remember into the expanse of the rainforest, so I say, *Mi vida, it's good to hear your voice. I've been worried about you every minute since Larksis. Have your friends managed to find out who's trying to kill you?*

I've made a number of people mad over the years, but specifically the shooter? Ga. Get me a list– Brill stops bubblechattering.

A recorded male voice repeats *You are in a No Call Zone* over and over in English, Spanish and Portuguese until I hang up. Well, no pues wow. *That's just great.*

I picture Brill out there, somewhere in the stars. It's a gran galaxy. And not exactly safe. The Galactacops do their best to keep order, but there are only so many of them in the vastness of space – and they still can't predict a crime before it happens. Humans tend to underestimate the danger of any situation, so in the days right after we went interstellar, we were blithely acting like rich tourists, visiting exotic fruit markets and megamalls and flufferific tension cloud amusement parks. Eventually, though, somebody got mugged for real. The story virafizzed so big that even now we all remember the baby-steps holo through the graduation footage of Jet James, first human murdered in space. By the time it happened, we were officially registered with the Galactic Courts as accepting Galactic protection. A dozen choco-addicted Galactic Inspectors jumped on the case. They were relentless, hunting the murderer across a tundra in the middle of a blizzard once they'd shot his ship out of the sky. Pero they brought the guy back alive, and turned him over to Earth's justice system. Claro está, the trial was carried out on Interface Station, since even a prisoner alien wasn't going to be allowed in Earth's airspace. But it proved that the Galactic justice system worked, and that Earth had been accepted as an equal.

The pilot doesn't say another word to me for the rest of the ride, even as we land and the helicopter's blades make gran-leaved rainforest plants bounce and flatten. Tawny emerges from the complex. She lifts a hand in greeting, but keeps well back from the flying bits of dirt and leaves. When the blades finally stop, the pilot gets out first and helps me to the ground.

"Bo! It's fabulous to see you again!" Tawny takes my hand and swings it back and forth, like we're little-kid best friends. I struggle to comprender this personality change as she leads me toward the blocky white multistory building. Given the flat roof, it looks a little like a shopping mall crossed with a hotel.

Princesa is here, I hear Tawny say.

"Disculpe?" *Huh?* I reply before I realize the sound was only in my head. I'm picking up crosstalk from her sublingual. That only happens if you're within three or four feet of somebody else who's using one. It's considered rude not to move away, but Tawny's still holding my hand.

She looks at me sharply, then hangs up. "Don't worry. Someone will get your bags. You must be hungry." Without waiting for an answer, she pulls me through the lobby, down a hall, and into a cafeteria. The upper half of the walls are decorated with rows of chevrons in brown and gold and orange in a sad attempt to create a festive look. A bald man walks past with a square piece of pizza that looks congealed. Blegh.

I double the fakeness of my smile, still wondering how she's able to make a call out. "I really just want a chance to freshen up, por favor."

"Suit yourself." Tawny still hasn't let go of my hand. "Let me show you to your room."

We travel through a maze of white-walled hallways, past dozens of identical doors. She lets go of my hand to pull a plastic card from her pocket. "Here's your room key."

"Gracias." I swipe the card and push down a lever to open

the door to my new temporary home, which is outfitted with worn avocado green carpet and stained orange Formica. It doesn't have a full kitchen – just a microwave, a hot plate and a mini fridge. I stifle a groan, brighten up my fake smile and ask, "So where's the householo?"

I don't see any obvious controls. Maybe it is voice activated?

"We don't have any." Tawny wrinkles her nose. "We find it distracts the workers. Productivity has increased nearly twelve percent company-wide since we removed them."

She babbles on about the state-of-the art exercise facilities and the neural enhancement modules that replaced the timewasters, then she finally leaves me solitaria. As soon as the door closes behind her, I growl in frustration. Fantástico. Not only can I not get instructions from Brill, I can't even find out what's going on in the outside world. I collapse onto the bed, burying my face in the scratchy comforter. I stay that way for a long time, right up until there's a soft knock on the door. Before I can answer, it opens, and a tall skinny guy pushes my bags inside. I've seen him somewhere before. The dark circles under his eyes are gone, but the thin shoulders and cool-toned black skin are the same. "Kaliel? Kaliel Johansson?"

He sees me and jumps. "Lo siento. Tawny said you'd be in the cafeteria."

I'm surprised he's mixing in Spanish when he talks to me, but he's making it sound natural.

"Está bien." I push myself into a sitting position. "I didn't see anything that resembled food in there. Do you know where I can get something decent to eat?"

"Sure. There's a restaurant on the south side of the complex, but you have to use your own dinero. Otherwise, you can go into Rio. You just have to have Tawny clear you for a gate pass. I recommend Primeira Taxa. They have the best Moqueca de Camarão in town." His pronunciation slides perfectly between languages.

I smile for real for the first time all day. "I've been there, and you're right. Absolutamente, we should go sometime, or maybe I can show you a few of *my* favorite places. I used to live in Rio."

"I didn't know that." He laughs, bringing warmth to his gray-green eyes. "It's funny how when someone's all over the feeds, you think you know what they're going to be like in person. You're not at all what I expected."

"Qué? Not what you expected how?" I clamber off the bed.

"For starters, you're being nice to me. After what you'd been saying on the feeds about IIGB in general, I guess I expected you to yell murderer and throw rotten tomatoes at me."

"Are you a murderer?" I look into his eyes, almost expecting them to change so I can gauge his thoughts, but the steady color reveals nada.

"You tell me. Everything happened just like I explained on the feeds. Still, I fired on innocent people." Kaliel runs a hand across his nearly-shaved head. "Despite what they're FeedCasting about me being exonerated, the prosecutor is pushing for seventy-two counts of murder one. If I'm convicted, I'll get a head shorter, real fast."

Ice races through my gut as I picture the guillotine blade slicing out through his Adam's apple, too vivid an image, too real a possibility. I swallow. My mouth has gone cotton-dry. "Sí. With all the spacejackings, they'd have to make an example out of you, and the feeds would love it, the bloodier the better." I shouldn't have said that so matter-of-factly. We are, after all, talking about a form of public execution where they strap you to a board and let your arterial red spray the cameras. "Lo siento, Kaliel."

He brings an idle hand up to his neck. "Don't be sorry for me. But do tell your roommate I regret what happened to her grandparents. I've memorized all the faces from the SeniorLeisure manifest, and sometimes I think I deserve the shave. I'm wandering in a nightmare. You want to know the worst part?"

I'm not sure I do, but I nod.

"Just like in the days of the Terror, they cut your hair short and snip off your shirt collar to make sure there's nothing to interfere with the blade. I think that's when it becomes real, when those cold scissors touch your skin."

Either that, or they dress you up for the cameras, if the execution's really high profile. Pero, I don't say that out loud. I try to smile, try not to think about how easily I could wind up taking a ride on that same blood-soaked teeter-totter if I get caught stealing cacao. I can't breathe in here. I move over to the window and open it, letting in vibrant scents of earth and green. It doesn't help. Nada, not one bit. "You don't have much hair, and you seem to favor T-shirts. So maybe it won't happen, no?"

He laughs. "See? Not what I imagined you'd be at all. Now that I've depressed you, I should get out of your way."

He turns, his hand already on the door lever.

"Oye, wait." I have no idea what I'm about to say, just that I don't want him to leave like that. "Do you know where I can get a map?"

Kaliel releases the door. "Do you have a handheld? They're not good for much else in this loco place, but you can access a few local files." When I pull the thing that looks like a chocolate bar out of my pocket, he laughs. "I think my little sister has one like that. She's twelve."

After he leaves, I close the window and visually scan the room for cameras. Then, I walk the perimeter of the space, the bug sweeper still hidden in my pocket. It doesn't find anything.

I exit my shabby excuse for a room. On my way to the restaurant, I find myself in a wider hallway where a long window runs along the top half of the right wall. A dozen uniformed school children are climbing on or leaning against a railing so that they can look down through the plastiglass.

I peer through the window into an open area one floor below. The robots, built like guys in jumpsuits with wedge-shaped silver faces, have a gauge running up the front, signifying battery life. These bots are nearing empty as they mush the husked pods, dropping the mess of puce-toned beans and white pulp into thigh-tall fermentation boxes. Camera drones float among the proceedings, allowing human eyes to keep close watch.

Up here, a tour guide tries to keep several of the niños from wandering off. She catches hold of one boy by his shirt collar, never losing her smile as she says, "You don't want to have to go through decontamination, do you?"

The boy's eyes go saucer-like. "No, por favor."

I don't blame the niño. Humans are not permitted to come into contact with the cacao beans until they've fermented, making them useless for anyone wanting to start an unauthorized cacao plantation. The chemical shower they give anyone who could have slipped a viable one into a pocket is somewhat toxic to the recipient, not just the potential trees.

Tawny strides up to me. "Oh, Bo! There you are."

I jump. "Sí. Here I am, right?"

"Did you want to take the tour?" She smacks herself on the forehead in a forced, kitschy gesture. "I didn't even think of that. I assumed you'd have seen the whole thing when you were in grade school."

I want to say no. I hate organized tours. Pero, it might be my best opportunity to case the place. So I shrug. "I wasn't old enough to appreciate it, no?"

She puts a hand on my arm. "If you want to join them, and then spend the rest of the day getting acclimated, that's fine. But tomorrow's going to be a busy day. The director needs to take some preliminary holos, so he can get a feel for your on-camera personality, and the stylists are excited to finally get to do something about your hair."

"There's nada in my contract about my hair." I feel that tension creeping into my shoulders again. My hair's long and luscious, my crowning glory.

Tawny clasps her hands together in front of her. "It's just that in the survey held last week on FeedCast Wannabees, eighty-six percent of respondents said you needed an updated look."

"I try to stay off that feed." I sound nonchalant, but inwardly, I cringe. Eighty-six percent? That's harsh. "I guess I could use just a trim."

"That's great." She takes my hand in hers again. "You're being much more cooperative than some of the other celebrities I've worked with."

I'm not going to ask her which celebrities, even though she's fishing for a chance to namedrop. "Why are we at one of the processing plants? I thought I'd be drinking something out of a pineapple by now, right?"

"My whole unit came to Rio to cover the Chocolate Festival. They sent you here instead of to corporate so that we could kill two birds with one stone, so to speak. If you're taking the tour, that actually works better for me. I can get a head start setting things up in town."

I grasp Tawny's hand, trying for a little girl-to-girl camaraderie. "Hablando de town, Kaliel said I should ask you for a gate pass so I can check out some of the local restaurants."

She pulls her hand out of mine, and the edge of the jraghite scratches me. "I don't think that's a good idea."

"Oh. OK."

I guess I must look shocked, because she straightens her top and says, "What I mean is Rio is a dangerous place. You've already been threatened once. Why give them another chance?"

"Pero nobody knows to be looking for me here," I protest.

"Let's be honest, Bo. You don't exactly have a history of

being discreet. We can't afford another incident that would show you haven't outgrown your wild ways. Maybe in a couple of days I can get Kaliel or Brandon or Rick to take you into town." She reaches into her bag, then hands me a different plastic card, this one bright yellow. "Why don't you go down to the company restaurant after the tour? My treat. This card will also get you anything you need from the commissary."

So now I at least know where I stand. Not exactly a prisoner, but close. I take the card. "Gracias."

I join the niños. While we're still looking down into the processing area, the guide points out the puffballs piled up in the corner with their upright doglike ears and oversized rabbit noses. "Those are cybernetic wombats. Their enhancements help them sniff out intruders."

Cybernetic wombats. The combination of those two words quiet the second graders for almost a whole minute.

"Why wombats?" one of the niños asks. "I thought they only lived in Australia."

The guide's smile warms considerably. "That's right, but wombats eat very little and can go a week without water. They are also difficult to deter once they have a target. Those claws can tear through most things short of concrete and steel."

The guide gets another respectful moment of silence when she points to the cabinet holding the just-husked cacao beans and explains that the titanium locks are connected to an alarm system that causes non-lethal nerve gas to fill the room, paralyzing any would-be thief. I swallow hard at that one, and struggle to get my legs going when it's time to move on. I can't get the image of myself lying helpless on the floor being eaten by wombats out of mi cabeza for the rest of the tour.

Still trying to come up with a viable plan, I make my way down to the commissary. It takes up a long hall in the left wing of the complex. I wander through the stores, touching silk scarves and soft sweaters, wondering if HGB cuts as many corners on the production of these items as they have on their buildings. I tug a black sleeve, fully expecting it to come apart in my hand. Instead, the garment springs off the hanger, which clatters back against the others.

I pack my shopping bag with seemingly random items. I start with some basic cooking gear, then add anything that looks like it might help me get into those cabinets, including a metal spreader spatula and a small meat tenderizer. I snag a reusable water bottle that will serve as a decent jar for transferring pulp. I pick up a pair of gloves and then three gauzy scarves from the little accessory store, figuring that they are long enough to serve as an improvised rope. I drop the items off in my room, then head for the restaurant, where I spot Kaliel sitting at a table with a couple of people. He waves me over as I come in the door.

"Hey!" He smiles as I approach. "How was your trip into town?"

"Oye. I didn't get to go. Tawny thinks I need a tour guide."

Kaliel points at the guy sitting next to him. "How about Rick and I take you tomorrow? I know I can get it cleared, because they'd love to have shots of me and you together. Assuming you don't mind partying with a dead man."

A lot of the FeedCasters had emphasized that Kaliel's only twenty-six. Two years older than me, and he's already staring at the end of his life. I shudder.

Rick, a Portuguese-descended Brazilian who's little older than Kaliel, gives him a sharp look. "You haven't been convicted of anything yet, and you won't be." Rick waves a hand at me. "Tell him all the Feeds say he's going to live."

I change the uncomfortable subject. "Take me to a grocery store, por favor, and I'll make you both a meal that will bring back hope." I gesture with my chin at their food. "Even with just a hot plate, I can do better."

Kaliel nods. "Sí. There's a traditional open-air market I'd like to see where they sell cool stuff during the Chocolate Festival. There's a lot of things I might never get another chance to do, so I'm determined not to let anything pass me by."

I don't have the heart to tell him that that's for the tourists.

Everybody else at the table has moved on to talking about their plans for the Chocolate Festival.

"You know what else I don't want to miss?" Kaliel stabs his fork into a greasy-looking mound of papas con chilies.

"Qué?" My stomach growls. I'm going to have to eat something soon, even if it is here.

"Tonight's meteorite shower. I have never just laid back in the grass and watched one."

Rick shakes his head. "You don't want to do that here. Too many snakes and poisonous bugs. Take the access ladder up to the roof. There are a couple of telescope mounts up there, and you'll find a bunch of employees with the same idea. I'm going. What about you, Bo?"

I don't have anything else to do until well after midnight, and it will keep me from going loco over not being able to communicate with the outside. "Sounds like fun, no?"

While loading my plate, I snag a couple of roasted sweet potatoes still in their skins, conveniently wrapped in foil, which I slip into the pocket of my cargo pants. I understand from the tour that wombats love them.

CHAPTER SIX

By the time I make it onto the rooftop that night, there's close to fifty people already up there.

Kaliel spots me and brings me a beer. "No, I didn't test positive for alcohol after the accident, if that's what you're thinking."

I take the bottle. I'm more of a wine person myself, but if a friend needs you to drink a beer with them to cheer them up, you drink the beer. "Claro. Nobody thinks that. And *you* need to start thinking about something else."

He points up, where a purplish light streaks across the sky, followed by two white ones. "They really are beautiful. But they just remind me how much shorter life can be than you expected, how desperately you need to–" His words cut off mid phrase. I follow his gaze. A larger meteorite, a real bola de fuego, streaks in our general direction.

"Check it out. It's your first light show, right?" Rick gestures me over to one of the telescopes, which happens to be pointed in the right direction. An object flashes across my view. Oye! I only get the briefest of glances but I swear it looks manmade, maybe a crashing piece of space junk. I look up and see it still streaking through the atmosphere heading down into the rainforest on the other side of the high stone walls, inside the cacao plantation. It sets off the alarms, and a dozen bird-shaped drones take flight from perches inside the wall.

"That was muy hermosa." *Very beautiful.* Kaliel opens another bottle. "I'll remember that for as long as I... well, as long as I can, anyway."

I hang out with them for another hour, but I decline the second beer Rick tries to hand me. I need my hand-eye coordination intact, no? When I finally leave, Rick's singing a Portuguese-language love song to some girl, and Kaliel's watching them. I don't say goodbye. They might see the guilt in my face. I don my gloves before I reach the outside access ladder we all climbed to get up here.

I start my descent. Laughter trickles down from the rooftop. I'm glad that I went to watch the meteor shower, not only for Kaliel's sake, pero because it gave me a chance to scope out this wall from above. A ledge runs along the entire length, crossing behind the ladder. When I reach the junction, I have a hard time making myself let go of the rung. I haven't done anything like this since the balance beam back in gym class, in those years when Papá had been the school's assistant coach, before his job got cut and he became a firefighter, and even then I remember my heart pounding, rápido. If it had been anyone but Papá asking, I probably wouldn't have been able to do it in class, either.

Still, I can't stay here all night. I take a deep breath and hold the air. Before I lose my nerve, I step over onto the narrow strip of bricks, gripping the wall through the thin fabric covering my fingers I inch across. I'm not that high up, maybe ten or twelve feet, so if I fell it wouldn't be life-ending, but try telling my corbarde body that. Sweat beads on my face as I shuffle toward the grate covering the ventilation shaft.

Once I reach the grate, I stabilize my balance and take out my Swiss Army knife.

I unscrew one corner of the grate. This is going to work, as long as nobody who's had too much beer comes down that ladder needing a pee.

A steel-toe boot clangs against the top rung. Dios mío. I flatten myself against the wall. The guy is still laughing and talking to someone on the roof. He looks down at his feet to make sure his exaggerated steps are landing solidly. He never even notices me. Once he reaches the ground, the sound of a zipper echoes in the still night and the guy starts taking a whiz in the bushes at the base of the building. I need to hurry, rápidamente, before he decides to re-join the party. Ignoring my pounding heart, I unscrew two more corners, leaving the grate swinging by one top tip. I climb inside the square metal shaft. I turn to peer out just as the guy zips up and looks back at the roof. He squints at the area where I am, as if part of his brain might be telling him something's wrong, pero it's too dark for him to figure out what.

A breeze flows over me, pulled by a fan somewhere farther inside. It's making a *choo-choo* noise parecido a the helicopter I arrived on. The shaft angles downward, and I start to make out the dim outline of the fan itself. When I reach it, I find and toggle the emergency off switch, but the blades are still too close together for me to step through. I unscrew one of them using the appropriate tool on my knife, then I rest the piece up against the frame. Hasta ahora todo va bien. *So far, so good.* Or is it maybe just a little bit too easy? I mean, that switch was marked.

I squeeze between the remaining blades and, just after the shaft levels out, find myself peering through the shutters of another vent at a grid of blue light, which marks a bionet that separates the shaft from the room below. Ay no! How am I going to get through that? No wonder they weren't worried about securing the fan.

I lean back against the side of the shaft and exhale through my teeth. I might as well go back up and have a few more drinks.

The louvres spring together at the top of the grate, like a window blind being pulled up, and the blue grid winks out.

"Mmpf!" I flinch away. Did I touch some hidden switch? I flip around and examine the wall. It looks smooth. Is this a trap? That seems un poco paranoid, even for HGB.

The bots keep their eyes on their work, cleaning their machetes and storing away the final few fermentation boxes in the airhole-studded cabinets. After the mechanoids leave, the lights go out and the cameras settle to the floor. Part of me wants to bolt back out the shaft, convinced this is about to go horribly wrong. But the rest of me's sure that part's paranoid.

Trying not to panic, I unwrap the three scarves from around my neck and knot them together. I tie the end of one around the louvres, then I rappel down them to the floor, landing silenciosamente. The cameras don't wake. Neither do the wombats still huddling together in the far corner.

As I sneak across the room, I take out my meat tenderizer and my spatula, puzzling over how to crack open the nearest cabinet without setting off the freezesmoke.

A high-pitched whine startles me so badly I drop the spatula. Not daring to pick it up, I turn slowly. A wombat the size of a gran rabbit stands looking up at me, emitting the mechanical noise. I hope the thing's not gritcasting video out its eyeballs.

"Nice wombie," I whisper, taking a sweet potato out of my pocket. "Nothing's wrong here. Nada."

The wombat chitters at me like a giant hamster, pulls the sweet potato out of my hand before I can even set it on the floor, then runs away. Tension drains out of my shoulders as I take a deep, calming breath. I take three more steps.

The cabinet I'm approaching explodes.

"Aaarrrraaaccckkgggh!" I bring up my arms to cover my face even as I'm knocked backwards, the adrenaline already racing through my system kicking into brain-numbing overdrive that makes everything seem to be happening slowmo, my connection to my own body distant and unreal until I hit the floor, hard. Pain jolts through my shoulder and the back of my head. Speckled with pineapple-scented pulp, I lie there for un momento before it hits me why the security measures turned themselves off. I've interrupted someone else's heist.

Oi! No! I push myself blindly up to sitting. My muscles are tensed for anything coming at me from any direction, and I can feel my heartbeat in my aching jaw. I can't really see or hear right. And I'm in the middle of the room.

What if this other thief has a gun? What if they don't like sharing?

I start crawling backwards, freaked that something's going to attack me while I'm helpless, pero after a few panicked seconds, the flash blindness passes. Stars still spot my vision, and when they clear I'm looking at a dented fermentation cabinet, one door hanging from the top hinge, the other blown to the floor. There's no one else in here, and the wombats are ignoring me. Eh? Maybe handing over that sweet potato got me on their approved-as-a-non-threat list.

Still scanning for the other intruder, I crawl forward to the edge of the mess, where I take the reusable water bottle and scoop up the nearest pile of seeds and pulp.

The far door opens, then closes again, and a black-clad figure edges along the sides of the cabinets. I freeze. There's nowhere to hide. The woman drops a backpack and starts filling something inside with double handfuls of the pulpy beans from the demolished cabinet. I think I recognize her.

"Meredith?"

"Qué?" She turns. Our eyes lock. Three cybernetic wombats – these more the size of Rottweilers than rabbits – move to circle us, chittering. My mouth goes dry as I get a glimpse of those strong, square teeth. Each womborg only has four incisors, pero, that's enough.

The meat tenderizer flew over against the far wall, leaving me unarmed, and I don't have another sweet potato to give Meredith. I shove the bottle back into my pocket and dash for my scarf rope, before I get back on the active threat list. As I grasp the colorful edge, an alarm sounds. The louvres release, tearing the top scarf apart. Ay, no! My escape route flutters down into my hands as the bionet flashes back on. "Aynh!"

"Aynh is right." Meredith's Spanish sounds like it is echoing down a tunnel, but that's probably just my ears post-explosion. She kicks at one of the wombats, then throws a device onto the floor. "Stupid junk Cyborg Mesmerizer. I guess you get what you pay for."

One of the womborgs bites the Cyborg Mesmerizer in half. My stomach clenches at the crackcrunch. See why I'm in cooking school? I'll take food over tech any day.

I wrap the scarves loosely around my neck, then grab the mangled cabinet door. "Maybe we can still get out of here if we work together." I think I'm shouting to be heard over the alarm, pero everything still sounds muffled.

"The security reset demasiado rápido. Deben haber mejorado." *They must have upgraded.* She pulls an aerosol can out of her bag. Is that bear spray? She looks back at me, even as she tries to dodge towards the exit. "I'm glad you're alive. I heard you got scuttlepunched just before touching down in Honolulu."

A wombat lunges at her leg. She dances backwards, dropping the bag to hold the can in both hands. She sprays the cybormonster. It flinches back. Despite my fear, I advance, waving the sharp edges of the busted door, trying to shoo the womborgs away from Meredith, but they don't even flinch. "Is that what's going out on the official HGB feed?"

"Of course not. But there's unofficial feed of your shuttlecrash."

Oye. Heat pricks at my eyes. I didn't know. That poor decoy shuttle crew. There's no way their fireballed deaths are my fault, nada, nunca, but if I hadn't come here...

"My sources theorize that they're pulling images of you from existing holos. Especially that stuff from your dorm. They've released dos ads already." She stumbles, and the wombats charge her.

"Noooooooo!" My heart squeezes and I gasp as she starts to go down. She sprays at one of the monsters with the can, and I hit another with the door piece. The shock reverberates up my arms, pero the wombat looks more annoyed than hurt. It turns and chitters angrily at me.

"Erghad!" My breath is coming fast, my heartbeat faster. "We have to get out of here!"

The third wombat jumps on Meredith's back, and the acrid smell of chemical fuel fills the air. The claws must have pierced the reservoir of her jetpack. The wombats back away from the fumes, allowing Meredith time to get to her feet, gracias a Dios. She makes a mad dash, but when she touches the door, she cries out in pain. "They've got the bionets back on."

Icy cold flashes through my chest. "No y no!" They've netted the doors, too. Fantástico. The light grid must be on the other side.

The wombats edge closer, finally seeming to register me as an intruder now that I've hit one of them. Those fumes won't hold them back for long.

"There's only one other way out." My voice squeaks on the last word. My hearing is clearing enough to register the tone.

We both stare at the processing equipment, and my chest prickles with dread. According to a display embedded in the wall, the roaster is still cooling from today's batch. The gauge says it's not hot enough to cook us, as long as we keep moving.

I spot a back-up jetpack in Meredith's open bag. I pull it out, making eye contact to signal I'm about to throw it to her.

Meredith shakes her head. "Take it! Mine should have a little fuel left."

She gestures for me to put the jetpack on. I don't argue. I

strap on the device, and it unfolds against my back. I activate it, screaming as it accelerates me up and over the womborgs while I'm still trying to figure out the controls, which seem to be tapping the same neural patch as my sublingual.

"Byaaaaaa!" I go flying into the roaster's open conveyer tube. Halfway along, I smack up against the bony backside of the only wombat smart enough to flee the nerve gas. En serio? Thanks to extra-credit-wombie-fan kid on the tour, I know this creature is using the same posture to block the exit as he would if this were his burrow. Helpful, no?

The sickly odor of the freezesmoke has followed me in here, though Meredith hasn't. I try to hold my breath, but I can't because I'm near hyperventilation. Annnnnd... the air I keep drawing into my lungs is getting hot. I already feel sluggish from the gas. If I don't do something right now, I'm going to pass out. And then I really will be muerto. I shove at the wombat's butt. "Move, you loco brute."

I might have enough room to squeeze past it. I take off the jetpack and hold it in front of me.

"Why did you stop, Bo?" Meredith has climbed on top of the last fermentation cabinet up against the far wall. That may buy her enough time to keep breathing until the guards come, but it's not a long-term survival strategy.

"I'm trying to get past this estúpido wombat." I wriggle forward, climbing over the wombat, blinking through the brainblur. No lo sé why she decided to sacrifice herself for me. I can't let her just give up. "You need to be heading this way, too. Prisa! You know what happens if the guards capture you in here."

"Be heading. Ha. That's cómico."

Her gallows humor chills me to my core, despite the heat. "En serio, why didn't you follow me?"

"My jetpack wouldn't start. The loco borg must have damaged the receiver." Meredith lets her cabeza drop back against the wall. "Be careful. Wombats will suffocate predators trying to get into their burrows by pressing them against the roof of the hole."

"Now you tell me." I'm halfway past the wombat when it pushes against me, the strong claws digging ruts into the softer conveyer belt. Searing pain hits my back as I roll against the heating unit. I cry out, but the marsupial seems intent on forcing the air from my lungs.

I try to breathe back in, but can only fit in a narrow stream of air. Between that and the heat and the nerve gas, it'll only take a few minutes for me to die. Icy certainty settles in my stomach, I am muerto. Pero, I keep fighting the womborg anyway. I turn on the jetpack, which I'm still holding out in front of me, angling the thrusters down, hoping they will either pull me free, or startle the monster into moving. Pero, those thrusters are safe enough to wear against your back. Nothing happens except that the jetpack starts trying to fly out of my hands.

Something pings against the wall behind my feet. I look back. Meredith throws something else. She hits her target, and the conveyer belt starts. Her voice sounds floppy, like she's talking around a mouth full of Novocain. "Hurry, Bo. I think I just turned the whole system on."

I slide against the wombat, which is using those powerful claws to dig backwards, releasing the pressure on my chest as he scrabbles hard to stay in place. I suck in precious air.

"Vamos! I'm not leaving without you! Somebody has to take care of your estúpido dog." Even as I shout, I know Meredith's not coming. I want to go back for her, but a clear heat guard is already dropping into place behind me, so I push my way forward before the wombat can block me again. He swings his head, looking just as scared as I am that this place has turned into a long oven. The jetpack pulls me free of him. It starts to gain speed. The wombat nips at my ankle but doesn't get through my boot. I kick it back, even as I zoom off the conveyer, into open air. My feet dangle into the intake bowl of the crusher at the end, designed to break the roasted beans into nibs. "Aaaaayyyyyhhh." I pull my boots up out of the way of the first rolling metal bar with inches to spare, relief flooding through me. The conveyer spills the wombat into the crusher. The chittering turns to an alarmed screeching that falls silent before I can get the jetpack disabled and the crusher turned off.

Guácala! Gross! I bring a fist up to my mouth as I wince. Poor wombie!

Trying not to look inside, I pull myself up against the crusher. "Meredith?" I peer across the conveyer belt. On the other side, I can just make out her still form on top of the cabinet.

The door bursts open and half a dozen guards, their faces veiled with gas masks, pour into the room, training weapon scope lights on her. Oye! I have to get out of here before someone sees me. As I drop down from the equipment, one of the guards says, "Did something move in there?"

Dios mío, I can't catch a break. The door in this room is locked down, too, pero there's no bionet on the chute that goes to where the nibs, having been ground into chocolate liquor, get pressed into cocoa powder. Other chutes lead to vats for making milk and dark chocolate, but the access points to those are obscured by tubing.

I must have breathed more freezesmoke than I thought. My coordination's shot. I have to stab a couple of times before I hit the button that opens the shaft. As I peer into the chute, the smell of cacao overwhelms me.

Voices sound outside the door, rapidly getting louder. Fear squeezes at my heart. *Be heading*. It's really not cómico.

Forcing my trembling legs to move, I leap into the shaft. It's a short fall, and I tumble onto a round plate, something like the bottom half of an oversized waffle iron, but instead of grooves, I'm lying on a strong fine mesh. The solid top half falls towards me, filling my vision, freezing my chest. "Gyaaaahhhh!"

My heart pounding, I scramble out of the way. The lid closes on the trailing end of one of my scarves. I pull it free just before the clamp secures itself on the press. I am smeared all over with dark chocolaty grit.

There's a smaller door in the wall here. According to the map, it leads to the garage, a convenient access point for attaching tubing to dairy tankers, important for making chocolate con leche. I use the long scraper meant for cleaning the press to force open the door. I manage to get it latched again behind me, which might buy me a little time. I try to slow my breathing, to relax my shoulders, but I'm still in panic mode. The arched tunnel smells rancid from old drips of dairy. It doesn't take long, though, to trade that smell for oil and exhaust fumes. Inside the garage, dozens of Jeeps stand parked in neat lines beside a lone tanker. I am tempted to take a road trip right now, but I have to be patient, stay calm. Tranquila. If I run, I'll never be able to set foot on this planet again.

I have the cacao beans I came for. Now, I just need to get back to my room and out of these clothes without getting caught. I've got a gate pass. When they decide to give me some time off, it will be just a matter of checking out a vehicle and slipping away to the spaceport. No one will ever know I'm the one who broke the monopoly. Estará bien. *It will be fine.*

I'm still shaking, my heartrate still noticeably high as I make my way back around the building, sticking to the shadows as laughter echoes down from the roof. I've never felt so solitaria in my life. Just a few hours ago, I was up there, with them, laughing and drinking. Now I've betrayed their trust. The thought makes me sick to my stomach, though that could just be aftereffects of the nerve gas. I remind myself that chocolate must be shared, to free Earth from dependence on HGB, though at the moment that feels a bit hollow. Poor wombie. Poor Meredith. Poor Earth.

When I reach my window, I pull on the sash which slides easily upwards. I climb inside and tug down the shade. I take off the jetpack and let it fold down on itself, then I strip out of my clothes.

I'm still trembling as I turn the knobs in the shower. When I close my eyes to let agua run over my face, I keep seeing Meredith, eyes closed, hair half in her face. There's nada I can do for her.

Once I'm clean and dressed and the adrenaline rush fades, I spread the cacao mess out on my counter and begin separating the beans from the pulp. My heart starts hammering again when I realize I'm picking out fragments. Meredith hadn't been professional in planning the explosion. Obviously, there was no one helping her. The group that had given her weapons probably doesn't even know she's in Brazil. I sort through every bit of the pulp, and I only pull out four beans that look whole. I wipe them clean and place them in the viability box. Only one chamber lights up green. Well, fantástico.

Cacao requires two trees to cross pollinate. The whole ordeal has been para nada.

CHAPTER SEVEN

The next morning, while I'm brushing my teeth, a folded piece of paper slides under my door. Ay, no. I rinse out my mouth, trying not to panic. I don't hear anyone still in the hallway, even as I approach the door. My hand shakes as I pick up the page, expecting a blackmail note or a police summons. If it says *I saw what you did last night*, my life is over.

I unfold it, blinking in confusion at the innocuous printed schedule, with a handwritten note on the back from Tawny that says, *Three scarves, Bo? Don't you think that's a little excessive? I know we go heavy on the air conditioning, but it's eighty degrees outside!*

I can't help but laugh out loud, there alone in my room, as the tension melts out of my shoulders. If that's all the reprimand I get, I think I'll live. I just hope Tawny doesn't ask me to model the scarves, no?

In the cafeteria I eat a couple of empanadas, which aren't half bad, before I trudge down to meet with my stylist. I'm guessing they want to show me off in town, because my trip with Kaliel and Rick is scheduled right after, before I meet with the holomercial director.

"Bo!" The stylist, a short petite forty-something, pats the back of her chair, gesturing for me to sit. "He estado ansioso en conocerte."

"Gracias." What else am I supposed to say? That I've been

looking forward to meeting her too? The chair swivels as I sit, throwing me off balance. My back presses against the cushion, radiating pain from the burns along the length of my spine. I manage not to make a noise.

The stylist, busy examining the raw canvas before her, doesn't seem to notice me grimacing into the mirror. She takes a thick lock of my hair in each hand and tugs on it. "Your hair is so dense and strong. We could do absolutamente anything with it. Have you ever had a perm? It would give you a little extra height for the cameras."

Judging by the mucho jumbo size of her own hair, it wouldn't be a body wave, either. I gulp. "No, por favor. I'm not ready for that, right?"

"No? Are you sure?"

I love the way my hair is naturally, but I finally agree to some dark red highlights, so she smears chemicals all over my head and wraps the strands in enough foil to prevent alien mind invasion – assuming we ever meet aliens who actually have that power. Once she's rinsed out the dye, she gets me back into the chair. She picks up a heavy pair of metal shears.

"We could remove a good bit of weight if we took your hair up into a bob. Maybe right here. Would that be too short?" She gestures with the scissors, laying them flat just above my shoulders. The tip of the closed blade touches my neck, sending a jolt of cold fear through my chest down into the pit of my stomach. *When the cold metal touches your skin, that's when you know it's real.* I flinch away, and the scissors' point leaves a fine red scratch.

"Lo siento!" She looks horrified. "Are you OK, Bo? You're so pale."

"I'm fine. It wasn't your fault." Damn Kaliel and his too-descriptive fears, fears I can't now shake, especially given the dividing line marked onto my neck. I force a smile. "Pero not that short, por favor. Just two or three inches more, OK?"

As she cuts my hair, chattering about her niños and how the oldest is about to make her an abuelita when she's too far away to help out, I try to remember why I agreed to this suicide errand. Things have to change, sí, but how did I convince myself that I have to be the one to do it?

The stylist trades her scissors for a blow drier, and as my hair loses moisture, mi cabeza really does feel lighter, which gets my heart thudding as I imagine it floating up off my shoulders. The stylist moves on to eye makeup and mascara. I cringe to think about what Meredith must be going through right now. There's only one way she's going to get a makeover, and that thought makes me sick.

The stylist dabs a coat of pink gloss onto my lips. After that, she sets me free.

I rush to meet the guys in the lobby. Kaliel's leaning back against the wall, and the hem of his jeans has shifted up, revealing a thick black band circling his right ankle. One look at the blinking red light that proves even now he's not free erases last night's doubts. The world is holding him responsible for all the problems hoarding chocolate has caused – the pirate attacks, the increasing poverty outside the chocolate belt, even the possibility of another war, todo, all resting on his thin shoulders.

Unaware of my thoughts, Kaliel smiles as he thumps the ident badge clipped to his shirt. "We're going to have to get you one of these. Otherwise, they won't let you back in the gate."

"You do that," Rick says. "I'm going to grab the Jeep." As he turns away, I catch the outline of a gun under his untucked shirt. I guess he's supposed to be our bodyguard for the day.

Kaliel points me toward a desk where a bored-looking girl sits chewing gum and staring at a computer monitor. She waves me over to a machine that looks like a pair of binoculars welded to a dart board. I have to peer into it until the green light practically blinds me again. Then she photographs me, adding blue dots from the flash to the assault on my eyes. Without speaking, she goes through a door and comes back a few minutes later with a completed badge. She tosses it on the desk, turns back to her computer, and without looking up, mumbles, "Tenha um bom dia." *Have a nice day.*

My vision has returned to normal by the time Kaliel leads me out the door, where Rick already has the open-top red Jeep idling, blasting samba on the radio. The trip promises to be fun, if I can just shrug off the lingering feeling of isolation. Kaliel hops into the back seat, and I climb in the front, then Rick turns the music down before he drives us out the gate. The pavement soon gives way to a red-brown dirt rut that barely qualifies as a road. The Jeep wends a serpentine path downhill, lush green falling away into the distance before us as we jitter our way through potholes and uneven areas. It's been a long time since I've been out here. I'd forgotten just how bumpy the ride gets.

I try calling Brill on my sublingual. I'm still getting that No Call Zone message.

When the ground levels out, Rick guns the engine and turns left, into a slow-moving shallow river. Both of the guys whoop, but I shrink towards the center of the vehicle as the tires kick up mud and agua as high as the doors. I ought to be able to let go and feel joy with them. El tiempo is precious to me too, and I don't want to waste it. I force myself back to the center of my seat and try to add a whoop of my own. It just sounds pathetic.

Kaliel asks, "Hey, are you OK?"

"Sí, I'm fine." I smile, and I do feel a bit mejor, just from looking at him. He's such a sweet guy. I'm going to take it so hard if he gets shaved.

We pull out of the river, onto an area that slopes uphill. I try calling Brill again, pero nada. There's no landmark here, and I don't even see the road until we've turned onto it. About ten minutes later, once we start to see little shacks near the roadside where people have hung their laundry to dry in the sun or have tethered their horses and goats to graze, I finally get a connection. A lone cow looks up at us reproachfully as the Jeep's tires hit a puddle and spray brown water in her direction. She moos, and for some reason, that makes me burst out laughing.

When Brill asks, *How's it going?* it's all I can do not to laugh hysterically into his ear.

I sum up the botched heist. *This isn't going to work. Get me out of here, mi vida.*

Ga. That's too dangerous. He sounds panicked. He pauses, then seems more in control when he says, *You'd break your contract with HGB, which would be as good as admitting your guilt. If you wind up having to run for the rest of your life, at least make sure you get the money to do it with.*

He's right about the dinero. The contract I'd signed, like everything else with HGB, is all or nada. If I break it, I might even wind up owing them money. Plus, no matter what I do, I'm not the only one affected. If they cancel mi mamá's feeds over my insubordination, no one else who pays their holostars enough to live off of would dare pick her up and risk upsetting whatever pull they have with HGB.

Then what am I supposed to do, Brill? I concentrate on keeping my face serene, acting for the benefit of the guys in the Jeep like I'm enraptured by the sight of high-rises clinging to the mountainside in the distance. Like I didn't live here for years.

Brill sighs inside my brain, like a soft breeze. *Shtesh. I said from the beginning that it would be easier to get the pods straight off the tree, but everyone told me I was nuts. Give me a couple of hours, and I'll find out what resources you need to get into the plantation.*

I shudder, remembering the predatory circling of those drones in flight. I shake my head. *I thought we decided* that *was too dangerous.*

Rick asks, "What?"

"Nada," I say. "Just been so long since I've seen Rio. It hasn't changed a bit, no?"

What? Brill bubblechatters.

I wasn't talking to you, mi vida. I wish you could be here with me.

I wish I could too, Babe.

I imagine Brill taking me in his arms, hugging me so close I almost feel like I'm being crushed, the way he always does when I'm upset. The smell of his leather jacket has come to be synonymous with comfort for me. I rub the fake leather of the Jeep's seat with my fingertips.

Listen, Babe. Give me until one o'clock, your time, then I'll ring you back. I'm going to call in some favors, see what I can do.

Peru– I start to say, but Brill's already hung up. Oye. I'm only scheduled to be in town from nine until noon. At one, I'm supposed to be standing in a holocube while some technician shoots preliminary bumpclips. How am I supposed to stall everything for a whole hour?

The rutted roads have given way to pavement again, and the farm animals to street vendor's carts. The smell of meats roasting over open charcoal grills are making me homesick despite the years I've spent insisting that Rio was never my real home.

We pass the old-fashioned town square with the park in its middle. An old man uses a levbot to string spaceship-shaped decorations between two wrought iron light poles. He turns. I recognize him, though I only know him by the nickname Dida. I used to watch him play dominos with other old men at the park's worn tables. I wave and he smiles, nodding at me while gesturing that his hands are too full to wave back. This warms my heart. There were some good times here, too.

"You'll see." Rick points ahead. "Not everything's stayed the same."

Kaliel hands his ident badge to Rick, who takes off his own. Rick nods at the glove compartment. "Let's leave HGB in there.

I'm more comfortable without a label."

I lock all three badges safely away. Rick takes us down a road leading to a twelve-story parking garage built up against Sugar Loaf Mountain. That *is* nuevo. Rick has to go to the top level of the garage to find an open spot. We get out and take the ramp leading into the cave-like opening carved into the mountain, to where there's an elevator with buttons labeled 1 through 72. Kaliel adjusts his pant leg so the tracker's hidden.

Rick presses 14 and says, "Welcome to the newest part of Rio."

Instead of going down, the elevator shoots backwards, into the mountain. Then it goes down. When it finally stops, the back wall slides open. Music pounds in on us, and a blue light pulses in time with the drumbeat. The bar's not wall-to-wall with people, but there's a decent crowd. It's still morning, but this is the first day of the Chocolate Festival, and Brazilians do love a good party.

Rick leads the way out of the elevator, shouting now to be heard over the music. "The whole mountain is riddled with shops and restaurants. There's even apartments, down at the bottom. Some people who live here never leave."

I lean closer to Kaliel and ask, "What happened to Moqueca de Camarão at Primeira Taxa?"

"Later." Rick turns back and pats my hand. "My girlfriend tends bar here. I haven't been cleared to get out of the facility for a week. Just give me a few minutes."

I was worried about trying to delay these guys for an hour? Soy ridículo. We'll be doing good if we get back today at all. Rick melts away into the crowd.

That leaves me standing with Kaliel, who takes in my new haircut. "You seeing anybody?"

At least he's thinking about something other than death. Pinpoints of colored light soar across the ceiling, highlighting people's shirts, micro-spotlighting the floor. A purple dot crosses Kaliel's forehead. I refuse to let it remind me of a sniper scope, of that close call with Brill.

"Sí, I am." I can't help smiling as I think about how jealous mi vida would be right now. After all, Kaliel is a good-looking guy, once you wipe the mopey frown off him.

"Want to dance anyway? Just friends?"

"Por qué no?" *Why not?* I let him lead me through the other couples to the center of the floor.

He puts a hand at the top of my back, lightly, just brushing the top of the burns. I try not to flinch. I can't explain where they came from, not even to him. I don't know how he feels about HGB, not really, and this place is too loud for sharing secrets. He's a really good dancer, gliding from the quick steps of a samba, into the hand-holding fun of a bachata, and back to a more serious, sizzling salsa. I get so lost in the music, comfortable following the cues of a partner who knows what he's doing, that when my sublingual rings, it startles me.

Hey, Babe. It's Brill, far earlier than he'd said he'd be. Brill can dance, but he approaches it more as an anthropologic experiment than something scintillating and freeing.

"Un momento, por favor," I tell Kaliel. "I'm getting a call, right?"

Before I've even crossed the dance floor, Brill's chattering in my brain. *This is going to be easier than we thought. A friend of a friend can get you a set of devices to disable electronic locks. He's also got a gizmo that should distract the drones. But Lula's smart. I just hope he hasn't guessed what we're planning. Try to think up something else plausible in case he asks.*

OK. I hug my arms across myself as I thread my way through the dancing couples into the relatively quiet hallway. The decreased noise level doesn't affect how the sublingual functions, but it does help me think. I don't dare use the handheld to record the directions Brill gives me, so I bum the stub of a pencil off a girl carrying a hunormous purse. Brill and I talk for a while, about nada really, but he still makes me feel better about being here, though I want more than ever to bury my face in his jacket and let go of all this secrecy, this responsibility.

Just when I think he's hung up, he says softly, *I'm sorry, Babe.* I blink. *For what?*

For putting the idea in your head to do this, for putting the weight of worlds on your shoulders. I wish I could be there to protect you. He hesitates. *Stay safe. Avell. Uan suavet.* Meaning, *Please. For me.*

When I get back inside, Kaliel is at the bar, a beer in front of him. I sigh. He needs a good and true amigo, not another dose of alcohol, and here I am about to lie to him. A girl farther down the bar's watching him, a secretive smile softening her lips.

I take the seat on the other side of Kaliel, not obstructing her view. "That girl's been checking you out since I left. Go ask her to dance already."

He tilts his beer bottle and peers into the depths. "She's a FeedCaster."

Ay no! I refrain from looking in the girl's direction. Not that that's going to change anything. Holos of me and Kaliel dancing will be available online in an hour.

He pushes the bottle away. "So, who called you?"

"My brother, Mario. I haven't seen him in years, but he lives in town." I can't look at Kaliel when I say this. My heartbeat's keeping up with the music, each thud accusing me. "I was wondering, if you and Rick are going to be here for a while, if I could borrow the Jeep and go meet him real quick."

He looks over at the reporter. "Just don't leave me stranded here all day without a dance partner. She might get brave and demand an interview."

I hate leaving him there, but as soon as Rick hands over the keys, I head for the elevator. Rick calls, "Stay out of trouble, or it's my butt." I'm grateful that he's the world's worst bodyguard.

I really am going to visit mi hermano, just in case they check. I've just managed to set a route that goes past the friend of a friend's business.

I drive the Jeep out of the parking garage into the too-bright sunlight. I can hardly see the buildings through the crush of people now lining the sidewalks in anticipation of the parade. A few are wearing traditional Brazilian garb, the women layered in bright colors like tiered cupcakes, but more people came in jeans – or dressed as aliens or chocolate bars. A tall man steps out of one of the shops, blinking at the crowd. His outfit makes him look like a cómico banana wearing a cape. I think he's trying for a Zantite. Now, I've seen Zantite warriors on the news feeds, and Zandywood stars in the holos. They're the definition of custurbing – cute yet disturbing, giant humanoids with rubbery skin, deeply lidded eyes and way too many teeth. If they saw this guy's weak imitation, they'd probably vaporize him.

As I inch forward in traffic, I study my hand-drawn map, trying to figure out where I can park that's in the same postal code as Lula's shop. I manage to find a spot where I only have to walk twenty blocks. The street mixes traditional architecture with ultra-modern steel and glass. Lula's place is on the traditional side – not to mention about to fall in on itself, with long cracks running up the walls and a wooden window frame badly in need of repainting. I open the door, and a little brass bell rings.

Drones and model airplanes and RC helicopters hang in angled frozen flight all over the ceiling, precarious, like one of them might drop on my head at any moment. Off to the side, a pyramid display of the latest sublingual devices sits in front of a clear booth with a dentist's reclining chair. My sublingual's old, but it's not the kind of thing you upgrade on a whim. I run the scar on the bottom of my tongue against the backs of my upper teeth. I'd gotten it as a teenager. Mamá took me for the install-op the day *M.O.M. Takes the Cake* came out. I think it may have been an apology for the toilet training story in chapter seven. Ay, that was a mal couple of months at school, with the sublingual still aching and all the girls giggling behind my back.

A burly man sporting a thick mustache comes out of a back room and leans against a counter covered with wires and diodes and half-assembled gadgets. "Bom dia! Can I help you?"

I take a step towards the counter. "Are you Lula?"

He nods.

"I'm an amiga of an amigo of Jack's."

His eyes narrow, and he purses his lips. "Jack who?"

I remember to answer in Portuguese, not Spanish. "Eu não sei." *I don't know.* I swallow hard. Did Brill forget to tell me which Jack? What happens if Lula doesn't believe me? Am I in danger here? "You're not expecting me?"

Lula tosses a small plastic box on the counter. "Put your thumb on here."

I comply. The box beeps, and my shoulders tense, but it doesn't explode or take my blood or anything.

Lula pulls a tablet computer from under the counter. He waits until *it* beeps, then reads something off of it. "No police report. That's good. Also, not a cop. Even better." He raises an eyebrow. "HGB spokesmodel? That's a new one."

I try to strike a model pose, but I'm still stiff and nervous. "It's new for me too, right?"

He rolls his eyes. "Come around that gap in the counter. What you want is in back."

The air in the back room smells of disinfectant, and the whole area is so well lit and dusted that it could be a clean room. Lula plucks two different white boxes off a rack of shelves, stacking them onto my arms, then he takes a smaller box from his pocket and places it on top. "Jack's friend already explain to you what these are for?"

"He said there'd be two devices." I gesture down at the boxes. "I'm not sure what the third one is."

Lula laughs. "Well, you know Jack's friend. He's always big on using little presents to keep the girls interested."

My cheeks go hot. "Qué?"

I know nothing of the sort. Brill's always seemed reserved around other girls.

Lula shrugs. "What do I know? I'm just an electronics geek who doesn't dare go offplanet."

The bell on the door jangles, so he goes to the front to help a lady who's having connection problems with her handheld. I'm not sure if I've been dismissed, so I lean back against the wall to wait. My handheld buzzes with a text communication from Kayla. I feel a flash of guilt. Everything happened so fast, I hadn't replaced her broken phone. She could have only gotten this number from one place: mi mamá.

Bo, I just watched a FeedCast of you dancing with the pilot who killed my grandmother. Please tell me it's holonique! The flying dork makes your spider guy look like a good choice. Also, have you seen this holo HGB released? My Mom saw it and went ballistic. It's horrible, but seeing our dorm has me missing school so much. Stephen was the only one I had to talk to for weeks on end on the shuttle here, and now my Mom is all freaked out about dealing with all of my grandparents' friends that showed up for the funeral yesterday. She gets so introverted, and expects me to be introverted with her, and I can't take much more of her tortured poetic side. I won't be back at school for a while yet. I hope you've been taking good notes.   KayKay

She's all over the place. She's still grieving – and she obviously doesn't realize I'm not taking notes for her for class. I text her back, letting her know I'm on Earth.

Lula still looks busy, so I play the holo. It starts with a banner ad of cacao in various stages of processing, centering on the text: *HGB Chocolate – There is NO Substitute.*

The image dissolves to a familiar room – the combined kitchen and living area of my dorm suite. From the angle, the camera must have been embedded in the vent-a-hood over the range. In the image, I'm holding an eyedropper filled with concentrated vanillin. As I allow two drops of the clear liquid to splatter across the dark surface of the glumpy mixture in the bowl, image-me sighs. "Why do we even have to do this? Nobody's ever found a synthetic substitute for chocolate. Why would some student be able to do the impossible?"

I remember trying to whisk the drops into the mix, but the mess had gotten so clumpy that the whisk just got a gran glob trapped inside it, while the rest wouldn't go through the wires.

"I know." The image expands. Holo-Kayla taps furiously at the touch field on her handheld. "I think everybody expected us to have *Star Trek*-style replicators by now, especially after half a century of interacting with aliens." Her mouth goes slack as she takes in the information she's just called up. "Your mom is coming, and she's bringing a whole shipment of chocolate."

"Qué? I mean, I knew she was coming, but how much chocolate?" My startled holohand squeezes convulsively, and the eyedropper spits its entire load into the bowl, ruining the experiment. I remember how the overwhelming scent of fake vanilla made me squint when that part of the holo was taken. Image-me steps away from the bowl. "Too bad she's not here already. We'd get an A if we melted some of the real thing."

The holo cuts away from us to a scene of HGB headquarters in Maui with the pineapple grove out front and a dozen hula dancers waving hello. A voiceover says, "Bo was so happy to be chosen as the new Princesa de Cacao that she joined us the next day in Paradise." Never mind that it takes three weeks to get back to Earth. "Don't let the tropical drinks fool you." The scene changes to a waiter carrying a tray of mai tais toward a pool, where presumably I am sitting in one of the lounge chairs. "Bo loves chocolate, and she's going to make it her mission to share that love with a deserving galaxy."

They have no idea. Nada.

Lula looks up from the handheld he's been fixing. "Are you still here?"

"I wasn't sure if I needed anything else."

"Here. On the house." He takes a screwdriver from a box on the counter. It's fancy, with multiple tips stored in the handle. "It's the one tool every thief needs. Think of it like your towel, Trillian."

I take it. "I thought that was my Swiss Army knife."

Lula laughs. "Amateurs."

I'm not going to get more information out of him, so I send Kayla a quick *Kaliel's-not-such-a-bad-guy* message in response to her shocked reply to my *I'm-on-Earth* text, then I head for mi hermano's house.

I'm not sure whether or not I want Mario to be home. I park in his crushed gravel driveway, and it takes me a moment to get the nerve to get out of the jeep. His house is a free-standing stucco structure, two story, in a pale green. I admire the hibiscus bushes flanking the door as I ring the bell.

He comes to the door in pajama pants and a T-shirt. His feet are bare. He's put on about twenty pounds since the last time I saw him. "Bo? What are you doing here?"

His cold tone hurts my heart. "I'm making an effort, mi hermano. You're at least going to let me in, no?"

"Oh. Yeah, sure." He backs away from the door.

It's quiet inside his house, save for the whirr of a microwave giving off the distinctive fragrance of my sister-in-law's chicken enchiladas. The architecture features real wood, designed to take advantage of natural light. Everything is so neat and tidy, you would hardly guess children live here, except for the drawings of ponies and kittens on the front of the fridge.

"Where are the niñas?"

Mario pours me a cup of coffee from the pot on the counter. "I'm on deadline, so Angelina took them to her mamá's house for the weekend."

"They're going to miss the Chocolate Festival."

Mario opens the microwave and pokes his finger into the middle of the enchiladas. He puts the timer on for another minute. "Angelina and her mamá will take them. I wouldn't want them there after dark, anyway. The festival's gotten rough the past couple of years."

I gesture at Mario's computer, open on his dining table. "What are you working on?"

"I'm down to the wire to turn in a draft of *The War over Cacao: A History of the Events Since First Contact*." The microwave beeps. Mario frowns. "I know you find my work boring, but you don't have to look at me like it makes you sick."

"I'm not..." I sigh. As a history professor, whatever mi hermano writes will undergo intense academic scrutiny. And I'm about to cast a shadow on a lot of that work. "Maybe you should ask for an extension on that deadline."

"Qué?" Mario takes the enchiladas out of the microwave. He cuts the end off one with a fork and blows on the tortilla before popping the bite into his mouth.

I can't tell him that chocolate is about to go galactic, that what I'm doing could well invalidate his book's premise. "It's just with everything going on with Meredith Vasquez – I think there's more to it than the Feeds are saying. I've been in the HGB facility, and there's definitely something about to happen."

Mario sets his plate on the table and stares at me like a wolf sizing up prey, seeking out weakness. "I know you better than anybody, Bo. What are you up to, Pequeña?"

"Nada." My ears start to itch as anxious tension builds in my chest. I blink, then look away. I never could outstare my brother. Trying to force my brain to come up with a safer topic, I realize why I'm here. "Does Nina still have that Princess Squidrider backpack I got her just before I left for school?"

His cheeks go pink above two days' worth of stubble already

threatening the return of his long-gone mustache. "That was a long time ago."

"So that's a no?" I've embarrassed him enough to let my previous comments go.

"It may still be in the garage with the boxes that are supposed to go to charity. Come on, we'll take a look." Mario picks up his plate and carries it with him down the short hallway. He flips the switch, and lights come on surrounding a super-organized work bench and his perfectly detailed black car. The boxes are stacked in a corner.

I open the top one and start digging around inside it. "Oye. This sketch pad belonged to Papá."

Mario coughs, like his food went down the wrong way. "It's been eight years. I finally decided it's time to move on."

"Well, you're not getting rid of this. Nunca." I flip it open. There's only one drawing in here – a half-completed landscape of the view from the living room window of our old casa, incomplete, not good art by any standards. But I still find myself clutching it to my chest. As the book shifts, a pen falls out of it, the kind that doubles as a stylus, just like the one Frank had back on Larksis. That's extraño – *weird*. The sketch had been done in pencil. I pick up the pen. The stylus end is all melted out of shape. "Hermano, do you have Papá's tablet that went with this?"

Mario shakes his head. "After the fire, when they found him, they said he had it clutched in his hand. I guess I always thought if I could figure out why, then I'd know what he was thinking in his last moments. I know it's selfish, but I always hoped he was thinking about me."

I smile, though my chest feels strangely too-warm inside. "I hoped the same thing." I set the book and the stylus aside carefully. Then I sort through the detritus of mi hermano's life. Finally, in the last box, I find the backpack. Princess Squidrider is the star of a Zantite tooncast. Even Zantite children must have secrets, because there's a hidden compartment in here where I hope I can fit Brill's presents, and that compartment has a scan-proof lining.

Once I've gone through the awkwardness of hugging Mario goodbye, I sit in the Jeep and take the devices out of their boxes. The door openers look like three large white cookies, with gray magnetic circles for chocolate chips. The drone distractor is about the size and shape of one of those fish-food sticks they sell to snorkelers, only there is a capped red button on one end, and it's made of something hard and black. I stow them in the backpack. When I get to the third box, the one that's a present from Brill, I hesitate. Ay. What did Lula mean *all the girls*?

I'd omitted a few things when Brill and I had had that previous-significant-others talk. It had been too embarrassing, once I'd owned up to letting the shallow soccer player devastate me, and gone through the litany of what was and was not true in what the Pops' malcasts had said about my love life after that, to talk about the quieter failures – the two relationships that hadn't gotten off the ground enough for the media to notice, and the three guys I'd gone out with, all briefly, since hiding away on Larksis. He hadn't asked *is that it?* or anything, so it hadn't felt like a lie.

Brill had only owned up to three previous girlfriends, all Krom. Could it be that he'd left out even more than I had?

I open the box and look down at a triple-wrap necklace with rectangular emeralds set in gold all along its three-foot length. It's muy bonito. I suck in a breath at the absolute extravagance, worried Lula's right about Brill trying to buy my loyalty. But it could just as easily be an insurance policy, something I can turn into spendable dinero or use to bribe a guard.

Feeling closer to Brill, just by knowing he's thinking about me, I put it on.

CHAPTER EIGHT

When it finally gets late enough, I walk outside the IIGB complex, trying to look casual. Kaliel is standing in front of the building, looking up at the sky again, yet another beer bottle in his hand. It's only been a couple of hours since I've seen him – we had gone to visit the open-air market, just in case he isn't around for next year's – but the time he's spent solitario seems to have caved him in.

I put a hand on his arm. "Are you OK?"

He flinches, then looks embarrassed. "I got a message of my own while we were out today. They set the date for my trial. It's going to be sooner than I thought."

My breath catches. Ay no! He has less chance to survive if the jury sees the victims' families' pain as still fresh. "How soon?"

"Two weeks." He looks me in the eye, and there's still some fight there, still the spark he's been trying to drown in alcohol. "Apparently, they want to make sure it all winds up soon after the Venezuelan woman's execution."

It's like he's doused me in ice.

"Meredith Vasquez is going to have a trial, too, no?" My words sound hollow, like the empty hope they are.

"Sí. On paper. For the feeds. But they caught her in the fermentation room." He looks up at the sky again as a single shooting star streaks toward the horizon. "You know what makes me feel horrible?"

I know what makes *me* feel horrible. I left her in that room, and after she'd kept silent about me being there, I'm about to take an even more loco risk, probably making her sacrifice worthless. "Qué?"

He takes a long sip of beer. "I keep wondering how her trial will affect mine. They might let me keep my head, but at the cost of her life. There's been enough blood already, don't you think?"

"Sí." I want to hug Kaliel, to kiss the sadness from his lips, comfort him the only way I know how, but I'm with Brill. I have to be loyal to my love.

I leave Kaliel drinking his beer alone, looking up at the full moon. Two weeks. Just dos. If the trial goes badly, he'll never see the moon swell to full again. Impulsively, I turn back and take his beer bottle away. Even though I know I shouldn't, I kiss him, tasting the bitter hops on his tongue, and it's one of the most intense, electric moments of connection I've ever had in my life. When I've absorbed as much of his sadness as I can, I end the kiss. I'm breathing hard, and my arms have wrapped tight around him. "Lo siento. I don't know how else to tell you to shrug off this walking death and live."

His body presses against mine, wanting life, wanting love. "I thought you said you were with somebody." He sounds husky, surprised, and broken all at once.

"I am. I... lo siento." I close my eyes and pull away from his embrace, feeling cold despite the humid air alive with sounds creeping in from the rainforest. I can still taste salt from his face on my lips. I open my eyes, but don't look directly at him. "Promise me you'll lay off the beer. You need to be sober for your trial."

"Sure, if it means that much to you." He takes the bottle from me and chucks it into the dark. It disappears into the tangled undergrowth beyond the building. "Too bad you're taken. I was starting to think I might have a reason to live, after all."

"Don't be loco. You want to live." I peer into his gray-green eyes. The spark's still there, brighter than before. "And this isn't about me. There must be people who care for you, who really know you."

He smiles, but that makes him seem even sadder. "My mom couldn't even look at me when she came to visit. She said she refused to believe she'd raised a murderer. My dad didn't even come."

"Lo siento." I kiss his cheek, trying to imagine what it must feel like to be facing death and being abandoned by your family, who must be feeling pressure from the sleazarazzi. My heart aches for him. "They're emotirated, but give them time. They'll understand eventually." Eventually. If he's got enough time. Two weeks. And a lifetime. I would love to stay here with him and be the amiga he so obviously needs, stand with him through the whole trial, celebrate with him when he's released or walk beside him to the inevitable end. "If I leave tonight – just know it wasn't you, OK?"

"What are you talking about?" Kaliel peers at me in the dim light.

I shake my head. "I'm just talking un poco loco myself."

I smell of insect repellant, despite the electrostatic bug defense ringing the perimeter of the building, and I'm afraid he's going to ask about it, but he doesn't. Instead, he tells me about his childhood, contrasting growing up in Sweden with the summer he'd spent with his grandparents, who had retired to São Luís, not that far from where I'd been in Rio. Then he talks about his pilot training in Mexico, which explains the Spanish.

Eventually, Kaliel heads back inside to get some coffee, and before he returns I slip away and make my way around to the back of the building. I walk parallel to the archway the robot workers use when they bring the boxes of pods inside for processing, right up until the passage becomes part of the plantation wall. The whole enclosed rainforest is ringed with a bionet extending from the top of the walls into the stratosphere. There's supposed to be an ultrasonic sound deterrent to keep living creatures from flying or leaping into it. The ecosystem inside has to be maintained, in order to keep the cacao trees pollinated. Nobody quite knows how this happens. Most botanists believe that midges, tiny flies with gene-ties to no-see-ems, carry out the task. Pero, nobody wants to chance being wrong. So they're terrified to lose an especies solitarias.

The small gate, about thirty feet to my left, is locked up tight, with a robot sentry posted at either side, each bathed in a security light, motionless. Like the workerbots, they have prominent power gauges. One of them is reading in the yellow mid-charge range. The other gauge is dark. Unlike the workerbots, these guys have oversized guns prominently displayed on their hips, hands frozen just above the handles. Fantástico. Brill obviously didn't take them into account when he set up the plan for me to infiltrate the plantation.

The partially charged bot activates, opening camera-lens-round eyes. Egad! I've been spotted. I didn't think I was that close. That gaze is alien and terrifying, and the bot's hand drops onto the handle of its gun. My heart misses a couple of beats. I start to back away.

"Are you from maintenance?" The sentrybot has no mouth. The words echo out from somewhere near where the slender neck joins the cabeza to the stockier body.

I freeze, weighing my options. It is more likely to shoot me if I run, no? I take the screwdriver out of my pocket and try to sound confident. "Sí. What seems to be the problem?"

"Oh, thank goodness. When I submitted the ticket, they said they might not be able to get anybody out here until after the weekend. Zero-one-zero-one-zero-zero-one here won't hold a charge. It's not surprising really. We are after all running on thirty year-old batteries. Please tell me you aren't going to have to retire him. We've been together as sentries for all of that time."

I nod, trying to look sincere, pero not too eager. "I can probably get you a replacement battery. There's a stock of spare parts in the building inside the plantation."

The bot moves to block my way. "I am forbidden to open the gate."

I put a reassuring hand on its cold arm, glad it can't feel my blazeblasting heartbeat. "I can open it, mijo. You just have to step back onto your charging pad and let me."

The bot casts a troubled glance at dark, silent Zero-one-whatever, then back at me. "This is highly irregular."

I shrug. "Then I should get back to headquarters so I can start the paperwork requisitioning a new sentry. Just imagine, you'll have somebody new to talk to, with a more advanced design. Fantástica, no?" I turn back toward the archway.

"Wait!" The bot holds out a beseeching hand. "You can really open the gate?"

"Sure," I smile. I walk up to the gate, slipping one of the devices that will deactivate the lock out of my bag. I secure the device in place, then I push down on the gate's handle, and the solid piece swings into the caged part of the rainforest, which is darker and wilder. The insect sounds, already a background hum to nights in Rio, get louder.

Before I even step through, one of the nearest drones takes flight. In a panic, I fumble the device from my backpack that's supposed to make me look like white noise. I get it turned on. The bird-like craft circles, then gives up and returns to its roost. I let out a long breath and cross the threshold. I take out my flashlight and make my way toward a corrugated-roofing topped station stacked neatly with empty crates and harvesting bags. The station has no walls. The tool cabinet isn't locked. Of course it isn't. Robots don't steal. Besides, tools aren't the valuable thing out here, anyway.

I rummage in the cabinet and take a machete from among the other tools just in case I run into anything feo out here.

A prolonged raspy click sounds just as I close the cabinet, and my heart goes cold. I must have activated a security system. Ay. I duck out from under the station's roof and look up, expecting a line of drones heading my way, but there's nada in the sky. When the noise sounds again, it's deeper, emanating from a tree frog sitting on top of the metal, complaining that I've disturbed its perch. Its red eyes glitter against my flashlight, then it hops away into the night. I let out a breath. Tranquila, Bo. Just because so many things could go wrong here, that doesn't mean they all will.

I approach the overgrown path leading away from the station, deep into the heart of the plantation. I'm nervous about using my flashlight, but more scared about blundering into a fer-de-lance, one of those aggressive snakes whose cabezas look like spearheads, in the dark.

I head down the path, clearing my way with the machete. It doesn't take long to reach a cacao tree. It looks healthy enough, at least by flashlight. I spotlight numerous pads along the trunk and branches, but not a single mature fruit. The harvesterbots must have been through here already. My heart sinking, I move along to the next tree, already knowing what I'm going to find. Nada. Nunca. Zip.

This plantation spans millions of acres. They can't have harvested it all. I sheathe the machete, sliding it between the jetpack and my back, which is still tender from the burns, then I put the pink backpack on backwards, so that it covers my chest. I activate the jetpack and get high enough to get my bearings. There's a building ahead and to my left. I let the jets drop me gently to the ground. I've got to conserve fuel.

Heading in the direction of the building, I bushwhack my way through the denser pockets of plant life, shining my flashlight up into the trees when I reach clearings. Bugs – and the occasional bat – flitter through my light. Mi papá would have loved this. He always used to talk about the wild places he'd journeyed through, all over the world, from the crater of the Irazú Volcano in Costa Rica to the frozen coast of the Arctic Ocean, back before he became a teacher and then a firefighter.

Taking courage from the fact that his blood flows in my veins, I keep going, hoping that the next cacao tree will mark the harvested edge of the plantation. Finally, one does. Cacao trees are undercanopy plants, and often the fruit grows at eye level. Some animal seems to have attacked the lower fruits on this tree, eating holes into the pods to get to the pulp, which is the natural way the cacao seedlings spread.

I jet up to the top of the tree, where the pods look undamaged. I don't dare try swinging a machete while airborne, so I grab onto a relatively thick branch that seems likely to hold my weight. My flashlight reveals a fruit that looks heavy and ripe, almost entirely red and gold. I slice it from the pad and shove it into the pocket of my cargo pants. When I go to sheathe the blade, a beam of red light bounces off it, and something starts chittering in the branches of the over-canopy tree above me. Slick dread slides hot into my chest. No, no y no. This cannot be happening.

The whole tree starts shaking.

One of the harvester robots, made to look like a capuchin monkey, leaps down, landing easily on the same branch as me, closer to the trunk of the tree, despite holding a full-sized machete in its paw. It bares metal teeth and activates those lasercutter eyes again, close enough now to be effective. I try to reflect the dangerous light back using the machete, but the laser cuts straight through. The blade drops into the undergrowth at the base of the tree, leaving me holding the useless handle. En serio?

"Nice monkeybot." My heart's thudding in my ears as I back down the slender branch. What would Papá do here? Probably fend the monster off using the machete, which he wouldn't have been estúpido enough to damage. There's a patch of something slippery on the branch. I lose my balance just as the wood snaps beneath me. Dozens of monkeys jump into the tree I've just vacated. I fall, managing to turn the jetpack on soon enough to catch me before I hit the ground.

Adrenaline and terror add urgency to the commands flowing over my neural patch as I zoom off in the direction I hope leads to the gate. Something thuds into the jetpack. I look back, ice replacing the heat in my core as two more machetes impact it, damage that otherwise would have severed my spine. The last of the strange-smelling fuel leaks out, wetting the butt of my pants. I scream as I crash, getting a face-full of mud and rotting leaves. I pull off the backpack, which is impeding my movement, and let the straps swing in my hand as I scramble to my feet.

I flitdash, even though I doubt I can outrun a horde of robots. The chittering behind me gets louder. Some of the monkeybots drop to the ground, while others bound along in the trees. The lead monkey's laser eyes flash on again, burning a deep gash into the rich soil beside me. Damn, he's getting close.

As I run over uneven uncleared ground, heedless of any snakes I might risk stepping on, I get the feeling something peligroso – *dangerous* – is watching me. The hairs along my arms stand up and a shiver runs through my stomach. I trip and fall face-first into the mud. I manage to flip myself over just as the first monkeybot drops from the canopy and lands heavily on my chest, knocking the wind out of me. I think the feo thing might have cracked one of my ribs. It raises the machete as more bots start landing on the ground near my head, on my legs, all over the place like malevolent raindrops. I thwack at it with my backpack, but before I can get a solid hit, two other bots grab my wrist, pulling down on my arm. The bot on my chest chitters, and I see my death staring at me with those creepy red eyes. My chest goes cold. It's going to kill me, and I don't think it even feels bad – even feels *anything* – about it.

"Oye! No!" I flinch, panic turning the edges of my vision sparkly as the blade starts to drop.

Then blade, monkeybot, and the part of my sweater said monkey had been holding in its metallic paw all disappear. The air smells of ozone. One by one, eleven other monkeybots zap out of existence, making for an even twelve shots.

There's a guttural curse, the quackpop of the vapgun being thrown to the ground, then something humanoid and familiar rolls across the path. Green eyes glitter in the dark, and suddenly I can't move.

I force my teeth apart. "Chestla?"

"Run for the building. We're almost there." She's managed to salvage two machetes and she's wielding them like swords. "I'll hold these guys off long enough for you to get there."

I can only force myself to move if I keep my eyes closed. I run blindly in the direction she seemed to be indicating. When I half-trip over something, I open my eyes and focus on the building. Something grabs me from behind. I scream before I register Chestla's voice. "You're moving too slowly, Bo."

She lifts me into a fireman's carry and bounds toward the door. It's locked. I try not to go paralytic, even though the monkeys are closing in and Chestla's breathing loudly near my face.

"Put me down!" As soon as my feet touch earth, I pull out the second device and activate the electromagnets, then override the lock even as Chestla turns to defend against the onslaught. My hands are shaking, my heart beating like a hummingbird's wing, but I manage to get the door open. We rush inside con rapidez. Chestla throws a single monkey that's clung to her leg back outside then slams the door. I shed the ruined jetpack and let myself collapse onto the floor.

"I cannot believe…" I break my words with a shuddery breath. "…that with everything I've just gone through out there, the thing I'm most afraid of is still you."

"Story of my life." Chestla laughs in the dark. "I do try to fit in, you know."

My breathing slowly normalizes. "What are you doing here?"

"Your mother hired me to look after you. I was trained as a protector on my planet, but I haven't gotten to use my skills, since I failed my final exam."

I nod, but don't reply. My mind whirls, and I can't land on one thought long enough to ask the question. If she crashbanged her test, how good of a protector can she be? Why did Mamá think I need looking after? How does Chestla plan to pass as human so that she can get offplanet? If she's protecting me, where has she been these past few days? Did she not leave Larksis soon after I did? "That meteor impact last night. That was you?"

"Titanium spitpod." Her go-dorm cheerfulness is back. "We had to wait for the middle of the meteor shower, and the guidance on a spitpod is garbage, so I wound up in the wrong part of the rainforest, and then I had to stop to put out the fire from when I crashed. I feel terrible that I almost didn't make it in time."

"But you did make it. Gracias, mi amiga. I owe you my life."

"Remember that next time there's a party." I hear Chestla moving. My eyes are still adjusting when she flips on the lights, the ancient type of fluorescents that cast a green tint on everything and blink a bit when they're coming on. We're in a warehouse full of filing cabinets and old office furniture, crates and labeled plastic tubs. She punches the wall, seems satisfied when her fist doesn't go through it. "We should be safe in here. Take a little time to regroup, then we can strategize a way past the gang outside. It's a good thing we found this warehouse."

"What is this place?" A pile of naked mannequins lays haphazardly – and somewhat obscenely – in the corner. Right near where I collapsed, someone has set four of them up in dance poses and dressed them in white ruffled blouses and long, multi-layered rainbow-hued skirts. I reach up and touch the fabric. "These aren't just ChocoFest costumes. They're vintage."

Chestla reaches into a box and pulls out a paper-wrapped lump. It crinkles as she unwraps a heavy gold pendant inlaid with black diamonds outlining the shape of a cacao tree. Yellow diamond chips and tiny rubies make up the fruit. "Is this valuable, Bo?"

I nod, though it's still not easy to move in her presence. "Muy. Brazil used to be known for black diamonds. Claro, that and coffee."

Chestla wrinkles her nose. "I never could develop a taste for coffee."

"What about chocolate?" I take the cacao pod from the pocket of my cargo pants. It's about the size and shape of a child's foam football, pero much heavier. "Have you ever tasted the pulp out of one of these?"

Chestla's face takes on a sarcastic sneer, which nearly makes me pee my pants. "No. Nobody's supposed to…" Then her eyes widen. "Wait. Have you?"

I look away. If I can convince my nerve endings Chestla's not here, I'll be able to keep moving. I pull out the seed viability box. "Just once, for an episode of mi Mamá's show." I place the pod on a nearby desk and hack it open with one of Chestla's machetes. The aggressive activity helps to short-circuit the prey instinct, at least enough for me to function.

The pulpy inside stands up from the bottom half of the pod like an oversized mushy ear of corn. I dig my fingers into it, pulling out a single pulp-covered seed. I pop it into my mouth, savoring the dance of sweet and tart, like a pineapple mixed with a rainforest breeze. Maravilloso! I strip the pulp with my teeth, then I spit the seed into my hand, wipe it dry on my pants and drop it into the box. When I close the individual chamber, the light turns green.

Chestla gestures toward the box. "Don't you need more than one pod to ensure generic diversity?"

"No, because every seed combines different genetics, especially when a plantation this size provides so many sources of fertilization. It's like when a house cat has a litter of kittens that look nothing alike, and you know she's been hanging out with different toms."

Chestla looks at me sharply. "What are you trying to say?"

I have to force myself to speak. "I'm not making a comparison between you and a cat. I know you know what I'm talking about. I saw you bookmarked ICanHazCheeseburger."

Chestla laughs. "I can't help it. Kittens are cute." She reaches towards the pod. "Can I really try one?"

"Sí." I nod towards the viability box, though the rest of me freezes at the sight of those sparkle-polish covered claws.

Chestla pops one of the pulpy blobs into her mouth. "This tastes nothing like chocolate. It is somewhat like a fruit we have on my planet, though ours is round with segments and tiny inedible seeds, somewhat like your oranges in appearance."

"Before people figured out how to process cocoa beans, they would eat the pulp and just spit the seeds on the ground. Then somebody figured out that you could ferment the pulp to make alcohol. It's the fermentation that kills the bean, but at the same time gives it that distinctive chocolate flavor. Litoll, no?"

I've used Brill's word for cool. Pero, Chestla knows it.

She nods as she spits her seed directly into the box. The light turns green. She grabs another.

We only manage to eat about half the pulp before we just start cleaning it off the beans with our fingers. We wind up with two more beans than there are chambers in the viability box. I double up the extras, then take out the little pouch Brill gave me to hide it in. I cover the box with more mundane botanicals, then I slide the shielded pouch into the backpack's scan-resistant hidden compartment.

Chestla watches me with troubled eyes. "Are we doing something illegal?"

I have to be honest. "Sí."

She looks away, down at the floor, and her long blonde hair falls over one of her eyes. I guess it wouldn't be too hard to make her at least look human enough to walk out of here through the ChocoFest.

Her silent judgment makes me look away. "Never thought you'd be protecting a thief, no?"

"I always thought I would be guardian companion to one of the Princesses of Evevron." She stares at me until I look back at her, and it's like those sharp eyes are peering into my heart. "But I don't get it, Bo. I've known you for years. You're a good person. At least tell me that, whatever you're doing, you have a good reason."

So I tell her, the way Brill told it to me, about how sharing chocolate with the galaxy will help rebalance Earth. When I'm done, I ask, "So, are you sorry you came here? Do you wish you hadn't stumbled into my secret?"

"I am sorry, for your sake. Evevrons are a very social race. We can't keep secrets to save our lives."

"I hope you can manage this one, or you could lose your life, just for being on this planet, much less inside the plantation." I don't want to think about death anymore. Besides, she already knew the danger when she agreed to breech the border.

Every part of my body aches, and the ragged hole in the front of my sweater reveals my bra in all its pink-lace glory. I'm covered in mud and scratches, but nothing seems to be broken. I hobble over to one of the doors on the far wall, which is marked with a symbol of two figures. Inside, there's a full set of baño facilities, including a shower in the corner. I turn the tap, and while the pipes creak, and the first burst looks a little rusty, the agua comes out cool. I strip off the ruined sweater and toss it into the trash can. I clean myself up and wash as much mud off my pants as I can. I grab a white blouse off one of the mannequins. "Ay no. I hate white. It shows everything." Including my bra. How am I going avoid shimmerpopping if I look like a refugee extra from Mamá's favorite old movie, *Romancing the Stone*?

A sound like slow hail echoes off the roof. The monkeybots must be looking for a way in. I turn toward Chestla. "Those things are modeled on real capuchins. They decided on robots when the cybernetic versions proved impossible to control, but they're still nimble enough to get through any opening. Let's just hope this place is as well sealed as it looks."

"How many of them are there?" Chestla moves over to the door, pressing her ear against it, listening for another wave of attack.

"Ni idea." The tour guide hadn't covered that. "But we could use some better weapons. Maybe this is an armory."

I open the next door to a blast of air conditioning. The lights in there are blue and cool, highlighting a row of sliding glass doors like a grocery store refrigerator. It's packed full of plastic cases about the size of my fist. "Chestla, mira."

She bounds into the room, looking back twice at the sentry post she's just abandoned. I open one of the cases and show her the contents.

"More cocoa beans?" Chestla sniffs. "But why can't I smell anything?"

"They've been deep frozen. Mas por que? Freezing destroys the bean's viability. Look at this label." I turn the neatly typed information towards her. *Theobroma cacao forastero – Rio 122. Prolific producer, low disease resistance*. "Someone's been collecting different varieties of cacao from all over this plantation, but there's only supposed to be the one growing here, HGB *Theobroma trinitario*. It's the hybrid that brings together the best genes of all the plants. Pero, why build a seed vault that can't be used to grow anything?"

She stirs the beans with her finger. "It could be used for gene manipulation. Or maybe, despite all they keep saying about how chocolate can't be replicated, they're working on a synthetic."

Surprised, I make eye contact. The prey instinct makes me jostle the container, and the beans scatter across the spotless tile floor. We bend to pick them up. As long as I keep my eyes on my task, I can ignore the raised hairs at the nape of my neck, no?

I drop a handful of beans back into the case. "This whole building doesn't make any sense. There aren't supposed to be any humans inside the wall, pero robots don't need bathrooms." I make the mistake of looking up at Chestla to see if she's getting my point. I scoot involuntarily back, knocking my rear end against a table stacked with cardboard boxes. The top one tips over, showering me with glistening dark brown wrappers, each stamped *Hershey's*.

Chestla pulls a bar closer to her. "Do you want to try one?"

I wrinkle my nose. "That's loco. You're talking fifty year-old chocolate, chica. How do we know it's even safe?"

Chestla unwraps the bar and breaks off a piece. "I've eaten survival rations older than this, and it hasn't killed me yet. It's like chewing history."

I look down at the chocolate in my hands. I unwrap it. The surface has grayed with age and developed the telltale whirls of bloom. Still, Chestla is right. When will I ever be able to taste a real Hershey bar again? I break off a square and pop it into my mouth.

It's overly sweet and gluey and kind of bends up against my tongue. It has a distinctive taste I can't quite place. "It's not bad, pero it is definitely not HGB."

"I like it. But what do I know? I eat potatoes for dessert." She closes the lid on the plastic case and hands it back to me. "What else do they have?"

After I put the bean sample back where I got it, we open all the boxes. Every one contains a different vintage bar, and we pull a single sample from each. We sit on the floor, the bars spread like a rainbow in front of us.

"Try this one. It looks like the pendant I found." She picks up a bar with a circular logo of a stylized cacao tree. It claims to be single-source chocolate from Ecuador. She unwraps it and we each break off a square. She spits hers back into the paper outer wrapper. "Yuck! That's not chocolate."

"I don't know what it is, but I'm in love. Estoy enamorada!" I suck on the square, letting it melt on my tongue, trying to comprender the nuance of this flavor, which is like coffee, like toffee, like cherries, like pecans – and like nothing I've tasted before. "Are there any more bars like that?"

"Enamorada? That sounds less committed than te amo or te quiero." Chestla pulls out a wet wipe and tears open the packet. She wipes a tiny smear of chocolate from her hand.

"That's because chocolate's just a flirtation. You know mi vida's my true love."

"Brill? I always thought he was just eye candy. Is there something deeper going on behind that rakish grin and self-important attitude?" She looks stern and genuine, the way any protector should when giving advice. She glances back down at the chocolate. "But I guess that's none of my business. There's a couple more bars with that same logo. The Venezuela and the Bolivia."

There's a lot more to Brill. I wish people could see that. He's a historian at heart, like mi hermano, and he loves puzzling things out, sorting events into context, looking at how one problem will affect everything else. For instance, he knows more about the history of tea as relates to Earth's Opium Wars than I ever thought I'd want to know, and he actually cared what I thought when he suggested Earth might be headed into a similar position by refusing to open the borders to alien trade and tourism. And then there's his exquisito taste. He'd appreciate being here right now, discovering these artisanal chocolates. The labels claim that chocolate should be as distinctive as champagne grapes, with soil and growing conditions contributing to a unique experience even from the same trees in different years. I taste each one. Venezuela is sweeter, but with a tannic aftertaste, like wine. Bolivia is smoky, nutty, almost leathery in a way that reminds me of Brill's aftershave.

I'm so enraptured, that I don't even realize someone else has joined us in the room until the guy says, "Oye! What are you doing in here? Get away from my research!"

At first I think he's talking to us, but then I realize he's waving at a monkeybot that just leapt onto the counter against the far wall. It burned through the roof with its eyes to get in. En serio. He chases it deeper into the room. Nervous fear flashes through my chest. We are about to get caught. Chestla's giving me hand signals, her rough plan for us to get away. I nod, then I sweep up the remaining bars and shove them into my backpack. We crawl around behind the tables, then dash into the flickering main warehouse. I hear more monkeybots dropping through the roof into the climate controlled clean room.

I grab Chestla's machete off the desk and make for the main door. "Vamos!" She looks confused. "Run for it!"

As we head back into the darkness of the rainforest, I tense for an onslaught I won't be able to see, but there's nada out here except trees. The bots must all be up on the roof, burning and prying their way into the building. The noise up there sends piel de gallina running over my arms. At least they aren't smart enough to strategize.

"Keep moving." Despite her words, Chestla pauses to pull a piece of corrugated sheet metal off an awning at the side of the building. It's oversized and awkward in her hands.

My vision is starting to adjust to the low light. "How are you going to run with that?"

"Don't worry. I'll manage."

"If you say so, chica." I head out of the clearing, into the tangle of plants. I have to stay ahead of her, or I will lose my ability to run. I'm not focusing on much else.

Running soon ceases to be an option. I have to hack at the undergrowth just to make a path big enough to walk through. Traveling through the now silent rainforest, I imagine small animals scuttling for their burrows at Chestla's approach, insects freezing in place on their branches. Finally, I break the silence. "Tell me about this test, por favor."

For a long time, she doesn't say anything, and I'm worried I've offended her, though I can't really see through the hunormous piece of metal. Her footfalls are silent. I might as well be alone.

"The hardest part is the obstacle course." Her voice startles me. "It ranges across a huge canyon, and you only get to try it once, during the test. I chose my route poorly, and I misjudged a leap. My family paid money they couldn't afford to have me rescue-flighted out. I had over a dozen broken bones, and when the boy I'd had a crush on since we were first unit sparring partners came to visit my hospital bed, I was so ashamed, I had him sent away. He'd just passed his test and been accepted as a gate guard. Before I recovered, he died protecting the king on a royal hunting expedition."

I can only imagine what they must have been hunting. Chestla's planet sounds muy terrifying. "Still, it comforted him in his last moments, no? Knowing that you loved him."

"I never told him."

"And you said you couldn't keep a secret."

After that, we lapse back into silence, trekking towards the wall, me missing Brill worse than ever. Who knows what Chestla's thinking about. Finally, I glimpse snatches of stone through the tangle of plants, and relief loosens the knots in my shoulders. We're almost out.

"I don't like this," Chestla says. "Someone's tracking us. All the little hairs on my neck keep standing up."

Overhead, one of the trees starts to shake, and robotic chittering echoes eerily around us. Apparently, robots have no prey response, because one of the monkeybots leans out of the tree to focus those lasercutter eyes on Chestla. She whirls around, holding the piece of metal in front of her like a shield. It won't take long for the laser to cut through it.

"Run, Bo." Chestla's voice sounds thick and urgent.

"I can't just leave, nunca." Despite my words, I find myself already backing away.

"What guardian companion wouldn't sacrifice herself to save her charge? Besides, I'll be fine. I refuse to die facing such a ridiculous enemy." The piece of metal comes apart in her hands, cut neatly by the lasers, and she flings one half up into the tree. The monkeybots lob down half a dozen machetes, one of which lands point first between her feet.

"Are you sure?" Several of the bots turn their fiery gazes toward me. My heart fills with ice. "Lo siento, Chestla." I run.

Her words follow me. "I'm the one who should be sorry, Bo. I haven't even taught you self-defense, let alone how to hide."

Chestla doesn't think I have the necessary skills to survive this. She's probably right. Without her, I would have died tonight in the muddy ground of an anonymous spot of rainforest floor.

The battle behind me sounds fierce. In front of me, the gate stands wide open. The device is still in place, but I thought I had closed that door on my way in. One of those frogs croaks again, the sound deep and ominous over the general hum of night noises. Leaden dread fills my stomach. Still, I don't have any other way out.

I'm within ten feet of touching the door when a figure steps from behind it. It's too shadowed for me to make out his face, but the gun he's holding is clear enough. It doesn't look like a vapgun. No sé whether that should make me more afraid or relieved. You're more likely to survive getting shot with a projectile than having your atoms vaporized, but bleeding out sounds much more painful. I skid to a halt even before the figure says, "Stop, Bo."

I recognize that voice. En serio? I blink, trying to make features form in the shadows. "Frank?"

"I don't want to have to hurt you. That wouldn't win me any points with your mom."

My heart's thudding with terror, but I try to keep my voice steady. "Because she's going to be so happy about your part in my upcoming execution, right?"

It hurts just saying that word out loud. *Execution.* So vague, so cold. I'd almost rather he shoot me right here, than have to face being paraded out for everyone to watch. This white blouse is so low-cut, it shows off a good bit of décolletage, and the word nut in my brain can't help but connect it, by way of the Latin root word *collum*, for neck, to decollate, an old-fashioned way to say behead.

He ignores my question, waving the gun like waving away my accusation. "This doesn't have to be that public. I feel like I owe you one, so hand over everything biological you've secured here, and I'll see to it that you get off light. You'll wind up with some intensive counseling and a little jail time, but you'll keep your head. I promise."

I've still got the machete, but no matter how grande the knife it's still not a good idea to bring it to a gun fight, no? I'm starting to see him better. His eyes are so cold, a shiver runs down my spine. "You were the one taking shots at Brill. He decided it couldn't have been you. He likes you, you know."

"It's a shame I missed, otherwise we wouldn't be here tonight. If you hadn't spotted the dot from my scope, I'd have nailed that second shot between his eyes."

How can he talk so casually about killing someone? And not just anyone, but mi vida, a person he knows? I shudder. I don't want to be in this monster's debt, not even to keep my head. There's something odd in what he said a minute ago, and my brain finally figures out what. "What do you mean, you owe me one?"

He sighs. "We've met once before, at your father's funeral. You probably don't remember, but you brought a flower out to a man standing at the edge of the trees."

"Sí." I do remember, sort of. Not his face or anything, just a long overcoat and a hand clasping the yellow blossom's stem. "Why weren't you with the rest of the group? How did you know him, since you obviously didn't really work together?"

Frank takes a step closer, the gun still aimed at my heart. "That was a long time ago, Bo." I get the impression he wants to say something else.

"You let my friend go right now." Chestla limps out of the rainforest, a machete in each hand. The end has been laser cut off one of them. Gashes bleed freely from both legs and one arm, and the slash on her cheek looks deep enough to scar. I can only imagine how the monkeybots must look.

Frank lets out a girlish squeak as the prey instinct hits him. Even though he's just proved that HGB hires assassins, reinforcing my belief that the monopoly must be broken, he's offered me a way out of this mess, and I only have seconds to decide if I want to take it. I know I'm in over my head. And still, I take off running. Gunshots follow me through the gate, one pinging off the metal inches from my head. Apparently, Frank doesn't owe me anything enorme enough to stop him from putting a bullet into the back of my skull – but maybe enough to keep him from trying all that hard. He doesn't chase me. Instead, from the other side of the wall he yells, "You! Alien! Surrender yourself!"

"You're just going to have to catch me first." Chestla sounds like she's proposing a Pep-Day game of hide and seek. "It's a big rainforest."

I run parallel to the wall.

"Hey!" The half-charged sentrybot jogs easily, keeping up with me. "Did you find a new battery?"

CHAPTER NINE

I race along the outside of the archway. While my communications are cut off, Frank's probably aren't. He could be calling for backup right now. There's got to be a way to make it to the garage and get a Jeep.

"Where are you going?" Kaliel is leaning against the wall of the main complex, his black skin all but invisible in the darkness, his light T-shirt highlighted by the contrast. He blinks, like he may have fallen asleep. After all, I've been in the rainforest for hours.

My heart clenches. I don't deserve this kind of loyalty. "I didn't mean for you to wait for me. You need to go back inside, before this gets feo."

I try to move past him, but he grabs my hand. "You're shaking like a leaf, and I heard gunshots. What happened in there?"

Heat bites at my eyes. "Por favor, let me go. You are in enough trouble already. If they think you helped me, we'll be in line for the teeter-totter together." I wrench away from him, then back away.

"But I want to help you. You've been the best friend I've had since I got to this place." He tosses me a set of keys. "The Jeep we took yesterday is still at the fuel depot."

"You're a lifesaver. Literally." I start running toward the depot.

He keeps pace with me easily. His gaze drops to the machete still hanging loose in my grip. "What exactly did you do?"

I shake my head. "There's no blood on this, if that's what you're thinking. Nunca."

"That couldn't be farther from my mind." He helps me into the Jeep. "Be safe."

"You are the best, Kaliel." I kiss him on the cheek.

He pulls me closer, tangling his hands in my hair. He kisses me, and this time it isn't about sadness. It's about need and desire and what might have been. My heart's not free to want what he can offer. Still, I find myself saying breathlessly, "Come with me. There are planets without extradition. Shadowpop and escape your trial."

He pulls away, steps back from the vehicle. "Don't think I wouldn't love to be with you, but running tells the world I think I'm guilty."

"Oh." Part of me is sorely disappointed. But mostly, I'm relieved. I still love Brill, need more than ever to get back to him.

Kaliel glances down at the pant cuff that hides his tracking anklet, and I wonder if that plays a part in his decision. I leave him standing there and drive the Jeep towards the gate, casually.

Any hope I have of a lowkey escape evaporates when two guards bar my way, shouting, "Halt!"

More are coming. No y no. I will not be caught here.

I gun the gas pedal and the guards scatter as I crash through the gate. Bullets ping off the back bumper and fly past my ears. I duck as best I can. My heart's already thudding with fear as I take the Jeep out onto the rutted dirt that serves as a road, and no one's even following me yet. At least there's only one obvious path. I feel like my teeth are going to jounce themselves out of my skull, and I start to slow down, pero the minute I do, I see headlights behind me. Grrrr.

Frank's voice comes out of the speaker Rick had been using as a radio. "Give yourself up, Bo. It's not too late for me to fix this, but it will be soon."

I have no idea if he can hear me or not, but I shout, "Not on your life, Frank. I'd never survive the capture. Nunca."

Is he even in the Jeep pursuing me? It doesn't seem likely. The headlights come closer again, and somebody takes a shot at me, shattering part of the Jeep's windshield. I scream. Once the glass stops falling, I shout at the speaker, "See?"

"What just happened?" Apparently, Frank can hear me after all. I don't answer.

I push the engine full speed despite the dangerous curves and the darkness. It feels like I'm diving down the hill. The vehicle keeps tilting like it wants to flip over. Each time, ice spikes through my stomach, melting more and more slowly. A chicken flutters desperately out of my way, but I don't dare slam on the brakes. "Lo siennnnntttttoooo!"

Feathers poof in the headlights, and a few float into the Jeep with me. I bat one away from my face.

"Stop screaming, Bo, and think. Where are you going to go? You're never going to get off this planet."

"Shut up, viejo." I'll admit, my escape plan had hinged on getting out without them discovering my thievery. I'll be flagged everywhere, and they even mapped my retinal patterns when I got my HGB badge. Pero, I can't think about that now. I've got to concentrate on not killing myself on this treacherous road.

My knuckles have gone white by the time I come to the river, and my heart feels like it's going to pound its way out of my chest. I've never driven through water, but I can see the outline of the road farther down on the other side. At least, I'm pretty sure it's the road. It was hard to make out last time, and that was during daylight. I take a deep breath and drive into the shallow agua. Ay! It keeps feeling like I'm going to lose traction and float away, but I make it out the other side, mud flying. I'm shaking from the adrenaline, grateful that I've reached flatter ground.

Eventually, the road becomes paved, and part of my brain recovers from the panic enough to start reviewing what just happened. Why was Frank at Papá's funeral, but not with the mourners? Could Papá have been an assassin, too? I can't imagine his gentle hands, which he used to brush my hair and change my sisters' diapers, choking the life out of somebody. But he did have the same stylus...

No. Nunca. I won't believe it.

The road takes a sharp turn and just where the arc levels out, there's a downed tree blocking it. Damn.

"Egayahhh!" I slam on the brakes, my brain screaming with soundless terror as the Jeep skids toward the obstacle. I'm not going to be able to stop. I jerk the wheel, trying to make it through the sliver of mud between the fallen tree and an upright one, but the Jeep pops a tire and flips onto its side. I scream as the world jolts and my stomach loses all sense of up in a way that prickles across my skin, pero the seatbelt keeps me from being dumped headfirst into the branches as metal rends and paint scrapes. At least I missed the solid trunk of the tree. The sudden stop has jolted all my injuries – especially my bruised ribs – and pressed hard on my burns, but nothing seems broken. I unbuckle the seatbelt and fight my way around the branches, ignoring the way they scratch at my hands.

Headlights poofbang into sight from farther back in the river. They'll catch up in just a few moments.

"Bo?" Frank's shouting through the speaker now. "What just happened? Are you OK?" And after a pause. "Say something!"

I don't answer. I'm too busy salvaging my backpack from where it landed in the tree. There's no way I'm going to get the Jeep back upright. Maybe that's bueno. The path is solidly blocked now, so unless they've got the chopper out looking for me, we're all on foot.

I jog down the road, the adrenaline blunting the pain. I'm sure that I'll hardly be able to move tomorrow, but right now I take advantage of the fear to keep myself going forward. Someone else is blundering through the undergrowth, but they're not shouting, and more importantly, not shooting. I try to move like Chestla, to think like her, confidently silent. A twig snaps close to me, so I freeze up against a tree.

"Bodacious?" a voice I don't recognize calls. Ay, he's close. There's no way he's not going to see me. I edge my way farther around the tree, forcing myself to breathe normally.

I grab that reusable water bottle out of the backpack. Two other guys start moving noisily towards us from different directions. The guy turns and gestures for them to be quiet. They stop immediately, then both shake their heads, gesturing that they didn't find me. While they're distracted, I chuck the water bottle deeper into the undergrowth, and it catches the guy's attention. He moves away, following the false trail. The other guys go with him. Gracias a Dios. I let out the breath I'd been holding, despite myself.

I sneak away before they can realize their mistake.

Soon enough, the sounds of the Chocolate Festival start drifting through the rainforest. I'm close to reaching the relative safety of the crowd. Muy close. I'm more watching to make sure those guys haven't circled around in front of me than watching my feet, so my heart tries to climb out my throat when something enorme with a lot of legs scuttles across my boot.

"Erghumph!"

It may have been a wandering spider. I don't look to see where it has gone. Brill's the one who's phobic about spiders. I have a healthy respect for a bug that can take down a mouse, but I'm a lot more scared of snakes. It may have something to do with Abuelita killing a snake on one of our camping trips and explaining how the cabeza can kill you even after being severed from the body. Those glittering scales had burned their way into my brain. A bodyless snake head clamping down on my arm had become a prominent feature in my childhood nightmares.

The three guys are farther down, scanning the edge of the crowd. If I hesitate too long, they're going to turn this way and spot me. I have to walk into the open and take about ten steps to join the party. Ay, it seems like miles.

I watch the people dancing, most of them turned toward the stage where a rock guitarist gyrates her hips, singing loudly about her broken heart. The shadows out here are even deeper, past the edge of the concert lights. A girl carrying a red cup trips over the legs of another girl who's sitting on a blanket, making out with a guy in a black T-shirt. Make out girl jumps up, and the two start gesturing angrily, probably shouting, though it's impossible to hear over the music. Cup girl slaps her. It turns into an all-out girl-brawl, but nobody moves to stop them. Mario was right. The Fest has gotten rough.

The Jeep guys, their attention drawn by the fight, aren't looking for me anymore.

Now's my chance. Tranquila, Bo. I try to slow my breathing back to normal. I force my legs to move normally too, not dashing too fast. I don't want to draw that lead guy's eye. I make it across, then look back over the cabeza of a niño who's crying about his candy apple, which is covered with dirt and leaves. The guy turns, and I think he spots me, but I melt deeper into the crowd, hurrying toward the open-air market with its maze of shops. I come out the other side without feeling like I've been followed. That doesn't keep me from looking behind me. I have to get off the street, muy rápido.

The party will last all night, and the streets are thronging with people, many of them dressed in costume and carrying peace-bonded weapons. Nobody bats an eye at my machete as I make my way toward Lula's shop. It's not open. Fantástico.

I bang on the door, but he's not there. I make my way around to the back and go in through the window. I don't know what time he comes in, but I'm willing to wait. I don't want to get in trouble, and I don't know who else I can go to for help. I try to call and check in on Chestla, but her phone's off. I hope she shut it down to keep them from tracking her, and not... well, I won't think about that.

I find a couple of jackets on a coat rack in the back room. I ball one up to use as a pillow and try to catch a couple hours' sleep on Lula's ratty break-room sofa.

I wake up to a rough hand shaking my shoulder and a gun in my face.

"Egah!" The shock squeezes at my heart and my bladder at the same time.

Lula asks, "What are you doing back here?"

"Lo siento. Por favor. Lo siento." My chest feels frozen. I manage to look away from the depths of the barrel pointed at my nose to make eye contact with him. "I need help. I can trade."

Lula laughs. The gun withdraws from the vicinity of my face, but he doesn't put it away. "What do you have to trade?"

"I have the necklace Brill gave me. These emeralds are real, no?" I take it off and hold it out to him, trying to hide that my hands are shaking again.

"Of course they're real." He sounds offended that I would question his merchandise's authenticity. He finally puts the gun into a drawer and locks it. "What do you need?"

"I have to fake my way through security at the spaceport. I assume you can alter my ident info, at least long enough for me to get offplanet."

"I could do that, but what prevents me from taking the necklace and turning you in to the police?"

My stomach goes cold. "I thought you were a homem de honra." *A man of honor.*

He laughs again. "So what if I am? You need to be more careful, if you're going to survive for five minutes on the run."

He's the second person who's told me that in the past twenty-four hours. I sigh. "You've read my stats-sheet. Does it sound like I've got a lot of experience in this kind of thing?"

"You know what? You have breakfast with me, and you tell me what it is like on Larksis, and with the necklace we'll call it even. But just so I know I'm not going to come back and find my shop looted, you stay in there."

He ushers me into a small baño at the back of the shop. He locks me in. En serio. What kind of loco bathroom locks from the outside? One designed to double as a holding cell, obviously.

I've made a terrible mistake. I try to pop the doorknob, but it isn't your average baño-door lock, either.

I woke up without my machete – I can't blame Lula for that one – and the best weapon I can come up with in here is a can of Glade. I can't find a lighter, but I bet it still hurts if you spray somebody in the eye. I stay on the back side of the door, tense, then bored, then leaning against the wall. It startles me when the knob turns. Ay! By the time I get the can up and into firing position, Lula's already giving me a disapproving look.

"Come on. I've got coffee, but only if you leave the air freshener where you found it."

I wash my hands at his break room sink before I take the coffee. He's offering strong, Brazilian roast dosed with chocolate syrup. It smells delicioso. It's been a long night, and any source of caffeine is welcome – even if he might have laced it with something. I only hesitate for a moment before taking a long sip.

"That shirt is practically see-through. I'd never let my granddaughters out of the house like that." Lula reaches into a white bag and takes out a yeasty roll that I can only guess is Pão de queijo, Brazilian cheese bread. He passes the bag over to me.

I take a roll for myself and bite into it. The layered flavors of sour cassava flour and bold buttery parmesan make me feel a little better. "My sweater got zapblasted. I didn't have a lot of options."

He laughs. "This is your first heist, isn't it?"

I nod. "I'm glad you didn't come back with the cops. Obrigado." It's hard to get the Portuguese word for *thank you* out of my mouth instead of a half dozen more natural options in several other languages.

He takes the bag back and pulls out a roll for himself. Bueno. I'm more convinced he's not drugging me. "When I saw you used to live around here, I looked you up with some of the locals. Dida said you were always a good kid. How did you get mixed up with Brill Cray, anyway?"

Well, that explains why he was gone for so long. "We met at a party, and he whisked me off across the universe."

"Sounds like the plot from *The Hitchhiker's Guide*."

I give him a sharp look. "I'm no Trillian. Nunca." That came out sounding way too sensitive. Still, I can't help picturing the fried-hair blonde smart-ditzy version from the classic BBC miniseries. "Brill's not perfect, pero we love each other. And what we're doing is noble. It's not like we've stolen the *Heart of Gold* for no good reason."

"I hope all of that is true, menina." He's used a word meaning little girl. I take it as an endearment rather than a comment on my maturity. Lula shakes his cabeza and has me put my thumb on the ident box. His tablet comes up with my picture, but a different name. "These credentials won't stand up to serious scrutiny, but they should get you through the spaceport. You made it sound like everybody's looking for you, but there's not a whisper of your name in the wanted lists. There's just a police bulletin to stop someone with your general description for questioning. Sometimes there are perks to being a star. HGB won't burn you publicly. You can work that to your advantage."

I swallow. Lula's not estúpido. He knows exactly what I've done. "And you're really not going to turn me in?"

"I don't care what people do with chocolate one way or the other. I'm allergic to the stuff. Besides, you pay more per hour than HGB."

"Good thing you didn't get our coffee cups mixed up." I take a long sip of mine.

"The better to keep me from drinking cyanide meant for you."

I splutter, and coffee goes up my nose. "Qué?"

Lula laughs. "Kidding. But seriously, menina, you've got to be more careful. The next guy you ask for help might not be a grandpa like me."

"I know. I just didn't know what else to do."

"You keep your end of my bargain. Tell me about Larksis."

Something about him really does feel grandfatherly, relaxing my nerves un poco despite the tense situation. Still, I know nada about him. "Why are you so interesado to hear my travel stories?"

"Because this keeps me grounded." He pulls at the leg of his trousers, revealing an electronic tracking anklet, just like Kaliel's. "It's been ten years since I've been allowed to leave Rio."

"What did you do?"

"I poisoned a gullible little girl with cyanide."

"Oye." He's not going to tell me what really happened. I wonder why he doesn't just deactivate it, if he's so good with electronics. Instead of asking, I tell him about the ocean on Larksis.

Lula asks questions until my handheld rings. I take it out and turn it off. "Lo siento. I mean eu sinto muito."

Lula frowns. "If you don't need that thing, I'd get rid of it before they start using it to track you." When I hesitate, Lula takes the candy-bar shaped device from me and pops open the back. He removes the battery. "Only put this back in when you find a secure location, and take it back out after you make your call. At least minimize the risk. I don't know what else to tell you that will help." He shakes his cabeza and hands me an envelope. "I'd hate to see a kid like you come back to Earth in a body bag. Still, there's no stopping this. You've taken a step too far, so you have to move forward."

I gulp at the words *body bag*, imagining a zipper slowly closing over my face. Ay-ay-ay. Frank had given me an out. I probably should have taken it. My mouth feels too dry to talk, so I take another long sip of coffee. "What do you want me to say?"

"Nada. You've got a couple thousand Earth dollars in cash, a plane ticket to Larksis 9 – and a spare ticket with an unspecified destination. It'll match the info that comes up under your thumbprint."

The doorbell jangles and Frank comes in, flanked by one of the guys from yesterday. Frank turns Lula's open sign to closed and quietly locks the door. That tiny click sends a cold chill down my spine. I flatten myself against the wall, able to see them through a one-way mirror.

Lula looks at me, and I can tell he's scared. He says softly, "Tell me you didn't leave anything in the rainforest that could be traced back to me."

Heat fills my face. Ay, no! I'd left that lock killer on the gate. "Pero they're untraceable, right?"

Frank pulls a gun and starts moving cautiously toward the counter. I whimper softly.

"Ordinarily, yes, but not to that guy." Lula sighs. "And neither am I. If I try to disable my tracker, it will pump me full of poison so fast I'll be dead before I hit the ground."

I do a double-take at Lula's ankle. Poison? En serio? Is that the same kind of tracker they've got on Kaliel?

Frank starts to move to the gap in the counter. As soon as he gets back here, he'll see me. My heart's pounding, and I shrink even farther back against the wall, my muscles tense, ready to run, only there's nowhere to go. Frank's between me and the door – and the window I snuck in last night. Lula's gun is locked away.

I'm trembling, though I can't help wondering if Frank's just full of empty threats. He seems so inconsistent, taking shots at Brill then letting him go, offering to help me tonight then shooting at me.

Lula gives me a dirty look, then he steps through the doorway. "Bom dia! Can I help you?"

Frank tosses the lock killer on the counter, his face serious yet calm. "I think you know what's about to happen."

Lula looks down at it. "You're going to torture me, and when I don't give up the girl, you're going to shoot me in the head."

"Or we could skip all that. You could just tell me what false identity you gave her. The thumbprint changed on me while I was looking at her records."

"What incentive do I have to do that? I'm dead either way."

When he says that, cold races through my stomach.

"But at least I'll make it painless." Frank pats his pocket. "I'll just cut your tracker."

Lula says nada. I don't know why he's protecting me, but the kindness brings tears to my eyes. My hand's still trembling as I wipe them away. Finally Frank sighs and gestures to the other guy, who's currently outside my field of vision. "Get him into that operating chair. Let's hope he talks quickly, before she makes it through any checkpoints." He hesitates, then looks at Lula, a question in his eyes. "Is that irony, since you use that chair to install communication devices? I never can tell."

Before Lula can answer, the guy puts a gun against his neck and drags him out of my field of view. My heartbeat loud in my ears, I drop to the floor and crawl to the gap in the counter. I peek around. Both Frank and the other guy are facing the chair. I can't see Lula's face through the tower of sublingual boxes, but his feet are visible – including his socks and that anklet. He makes a grab for one of the instruments, and tries to cut it himself, but Frank shoots him in the arm. The gun's suppressor isn't a soft thud, like in the holos, more still a bang – just not loud enough to disturb the crowd partying outside.

"You don't get to do that before I get my information." Both Frank and his colleague are focused on Lula.

The sound of that gunshot still echoing around in my brain, I dash for the door. It takes a few seconds for my shaking hands to unlock it. I hear a struggle and then another gunshot. Frank growls, "Great. He's dead."

As I open the door that tonta bell gives me away, pero I'm through it before bullets start to hit, shattering the glass.

Frank races onto the sidewalk, but I'm already running flat out. "Bodacious! Stop!"

Like that's going to happen. Idiota.

I don't even look back. He won't shoot, not with the street this crowded. I turn a random corner, going slightly downhill. This puts me back into the middle of the festival proper, so I make for the market. A merchant has left one stall unattended. I hop over the counter and duck down. Once I've stopped moving, I realize that tears are streaming down my face. Lula's dead, and it's my fault. Just like Noodles. And the crew from the decoy shuttle. I sit there, trembling, trying not to start seriously bawling. I still can't believe Frank killed him. Frank really would have killed mi vida if he'd had the chance. How on Earth had Brill survived that little fishing trip?

I wait a while, but the merchant returns. "Oy! What are you doing back there?"

I try to shush him, pero he starts shouting louder. I run out of the stall the same way I came in. On the street, I slow to a walk. I'm looking for trouble so hard, I step on someone's foot.

"Oy!" The guy glares at me through hue-changing contacts. They switch colors all at once, randomly, about every ten seconds, and don't look anything like real Krom eyes.

"Lo siento, por favor." I realize too late that I've slipped back into Spanish.

"Estúpido!" He spits on the ground.

He's the one looking stupid and impolite and still has the nerve to look upset as he walks away. Still, the brief encounter gives me an idea.

Lula was generous, considering the position I'd been in. He could have taken the necklace for just the credentials, but he'd given me the things I need to make the credentials work. Trying not to picture his face, which only brings pain, I buy a new black sweater and duck into one of the cement restrooms to change. Then, feeling a lot less visible, I wander through the booths, picking out a pair of zebra-stripe sunglasses and a blue wig. If I'm going to hide in plain sight, I might as well go over the top, no? Because if you shimmerpop like a crazy person, nobody looks too close. I add a pair of glitter-covered antenna attached to a headband. I just hope I don't have to tell Brill about it. It would be demasiado humillante – *too humiliating*. He'd find those sparkly spheres demeaning to aliens everywhere.

I buy more chocolate bars, some of them HGB dark, the rest a variety of kiddie bars full of caramels or krunchies or nougat, and a clear temp-and-humidity control bag to keep both my vintage bars and the new acquisitions from melting. Chocolate may be better than Earth currency once I get offplanet. I make my way through the crowd, and as soon as I can, I hop onto an open-air bus taking tourists – who often make the ChocoFest a jumping off point for an offplanet vacation – to the spaceport. I pay cash, so nobody scans my thumb.

The breeze makes me happy for the sweater, and I cross my arms over my chest as I stare at the seatback in front of me, numb, trying not to deal with the violence repeating itself in my brain. I try to think about anything else, and all that I can come up with is Kaliel. I still can't believe I let myself kiss him. Twice. What am I going to tell Brill? Or does he even have to know? I haven't talked to mi vida since I was at the bar.

My sublingual rings, and I'm terrified it's him. Or Frank.

When I answer it, and Mamá says *Hola Bodacious*, tears prick the back of my eyes, for so many reasons. She continues, *I got a call from Little Mario. I am so glad you went to see him. He said he hopes you come back when the girls are home. It has been so long, you might not even recognize them.*

I keep seeing the holos you send, right? I take a deep breath. She's going to prickle at my question, pero I have to ask it. *Mamá, how much do you really know about Frank?*

It's so quiet inside mi own cabeza that for a moment I think she's hung up. I was asking about her research into his current occupation, but is it possible that she knew him from before, that Papá really was involved in something sinister? The numbness vanishes, replaced by anguish. Nooooo!

Why do you always try to ruin my love life, Bee? She only calls me that when she's exasperated. I don't care. I'm just relieved that she's angry at me, rather than hiding something horrible. *Frank called me today asking if I had heard from you. Are you trying to steal another of my boyfriends?*

Ewwwwww. He's like a million years old. *En serio, Mamá. He's a spy or something. I saw him kill a guy.*

Bo. Do not start making things up.

I'm trembling at the memory, cold with the idea of Mamá calling him and telling him what I've said. Could that get *her* killed? She really should know me better by now, but she still doesn't believe me. *He's not there with you, right?*

Well, no. He had to go home to take care of his granddaughter. She has the flu, and they will not take her in school until her fever has gone.

If Frank has a real granddaughter, I'll eat the glitter-covered Styrofoam ball at the end of my antenna's left spring. *OK,*

Mamá. Maybe I was wrong. Maybe I saw somebody else. But in case I'm not, be careful por favor.

OK, mija. But you need to be careful, too. HGB can give you a wonderful career, but you have to be on time from now on.

Now I just want to tear off that spring. *Did you get a call from Tawny, too?*

About an hour ago. She was worried something might have happened to you in town. I told her you knew your way around, that you used to live there. For some reason that only made her more hysterical.

HGB really must not know where I am, if they're calling mi mamá.

We chat about her FeedCast, about unimportant things. Eventually, I let Mamá go as I rub at the tension knots in my own shoulders, trying to force them to release. The bus stops and more people get on. I sigh as I get squashed in between three children and an elderly lady. I pull out the handheld. What would happen if I called Minerva's phone number?

The bus pulls into the spaceport, and everyone starts unloading luggage from underneath. I'm just carrying the pink backpack, so I hop off and walk toward the brightly lit building. I swipe my thumb to enter the door. I've never seen so much security all in one place in my life. Nunca. And they don't know it, but they're all looking for me.

Good thing the Privacy Protection Coalition got it made illegal to scan bio-responses, because my blood pressure and respiration just shot way off of norm. Tranquila y tranquila. Trying to slow my breathing, I pocket the ticket for the ride back to Larksis 9 and pull out the standby anytime anywhere one. I have to go up to the counter and get assigned to a flight.

The doors open and I freeze, my chest a hollow cave of ice. Dios mío, Frank's here. I can't breathe. Lula's blood's all over his shirt. People keep glancing at him, trying to see if they're really seeing what they think they're seeing, while circling out of his path. Hands balled into fists close at his sides, he's scanning the waiting area of one of the boarding gates.

My mouth goes dry. Every instinct says to bolt back through the door. Instead, I turn my face away and step up to the counter. The hologram, a girl with a hunormous mass of curly red hair pulled back in a clip, gestures for me to swipe my thumb. Good thing holograms don't notice things like trembling fingers as I comply then hold up my ticket for her to scan.

"Gracias, Senhora Perez Chaves. Where is your destination?"

"I need to get to Krevia." Brill is waiting for me there. It's going to take days to get to him, long nerve-racking days.

She looks at a virtual schedule and says, "The next transport for Krevia leaves in sixteen minutes. If you hurry through security, you should just make it."

Security might take longer than that. I glance over at the line of people waiting to get scanned, then at Frank, who's working his way through the next closest gate.

"When's the next one leave?"

The pleasant smile never wavers as she says, "Twenty-nine hours, thirty-two minutes."

Well, fantástica. I can be dead by then. "I'll take the first one, muchas gracias."

"Have a nice flight!" A boarding pass pops out of a slot in the counter.

I take it and join the line waiting to be cleared. Brill promised the beans won't show up on the scanners, but when my turn finally comes, the guard waves me to the side for a physical inspection. Cold blazebangs through my chest. I almost bolt.

He points at my backpack. "We're detecting high levels of theobromine in your scan. We believe you may have a number of chocolate bars in that bag. If this is the case, you will need to fill out a declaration form, and then I will need to match the numbers on the form to the number of bars a physical search reveals."

I nearly swoon with relief. I glance back. Frank has just reached the counter where I checked in. Ay! There's no way I can elude him for the next thirty hours. The minutes are ticking away before the shuttle leaves, and the paperwork is slowing me down. I have never typed so fast in my life.

The guard lets out a low whistle as he pulls out bar after vintage bar. "Lady, you must really love chocolate."

I take them back once he's counted and cataloged them. "You have no idea."

I have to run across the spaceport to where the shuttle is boarding.

I glance back to make sure Frank's not following, and a guy bumps into me. He turns. "Sorry. Sorry." It's the guy from the Jeep, the one who nearly caught me. My chest freezes over. I literally cannot breathe. I am so muerta. He looks straight through the pink lenses of my sunglasses, but doesn't recognize me. How is that possible?

I lag by about a beat, then finally manage to draw in air. "No worries!" I try to sound vaguely Australian or something. I pat his arm briefly, then I rush onward, making it to the gate just as a uniformed hologram calls out, "Last boarding call for Krevia."

CHAPTER TEN

I've been using the seat-mounted system to watch holos of Mamá, not her show, but candids the Pops took while she and mi hermanas were doing ordinary stuff. I used to angerzent how we never seemed to have any privacy, how every minor mistake could wind up virafizzed, but now, these brief glimpses of normality are keeping me sane. Mamá and the girls at the pool: Isabella, who is fourteen now, trying unsuccessfully to balance on a blow-up seahorse, while Sophia, who's twelve, shoots the FeedCaster with a waterblaster. Mamá helping them pick out libros at the library – and having a second FeedCaster photobomb this one. Mamá buying a pair of sunglasses not too different from the ones I'd gotten at the ChocoFest – with the camera hidden in the display. I guess the salesperson's a fan.

Pero now we're landing, and I have to let go. I run my hand through the holo, as though I can touch Mamá's face, but the light just reflects on my palm, destroying the illusion. Heat fills my eyes and nose, but I will not cry again.

Given the nonexistent security at the spaceport, I have no problem walking off the shuttle into a new world of unpleasant aromas. A gray haze hangs over patches of stunted trees and expanses of cement. It's all muy desagradable – *so, so disgusting*. I grab a map of the city from a rack. The restaurant where I am supposed to meet Brill isn't far, but it's cold enough here that my breath fogs the air, so I go back into the spaceport and pay too much Earth cash for a dove gray hoodie made of a reasonably cotton-like material. I zip it all the way up, pushing the collar as high as it will go, trying to capture as much warmth as I can without using the hood. Brill hasn't seen me in a while, and I want my hair to look maravilloso. The cargo pants, which I'd chosen for practicality, really flatter my backside, and the black sweater underneath the hoodie is soft. He'll be wowed enough to forgive me. I hope.

As I walk, my surroundings keep getting seedier and seedier, the mix of peoples from far-flung planets more unfamiliar, and unease builds inside me. A guy walking against traffic on the opposite sidewalk looks like an eight foot-tall humanoid fer-de-lance, and the thought of him crossing over here turns my chest cold in a way the weather never could. The moment I've processed this thought, I feel guilty. He's not *actually* a snake, even if the flat diamond shape of his head keeps raising the hairs on the back of my neck. No y no. The guy's minding his own business, and despite the black leather jacket – not so different from Brill's, after all – and the ball cap with the *Blaster's Emergency Clinic* logo on it pulled down close over his whiteless golden eyes, he could be just as nice as Chestla on the inside. There's only so many viable patterns for carbon-based life in the galaxy. It's not like this guy's venomous or anything. He can't help it if those shimmering gray scales hit something primal in people from planets like mine.

Brill must have checked the time of my shuttle arrival, because when I reach the restaurant, he's just gotten us a booth. My heart's beating un poco fast, and my palms are clammy, I'm so nerviosa. I've decided I'm going to tell him about kissing Kaliel, some time before we leave this restaurant. I don't want to hold another lie inside me. I slide in opposite him.

The place is nicer inside than I would have expected, given the neighborhood, with lightwalls ombred from red to yellow, overlaid with geometric openwork wood patterns, and light patterns in the table that respond to movement and warmth. The deep brown cushions on the booth look brand new. Despite the swank, we're practically the only people in here.

I can't decipher the strange look on his face. I whisper, "I've missed you."

He grabs both my hands in his, squeezes so tight it hurts. "I've missed you too. I was so afraid you weren't going to make it." He realizes he's hurting me and lets go. "Sorry. We need to talk about your future, now that you are a fugitive of Earth. Once we leave this planet, you could go anywhere that doesn't allow for extradition. I don't recommend Krom. Too many people there consider Earthlings savages. You wouldn't be treated fairly." He grimaces, the way he so often does when talking about his home planet.

"You don't have many happy memories of Krom, do you?"

He looks surprised. "Ga. That's not true. I have lots of happy memories. Just… there are a couple of really unhappy ones too."

Sí. The painful ones must have to do with his family, the one thing he never wants to talk about. Now's not the time to push him about what happened to them.

I nod. "Tell me about this buyer, por favor. I need to be sure that we're giving chocolate to someone who will take care of it."

"Haza." *Fine.* Brill's leg bumps into mine under the table. He lets the outside of his knee rest against the inside of mine for a moment. "They're Krom businessmen. They will clone the beans and create price competition."

Only, that's not going to work. No y nunca. There's something engineered into the DNA strand of HGB *Theobroma trinitario* that makes it turn to mush in the face of that kind of gene-doctoring. Brill has to know that. Or does he? His eyes are teal, appropriate to what he's been saying.

"Venezuelan bio-grammers tried that, early on after the war.

It can't be un-mushed. You have to start a cacao plantation the hard way, letting the trees grow to maturity and planting the resulting seeds."

"Krom scientists are a little smarter than…" He looks down at the table, takes his napkin in both hands. The light dances in the table's surface, like he's gotten warmer all of a sudden. His knee bumps mine again, but this time I don't think it is intentional.

My mouth hardens into a line. "Go on, say it. Than us imbécil Earthlings."

"Babe, that's not what I meant."

It was, though. He is, after all, a product of the planet he just warned me away from. Krom may be physically superior, they may have a grander history, better neural enhancement and more technology, but it doesn't give them the right to look down on humans.

Brill's eyes go violet, then bright pink. Whatever he's thinking of saying, it's a lie. Then he shakes his head, and his eyes shade towards gray. "I'm sorry. Lo siento."

Like saying it in my language is going to help. The words just come pouring out. "You guys are the ones with all the time in the world. By the time chocolate grows into a thriving industry anywhere else in the galaxy, I'll be an old woman, if I'm not already muerta."

And Brill won't even yet be middle-aged. That fact sits there on the table between us, feo and out of place, like a misshapen toad. Brill tries to take my hand, but I pull away. The lights follow our movements.

"And by then, mi vida, you will have found some other girl the age you look."

"Bo, I promise you, I won't–"

I stop him with a look.

He lets tangerine anger bleed into his eyes. "Is that why you decided to have all your romances at once, to make up for what

I might do in the future after you die on me? Two hundred years of broken-hearted devotion is a lot to ask for, *mi vida*, if you can't control your own heart for a couple of weeks."

Confusion blunts my anger. "What are you talking about?"

"You and that kek," meaning *idiot* or *jerk*, sometimes both, "melting into each other on the dance floor. It's being played all over the feeds, with a variety of tacky polls. Don't try to tell me you weren't attracted to him off the dance floor, too."

Heat flares in my cheeks, shame and sadness mixing with the blunter anger. "Verdad, Brill? Sí, I kissed him. I didn't think it would matter, because I was saying goodbye. Chances are he's going to be dead in a couple of weeks, and I couldn't stand for him to be so alone. If I have to stand trial, I'd want–"

"That is not going to happen, Babe." His eyes are still light orange, but there's compassion in his voice. "Ga. I'll take you to Krom if I have to, but I won't let that happen."

"I don't want to go to Krom! Nunca! It's been hard enough getting your amigos to like me, loco boy. I'm not ready for a whole planet of Gavins." I feel my hands clenching into frustrangerated fists. I try to relax them before I speak again. "I probably got Kaliel in more trouble, and he still won't leave Earth. Chestla came to Earth to try and help me, and she's being hunted in the rainforest, if they haven't captured her already. Meredith will be found guilty of treason, and she's beyond rescue at the Global Court headquarters in Switzerland. Ay no, Brill. None of them thought they would be facing the shave."

"Suavet ita hanstral." Brill looks subdued, his eyes edging toward a worried gray. He bows and gives me that super-formal closed fist salute. Then he takes both of my hands in his.

I pull away. "You're sorry? That's all I get? My life could be over, no? And what did you risk?"

For a long time, he doesn't say anything. His eyes change color like a fireworks show, first gray then red then gold then orange. "I risked my heart. I've never let anyone in like that before. Tesuaquenell." Literally, *my heart halved*, but it means *I love you*.

He's never said it in Krom before. English, Universal, Spanish, even in Tondorgian once… but never the language of his heart. Heat floods my face and tears blur my vision. I blink them back.

"Then help me do the right thing. Those three people all rescued me, mi vida. I have to do something to save them. Por favor. Maybe we can get them better lawyers, or find someone willing to smuggle them offplanet–"

"You have to complete the cacao buy. Then what those people have done won't matter so much to the courts." Brill holds out his hands in a placating manner. The lights waver under them. "I can't guarantee that, but historical precedent strongly suggests it."

I put my hand over his on the table, needing that to be true with all my heart. I realize he's just guessing, but it's a good guess, no? "How do you know these business guys won't just hold the cacao beans ransom and sell them back to Earth?"

"Shtesh!" Brill's eyes sink all the way to a brown that matches the booth seats. "Where would be the honor in that? I don't think you understand Krom at all."

My mouth pops open, but no words come out.

A waitress comes by and sets a glass of agua on the table. In Krom, which is, after all, a common trade language, she asks, "Do you know what you want?"

Was she eavesdropping on our conversation? No. She probably just noticed Brill's eyes.

She blinks and repeats, "What you want?"

That used to be such a simple question. I say, "Ga. Not yet," at the same time as Brill says, "Can you give us a few minutes, avell?"

He takes the agua glass away from me. "You really don't want to drink that. Nothing but alcohol and overcooked food while you're here, OK."

"OK." I eye the glass. It's been a long time since I've been in a place that doesn't sterilize the tap water.

Brill takes a sip of his own glass of wine. "I guess I was just afraid that when you went back to Earth, you'd realize how boring Krom are, and you might not want to be with me anymore."

Could such a supposedly superior being really be that insecure? I look into his eyes, trying to comprender. "I spent the whole time wishing I was back in your arms, mi vida."

Brill moves from his side of the table over to mine and wraps his arms around me. "Better now?"

He's mastered that perfect level of cheesy romance that always makes my heart glow. I let myself melt against him, the smell of his new leather jacket bringing comfort, but the flight to Krevia gave me a lot of time to think, to examine each event that led up to this moment. I need to make everything clear between us. "Lula said you buy baubles for all the girls. How many have there really been?"

His arms stiffen, then come down to his sides. "I never lied to you about that. You know how a guy's reputation tends to get exaggerated."

"Sí. Of all people, I know how that happens." Heat flames into my face as I think of all the unkind things the FeedCasts have said about my own "exploits."

He brings his arms back around me. "I've spent my life afraid of getting hurt. My relationships have been more about what the girl and I could do for each other – until I met you."

Which sounds sweet. Pero it brings up something else I've been worrying about. "What were you doing on Larksis that night in the first place? Because none of mi amigos could ever remember inviting you to that party."

His lips brush my neck, one step away from us making out in public. "That was a long time ago. The whole Larksis system produces cheap goods for export. I guess it was just random chance that brought us together."

"Sí. The random chance that you speak English, out of all the languages in the galaxy, no?"

"It's a trending new trade language on this side of the galaxy. The cool factor that comes with coffee, you know."

"But not near Larksis. Which is about as far as you can get from here."

He shrugs. "Which makes for long solo flights with nothing to do but read, hit the treadmill or run linguistics feed. Coincidences can be amazing, su."

I want that to be true. I want things to be like they were, where I would have just teased him about how many people are watching him play with my hair, then kissed him in this empty restaurant. But things aren't that easy anymore. I pull back so that I can see his face. "Was it random? Or did you come to that party looking for me because you thought I could get you closer to chocolate?"

"It was always about you, Babe." His eyes flick all the way to a selfish brick red, then snap back to the gold. My heart feels like he's shot a poisoned dart into it, darkening the glow. He's lying to me. And when it comes to something he deeply feels, he's *not* very good at it.

"You kek." I shove him away, but he's blocking my exit from the booth.

"What did you expect me to say?" He puts a hand on my arm. "Haza. Frank was right. Back then I wouldn't have dated an Earthling, but that was my prejudice and my loss. The first time we kissed, I remember thinking that you had the capacity of caring more deeply than anyone else I've ever known. I really do love you. That's not a lie."

His honesty knocks the breath out of me. I pick up his wine glass and drain it. "Then let's get this over with, so we can get *us* back on track."

I still find myself melting against his shoulder as we walk hand in hand toward the water-front park where we are to make the exchange. We're facing this planet's super-bright sun, so I take out the sunglasses I bought at the Fest.

Brill stops. "Ga. You can't wear those, Babe."

I look down at the frames. They don't have any weird designs or logos or anything. "Qué? Why not?"

"Sunglasses are taboo on Krom. They imply that you've got something to hide, or that you can't trust the person that you're talking to with your emotions."

"Oh." I tuck the sunglasses into the pocket of my hoodie. I don't really know much about his home planet, do I?

As we approach the agua, I begin to see why Brill doesn't want to eat or drink anything connected to that murky brown sludge. An automated garbage scow floats by, dropping some of its overloaded jetsam into the water as it goes.

We sit down on a bench at one of the piers to wait. Niños throw rocks into the water, careful to never fall in themselves. A man walking what looks like an overgrown cat with purple fur picks the animal's dung off the pavement with a rag and tosses both rag and waste into the water. The tall guy in the *Blaster's* hat, now doing laps on the park's track, gives him a dirty look that springs goosebumps up across my arms.

Two Krom wearing suits approach and sit down on a bench opposite us. One of them is carrying a secure bankpad reader. The other has a loaf of bread. He starts breaking off chunks and throwing them into the agua, as though feeding ducks or fish or something. Claro está, we all know there's nada alive in there, but the currently blue-eyed Krom seems happy enough with his pretense.

I lean in towards Brill, like I am going to kiss his cheek. Instead, I whisper, "So, how do we do this?"

He says into my ear, "One of us goes over there and shows them the merchandise. Then one of them comes over here and shows us the bankpad so we can verify our account numbers. Yours is the day and time we met, down to the minute. Two thumb prints on the pad, and the money gets transferred, half to each account. Litoll?"

"Lo tengo. Sounds easy enough." I swallow back nervous fear.

"Now go over there and show off those beans." Brill pats me on the leg.

As I approach, the two guys slide apart from each other. One of them gestures for me to sit down. I pull off the backpack and start to access the hidden compartment. Before I can produce the beans, a raspy voice shouts, "Freeze!"

Oi! *Blaster's* guy has come up behind us, a gun in one hand and a badge in the other. His entire body springs forward, taking him somewhere upwards of ten feet tall, overloading my heart with instinctual fear.

"Engyaah!" I couldn't be more incoherent.

The boost bares his midsection at my eye level, showing off an intricate pattern of olive green scales interwoven with the gray ones between the bottom of his jacket and the top of his jeans. He's lost some scales here and there, and a mass of scar tissue takes up nearly a foot of his abdomen. My heart pounds, pero I'm frozen in place, more scared of him than of the gun. I have to pee. I miss Chestla.

A smaller humanoid runs towards us, also brandishing a weapon.

The Krom sitting to my right frowns at Brill like this is all his fault. Both Krom stand up muy slowly, with their hands out in front of them, palms up. It takes all my will to force myself to move, but I copy the gesture.

The Krom to my left says, "What can I do for you today, officer?"

In Krom, *Blaster's* guy replies, "I, Gideon Tyson, Galactic Inspector, hereby arrest all of you for–"

I lock gazes with Brill, and in his horrified expression I see the guillotine blade dropping. He cuts his gaze toward the path leading out of the park. He's telling me to run. Pero, a garbage scow's coming fast, and I have a better chance of getting on board than of beating Tyson in a footrace. Using everything I've learned from hanging out with Chestla about managing the prey instinct, I close my eyes and sprint for the end of the dock.

"Stop or I'll shoot," Tyson shouts.

I leap. I don't really believe he'll do it, not in public. After all, I'm a celebrity, and cops don't shoot celebrities, nunca. Furthermore, I am a girl. But just as my feet hit the pile of garbage, I hear Brill shout, "Don't, Tyson! Avell! Avell! Ga!"

The gun goes off. A searing pain burns through my body. Apparently, cops will shoot you. Even if you are a celebrity. Even if you are a girl.

I crumple into the pile of garbage, already woozy from the shock. As darkness fills mi cabeza and blood smears across my hoodie, I lose consciousness.

I wake from a nightmare about fire and fangs. The craft slows, as though it has almost reached its destination. I've got to get off before that happens. I sit up. The backpack rests near my hand, but as I move it falls overboard, into the water. The gunk is so thick, it floats. I reach out, catching hold of the strap. Then, despite the burning pain in my shoulder, I manage to step from the scow as it passes an exceptionally close dock. I crumple against the dock railing.

I must have floated a long way downriver, because I'm outside of town. It's greener here, but in a sickly way.

I've got to get to a doctor. Pronto. I call Brill, but he's shut his phone down. I can't even leave a message. I call the hotel. They say he's checked out. I call the spaceport, asking to be put on the same transport as him. They say he's already left.

My chest cold with fear, my heart breaking with abandonment, my shoulder on fire with pain, I put the battery back in my handheld long enough to show a holographic map of the area, dragging up a layer of pins for medical facilities. The device dings with a message, but I ignore it. I grab the nearest pin. It turns into a gran, white mental hospital. Well, that won't work.

I grab another pin. A holo of an elderly man who looks humanish – barring the single eyebrow that goes over both his eyes like a Muppet-style sideways parenthesis – pops up. The search voice tells me that I am looking at one Dr Nurry Ulilt. "Why should they choose me? Oh. OK. I've been a physician and veterinarian here on Krevia for over thirty years. I treat the whole family, from the grandparents to the toddlers, as well as the four-, six- and eight-footed family members too." He's speaking an archaic form of Universal Standard. Not that Universal really is all that standard, given the distance between the planets that use it.

Let's just hope Dr Ulilt isn't out making house calls, por favor. I'm going to have to walk there, and we're talking maybe a quarter of a mile down a dirt road. I stumble along until I'm too weak to keep going. I sit down, putting mi cabeza between my knees. Gracias a Dios. I'm close enough to see the cinderblock building that must be Dr Ulilt's clinic in the distance. Tears of frustrangeration fill my eyes. I'm about to bleed to death here, in sight of help. If I rest for a minute, maybe I can gather the strength to crawl.

A door opens in the building, and a niña carrying a paperboard box starts walking up the dirt road. I call out, and when she sees me, she turns around and rushes back inside.

That's just increíble. I'm feeling woozy again. I close my eyes, and my balance goes wonky, and suddenly, I'm lying on the ground. I open my eyes to find the niña and Dr Ulilt leaning over me. They lift me onto a flat panel, and the niña places my backpack beside me. I wrap my hand around one of the straps.

My panel drops onto a table, and Dr Ulilt comes around to talk to me. "You're going to feel a nudge right here inside your elbow. I'm starting a saline drip to keep the blood you've got left dancing. Do you want to speak me what happened?"

I don't dare tell the truth. For all I know, the good doctor might just let me die so he can take the beans. Universal's linguistically derived from Krom, so I sound halfway decent speaking it. "I was just playing around with my boyfriend's gun. It was an accident."

"Uh huh." Dr Ulilt frowns. "And I suppose you don't want this summarized to the constabulary. That costs extra."

He gives me a shot of something. After a few minutes, the wooziness passes. Dr Ulilt shines a light into each of my eyes. He helps me to sit up, which hurts immensely, then he takes off my hoodie and cuts away a good portion of my sweater. He moves around to get a look at the back of my shoulder. "It could be worse. The bullet went straight through. Do you want a local anesthetic while I darn, or do you want to be inert?"

I puzzle through his strange word choices as the niña wheels in a metal table laid out with shiny instruments and stacks of gauze. It doesn't take that long for dictionary meanings to shift, and this planet hasn't been a galactourist stop for a long time, if ever.

"Local," I croak. I don't want to give these two a chance to look through my things.

Dr Ulilt tells the niña something in a language I don't comprender. She picks up a device that looks like a caulking gun filled with yellow liquid and hands it to the doctor. Ay. Anxiety kicks my heartbeat back up. I look away as he plunges the device into my wound, gritting my teeth as pain rips through the entire area, sending my heart racing in panic. Across the room, the paperboard box the girl had been carrying wobbles, emitting a whining noise. Then the box tips over and six little purple-furred cat things tumble out.

My shoulder goes numb, and my hand won't move. My rapid heartbeat slows dramatically, and I'm afraid that maybe he's injecting too much of whatever it is, too close to my heart. I could die from a dose his people find normal. But despite the slow rhythm I stay conscious, and I'm not in pain for the first time in a week.

The niña hurries over and gathers the cat things back into the box. She holds one of them up and says something to me.

Dr Ulilt translates. "She wants to know if you yearn for one. Her vikklet had kittens, and her mother modulated she must give them all away. She's just picking them up from being spayed."

"Tell her that's very sweet, but that I couldn't possibly have a pet right now." I turn my head toward Dr Ulilt as I am speaking, and I get a look at that enorme metal cylinder coming up out of the hole in my flesh, dripping blood-flecked foam that rapidly solidifies on the tip. Well, that makes me nauseous.

I turn back to the niña. She brings the kitten over to the panel and sets it down beside me. Her hand over mine, she helps me stroke the coarse purple fur. The kitten rolls over, and waggles six paws in the air. I reach down to pet its belly, and the paws close playfully on my hand.

The niña says something else. I don't look back around as Dr Ulilt says, "She modulates that petting an animal is calming. It is almost as good as medicine."

The kitten makes a little growling noise and bites at one of my fingers. I wish I *could* take it with me.

"So, how will you be paying today?" Dr Ulilt asks.

I have dinero. "Will you take Earth currency?"

The eyebrow goes lop-sided. I guess that's his version of arching it. So that's a no.

"How about trade? Two standard size chocolate bars, one dark and one milk?"

I can hear the excitement in his voice. "That will just about cover it."

Oi! I should have just offered one bar, but it's too late.

I hear the snap of Dr Ulilt stripping off his gloves. "You're all done. Just don't move that shoulder at all for three or four days, and take one of these when the pain modulates to you."

He places a bottle of pills on the panel next to me. I wait until he steps back before I unzip my backpack and extract two chocolate bars from their sealed plastic. I try to make sure he doesn't see the other bars.

There's a knock on the door. It cannot be a coincidence. Of course, they'd be checking doctor's offices all along the river. Dios mío, I still cannot catch a break. I scramble off the table and into a corner, cold flashing through my stomach while my heartbeat stays unnaturally slow and steady. Dr Ulilt's eyes widen, pero he says nada as he moves to answer his door.

"Have you seen this girl? She's wanted for questioning." It's Tyson's partner, speaking halting Universal.

Dr Ulilt takes a handheld, peers at the holo. It's an unflattering likeness, from when I passed Tyson on the street. His eyes flick to me. "I'm not sure."

I use my non-numbed hand to pull two HGB kiddie-bars out of the plastic. I wave them so that Dr Ulilt sees them.

"Let me think. There was a girl in here earlier," he says slowly. But he raises four fingers behind his back.

En serio? What a kek. Still, I'm in no position to argue. I pull two more kiddie bars out of my backpack.

Dr Ulilt shakes his head. "No. It wasn't her."

After the police leave, I trade four more bars for fresh clothes, a two-minute shower in a contraption where you pour bottled water into a tank at the top, and no-questions-asked transport with his son, Uke, who is making a three-day flight to Kranar Prime to pick up medical supplies. It sounds perfect, because that's just about the amount of time Dr Ulilt says it will take for his miracle foam to make my shoulder at least stable again – though he's warned there's going to be muscle rehab involved before it's anything like good as new.

So I spend mucho tiempo lying in a bunk, watching the ship-mounted holo aboard Uke's shuttle. Mostly news, trying to get a better picture of what's going on out here. I stay away from the novelas, because it just doesn't feel right at the moment to escape my problems into fiction. Pero, I binge through a holocade of Meredith's feed. She's obsessed with Pure275, and she will interview anyone, no matter how loco, who has a connection with it. There's this one CastClip, labeled *Tainted Chocolate*.

The woman she's interviewing just looks loco, fidgety, with unfocused eyes that seem to be staring off in different directions. She's wearing solid black, and is at least Mamá's age. The name she's being interviewed by is Jane Smith, pero her accent says she's Mexican.

Jane talks about a raid she and her group did, recovering samples of Pure for independent testing. The group has since disbanded, and they don't seem to have been affiliated with CyberFighter's gang. In fact, she claims they were working as contractors on an undercover investigation for the Global Court.

Then Meredith says, "Jane has promised to show us some amazing feed she took on a different raid, where she uncovered tainted chocolate." She pats Jane on the hand. "Let's set this up for the viewers, por favor." Turning back to the camera, she says, "It's eight years ago, the night of the full moon on a sweltering day at Heebie-Jeebie Central in the Yucatan."

"Heebie-Jeebie?" Jane interrupts.

"HGB. You were at HGB's Yucatan headquarters." Meredith looks frunoid – both frustrated and annoyed. "Anyway, one of the group's members had gone missing, and you'd… they'd gotten an anonymous tip that there was tainted chocolate being kept on site. Let's watch."

"We're on the ground and inside HGB-owned property," past-Jane narrates softly, filming as she walks. Her footsteps sound loud, until you realize there's maybe half a dozen people with her. "The unofficial news is that HGB tainted that chocolate with herbicide by accident, that they've pulled it in a secret recall after several people died up north."

They walk onto a manicured lawn, and my heart squeezes with purely emotional pain. "Oi," somebody says, and I agree. The dorm that had caught fire the night mi papá died is still smoldering behind them. I recognize it from all the footage covering the fire. It had taken days for it to cool enough for anyone to even get inside the ruined structure. It is possible Papá's body is still inside at the moment this holo was taken. I feel nausea rising, being hit so unexpectedly with this reminder.

Jane continues, "However, we fear that they could be stockpiling this chocolate as a weapon, to weaken unsuspecting elements of any country that resists HGB control, or even to be shipped to a secret enemy out in space."

"Not all of us believe that," a voice interjects from somewhere behind the camera. Jane scowls at whoever it was.

"I have to be quiet now. We're going into the warehouse where the tainted chocolate is being kept."

There's a lot of sneaking, and some *that-was-close* action involving a spotlight and a couple of sentrybots. Jane shoots the bot that's guarding the warehouse door, taking it out cleanly enough that it probably didn't even send a distress call. One of Jane's companions steps over the slumped metal body to pry open the door. An alarm goes off, and the entire group rushes into the warehouse.

I find myself leaning up in bed, in anticipation. Only... ay, it is empty, spotless, ready to be filled. There are no crates of chocolate, or anything else.

"No. It can't be." Jane's voice sounds panicked, even over the wailing alarm.

"Vamos!" one of her companions shouts. "We have to go."

Jane stands rooted to the spot, until one of her friends drags her away. The holo cuts there.

"So what you're saying," Meredith says slowly, "is that you discovered an empty warehouse. Did you ever find the poisoned chocolate?"

Jane shakes her head. "It was moved. Don't you see, it's just one more level of coverup."

Meredith ends the interview as quickly as possible, and in the comments section scrolling by her face, she's typed, while still giving the interview and smiling, *Lo siento chicos, I've got to start watching these feeds before I agree to the interview.*

Such a waste of time. Like me, lying here wounded, unable to do anything useful.

I should have learned better from Lula about not trusting strangers – especially the kind who would extort chocolate from an injured woman – because when the shuttle touches down, the door opens on the silhouette of a certain Galactic Inspector, gun drawn, a smile on his reptilian lips.

Claro! I force my own suddenly stiff mouth to move. "Tyson."

He dips his head at me, bringing it against his chest with that unnerving flexibility. The scales on his forehead glisten in the light, almost like flowing quicksilver. Despite the wedge-like flatness of his face, Tyson's hands aren't lizard hands. No y no. They're boxer's hands, and today each flexible digit is graced with an engraved silver ring that gives the same effect as brass knuckles. When he parts his lips, I can see his tongue because the guy's got no front teeth. You have to have front teeth to say TH's. Tyson can't. Otherwise, he speaks perfect English.

"Hi, Bo. Tis is such a beautiful day for a trip back to Eart."

CHAPTER ELEVEN

Tyson barely frisks me before he picks up my backpack, while keeping one surprisingly warm hand on my arm. My heart freezes as he makes a cursory inspection of the contents. He pockets my screwdriver and the devices Lula gave me before slinging the bag over his shoulder. Not that it matters. No. Someone's bound to tear that backpack apart, looking for either evidence or souvenirs, once I'm back on Earth. They'll find the cacao beans.

I try to cover my fear. "So what happened to your partner?"

He shrugs. "I usually work alone. Te big cases, we team up."

Spacecases, guys who spend too much time alone in transit between stars, can be unpredictable and dangerous. So this should be fun.

He cuffs my hands behind me, gunshot wound or no, and doesn't let go of me until he's marched me across the tarmac to his ship, which looks more like a flying saucer than a transport shuttle. I glance up at him.

He blinks. Ay. Ga. He's not even looking at me, but those translucent lids dropping over his golden irises send my heartbeat skyward as my flight response hits.

"Ergahahaa!" I flinch away, and his grip on my arm gets even tighter.

He looks at me like, *what?*

I try to force my breathing down to normal as I study my

boots, and I feel my heart rate slow un poco in response. Tranquila, right? Panicking won't help. I need to get him talking, to see me as a person, rather than a checkmark in his ledger of criminals. I nod at the saucer, then force myself to look at him. My lips only quiver a little as I say, "Your ship is muy litoll. What's her name?"

"*Te Open Grenade Party Sunshine*." He licks at his top lip. "I understand it loses something in translation."

I'd wondered how he had such an Earth-sounding name. It must be a translation of concepts into English, too. The door slides upward and a ramp descends, just like in every bad science fiction movie I've ever seen. My chest goes cold. I cannot get into that ship. No y no y no y no. Y no. I back up, bumping against Tyson, feeling the panic rising inside me again, demanding that my feet run, pero he doesn't even seem to notice me trying to wrench my arm out of his grip. "Can't we at least talk about this? I can pay you, or I'll do whatever you want."

"You're confusing me wit a bounty hunter. I'm an officer of te law, and while I do get a commission for each case I close, I'm not in tis for the money. I protect te galaxy from green mucus hate garbage dangertype." Tyson pushes me ahead of him up the ramp, giving me an unobstructed view of the ship's rounded white walls, of the bank of unfamiliar equipment making up the pilot's station. Not all Galactacops are this noble. Why'd I have to wind up with one that can't be bribed?

"Dangertype? Look at me! Mira! Do I look dangerous to you?" I try to keep him from pushing me through the door, pero I only manage to trip myself. He lets me go as I sprawl onto the ramp, probably to keep from hurting me. I scramble to my feet and try to dodge past him, listening to my heart's demand to run away, run away, run away.

He catches me by my good shoulder. "Looks can be deceiving."

He pushes me over the threshold in front of him. Inside, there's not a speck of dust, and all the metal gleams, especially the bits on the cell that takes up the back arc. I can't look away from those bars.

"Por favor." I turn toward him. "I said I'll do anything."

He scrunches up his face in a truly alien way I can't read. Pity, maybe? Disgust? His voice is hard. "I don't need anyting from you, and trust me, little girl, I'm not your type."

He removes the cuffs and forces me into the cell, tossing my backpack in before he closes the door with a clang.

Despite the prey instinct's objections, I reach a pleading hand out through the bars, catching the edge of his leather jacket's sleeve. "Do you know what's going to happen to me once you turn me over?"

"Don't care." He pulls away from me, then sticks earbuds into divots in the sides of his blade-like head. He turns the music up loud enough that I can hear it.

"Well, be that way, muchacho." I flop onto the surprisingly comfortable bunk molded into the wall. He's sprung for decent sheets, which smell like they've just been washed, and a large, soft pillow. I suspect a guy who does that really does care.

The ship takes off. He's guiding it using something that takes both hands, but looks like an oversized trackball ringed with buttons. I wouldn't have the vaguest idea how to fly it, even if I could get out of this cell and somehow subdue him. After he sets our course and gets us out of the populated area of space, he climbs a ladder, likewise molded into the wall, and goes through an opening in the ceiling. He must have some sort of loft quarters up there, no? I can hear him moving above mi cabeza. He comes back with a box of ration packets and holds two of them through the bars. "Take your pick."

He's still got the headphones on, making it clear this isn't a discussion. The text on the labels is written in six different

languages, one of which I can comprender. I pull the pouch
that roughly translates as *Blissberry Muffin Yum Fun Breakfast
Surprise*. Tyson hands me a couple bottles of agua, then nods
towards a button in the wall. "Tat'll access te suction toilet.
Don't worry. I won't look."

He returns to the controls and turns on a bank of heat lamps
that surround his command chair. Does that mean he's coldblooded after all? Or maybe he just gets cold easy – it is chilly in
here – or needs simulated sunshine for Vitamin D. I'm not going
to find out, though, because he ignores me for the next twelve
hours, when he repeats the offers of food and agua. Despite his
size, his species must eat significantly less than humans do. I
take both the Stew Supreme Happiness with Surprise Dessert
for now and the Hardcracker Dairyspread Sandwichtype Joy
with Random Flavor Sweet Jelly for later. Tyson doesn't seem
to mind.

I try calling Brill again on my sublingual. He's gone dark. He
abandoned me, despite all the messages I left telling him I was
alive and in need of help. Tears prick at my eyes, but I press my
index finger and thumb against the lids, forcing them back. I
can't dwell on how much missing him hurts.

I try Chestla again, for about the millionth time. This time
her voice fills my head. *Make it quick, Bo. It won't take long for
them to triangulate the call. I only had this on to pull up a map.*

I feel the knots in my shoulders relax, just a little. She's alive.
I just wanted to make sure you are OK.

She growls. Then sighs. *As OK as I can be inside a rainforest-
sized cage. I've cracked the security on the computers in the facility
we found. I was trying to find a way out of here, but so far the only
interesting thing I've come up with is information on something called
Pure275. They're trying to hide the fact they weaponized it about forty
years ago.*

Forty years ago was around the end of the First Contact War.
I want to ask her what she means – and what she did with the

guy who was insisting it was his facility – pero she hangs up.

Pure275's the same stuff Meredith was talking about, that poisoned an entire town, that may or may not have been accidentally introduced into a batch of chocolate. But as an intentional weapon? While there's no way I can contact her directly and ask, there must be more information about it on her Feeds.

Tyson's humane enough to give his prisoners screen-access, though it's partially locked down, and due to space constraints the field's showing sideways against the ceiling. I amend the search I'd done on Uke's shuttle to include the term weaponized, then I pop up one of her holos with a likely-sounding title.

Meredith is sitting with an elderly woman who has wiry short gray hair. The woman is wearing a red day dress. They're in the cafeteria of a hospital or a nursing home. There's a plate of empanadas between them, and they each have a steaming cup of coffee, so I guess it's a nice nursing home. The woman takes a drag from an inhaler, then pounds a fist on her frail looking chest. "It's the lungs that got hit the worst, you know. The one thing they still can't replace."

Meredith makes a sympathetic face. "Before we get into that, let me introduce you to my audience. Chicos, this is Anita Garcia. She's a survivor of Montoya's Folly, the battle that most believe lost the war for the Independents, and one of the few civilians in La Flor de La Guajira to live to tell of her pain."

They discuss the war for a bit, how by that point Columbia was already allied with HGB, how the war was already over, really, and how many lives could have been saved if Montoya had just surrendered. How we should have just come together to figure out what was going on outside our solar system, instead of tearing ourselves apart from inside it.

Finally, Meredith brings up Pure275. "So you claim Consolidation forces used the herbicide as a weapon. Do you have any proof of that?"

Anita looks down into her coffee. "I've had my DNA tested, and the markers are there, but my insurance claims they aren't any different from those of anyone else living in the chocolate belt. Pure's supposed to be harmless to humans, unless you ingest grandes quantities of it, over time." She casts an embarrassed look at Meredith. "But I suppose you know that better than anyone."

"Sí. It's OK," Meredith says softly. "Go on."

"No hay pelos en mi lengua." *There are no hairs on my tongue.* Meaning the old lady plans to tell it like it happened. "The crop planes started spraying the town, even though soldiers on both sides were fighting in the streets. Nobody had uniforms, and there was no easy way to tell Consolidation from Independent. We didn't expect them to turn on their own. They'd been making wholesale passes over the rainforest, trying to take away anything worth fighting over. But when they turned towards us, the people who were outside ran for cover, but most of them didn't make it. It was like a cloud of sticky, cloying smoke, even for those of us cowering inside."

"That's horrible. Lo siento. Truly." Meredith puts a hand on the old lady's. "So how does no one know about this?"

"Because when it was done, they came back and shot the corpses." She moves her hand, takes a long sip of coffee. "Claro. We already had the markers in our DNA."

They chat some more, and finally Meredith says she has to go.

"Aquí," Anita says, wrapping a cloth napkin around the remaining empanadas. "At least take these for your little dog. He's my favorite part of your show. It's triste they wouldn't let you bring him in today." And that's the end of the holo.

It's a horrible story, but does it change anything? Anita never said HGB was responsible for those crop planes, but Chestla claims the Triumvirate was the one to weaponize Pure275. So maybe HGB didn't stay completely out of the war – maybe their not-a-single-shot-fired claim was a lie. They still wound up on top. I send Chestla the link anyway.

Tyson sleeps on and off in his pilot's chair, close enough to the computer to make course corrections. I eat a couple more rations.

I've just started another holo when the ship jolts and the lights flicker and we lose grav just long enough for me to feel a cold dip in my stomach and my phone to lift off from the bunk, only to come sailing right back down. Tyson seems to sleep through it, leaving me to panic, alone in my cell. It doesn't quite seem serious enough to wake him up, but I can't shake the thought of dying in space in a crashbanged saucer with no air to breathe... sharing my last moments with this dork.

When he wakes up, Tyson looks at the big ball and says something softly in what I can only assume is his native tongue.

"What's wrong?" I ask.

"Nothing tat concerns you." He doesn't even turn around from whatever he's doing with the instrument panel. He bangs at the side of the ball, then lets out an unhappy hiss. "We're about to land, anyway."

I'm expecting this to be the Moon, the closest Tyson's going to get to dropping me off on Earth. I steel myself for the yammering paparazzi, or for a quiet circle of rifle barrels, or whatever lies in between, but Tyson ignores my cell and exits the ship. Claro. He comes back with a short non-human humanoid who's wearing a toolbelted jumpsuit and carrying a toolbox. Which means this isn't Interface Station, the Moon base where business and legal transitions take place in the near vicinity of Earth.

Tyson points to one of the control panels and speaks in Universal. "I tink it's te splebergyro, but you're te mechanic."

A gushing noise precedes a rhythmic pumping somewhere inside the walls. We must be at a refueling station.

The mechanic pulls open the dashboard and starts fiddling with the wires and parts inside. There's a soft hydraulic hiss, as the lock to my cell disengages, the silver bar holding the door closed sliding away, leaving a tiny gap of freedom. I suck in a breath and look from the mechanic to Tyson. Neither of them heard it over the pumping and clanging. The mechanic takes the ball out of the workings. It fills his arms. He stares unabashedly at me. Kek. I take a nail file out of my backpack and pretend to be absorbed in giving myself a manicure. He lets out a low whistle. "You know there's an unofficial bounty on that one, dead or alive. It'd pay a lot more."

Tyson shakes his head. The movement's almost hypnotic. "I don't mind paying you for information, Elgnrad, but I keep telling you I'm not about to turn bounty hunter."

Elgnrad drops his voice, but he must assume humans have horrible hearing. "I don't know why you don't just finish her off now. She'd be so much easier to transport dead. Cheaper too, since you won't have to feed her. It's not like her life's worth much to her. They're going to execute her for treason the minute she sets foot back on Earth."

Ay! My heartbeat goes way up. Tyson's already shot me once. He might well have no objection to marching me outside – I can't imagine he'd spray brain matter over the interior of his spotless ship – and putting a couple more bullets into me. I can't help picturing that body bag Lula was talking about, the zipper sliding shut on whatever is left of my face. Cold fear flashes through my stomach again. It's starting to feel familiar.

I hold my breath, waiting for the scaled Inspector to agree to Elgnrad's logic.

Tyson shakes his head again. "If tat is her people's justice, ten so be it, but I don't kill criminals I have already subdued."

"Suit yourself." Elgnrad gestures with the ball. "I need to check the charge. Come with me. There's something I have to show you for another case that might be worth your while."

"Wort you some cash, you mean." Tyson follows him out. The doors close behind them.

The adrenaline rush has my hands shaking. I'm still half-convinced that Elgnrad will change Tyson's mind, that he'll come back in here and... I don't want to think about it. No y no.

I put a hand on the cell door and push. It swings open. Now, all I need is a map, and I can be on my way. I put the battery back in my handheld.

It dings again with the same message, probably whatever was coming in when I shut the unit off the first time. It's from Minerva. In the holo, a blonde niña with thick bangs and the rest of her hair pulled back into a ponytail blows her nose into a tissue. Eh? Does Frank really have a granddaughter? She sniffs, then addresses the camera. "Hi, Bo! I'm sorry I didn't get a chance to meet you while you were visiting Earth, but I've been sick. Thank you for asking after my health. I'm much better, honest. Grandpa says now that I'm not contagious, I can go play with Isabella and Sophia again. He says we're going to stay with them for a while, until you make it back and join us. Won't that be fun?"

My heart turns to ice. The threat couldn't have been much clearer. Minerva babbles on about wanting a pony and how she wishes *she* could be the Princess of Chocolate, while I have to work just to manage to breathe. If I don't escape, I'm as good as muerta. If I do, though, what's going to happen to mi familia?

The handheld rings, claiming to be Minerva. More likely, it's Frank, seeing I've finally received his message. I try to remind myself that he can't shoot me through the phone, but that doesn't stop my hand from trembling as I hit the button.

"Hola?" My tongue tries to stick to the roof of my mouth. I step out into the main body of Tyson's ship, crossing to the exit door with the phone up to my ear.

A kid giggles into the phone. "Are you speaking Spanish?"

"Sí, but I'm just as fluent in English." I push the button, and the door opens. I hop through before the ramp even has a chance to descend. I can't figure out how the door is supposed to close, pero Tyson could be back at any moment. If he sees I'm gone, at least I'm gone. "You're Minerva, no?"

"Sure am. My grandfather showed me a holo of you. You're pretty. I hope I get to be as pretty as you when I grow up. I probably won't though, because I'm not a princess."

I guess I'd have to eat that sparkly sphere of Styrofoam after all, if I hadn't ditched it back on Krevia. "Don't worry. There are all sorts of princesses. Some day, I'll sit down and help you figure out what kind of princess you want to be, but right now is your grandfather there?"

"Grandpa!" She's screaming at somebody across the room, but she's still got the handheld up to her mouth. I move the phone a few inches away from my own ear.

Frank sounds close, but he's not yet speaking into the phone. "OK, honey. Go tell Isabella you want to watch a movie. You girls stay in the TV room. Ask Isabella's mom to make you some popcorn."

"Who let a coldblooded killer like you have charge of a niña, Frank?"

He laughs. "Just because I happen to have a job that isn't pleasant to do doesn't make me a monster."

"And who do you work for again? HGB? The police? Some government?"

"That's not what's important here, Bo. Look, you–"

"Oi!" I freeze. Tyson's headed this way. He's got his head down, peering intently into the contents of an antiquated beige paper folder. "I gotta go."

"Call me back, Bo. Your friend Kaliel's anxious to hear from you."

Cold knifes through my chest again. "Don't do anything to him. Por favor." I have to hang up, but it's hard to make myself push the disconnect button. My heartbeat's pounding again, half raw flight response, half terror for Kaliel. I'll never forgive myself if Frank kills him. Nunca. I slip under the nearest starship and crawl out the other side, trying to look casual as I search for the exit to this spaceport, which is basically an oversized piece of tarmac with refueling hoses sticking out of it, ringed by walls too far away for me to spot over all the ships.

Tyson's yelling. He must have looked up and realized the ramp to his ship was down. The mechanic replies, then the ramp clangs as both pairs of boots race up it. Well, fantástica. I keep moving in the opposite direction.

A few seconds later, a female voice comes over the loudspeaker, speaking first in Universal Standard, then Krom. "Excuse me. The Greegarrngy Refueling Depot is now experiencing a lockdown." A green grid goes on overhead, sectioning the sky. "A dangerous fugitive has escaped custody. Please remain inside your ships. If you are not currently in your ship, please report to the central hub for identification check."

About the time she starts repeating herself in a third tongue, I pass a pequeño red ship where the hatch looks slightly ajar. Bueno. Eventually they'll have to drop the force field to let more cops in. Maybe this ship is quick enough, I can use it to escape. I pull the hatch the rest of the way open and slip inside. It smells weird in here, spicy in a way that reminds me of an Indian restaurant, but the spices are not of Earth, and underneath, there's an odor of sweat socks. I hope this thing is easier to fly than Tyson's saucer. I'll look for an instruction manual as soon as I've sorted things out with Frank. I lean against the wall and take out the phone.

When Frank answers, I ask, "Are you holding Kaliel hostage, viejo?"

He laughs. "Me? This is all you. Kaliel's tracking anklet puts him outside, waiting for you the entire time you were inside the perimeter of the plantation. Then you exited the facility in a Jeep checked out to him and Rick. They're keeping it quiet, but when Kaliel's trial starts, he's getting a charge of treason added for helping you. Rick might even get one, too."

I can hear my blood rushing in my ears. "But that's not fair. Neither one of them deserves to get shortened over this. Rick wasn't even there, and Kaliel had no idea what I was up to. Nada. Nunca."

"So he keeps saying. If you come home and testify, they might even believe him."

I remain silent, trying not to remember how strongly Kaliel's body had pressed back against me when I'd kissed him, how sweet his lips had tasted after we'd washed away the bitterness of the beer. On top of that, he's a good guy. Turning myself back over to Tyson sounds noble. Only, sacrificing myself won't save Kaliel. There's a good chance now that they'll vote for execution on his other charges. There has to be a better solution, if I can just figure it out.

"If you won't do that, at least give us Brill's location." Frank sounds exasperated.

"I can't. No sé where he is." There's that tug of my heart breaking again. "I know I have no right to ask this, pero what you were going to do for me? Pulling enough strings to at least let me keep my head? Forget about me. Do it for Kaliel."

There's a pause as Frank considers this. "Take a holo of the biological material, and send it to Minerva. Then I'll think about it."

I hesitate. "How do I know you won't use it as evidence against him?"

"I promise I won't." He sighs. "You need to learn who you can trust, and who you can't."

Two voices outside the ship start speaking a language I don't comprender. I recognize Tyson's gravely baritone. The other voice fades as its owner moves farther down the row.

I drop to a whisper. "I'll try. If I survive the next five minutes, you'll get your holo, lo prometo." *I promise.* I hang up and flatten myself against the wall. My hand bumps a two-foot-long metal canister – maybe an emergency oxygen generator, maybe a fire extinguisher, maybe something else entirely – clipped to it. I pull it from the wall.

The hatch opens, and Tyson starts to climb into the small space. "Bo? Don't run. Tat's my last warning."

Dios mío, how did he even figure out I was in here? I take a deep breath and duck behind the pilot's chair. I have to get around him to reach the hatch, which means I'm going to have to smack him with the canister. There's no other way out, and I'm not going back into that cell. Tyson's head swivels, searching, as he pulls his boots up into the ship. His spine flexes in near-impossible ways, so I wait until he's mostly facing away from me, then I hit him between the shoulder blades. The hard, heavy thud reverberates back up into my arms. Ay. He goes sprawling and lets out a groan. For a second, I'm frozen in shock. I didn't really expect that to work.

I drop the canister and dash past Tyson, but his body lengthens out, and he makes a grab for my ankle. I kick his fingers away, accidentally stepping on his hand. He bites my calf, and oi, it's like being hit with twin hypodermics full of liquid fire.

I cry out in pain, and his fangs release my leg. I stumble backwards out the hatch, falling heavily onto the pavement, jarring my gunshot wound. The impact knocks the breath out of me. I managed not to hit flat on my back, so hopefully, inside the cushioning layers of the backpack, the cacao beans are still intact.

"Stop, Bo." Tyson's climbing out of the hatch the civilized way. His jacket swings open, and I catch a terrolting glimpse of the gun that shot me.

"Qué? What the heck?" Sucking in air, I scramble to my feet, despite the protest from mi pounding cabeza and abused body.

I take off, desperate to make the cover offered by the flying storage pod the next row over before his feet touch the ground. "You bit me!"

"Just so you can't run again. I'll give you te antivenin when we get to Eart."

"The *what*?" I'd felt guilty earlier for comparing this guy to a fer-de-lance, but now I find out he's actually venomous? And he bit me? En serio? I mean *really?* I poke my head back around the corner of the flying packing crate.

He's drawn his gun, but he isn't aiming it at mi cabeza, just holding it loosely in his hand. He makes eye contact, and despite the shape of his face, I can see he's trying for a reasoning-with-the-dangerous-suspect expression. "It was mostly a dry bite. Tere shouldn't be enough venom in your system to kill you right away. Even witout treatment you've got five, maybe six days. But tose last couple of days, you'll wish you were closed dark peaceful."

That's more vivid of an image than I can take right now. "You kek! That's worse than when you shot me."

He takes a step towards me. "Just come back to te ship. I'll give you te antivenin before tere's any liver damage. I promise."

"So they can cut off my head? No por favor!" I run for it. He's faster than me, would be even if my leg wasn't bleeding from the holes he's drilled into it, even if mi cabeza wasn't throbbing from the toxins racing through my system at the behest of my pounding heart. I dash between ships, trying to lose him, pero it isn't working. I make it into an aisle where the vehicles are packed closer, in line for maintenance. I roll under a replica of the *Millennium Falcon*, one of that limited edition production the historic film conglomerates authorized for the galaxy's many cult-classic fans of Earth art.

I'm not sure if Tyson saw me or not. I hold my breath as he pounds towards me and keeps going. He said there'd be days before liver damage set in, but mere minutes later, my internal organs feel like he's set them ablaze. I throw up, pero that only makes me feel worse. "Sorry, Hans."

I wipe the spit from my mouth. I'm dying, no? Maybe that bite wasn't as dry as he'd meant it to be. I curl up on my side, wrapping my arms around my chest as fire dances through my gut, ice through my chest, waiting to slip into darkness. I think about calling out, begging for antivenin, pero, Tyson's gone. And darkness doesn't claim me.

In fact, the worst of it passes.

I force myself to my feet and limp back the way I came, hoping Tyson won't expect me to retrace my steps. I'm not OK, by any means, pero I may have those few days Tyson was talking about to square things with Frank, and find a way to keep living.

I climb the maintenance ladder on the outside of the flying storage pod. My arms are trembling, and my stomach keeps trying to heave up my guts again, but I manage to hold on to the rungs.

Toward one end of the green grid, there's a luxury transport appointed all in gold, built like an oversized cruise ship mixed with a packing crate. It's so grande it's taking up a row of parking spaces all by itself. I take a closer look at the boxy, angled golden front, where a band of windows arc across near the top, pero I don't make out any trade confederation markings. Nada markings of any sort, actually. The hull, built of hard black metal, is likewise unmarked. It must be a privately-owned vessel. Surely they'd have parked that thing as close to the exit as possible, to let passengers who could afford such lux accommodations relieve themselves of some money at port-side shops and restaurants. I tremble my way down the ladder and start in the direction of the cruise liner, keeping alert for Tyson, trying to puzzle out how I'm going to get through that exit.

Just before I reach the obsidian ship, I turn a corner and come within three feet of bumping into the little mechanic. Ay!

"Mpfh!" I squeak. He's holding a gun, and I don't doubt he'll kill me for the bounty if I stay still long enough to let him. I run, if you can still call it that, given my rapidly stiffening knee. He's facing the other way, so I get a few seconds' head start as he turns and registers who I am, before he fires a couple of shots and shouts, "Hey! Earth girl! Come back here!"

He chases me, but he doesn't move fast, given his short legs, encumbered as he is by his equipment, and he seems hesitant about firing into the ships, with their varied fuel sources. Out of breath and nauseous, I turn a corner, coming up against the straight line of the cruise liner. The exit is probably on the far side of it, and I'm not likely to make it that far before estúpido Elgnrad, the greedy little kek, gets a clean shot.

I run parallel to the obsidian ship and duck through a set of double-doors into the first-floor lobby. Cool, lightly perfumed air blasts down at me as I search frantically for a place to hide, pero I just see silver metal walls, plush red carpet, and part of an elevator door just on the other side of a bioscanner that will surely flag me as an intruder. A hatch in the wall opens on my side of the scanner, and a series of open-top, box-like metal carts trundles out, the automated kind luxury hotels use to take guests' luggage up to their rooms.

Fantástico, no?

I hear voices coming from somewhere up the red-carpeted hall. Outside, Elgnrad asks someone, in yet another dialect of Universal, if they've seen me. I'm stuck in the middle, my pounding heart still racing venom around my bloodstream.

Wondering why Elgnrad didn't check inside the doors, I climb into one of the silver-toned luggage carriers. A small sign on the inside rim of the cart details weight limits, loading and maintenance procedures, and prohibited materials in a language we studied at cooking school for diplomacy – Zantite. I can only read about a quarter of the words, but my heart still goes cold, at the same time beating even faster.

I bring both hands to my face, squeezing my temples. "Noooooooooo."

It's a whisper, a sigh. My breathing is coming hard and desperate. Por qué yo? Por qué aquí? *Why me? Why here?*

I haven't stumbled into a cruise ship. This is a Zantite military vessel. Rumor says they eat stowaways. But that can't be true, no?

I peek over the edge of the cart. Two Zantites in black uniforms are marching toward the double doors. The taller one, a full nine feet at least, wears gold insignia on his shoulders. Gold fringe rims his shirt pocket and several red bars of rank go down the center of his chest, reminding me of the power bars on the robots back at HGB. I've watched Zantites in the holos fall in love, dance, tell jokes – pero in person these lemon-yellow-skinned giants with the double rows of pointy teeth are scarier even than Chestla. Oddly, though, their presence doesn't produce the same paralytic effect.

I duck down, holding my breath as they walk past me. They'll leave the ship, then I can sneak back outside, no? Erm, no. They stand just inside the double doors, watching for something or someone.

The bigger one says softly, "I don't understand why we're still here, private. Or why you felt the need to get me involved."

The private's face goes green, blue Zantite blood rushing through the veins in a typical, if a bit overstated, blush. He runs both hands over his bald cabeza – all Zantites are bald, and I never get over how cool it is the way their skin moves like rubber when they do that. "I do apologize most thoroughly, General Crosskiss, sir. As I explained in my ekkerdg, the refueling station has gone into qwep. They refuse to deactivate the forcefield or grant us permission to leave until a female who has escaped from the Galactic Inspectors is recaptured. I filed a complaint, and a representative from station security is on his way here to discuss it."

I caught most of that, but Zantite isn't my most fluent language. There were at least two words I couldn't even fill in through context, not for sure. *Qwep* could be lockdown. Or it could be panic, no?

Crosskiss's wide lips curve into an exaggerated frown. "What could this nrawg possibly have to do with us? Nobody is stupid enough to stow away on a Zantite war vessel."

Well, almost nobody. Oye.

"Look, sir. He has arrived."

Another four-foot-tall humanoid of the same species as the mechanic steps through the double doors. This guy's wearing a solid green uniform. He says something in that language I can't comprender and holds out a tablet with a holo of my face floating above it.

The private looks increasingly green as he translates. "The conditions of the qwep are non-negotiable. He demands permission to bring a crew of security nerkggs aboard to search our ship for this woman."

Sí, qwep definitely means lockdown. I can only hope nerkggs aren't telepathic dogs or anything.

"Private, please remember we are on a schedule. If we are late meeting the diplomatic convoy, the consequences could be disastrous for me. Imagine what they could be for you." Crosskiss's mouth widens even more.

The private whimpers, and all the color drains from his face, leaving it a creamy chiffon tint. He starts speaking rapidly in that incomprehensible language. The other guy holds out the tablet, poking a finger right through my face for emphasis. Crosskiss makes an unhappy growling noise. The private grabs the guy's tablet and does something to it. A moment later, it starts translating the conversation back into Zantite. The private cuts his eyes back at Crosskiss, checking to see if he's been appeased.

"You must understand," he says in gibberish, which gets translated right back into Zantite. "Someone choosing to stow away would not pick this vessel."

The other guy laughs and says something that roughly translates to, "Look, you presumptuous shark-faced know-it-all—"

"Enough!" Crosskiss looms over the private, as the tablet translates his words into a mish-mash of sounds. "Private, you have failed me for the last time. You know your record of mistakes. Have you any complaints?"

The private's chin trembles, but then he slowly shakes his head. "Please, sir, send my courage home to my family." He falls to his knees, arms crossed in front of him. Even at that, he can't still his trembling hands. He bows his head. "I want my wife to know I did my best, with all my might."

This is getting un poco over-the-top dramatic, like on *Kiss Me Slowly*, one of the best Zantite soap operas. They bring you right up to the moment where there would be violence – then the cameras cut away. Zantites won't put anything gritty in their feeds. This loco situation makes even less sense than the ones on the soaps. We're talking about a translation issue with a security bureaucrat. It isn't like the delay is the private's fault, and it's sounding almost like Crosskiss plans to execute the guy, who is silently weeping.

"You have tried, private, more's the pity. I'll see that it's done." Crosskiss unhinges his jaw, opening his mouth impossibly wide, showing off both rows of feartastic teeth. Oi! In one quick movement, he dips his head, engulfing the private's tear-splotched face, closes his lips around his victim's neck and twists his own torso, ripping the private's cabeza from his body. Azure blood spurts onto the carpet and the whole world's gone silent save for the pop of Crosskiss's jaw going back in place.

Mnugh! A chill spikes through my gut. No wonder they won't put this on camera. It's too horrifying. I start silently dry heaving, but there's nada left in my system to throw up.

Crosskiss swallows, then pulls a communications device from his pocket. "I need a replacement down here for Private Chlaf. Preferably someone with actual negotiation skills."

The guy in the green uniform shakes his head. The front of his trousers are wet. He speaks slowly and clearly into the tablet, which translates, "That won't be necessary. The lockdown is cancelled. You will be cleared to leave immediately."

Crosskiss leans down and bites a chunk out of the private's side, watching to make sure the uniform guy saw him do it. He finishes chewing and wipes his chin. "I will come finish any further negotiations myself."

The guy squeaks, snaps out a salute and runs for it. Crosskiss just stares down at Chlaf.

I feel faint.

Several more Zantites appear in the hall, moving to circle the corpse. Were they drawn by the scent of blood?

Crosskiss sighs. "Preserve the heart, wouldya, Doc. He wanted it sent to his wife for burial. If there's not too much blood on the boots, send her those too."

"Are you certain?" The one answering to Doc is dressed just like the rest. Though still massive, he's thinner than the others, like an oak tree among ginormous redwoods. "If we send the boots, I'll have to list that he died in combat. That will look inconsistent on the report."

"He had a kid, right?" Crosskiss looks almost wistful. "Go ahead. I'll explain it well enough for them to get the bonus benefits. He took his death with a surprising amount of honor, despite his incompetence."

"I'll take care of it." Doc lifts the bleeding body under the armpits and gestures in my direction. I flatten myself against the bottom of the cart. Ay, I can't breathe. All they have to do is look over the edge. There is no way they're not going to see me. I'm already trying to figure out how to plead for my life in Zantite, even though it won't help. These people really do eat stowaways.

Someone else grabs the dead guy's feet and helps Doc toss him into the cart with me. One oversized thick-fingered hand flops into my lap. I push it away, fighting the scream trying to claw its way out of my throat. Irrationally, my loco brain insists that biological fluids, like the blue goo leaking from the body, are listed as prohibited substances for automated transport.

I hear everyone moving away, so I edge up high enough to see what's going on. The four Zantites march back through the biological scanner. As soon as they move out of sight, I start to pull myself out of the cart, away from the dead guy. I'll have a better chance sweet-talking Tyson out of that antivenin than I will of surviving here.

A steady thrumming comes from under my knees, vibrating the metal cart edge gripped in my trembling hands. The doors swing shut, and I hear an outside hull plate slam down over them.

Qué? Nooooo! We can't be taking off!

The cart jolts forward, throwing me off balance. I land on top of what's left of Private Chlaf. Erugh! I scramble back up as the cart crosses through the hatch into the cargo transport system. The hatch shuts, sealing me into absolute darkness. Oi! I have to get out of this cart before it gets to whatever serves this ship for a morgue.

CHAPTER TWELVE

I activate my handheld, putting on a random holo for light. The last thing I had queued up was the choco-ad starring me and Kayla. I'd been horrified when I'd first seen it over the invasion of privacy, pero that Bo, the one that hadn't been shot, injected with venom or touched by a corpse, didn't even know the meaning of the word horrortastic, en absoluto. The cart's path intersects another hallway, and a second cart bumps into mine. Ay! I muffle a terrified squeak as Chlaf's leg bounces up.

The other cart's full of frozen bags of what, in this dim light, looks like assorted vegetables. I'd rather wind up in the galley than in sick bay or the garbage. I scramble over the edge and slither onto the top of the bags, which shift under me like I've climbed into a ball pit. The more I move, the more I sink, so I freeze, take a few deep breaths. Tranquila, right? I close my eyes and try to relax my trembling muscles. Maybe the chill will slow the progress of Tyson's venom. Frío against my feverish leg feels so good, I moan. I don't even care that I'm contaminating several hundred pounds of precious food with the private's gore. I dip my face so that one of the bags rests against my forehead.

A hatch opens somewhere ahead, filling the corridor with light. Chlaf's cart shifts off the main track and rolls through into what looks like sick bay, just like on any other ship. Do they even have a morgue? Two assistants pull the poor guy out of the cart.

As the hatch closes, I hear somebody say, "What are these tiny handprints? It's like a child has been finger-painting with his blood."

A chill dances down my spine and my stomach clenches again. No pues wow. Now they're going to be looking for me.

About thirty feet down the tracks, my cart transitions onto a hydraulic lift, which takes me up several floors. A hatch opens, and cold wafts over me even before the cart rolls inside a muy grande walk-in freezer. My little vehicle stacks up against the wall in a line with half a dozen other carts, all filled with various foodstuffs.

There's lighting in here, pero it's dim, the kind someone leaves on so they can find the real light switch later. The hatch closes. I rub the condensation from one of the bags onto my hands, then I wipe my palms on my pants, cleaning them as best I can. Eeugh! I make my stiff muscles move enough to get me out of the cart and over to the wall. There's no obvious way to open the hatch from this side. I'm stuck with my choice.

I get a holocall from Chestla.

"Hola?" I whisper, about to ask her advice on how to exit a Zantite warship when she says softly but urgently, "Hadaxia huro you answered! I don't know what to do, and your little sister told me your mother is at some nail salon."

It's night where she is, and her face is shadowy, though there's light coming from somewhere to her right.

"What's wrong?" It must be something gigantesco. She hasn't even noticed I'm inside a freezer, or that I'm covered in blue ick.

The same researcher we had fled from the night of the monkey attack walks into the image. He puts a hand on her shoulder as she leans closer to him. Eh? Is he immune to the Chestla Effect? Mud cakes the guy's kaki cargo pants and his boots. He stage whispers, "There appears to be someone spraying herbicide *inside* the plantation walls. This is highly irregular."

Chestla smiles, though the expression's tense. The cut on her cheek has healed into a thick red scar. "That's Eugene. He's been out here on his own for years. HGB forgot about him." She turns the camera around, and the holo gets even grainier. Pero, there's another light in the distance, and someone holding it. They're doing something that I can't quite make out. Chestla says, "I don't think any of the HGB guys have come inside the wall looking for me. I guess they're more afraid of someone making off with more of their precious plants than they are of me being in here. But there's a lot of commotion on the other side of the barrier, and this guy used it to get in. What do you want me to do, Bo?"

"Me?" I squeak.

"Well, yeah. I work for you, don't I?" The camera view edges closer, bringing the guy into sharper focus. "Besides, I don't understand Earth's situation. Is this guy one of the good guys or not?"

"Chica, if he's trying to destroy one of Earth's last reserves of cacao, then probably not."

The guy's head comes up, like he's heard something. He turns and draws a weapon, and Chestla hangs up the phone. Oye.

There's nada I can do but wait for her to call back.

I look across the freezer, past hanging sides of meat animals and whole bodies of feet-on headless birds. Who knows who's on the other side of that wall. I make my way across to the door and push on the handle. It turns but the door doesn't open. It's probably padlocked from the outside. Should I call for help? If I'm not found, I'm going to freeze to death. Pero, if I am rescued, whoever finds me may well bite mi cabeza off. Either way, I owe it to Kaliel to take that holo and send it to Frank before my time runs out.

I grab an empty cardboardish box and flatten it so I don't have to sit on the floor. My butt and thighs still start shivering within seconds. The only thing contenta in here is my throbbing leg. I take off the backpack, which is miraculously free of blue splatter. I spritz hand sanitizer over my hands and wrists before I remove the pouch from the backpack's hidden compartment. I take holo of the edible jewels, still sealed in the viability box, then send the footage to Minerva.

Moments later, the phone rings.

"Hola, Frank." I almost blurt out what is going on with Chestla, but I'm afraid he might use the situation to capture her.

"Hola, back at you. I was beginning to think you'd given up on Kaliel. Or that somebody'd killed you."

I look down at my leg, swollen and tender, and tears try to jump into my eyes. "I'm not sure yet that they haven't."

"I don't like riddles. They put me in a bad mood."

My throat feels thick. "You wouldn't happen to know a Galactic Inspector that looks like a fer-de-lance?"

"Gideon Tyson? Yeah. Good guy. Even bothered to learn English when he took up a post on this side of the galaxy."

"He bit me."

There's a beat of silence. I'm hoping Frank's about to express outrage on my behalf.

"And you're still alive?"

So much for sympathy from Brill's would-be assassin.

"Sí, viejo. Tyson claims it was a mostly dry bite, but I've got less than a week to live unless he gives me antivenin. Where else can I get it? Or what can I use instead?"

The silence drags on un poco longer this time. "I've never heard of anyone surviving an attack by a Myska long enough to need antivenin. If you can, get a tetanus shot and an antibiotic, just like for any biological bite. You might be able to slow the effect if you can get ahold of some yewstral."

"Qué? What's yewstral?"

Frank snorts into the phone. "Brill never gave you any? I thought it was some sort of love gift on his planet. Or maybe it's a friendship thing. I can't remember for sure. It's alcohol made from a berry native to Krom that neutralizes certain neurotoxins."

Ignoring the implication that my boyfriend's not very thoughtful, even by Krom standards, I weigh the odds of finding something like that on a Zantite vessel. "So I'm pretty much muerta."

"Unless you can find another Myska willing to sell you antivenin. It'd look better if you came back on your own, but if you have to let Tyson bring you in, at least you can trust his word."

"This from the guy who's done nada but lie about who he is. You're going to break Mamá's heart when she figures it out."

"That's the last thing I want to do." He sighs. "You've put me in a difficult position. I really do love your mother, but my superiors want me to leverage her against you if you don't come home."

"You love her?" I repeat stupidly.

"Don't get your hopes up. If you make me choose between my heart and my duty, I'll choose duty. Don't imagine I'm not capable of destroying something I love."

I hope that's falso. I feel there's a spark of humanity in him. He had sounded concerned about me when I'd been in that jeep, no?

I take a deep breath, swallow back snot. This might be my last chance to ask Frank questions. "Mi hermano showed me the stylus they found in Papá's hand after the fire. It was just like yours. Since I'm probably going to die here anyway, tell me how you knew mi Papá. Was he a killer like you?"

Frank hesitates. Just when I think he's going to ignore my question, he exhales noisily into the phone. "Actually, he was more like you. Your father stole research from HGB. It was my job to get it back. And to silence the information leak. Permanently."

Is he saying... I mean... Ayyyyy. My whole world collapses in on itself. I can't even breathe. My mother has been dating the man who murdered my father. Frank gives me time to process this.

"Pero Papá's death was an accident." That comes out as a whining, protesting plea for him to tell me I'd misunderstood. He doesn't. The silence drags on.

And in it I have a loco idea. That burned out building, still hot from el fuego, had been in the background of Jane Smith's holo. "Did this have something to do with the chocolate with the Pure275 mixed in?"

Frank growls again. "No. Your father took several vials of something too precious to let burn with him." That sends chills down my spine and into my gut, and it only gets worse when he says, "I've never heard of there being a batch of poisoned chocolate. Where are you getting your information?"

"Just something I saw in a conspiracy theory HoloCast. Someone was looking for it, there, about that same time," I say vaguely. "It just seemed a grande enough coincidence it might be true."

"Was it supposed to be HGB dark? Mario had a brick of that on him at the time. I did think that was odd to bring into a fire." How can he talk so matter-of-factly about this? I want to close my ears, to run away. Frank continues, "I don't like being out of the loop on something that big. Do you have any more information?"

Papá was murdered. Papá knew there was something wrong with HGB. I'm horrified and justified and proud and angry and confused. There isn't a single blended word that could cover all of that, and I'm sure if I was Krom, my eyes would look like a Pink Floyd show. It doesn't matter if there really was tainted chocolate or not. Papá had been in the right place to find *something* important.

Finally, Frank gets tired of waiting for me to say something else, so he says, "Your father's resumé never added up. Even you have to realize that. The guy's a travel photographer, only he quits that to get married and become a gym teacher? And when that's played out, he becomes an HGB firefighter, and gets himself transferred to every Headquarters Branch on this side of South America? It had to be a cover for something."

"How many covers have *you* had, viejo?"

"More than I care to count. You wanted to know who I am. Now that I've been brutally honest, maybe you'll trust me."

"That's loco! I'm hanging up on you."

"Wait, Bo!" His voice sounds urgent, rushed. "I know the first thing you're going to want to do is call your mother. Trust me, you'll regret it if you tell her your father was assassinated. If she says anything, everyone around her could be in danger."

"Haza." I'm surprised to find myself using the Krom word for *fine* instead of the Spanish. My breathing is coming heavy. I'm trying to fake OK until my reality stops cartwheeling. "I did ask for honesty."

Something happens in the background, then there's the sound of a child crying.

His mouth moves away from the phone. "Isabella, honey, go get that little knife."

My chest goes cold again, then flames with outrage, though some of that may be the effect of the venom. "Don't you dare touch those sweet little niñas!"

"That wasn't a threat, Bo. Your nieces are here, and the little one got gum in her hair again. What kind of sick jerk do you think I am?" Frank's chin scrapes against his phone. It sounds like stubble, like he hasn't shaved.

"No lo sé." Exactly how heartless is he? "Why did Brill come back alive from that fishing trip, when you tried to kill him again right after?"

"You called him." Frank sighs again. Is it possible that he couldn't do it because he knew the two of us were so in love, after listening to us on the phone? "He told you where we were and, well, I didn't want Lavonda finding out I'd killed her daughter's boyfriend. I couldn't wreck my cover."

So much for the true love theory. I wrap my hand around a bag of frozen fruit so hard it pops, spilling fluorescent pink berries. I'm from a tropical climate. For me, freezing is about the worst way to go, but my lips already feel like ice. "Por favor, Frank. Don't hurt Mamá if you lose contact with me. I've been shot, then poisoned, and I'm currently locked in a freezer."

"Tyson locked you in a freezer? That doesn't sound like him. Where are you?"

"He didn't..." I'm not ready to tell Frank where I am. If the phone's not tracking me accurately, that's his problem. "Just... at this point, I couldn't get back to Tyson even if I wanted to."

There's another long silence. "I need to talk to my superiors about what happens if you don't survive. Don't think you can escape the consequences of your actions by pretending to die. We'd need proof."

"You want me to provide proof that I've died once I'm muerta?" My voice squeaks on the word *muerta*.

Frank laughs. "I didn't say it made any sense, but things have been set in motion. You're the one that created this mess. Do your best to keep in touch."

The freezer door opens.

I drop my voice to a whisper. "I gotta go." I hang up.

I shove the viability box back into the backpack's secret spot, then zip the spice pouch in the main compartment, just as somebody steps into the doorway. My scalp prickles, anticipating more danger. I might die in the next few minutes. I start to call Frank back to stream him potential proof of death, but the lights flick on, startling me, and I drop the phone. I duck behind a stack of boxes, but I've already been spotted.

"Who are you?" The guy's speaking Zantite, but not with a Zantite mouth. I take in his broad shoulders and tapered waist, his curly black hair, chiseled jaw and curious violet eyes that are taking on a hint of blue. Fantástico. Exactly what I need. Another Krom.

Wait. Another Krom's exactly what I need. I ask, "You wouldn't happen to have any yewstral?"

"So what if I do?" His eyes lighten until they reach pale tea green, almost like the tea bag hasn't been left to steep long enough. Sheesh. That unassuming color signals casual flirting. He's not going to hurt me. He's just happy I'm a girl. I come out into the open to retrieve my phone. He blinks, the color deepening to a worried pearl gray. "If you won't say who you are, maybe you'd care to explain why you're covered in Zantite blood."

"That's a long story, muchacho." I look down at my ruined clothes, repulsed all over again. "The upshot is I watched your general eat somebody."

"Again?" The Krom looks down at the floor, inhaling for what seems like forever. "Did you happen to catch the guy's name?"

"Chlaf, I think."

A sound system echoes into the freezer from somewhere outside the door. "Attention! Please be aware we may have acquired a stowaway at the last port. She is female, with dark eyes and chemically altered dark red hair and is wanted by the Galactic Police. Please note, there is a reward."

"That you?" The curious, amused violet's back. I may be biased, but Brill's slightly hotter than this guy, with higher cheekbones and more refined features. Pero, it's really close.

"Sí, that's me. You planning to turn me in?"

He scratches dramatically at his chin. "That depends. What'd you do?"

"I'd prefer not to say, no?" I look down at my clothes. Who knows what he's thinking. "But I'm not dangerous. I didn't kill anybody or anything."

He gives me a devastating grin. "You'll tell me when you're ready."

I doubt that. Pero, at least it sounds like he's going to wait on claiming that reward. The nausea hits me again and I cross my arms over my abdomen, dry-heaving unattractively in front of a super-humanly hot stranger. Ay! Por qué yo?

"Are you OK?" He steps closer and puts both hands on my upper arms, holding me up, despite getting drying blood on himself. His skin tone's a warm brown almost the same shade as mine, a lot darker than Brill's.

Even in this freezer, sweat starts beading my forehead. I manage a wry smile. "About that yewstral, chico... I can trade. I have Earth spices. Or Earth cash. Or chocolate."

"You didn't say you needed it medically." He keeps one hand on my arm and with the other unfolds a step ladder. "Sit here for a second."

He goes into the galley, which is all sleek silver, with black countertops and red cabinet pulls. I can see him bending over, hear the clink of bottles as he searches a lower cabinet for the right one. I hate to admit it, but it's a nice view. I look away, at the still animal corpses waiting to become dinner, which helps me refocus. I'm still with Brill, I think. At least, he hasn't given me a chance to break up with him yet. He did leave me on Krevia and cut all communications. It's hard to think when mi cabeza feels like this.

The Krom comes back with two human-scale champagne flutes and pours the rust-colored beverage into them. "This came from the ship's stash, not mine, so you don't owe me anything for it, but I always insist on knowing with whom I'm drinking."

Smooth. This one's a charmer. Pero, he's a Krom, and look

what I got with the last one. I take the glass. How'd he chill the yewstral that fast? "I'm Bo Benitez."

He blinks, his own glass halfway to his lips. "Why do I know that name?"

"Bodacious Babe Benitez." I take a sip of the yewstral. It tastes citrusy and light with bubbles that tickle my nose. Under different not-so-covered-in-blood circumstances, this would make a magnífico first date. I scrunch up my nose. "Princess of Chocolate ring a bell?"

He laughs, his eyes lightening toward pale tea again. "I bet you–"

"Jeska? Are you here?" The guy banging around in the galley cabinets is speaking Krom, but with a growling accent I guess is Zantite.

"I'm in the freezer!" Jeska drains his glass. "That's my roommate. You can trust him. He's a good guy."

Apparently, there's no shortage of trustworthy guys today.

"On my planet, Jessica's a girl's name." I shouldn't be teasing him, but the smile I get in response is gratifying. I know it's pronounced Jess'ka, with the elongated *s* and the hesitation in the middle. I've heard the name somewhere before.

"Jeska means son of foresight. I think I'm OK." Jeska touches my hand. "You're freezing. You can't stay in here much longer. Bring the yewstral. Maybe V can help me figure out where to hide you."

The galley's un poco bigger than I would have expected, longer than it is wide, with a grid of burners embedded into one end of the island in the room's center and a triple basin sink in the other. The whole space has been efficiently designed for storage, except on the opposite long wall, where several flat panels go from the countertop all the way up to the ceiling. On the same wall as the freezer, there's a door that opens into a pantry, and two wide black doors that probably front a refrigerator. The far short wall has another door, which has to be the way out of here. Not that I'm in any condition to take it.

Without looking up, V, who's even taller than Crosskiss, says, "I can't remember if I put salt in the eggs or if I just got out the box."

Jeska hands him the box. "Put more anyway. You never put enough."

A Krom asking for more salt surprises me. What about Jeska's delicate cardiovascular health?

I pull out my lipstick and slide on a coat out of habit – mi mamá taught me early that lipstick equals confidence – not that it is likely to make a difference given the state of the rest of me. I pocket the coppery tube.

V sticks out his bluish tongue, which makes a striking contrast against his yellow skin. His face is longer than the other Zantites I've seen, his chin more defined. His flat nose comes up more off his cheeks, too. "You wouldn't know good food if I smacked you with it."

"Go ahead and hit me with some, then." Jeska peers into the bowl, looking oddly out of scale. The counters are higher than a human would have put them, but not impossible for Jeska or I to work at. "At least that way, I'd get something decent to eat."

"I've got dill, if you want some." I rummage in my pouch and pull out a circular plastic container.

V turns to look at me, huge thick-lidded eyes intent and unblinking. His frown is just as wide as Crosskiss's, and I flash back to the general's teeth cutting through his subordinate's spine. V starts to open his mouth. I squeak and stumble backwards. Jeska catches me. "You don't need to be scared of V. He's an artist at heart."

V stares hard at Jeska. "Please tell me that's a female Krom you smuggled on board and not the stowaway Crossbow's looking for."

"Have a heart, would you, roomie?" Jeska pulls my hair back from my cheek, smoothing it along the back of my head.

Portuguese actually has a word for that, cafuné, meaning to tenderly run your hands through someone's hair. It's comforting and sexy at the same time. I hate Krom. "She's just a kid. She's hurt and scared."

V leans close and sniffs me, and I nearly pee my pants. After all, his nostrils are the size of my fist. He wrinkles his nose. "Then whose blood is that all over her?"

"Orlux." Jeska dips his cabeza for a moment of respectful silence, making that close-fisted salute, though Orlux – which I guess was Chalf's first name – isn't here to direct it to. "Crosskiss ate him in front of her. Ate part of him, anyway, I expect. That guy never finishes anything he starts."

"Oye." I pull away from Jeska's touch. "How can you talk like that? I'm going to be scarred for life."

Jeska gives me a wry smile. "I've been here for a long time. The ship's doctor usually finishes up for the general. In their culture, approaching execution the way he does is considered disrespectful. I mean, how would you like for your family to get back a half-eaten corpse?"

"Mnghh." I picture Mamá's shocked face peering into a body bag. "It's worse to have to *be* the corpse, no? Crosskiss is still looking for me."

"Suavet ita hanstral." Jeska turns away, starts digging in a drawer for a whisk for the eggs. I can't see his eyes, can't tell what's going on inside him. "That was insensitive. I wasn't thinking about what the big guys do with stowaways. We'll make sure that doesn't happen. Right, V?"

"Right." V leans down to my level and smiles, showing a lot of his teeth, razor sharp and blindingly white. "My name's actually Varnex, but you can call me V too, if you want."

"Egahhh!" I fall on my butt, scrambling backwards, heart thudding, bladder desperately wanting to empty. My cheeks flame with fever, fear and embarrassment. "Lo siento. That was an instinct."

I'm sure he didn't understand the Spanish, but Varnex says, "I am the one who should apologize thoroughly. I did not mean to frighten you." He cocks his head, listening. "Mertex is in the hallway. I'd recognize that clomping walk anywhere."

"Murry would turn you in in a heartbeat, even if there was no reward." Jeska looks around, finally pulling open the door to a golden four-foot cube sitting just outside the pantry. The door has the relief of a loaf of bread embossed across it, like on some European Earth antiques. "Naramoosh!" *Quickly.* "Get in the bread safe."

"The what?" I cast a confused look at Varnex, who takes my glass.

Jeska pushes me into the empty cube. He hands me my glass and pats the bottle of yewstral. "I want you sloshed by the time I get you out of there, Bo."

A Krom who not only has no problem calling me Bo even though we've just met, but also seems to have a nickname for everybody? That's even stranger than his love for salt. I look down at the bottle. "How much of this do I need to drink?"

"That depends on what happened to you."

"A Myska bit me. He said it was a mostly dry bite."

Jeska's eyes go solid black. For a long moment, he doesn't breathe. "The whole bottle, but slowly. You don't want to add alcohol poisoning to your system. After that, we'll see."

Jeska closes the door to the safe, leaving about a finger-width of light and air.

I still hear Varnex whisper, "Then what's she doing alive?"

The door swings open, and Mertex comes in. He walks across the kitchen and washes his hands. His face is round, his eyes un poco oversized, his skin tone more old newspaper than lemon. He turns off the agua. "It smells good in here."

I agree. There's daragori bacon cooking out there, and biscuits. My mouth fills with saliva. I wonder if I could keep food down at this point, after my body's insistence on emptying itself so thoroughly earlier. I take another sip of yewstral, which seems to be quenching the fire in my stomach. Sí, I believe I could.

Jeska uses his dishtowel to wipe the counter. He shakes a little spilled salt into the sink and casually asks Varnex, "Are you going to see the holo later?"

"I'm going." Mertex pulls out a scooper and starts putting little balls of butter on the edge of the breakfast plates. "It's starring Minda Frou. And Gefex Gee."

Minda Frou's even famous on Earth. Her antics regularly show up on our gossip fluffcasts.

"You guys almost let me forget about the biscuits. Again." Varnex turns the heat off under the industrial-sized skillet, so I guess the eggs are done.

I hear the door open again.

"Where's Plelix?" The speaker is standing out of range of the slice of room revealed by the narrowly open bread safe – if that's even what Jeska actually called it. The familiar voice sends me to trembling so badly the surface of the yewstral takes on eddies.

Varnex's eyes widen, and he snaps a salute, three fingers up and wiggling at the forehead, thumb and pinkie flat across the palm. "General Crosskiss, sir! What a kindness you have done us by gracing our galley with your presence. Major Sa is registering the adex for all the supplies we received. He should be here any moment."

"Are you sure he's not just decided to take the morning off?" Crosskiss's question snaps like a double handful of dry spaghetti. "After spending too late a night playing cards?"

"I'm here, sir." Plelix, wider across the chest than the others, his body solid muscle, rushes into view and snaps a salute. He looks like a warrior or an athlete, who accidentally got dressed in a black chef's uniform. A scar runs across the right side of his head, where a human's ear would have been.

Crosskiss clears his throat. "You're in charge of this shift. Do you trust these men to prepare our food on their own?"

Plelix's yellow skin goes a shade toward aquamarine. "Actually, I do, sir. I've trained them well."

Crosskiss steps closer. I can just see the toe of his shiny black boot, which sends a shiver down my spine. Varnex and the other two cooks become intent on making breakfast. Jeska had better be more careful slicing the fruit, no? It isn't safe to operate a knife with such badly shaking hands. And Mertex, the shortest of the Zantite cooks, keeps shifting his eyes towards the scene, trying to stare without being noticed.

Crosskiss leans towards Plelix, and I can see that gran mouth widening into a smile. I cringe back, closing my eyes. I refuse to watch him cannibalize another crew member.

"That's excellent, major. We will be rendezvousing shortly with a convoy of delegates who will be using the *Layla's Pride*'s conference facilities over the next two days. As your shift has the reputation for providing the best chow aboard this vessel, I've chosen you and your men to provide all required meals and snacks for our visitors. They will be coming from all over the galaxy, so make sure it's something everybody can eat. I am certain you will do me proud."

He's not going to eat him, gracias a Dios. I let out a long, silent breath, and some of the tension drains from my shoulders.

"I'll do my best, sir, with all my might." Plelix sounds confident.

Though the words he uses are formalized phrases, Crosskiss accepts them earnestly, touching hands with Plelix before replying with the culturally expected, "Your success is guaranteed." He adds, "I apologize thoroughly for the short notice. We only received the orders a few hours ago."

As soon as Crosskiss's boots have clomped their way out of the galley, Mertex emits a loco high-pitched wail. Three pitchers of fruit juice shatter simultaneously.

Jeska moves to him, lightning fast, and takes him by the elbows. "Pull yourself together. It's going to be OK. We can–"

"How is this going to be OK? There's bound to be some sort of error." Mertex's voice is shaking, but at least he's stopped wailing. I take my fingers out of my ears. I don't remember sticking my fingers in there. It must have been part of some self-preservation instinct. Mertex points at Plelix. "Of course he looks all confident over there. He's an officer."

"We're going to survive this, Murry." Jeska grabs a towel and starts mopping up confetti and juice. "We've been cooking together for years. So Crossgarters wants something special. We can handle that."

"It's not just that. I thought I saw something move in there, but I didn't want to say while the general was here. What if whatever it was has damaged the ceremonial loaf starter?" Mertex points to the bread safe. He pulls the door open the rest of the way, and as he leans towards me, I cringe back. No y no! This cannot be happening.

His brow crinkles. "You're the stowaway!"

I'm trembling, even though I've got my arms crossed. Just like Private Chlaf. "Please don't eat me."

"Why not?" Mertex bites at his spongy lip as he reaches in a hand and pulls me out. "You might be delicious."

I try to hold onto the edge of the bread safe, ready to break my glass and poke him in the eye with the stem. Mertex lets go before I actually do it.

"He can't eat you." Varnex tosses him a biscuit, instead. "He's not an officer. He'd have to challenge you to a duel. Now Plelix, if he wanted to, could execute you as a stowaway. But he won't, because he's a nice guy."

Plelix holds up a biscuit stuffed with egg and about ten pieces of daragori bacon. "How does that old joke go?"

In unison, he, Varnex and Jeska say, "You can't eat officers. The brass gets stuck in your teeth."

Mertex rolls his eyes. "I'm taking you to Crosskiss. If there is an error later, it will help to already be on the general's good side. Plus, there's a reward. Any idea how much you're worth? I bet it's a lot." Without waiting for an answer, he picks me up. I manage to break the glass against the safe, but it's confettiglass, just like the juice pitchers, and the piece that doesn't shatter has no sharp edges. Dios mío, I should have held onto the bottle. He tucks me under his arm and rushes through the door into another red-carpeted hallway. His skin feels like silk, despite the rough way he's holding me.

We catch up to Crosskiss, who is talking softly into his communicator as he walks.

Instead of waiting for the general to finish his conversation, Mertex blurts out, "General Crosskiss, sir, I have captured the stowaway."

"I'll call you back." Crosskiss turns, cold irritation in his eyes.

Mertex holds me out in front of him, like a cross between an offering and a shield. One of his thumbs comes painfully close to choking me. "She was hiding in our galley, probably preparing to poison us all."

"Por favor." The words come out half strangled. I manage to pry his thumb off my neck. "I was not! Poisoning anybody, I mean. I'll admit I was hiding."

Crosskiss's gaze drops to me. "You speak Zantite. Your accent is atrocious, but I can mostly understand you."

"I was studying to be a chef, which requires linguistic proficiency." Was. Because I'm not making it back to Larksis 9. I can see in Crosskiss's eyes that I'm going to die right here in this hallway, amidst the scent of flowers and soft orchestral background music.

"Put her down, corporal."

Mertex sets me on my feet, pero he keeps a hand on my shoulder to stop me from bolting. I look around for any source of escape and realize that Jeska has followed us. The

Krom's irises are solid black, but his set jaw looks determined. Determined to do what, I'm not sure. I just hope he doesn't wait too long to do it.

"On your knees, stowaway. It has been established that you are a nrawg and are ukkat to be aboard this vessel. The Galactic Police will be notified of your capture. Have you any complaints?"

I don't even comprender the charges against me, pero he probably just said a synonym for stowaway, and that much is true. "Por favor. I can't just disappear. People I love will die if I don't come back and you don't provide proof of my death."

Crosskiss hesitates. "Usually, when people beg, it's for me to let them live."

"Does that ever change your decision?" I try to look him in the eye without staring at his mouth – that wide, all-consuming mouth. A chill runs through my gut. I really wish Mertex would relax his grip just a little, so I could run.

"No." Crosskiss takes out a device and tosses it to Mertex, who catches it one-handed. "Take holo of the execution, and save the hands. They should be able to use the prints for identification." He gives Mertex a sharp look, like the guy might get carried away and chompcrush my fingers. I guess he's going to let a non-officer help after all. He looks at me, and I hold the eye contact. He gives me a half-smile. "Save the heart, too. This one really is brave."

I pull the chocolate-bar-looking handheld out of my pocket and toss it to Jeska. "Please. Send a copy of the file to Minerva. It's muy, muy important. If you can, por favor, send my backpack home, too."

I flash back to that last beso with Kaliel, so warm and tender. He may well keep his head, now that I'm about to lose mine. I close my eyes, letting my moment with the tragic pilot go, remembering instead my first beso with Brill on the beach. I can still feel the scorch of his lips on mine, but maybe that's just the fever. I would give anything for him to be here with me right now, holding me one last time.

"On your knees," Crosskiss demands again.

Mertex lets me go, pero the way his hand's hovering near my shoulder, I can tell he's waiting to catch me if I run. Better to get through this with a little dignity.

"Sí. I apologize thoroughly. I just need a moment to prepare my heart." Said heart is trying to pound its way out of my chest, and the moment in question doesn't feel real. I can't make myself sink to the carpet the way Private Chlaf did. The knee swollen to frozen by Tyson's venom won't bend anyway. My sublingual rings.

It's Mamá. *Mija, Frank said I should call you right away, that you might not have much time, but he wouldn't say what's wrong. Was there some kind of accident?*

A lump sticks in my throat and I have to swallow hard, just as Mertex kicks the back of my legs. My venomized calf sends screaming pain through the rest of my body as I fall to my knees. Tears spring into my eyes. I don't want to die. It's only a small consolation, but at least Mamá won't be alone when she hears the news. Frank must love her after all, if he told her enough to give her a chance to say goodbye.

Eh? Have I that easily forgiven the man who killed my father? I'm supposed to hate him right now, no?

He's just being overdramatic. Everything's bueno. I just told him you weren't taking my calls.

I am sorry, mija. I didn't know I really hurt your feelings.

I love you, Mamá. No matter what, you remember that. And tell Frank gracias.

Crosskiss takes a step toward me. I hang up the sublingual. I don't want her to hear me scream.

"Wait!" Jeska steps between us, and for a moment I think Crosskiss might snap his cabeza off instead of mine, just out of frustrangeration. He holds out a hand toward the general. "You don't want to do this, sir."

"Why? Because you haven't seen a compatible female in the last five ports? Stop thinking with your nether regions and get out of the way." Crosskiss unhinges his jaw. I can see into his blue-tinted throat, which looks flexible and cavernous. Suddenly it doesn't seem so impossible for him to eat a being his same size. I'm not even half that big. A chill runs down my spine, and it strikes me cold that I'll never feel that sensation again once Crosskiss severs the vertebrae. Nunca.

Jeska's hand is trembling, and he tries to steady it by squeezing harder on my handheld. He'd better not break the thing. "No, sir, General, please. I am trying to save your life. This woman was bitten by a Myska, and there's enough yewstral in her system to knock out a ganggevsplat. I'm smaller than you, but if I ingested all that, I know *I'd* be dead."

While he's still speaking, Crosskiss's mouth covers my head, blotting out the light, engulfing me in the scent of mint. He must have brushed after the last execution. My heart's pounding so hard my vision's narrowing, but there's no escaping this. His teeth scrape against my back, snagging my sweater. I take in a final breath, to be let out as a scream.

Pero, he hesitates as he registers Jeska's words. Those double-rowed picket-fence teeth shred my sweater as he pulls back, leaving my spinal column intact. My face is damp from his saliva and my own sweat. I'm shaking all over. It takes him a long moment to get his jaw back into position enough to speak. "Bitten by a what?"

"Myska. They're venomous people from the Bremes System. Just look at her leg." Jeska pockets my handheld and pulls out a small knife which he uses to cut the cloth of my cargo pants away from my calf and knee. The injection sites have turned deep red, with an underhint of infected green – ay, that was rápido – and the rest of the leg is swollen like a sausage about to burst out of its casing.

"I can see the advisability of delaying the execution." Crosskiss has turned un poco green himself. "But you know we don't have a brig. What do you suggest we do with her?"

"Cut off her hands and toss her out an airlock?" Mertex suggests.

Jeska and I give him muy similar dirty looks.

The Krom says, "If we're going to keep her alive anyway, we might as well get some use out of her. She's famous on Earth. We might be able to trade her for something. Or she may have some information we can use."

He sounds like a trained public speaker, but even I can tell he's grasping at straws.

"I also cook. I'm getting sicker, but as long as I can stay on my feet, I'll help out. It sounds like you can use all the competent hands you can get, no?"

"I object." Mertex grabs my shoulder again – this time the one still recovering from the bullet wound. "What if she tries to poison us?"

I stifle a cry of pain.

"Then I'm holding both you and Corporal Hayat responsible. Get her down to sick bay and see if there's anything Doc can do to keep her mobile for the rest of the day. Make sure she doesn't have any other communication devices, or any weapons. I'll interrogate her tomorrow, and then we'll see about the advisability of an airlock." He turns to me, pointing one hunormous finger right at my face. "Don't even try to leave this ship, stowaway. The guards will have orders to shoot you."

So my options are getting shot, wooshwashed out an airlock, or crunched. Perfect, no?

"Come on Bo, let's go see Doc." Jeska holds out a still-trembling hand to help me up off the floor. I take it, wondering why he'd risked his life for me. His eyes are cobalt blue, a form of happiness I can only interpret as relieved.

"Gracias," I tell him. "Thank you. For everything."

"No you don't." Mertex presses hard into my fragile half-healed flesh, determined to keep me from ducking out of his grip. "I'll take her down to sick bay."

As I pass out, I hear Jeska say, "We'll take her together."

I dream about fire. It's a familiar nightmare, one that I've had a lot more since I've been together with Brill, spending all those nights with our toes in the sand talking about being heroes. In the dream, I'm usually standing behind a transparent barrier watching my father throw that little girl down to safety. He turns, and looks at me, and his eyes melt from their sockets, replaced by flames as he burns from the inside out. I bang on the barrier, trying to get him to let me lead him out of there, but he won't look, just melts like he's made of wax. This time in the dream, the barrier evaporates. I'm with him in that fuego, and when his eyes start to burn, he wraps his arms around my waist and the fire jumps from him to me, and I'm the one turning to wax.

I wake with a soft cry. I'm lying on an oversized exam table. The same Zantite who had thrown Orlux Chlaf's body in on top of me now wears a benign smile as he injects something into my leg, and suddenly I feel a lot less feverish. His eyes are sapphire toned. All the other Zantite eyes I've seen range from black to warm brown. Given the color of their blood and his thinner form, I wonder if he's something like an albino, despite his vibrant yellow skin. Claro está, for all I know, he could just be from a different part of Zant.

"I'm Waylux Tassiks, but everybody just calls me Doc."

I look over at the wall, at shelves stacked with bottles and pills and instruments. On the bottom one, a cube of something like permaplaque surrounds a heart, más grande than a human's, but not so different anatomically. A shiny pair of boots sits on the floor below. I feel queasy, have to look away.

Doc moves his hands up to check my lymph nodes. "I've

done what I can to slow the venom's destructive power, but I cannot stop it. I am thoroughly sorry for your loss."

His fingers feel muy, muy cold.

CHAPTER THIRTEEN

I turn the edge under again on my already double-cuffed borrowed uniform pants. They're still too long because Jeska's about six foot four, and he had to notch the belt so they'll stay up. The shirt smells spicy and citrusy, a soft cologne that's all guy. It's nice to be clean, even if I am still dying.

Pero, I'm not dead yet. My stomach growls loudly, as a reminder. "Do you guys think I could have some breakfast?"

Plelix's eyes get this soft concerned look. "Oh, you must be starving." He sounds oddly like mi mamá, which I cannot reconcile with all those teeth.

Jeska scoops out an enorme portion of eggs for me, which I eat as fast as my still uneasy stomach will allow.

Everything's un poco too grande here, not just the industrial sized cooking equipment and the plates. The biscuits themselves are just large enough to be out of scale with the human mouth, but not pie-plate sized. Perhaps it's a concession to the non-Zantite members of the crew.

"Can we just get on with this?" Mertex scowls at me. "Or can't you actually cook?"

Kek. I place the empty plate into the sink. "Oh, I can cook."

Even if the stores of a Zantite galley aren't inspiring. There's coarse flour made from unidentified plant sources, cheap cheese and economy sized cans of peaches and sopupousa sauce and lard. The peaches are stamped *Product of Earth*, which means they must have been going muy cheap to have been exported all the way out here. They passed their expiration date some time before I was born.

"So how come you guys have so much Earth food on board?" I feel more than hear the collective gasp behind me as I reach for the proper blade to cut pieces of breck for the first dish on Plelix's hastily assembled menu.

Plelix clears his throat and leans close to me, putting his big hand over mine. "Maybe you had better let me do that." He gently levers the knife out of my grasp and into his own.

"En scrio? I mean, seriously?" I put both hands palm down on the counter. "What am I going to do, muchachos? We're in space, I'm outsized and outnumbered, and half of you guys helped save my life. The only thing I'm good at is cooking. My knife skills are legendary."

"Perhaps once we get to know you better. For now, why don't you open those peaches?" Plelix points with the knife toward a can opener already sitting out at the end of the counter. "To answer your question, this vessel has been on a drekk looking into settling a colony on one of the dwarf planets at the edge of the Sol system."

The little hairs at the nape of my neck bristle at the thought of cannibals moving in right next door to my home planet. "And we were still willing to trade with you?"

"As far as I know, nobody even realized we were there." Plelix pokes the knife into the breck, moving more like he's attacking the already-dead bird than butchering it. "We traded with pirates, probably some of the same ones that will be bringing supplies today."

I press my lips together to keep myself from trying to take the knife back as he starts to hack the meat into pieces. He may be a good leader, but he's not a trained chef. They probably transferred him to the galley when he made officer just because that's where his rank was needed. Still, his crude technique is getting results, and the pieces of breck are reasonably even.

I move farther down the counter, to my station. Estúpido can opener. "Are we close to Earth now?"

"Close enough." Plelix tosses the carcass, which still has lots of meat clinging to it, into a pot then moves on to the next breck.

"We just left the same fuel depot as that tourist vessel of yours that got blown up." Jeska gestures with a spoon coated with something resembling mayonnaise. He levers the spoon back into the jar and blops out more mayoishness onto the top of something green in a big bowl. I watch as he starts to crumble bacon left from breakfast in the mixture.

"You're not planning to eat any of that when it's done, right?" As strong as Krom muscles are, their cardiovascular systems truly are equally fragile. Brill wasn't exaggerating.

He looks at the grease on his fingers. "Wal, su. I gotta eat. The Zantites feel they're making enough concessions by stocking iron supplements and Krom-origin vitamin tablets. They aren't likely to spring for frughro or other vegetarian dense-proteins. It's all about what they can get close at hand, cheap." He picks up another piece of bacon and pops it into his mouth. The whole vegetarian thing also plays into the Krom don't-eat-it-if-you-can't-prove-it's-not-sentient   philosophy, which has helped keep them out of trouble on the many planets they've visited. Pero, I guess Jeska's not worried about that either.

"You can't talk that way." Mertex's gaze cuts to the ceiling. "Think about where you are."

Plelix makes a guttural hissing-splatting sound. "Those cameras went out ages ago. Nobody fixed them because nobody cares." He hefts a chunk of greasy, yellow cheese.

My handheld rings in Jeska's pocket. He holds up both bacon-grease covered hands. "Sorry, I forgot to give it back. If it's urgent, you'll have to rescue it yourself."

I snatch the device from next to his well-sculpted hip. Ay-ay-ay. "If I go out an airlock tomorrow, I still need you to make sure this doesn't go with me, por favor."

"Hey!" Mertex snaps. "You can't give her that. Crosskiss said she wasn't to have communication devices."

If he'd realized I have a sublingual, Mertex might have demanded Doc cut it right out of my throat. Nobody had checked for such a device because, other than humans, there aren't a whole lot of people who use such invasive tech.

"What difference does it make? She might have people she wants to tell goodbye." Plelix's eyes look compassionate, but his words make me feel like I've swallowed a rock. He's offered no illusions about me making it out of here alive. "Besides, do you want to be the one to tell Crosskiss?"

Mertex's gaze drops to Plelix's rock-solid chest and built biceps. He swallows visibly, probably imagining his odds of escaping execution if he defies the only officer in the room. "I guess not, sir." Nobody else has called Plelix *sir*.

The phone's still ringing. I don't recognize the number, and the caller hasn't listed a holo. I answer it anyway.

The voice belongs to Gideon Tyson. Frank must have given him my number. "Time to stop frenetic feartype bounce bounds, Bo. Tree ships took off in defiance of te lockdown, and tey're all headed different directions. If I guess wrong, tere's no way I'll be able to get you te antivenin in time. I know te warrant says dead or alive, but I always prefer alive."

I put a hand over the mouthpiece. "I suppose there's no chance I could get a little privacy?" The switching between Zantite and Krom and now English is not helping my headache.

Plelix shakes his head. "I am thoroughly sorry, but I can't explain to Crosskiss if he were to find you wandering the halls with a phone."

I say into the handheld, "Now you're all concerned? You could have thought about that *before* you bit me, no?"

"I explained tat, Bo, and you've got plenty of time to turn yourself in. If you die because you won't let me help you, you can't blame me."

"Pero, I bet you'll blame yourself." I'm being sarcastic, not really expecting him to react. I scoop the peaches into a saucepan, to which I add something that smells a little like red wine.

"Go careful on that," Plelix warns as the crimson fluid falls from the bottle. "It's grewkpl."

"Qué?" I stop pouring. What's grewkpl? Expensive? Toxic?

"He means rationed," Jeska says.

"Oh. OK." I pour in a little more. Then I duck back into the freezer to rescue my backpack. I unzip it and take out the spice pouch, tucking the backpack into the bread safe, which one of the guys had cleaned while I was taking a shower.

Tyson breathes in my ear, and I realize he's been silent for a long time. "To be honest, Bo, I will blame myself. Early in my career, I killed a kid, a Krom barely twenty years old, out on his Voyage of Discovery. He had been innocent. Since ten, I've managed not to kill anoter innocent man. I've been all trough your file, and it doesn't make any sense. I get tis feeling tat you are eggshell clean-hands powder fun, when you're clearly not. I need to take you home so you can straighten your life out, find justice. Once you have paid for your crimes, you can find peace."

"There's no justice waiting for me there, Tyson, only death. If you don't believe me, look up Meredith Vasquez on the Earth feeds. Check what the polls predict for her. It's muy feo." I really want to live long enough to find peace, and he's right, I can't blame anyone for the fact that my life is ending except myself. I knew the consequences when I ran from Frank in the rainforest. Frustrated tears are trying to cloud my vision. I blink them away as I place the spice pouch on the counter. One handed, I withdraw a cinnamon stick and the little grater.

Mertex lets out another high-pitched squeal, not as loud as before, but still disconcerting enough that I drop the grater onto the counter.

"What was tat?" Tyson asks.

"I'll tell you later. I've got to go, chico." I hang up the handheld just as Mertex sweeps my pouch up off the counter.

He pokes around at the contents. "I told you guys she was planning to poison us!"

Indignation burning in my chest, I pick up the cinnamon stick. "Mira! Smell it. It's cinnamon. I was just trying to help. I didn't see a spice cabinet or any herbs anywhere in this galley, so I thought I'd share mine."

"She's being incredibly generous. That stuff is worth a fortune out here. It's one of the Sol Four." Jeska's moss-toned irises reinforce the feeling of approval in his words.

Mertex gives no such clues to what he's thinking. Nada. "I'm going to hold onto this pouch until I've had the contents tested for poison. While I'm at it, I'm going to have that backpack checked for explosives."

The cacao beans are still in the backpack's secret compartment. I have to make a bid to keep it, but I can't sound too desperate. "Take the spices, but the bag was a gift, and it reminds me of home."

Jeska gives me a look that says *Princess Squidrider reminds you of home?*

I give him one right back that means *Can you prove she doesn't?*

"That cartoon's from my planet." Mertex closes the pouch and grabs the backpack. "Not yours."

Oi! There's nada I can do to stop him.

Plelix gestures toward the bread safe. "Hand me the starter box while you're in there."

Jeska isn't going to intervene. My chin dips toward my chest as my eyes focus on a random spot of floor. Ay, I gave away my life to get those beans, and now Mertex is just taking them.

Mertex bends down to the level of the safe. "The starter's not here."

All the cooks exchange panicked looks, then turn toward me. My heart starts beating faster, though no sé what I could have done wrong. I stare back. "Qué?"

"Wasn't there a gold box about this big in the safe when you hid in there?" Plelix holds his hands about eight inches apart.

I shake my head. "No, no y no. I'd have noticed. I'd have been sitting on it. You guys cleaned it. You didn't notice something was gone?"

Jeska's eyes blend back and forth between lilac and gray, finally settling on the color of curiosity. "The safe was open when I shoved Bo in there. I bet somebody took it as a practical joke. We'll find it in time. If not, maybe we can fake a new batch of bread starter."

"From what?" Plelix asks. "It takes time to breed yeast."

They all look stumped. Underneath that, there's a hint of fear, the way Private Chlaf had looked just before things had gone terribly wrong.

Their nervousness is echoed in my own voice when I ask, "Por qué is it so importante?" They look confused, so I repeat myself completely in Zantite.

Plelix closes the safe. "In Zantite tradition, all ship bread comes from the One Loaf. It is passed by starter from our home world, then from ship to ship. A golden box of starter is kept in the safe, along with two baked loaves. Honestly, it's nasty. We dehydrated the loaves years ago, so we wouldn't have to keep replacing them. The starter itself lives just about forever. Nobody's looked at it in months."

Mertex clutches at my backpack. "But now that the king is here, he's going to have to eat it in front of his guests. I told you guys an error would be made. Think what'll happen when that doesn't happen." He stalks from the room, probably to go hide my property in his dresser drawers.

Jeska watches him go. "Kek." Then, shaking his head, the Krom grates a goodly amount of cinnamon in with the peaches. "So why did you stow away, when you obviously had enough money to buy transport?"

I try to look him straight in the eyes, which have turned green again, only lighter now, like sea foam. I love the sea. I find myself blushing. "It was an emergency."

"Wal, su. It would have to be." Jeska nods. "I'd—"

Without warning, Varnex's face and half his bald cabeza turn a brilliant shade of chartreuse. He's got a spoon in his mouth, and at first I'm worried that he's having an allergic reaction to the cinnamon, but then he claps his hands. "By Garfex, that's beautiful! I have never tasted cinnamon before. It's like Boskcetek's third symphony."

I glance at Plelix, who doesn't seem shocked. For all I know, Varnex could get this emotirated regularly. I stammer out, "I'm glad you liked it, chico."

Varnex asks me questions about Earth spices for several minutes. Mertex walks back in and gives me a dirty look for being happy. I refrain from sticking my tongue out at him. He hands my father's thick-papered sketch book, which I've started using as a journal, over to Varnex, who clutches it to his chest.

"Thank you thoroughly, Bo." Varnex flips the book containing all my private thoughts open right there in the middle of the room.

I can feel my cheeks going hot, even though the chances of these guys reading Spanish are slim.

"You'll have to forgive Varnex." Plelix washes his hands then steps closer to me. I can already tell from his expression I'm not getting that libro back. "He doesn't want your secrets, just the paper. Canvases are hard to come by in spaceport towns, so he paints on anything he can find. He was in art school when he enlisted."

Jeska doesn't say anything about my property or how they're dividing it up before my impending death. He just mimes for Mertex to pick up a mallet and pound the breck pieces flat.

I raise one eyebrow at Varnex. "Then why did you enlist?" I think I mispronounced the key word. I run my hands under the faucet again, wishing I had some moisturizer. I wash las manos almost constantly when I'm cooking.

Jeska laughs. "I don't think I've ever met anybody who *wanted* to enlist." Yeah. The word's *tekkit*. I'd said *tokkit*, which I hope doesn't mean anything horrible. Jeska shakes his head. "Personally, I got drunk with my brother's best friend and I woke up in a burlap sack."

"Oh, that's nothing." Plelix waves a dismissive hand. "My baby sister hit me over the head with a flowerpot and forged my name. She was mad because I hid her dolls." Plelix looks at me. "If a recruiter wants you, they find a way to make the volunteer paperwork happen. Usually somebody with social clout needs you out of the way, but they don't object to windfalls like me getting pulled up to their office in a little-kid wagon. Guys like Jeska, they buy, but only from their own people, usually blood relatives. It prevents interplanetary incidents."

"How much were you worth?" Varnex drinks another spoonful of peach juice. "I've always wanted to ask."

Jeska shrugs. "I have no idea, V, but probably more than all three of your worthless butts combined."

The guys – excepting Mertex – all start snagging leftover biscuits from the tray and drizzling peach juice on them.

"How old was your sister?" Jeska asks.

"She was seven." Plelix is talking around a mouthful of biscuit. "I was seventeen."

Varnex sighs dramatically. "I'd just given my first show, my first year in the school. A couple of the guys who were about to graduate were jealous that I'd gotten picked over them. I was still in my formalwear when they shoved me into their car."

Varnex cuts his gaze at Mertex, like he's expecting the shorter Zantite to break in with a story of his own.

Plelix licks his fingers. "So how did they get you?"

Mertex just keeps pounding those pieces of breck. I think he's decided not to answer, nunca, but finally the mallet stops. "I volunteered."

The laughter in the room evaporates.

"Why?" Jeska's eyes shade toward eggplant in puzzlement.

"Well." Mertex bites at his lip. How he doesn't cut himself with all those razor-sharp teeth, no lo sé. "There was this girl. I found myself with a sudden need to get as far away from her as possible."

Just like that, the laughter's back.

Plelix chucks Mertex on the shoulder. "Well, I can understand that."

"Regret it now, don't ya, su?" Jeska starts stuffing the bacon-mayo mixture into pockets he's making out of the flat pieces of breck. Then he washes his hands and goes into the pantry to get ingredients for the sauce.

Two guys, both humanoid, neither quite human, come through the door carrying large cardboard boxes. Bricks of HGB dark poke out the top of one box, carried by a tall willowy guy with green-tinted skin. I swear I recognize the guy who's bringing in booze – yet another Krom – but that's impossible.

They stack the boxes against the wall, leaving room for the freezer door to swing open, then go back into the hall and return with more supplies. They're efficient, sí.

Something knocks against the galley door. Varnex opens it. A guy totters through carrying an impossibly large, currently empty, chocolate fountain. It obscures everything but his legs. Brill owns a pair of shoes like that. I sigh. Ay de mi. If he was here right now, I'd melt into his arms, and he'd tell me how to fix this.

The guy holding the chocolate fountain asks, "Where do you want this?"

My heart squeezes at the sound of that voice. "Brill?"

He lowers the silver piece enough I can see the shock on his face. "Babe?"

I'm too shocked myself to move. "Qué? What are you doing here?"

"Delivering a supply order." He puts the fountain on the counter and rushes over to me, moving so fast it's hard to follow. He wraps his arms around me, crushing me in his embrace. "Shtesh, Bo! I thought you were dead!"

"Obviously not, loco boy." I close my eyes, trying to melt into him, but the pain in my shoulder makes it difícil not to pull away. "Not that you stuck around to find out."

"I'm so sorry. Ita, ita, ita hanstral." He kisses the top of my head and more or less carries me out into the hallway.

I rub my hands against his back. "I called and called. Why didn't you ever pick up?"

Plelix pokes his cabeza out through the door and gives us a stern frown. "I'll give you five time segment partitions. Don't go anywhere."

We nod our assent, and the warrior-chef disappears back inside the galley.

"I had to burn that phone, Babe. I saw you go down, and you didn't move, and there was so much blood. When Krom bleed like that..." He shudders. "Forgive me for assuming the worst?"

I nod into his chest. Despite the tears in my eyes, everything's going to be OK now. "You would not believe what I've been through. I didn't have a way to get ahold of any of your amigos or anything."

His arms stiffen around me. "It's just that Gavin didn't want–"

"I know. Gavin was afraid that someone might find out he had an Earthling's phone number. And Zarak was too scared

Gavin would find out."

Brill's eyes go an embarrassed pink. "And I'm sure they also thought it would be weird to have somebody else's girlfriend in their contacts. Krom from the homeworld can get a bit... jealous in our relationships."

I manage a smile. "No kidding?"

Pero, he knows I'm right, too.

He changes the subject. "Did you hold onto the beans?"

My heart freezes. I look up at him. His eyes aren't the selfish color of sangria, like I feared. They're gold. He really is thinking about what's best for me. "They're here, on the ship. The nerdy one has my backpack, pero I don't think he's found the secret compartment."

"Wal. Wal." Brill probably doesn't know what backpack I'm talking about, but he nods anyway. "Let me see who we're dealing with." He pulls away from me and steps back through the door into the galley. He makes eye contact with Jeska, who's busy whisking that sauce to go on top of the breck. The rhythmic clicking of the whisk against the pot goes still. The absence creates a momentous silence.

"Brill Cray. I never thought I'd see you again." Jeska throws the whisk into the pot, heedless of hot liquid or remaining lumps.

"Jeska." Brill gives the other Krom a cold smile.

I'm frozen in amazefused shock, still in the doorway. Qué? These two know each other?

Jeska walks over and punches Brill in the face. Brill staggers backwards then brings a hand up to his right eye. When he moves it away, the colors are spinning like a kaleidoscope.

Both of Brill's companions draw sidearms, pointing them at Jeska's head. Jeska's glare should be enough to melt the gun barrels.

"Don't!" Brill steps into the line of fire, waving the guns back down to the men's sides. "Shtesh! I deserved that."

"You're with *that* guy?" Jeska shakes out his bruised hand even as he tilts his head to look at me. "Remember how I said I went for drinks with my brother's friend and wound up here? Brill's the one who sold me to the press gang." He looks back at my boyfriend. "How is Darcy, by the way?"

Press gang? Who's Darcy? I thought I'd met all of Brill's close amigos, but that name's not ringing a bell.

The kaleidoscope effect in Brill's eye is slowing down. "Not in prison, no thanks to you. He's–"

"I never did anything you could go to prison for. Unlike some people."

"No. You were just a failure and a traitor to your race. If my Bodacious is helping out here, I think I'd better stay."

"Integrity and failure aren't the same thing." Jeska puts a hand on the counter, not noticing that Varnex is discreetly moving the knife block away. I wish I could say something to stop this from escalating, but I'm not even sure what they're arguing about. The subtext bridging it all is skipping past me.

Plelix steps between them. "I am honored to make an initial impression of you, Brill." He pauses, but Brill doesn't respond with *And I also,* either because he doesn't know it's expected or he's too angry to care. Plelix continues, "I'm glad you came aboard. We can use an extra set of hands getting everything ready. Wash up and grab that bowl." He smiles at Brill's companions, showing more teeth than strictly necessary. "Care to unload the rest of those supplies?"

Gavin picks that moment to come through the door with yet another box. He's slightly built for a Krom, with a more delicate face than either Jeska or Brill. His lightly hooded eyes go gray as he takes in the scene. He stares in frank disbelief at Jeska, then arches an eyebrow at me. Our relationship's been... difficult, but I respect the guy, even when he shakes his cabeza and whispers, "I'm not getting in the middle of this," then walks back out the door.

The gun-toters follow him out, presumably to fetch more boxes.

"Hey." Brill takes a step backwards, away from Plelix. "I'm a trader. I don't cook. Ask Jess."

Plelix picks up the bowl, ponders the distorted reflection in its depths. "If this event doesn't go well, then everyone in this galley will be sliding down the general's gullet in bloody pieces. If you're still here, that includes you."

Swallowing hard, Brill takes the bowl. "I see what you mean, su."

I finally get my brain to unfreeze enough to process the shock. "You really sold another person? Like they were a cow, or a stock?"

Someone he was once close enough to that he's comfortable using a shortened name.

"Don't look at me like that, Babe. It's more complicated than it sounds."

"I need a minute to think about this, Brill." My heart's pounding, which is making mi cabeza pound. Doc told me the more excited I get, the faster the venom will do its work. I need something to help calm me down. When I tug on his uniform sleeve, Plelix agrees to let me revisit sick bay, as long as someone comes with me.

It might as well be Mertex, since he'll demand to go anyway. I put a hand on his arm. He jumps. "Watch it, stowaway."

"I am going down to sick bay for some antianxiety meds. I asked permission, so don't grab me again por favor."

He moves to block my path. "Crosskiss only let you live to help us cook. I haven't seen you do much of that yet." He's a lot less intimidating now that I've figured out he's a coward who has absolutely nada authority to execute me.

"Come on, chico. At least earn your reward money." I walk around him, then out the swinging door. We're halfway to the elevator when my sublingual rings. I ignore it. Let Brill see how it feels not to get a response.

Mertex steps ahead of me, trying to get me to walk faster, but my heart is already pounding. I stop, leaning against the wall, swallowing back nausea.

"Why are you stopping?" Mertex snaps.

In response, I throw up my breakfast all over the carpet.

He makes a disgusted face. "Don't think I'm cleaning that up."

My sublingual rings again. I'm too frustrangerated not to answer. *Qué?*

Come on, Babe. We need to talk. I stepped into the freezer to get some privacy. It's kalltet cold in here.

I roll my eyes. *Don't expect me to feel sorry for you. I was locked in there for a while before you got here.*

He makes a sympathetic noise that echoes in my brain. *I'm sorry that happened. Gavin and the rest of the guys headed out for our other job, but before he left he said he saw a guy on board who is in the market for cacao beans. We may be able to set up the buy here on the ship. Maybe we can talk about it while we warm each other up.*

My heart's still thudding, from being sick, from getting emotirated, from what he's just said. *I'm not so sure, Brill. Gavin never thinks things through, and he obviously doesn't check his facts, no? Además, I don't think he sees me as enough of an equal to care whether he's putting me in danger.*

He makes an unhappy noise that echoes in my brain. *My best friend wouldn't be somebody that callous, Babe. I really thought you believed better of me.*

I want to believe him. Pero, I'm not sure what to think. I wipe at my mouth and tell Mertex, "I need to get down to sick bay pronto."

Why are you going to sick bay? Do you have frostbite?

No, Brill, I'm dying, but you didn't even seem to notice. I know I sound overdramatic, but I don't care, no? I'm living through overly dramatic events.

I just thought you were dealing with the aftereffects of being shot. Jrekt! What do you mean, you're dying? He pauses. *Bo.* He pauses again. *Say something, Babe. Please.*

I close my eyes. *After you left me on Krevia, the Galactic Inspector captured me. When I tried to escape, he bit me.*

Tyson bit you?

I open my eyes, staring at Mertex's uniform shirt. The way Brill said the Inspector's name sounds un poco too familiar. Heat builds in my chest. *How do you know Tyson?*

He may have arrested me once. Or twice. Brill's sigh resonates through my brain. *OK. He probably only showed up on Krevia because of me. I'm sorry, Babe. I wasn't looking out for him because I was too busy trying to find out who's been trying to kill me.*

I laugh out loud. Mertex looks at me funny. I ignore him. *That was just Frank. You don't have to worry because right now he's too busy deciding whether or not to leverage mi mamá against me.*

By leverage you mean he's taken her hostage?

I mean he's threatened to kill her.

Brill hesitates. *We need to talk about Frank. I had a friend look into him, and he's connected somehow with the fire that killed your father.*

That's because Frank assassinated mi papá. I can't believe how calm that sounded.

You knew that?

Sí, I just found out.

"Come on, then." Mertex picks me up and tucks me under his arm again. He's gentler this time, but I still can hardly breathe as we jounce along the hallway. I unintentionally hang up on Brill.

We round a corner, and Mertex hesitates. He sets me on my feet. Crosskiss is standing in the hallway talking on his handheld, a separate device from his shipboard communicator. Mertex flattens against the wall as best he can, listening.

I whisper, "You little eavesdropper."

"Oh, shut up, you want to hear this too, stowaway." He puts an arm across me, holding me up.

Crosskiss growls. "Galactic Inspector? No, don't change course to intercept. I don't care if we do have what he's looking for. He can wait until the diplomats leave." There's a beep as he hangs up.

My heart starts hammering again as I picture Tyson, angry at being made to wait.

Crosskiss starts talking on the handheld to someone he keeps referring to as "Aunt Layla." He's using a lot of words I don't comprender, pero she doesn't seem to be all that keen on helping him. Finally, in an exasperated tone, he says, "I don't care if you don't want to dweezle snokz. Can you at least bring those cookies I like? The chocolate chip ones in the red package that come from Earth."

He's begging for Mrs Field's? That's just extraño. When Crosskiss hangs up, we head the other direction, taking a roundabout route to a different elevator.

Once we're inside, Mertex sets me on my feet again. We stand in silence, surrounded by soft music all the way down. He helps me through the doors, and we make our way to sick bay.

"Doc's busy." The Zantite medic barely looks up from the card game he's playing with a private young enough to still have green pimples erupting all over his face. "Anything I can help you with, or do you want to wait?"

"We can't wait long, Quayex." Mertex studies the game, not the guy. "I just need to get her functional so we can get back to cooking."

Quayex sighs. He eyes the cards, then places them face-down on the table, admonishing the private, "Don't look." He turns to examine me, but gives up after about ten seconds. "I don't know anything about Earth physiology. Let me see how long he's gonna be."

I shudder as Quayex disappears through the door into a secondary room that looks like an operating theater. I catch a glimpse of Doc's back, but it's deathly quiet, matching how numb and hollow I feel inside. I hope he's not eating another patient in there.

The young private helps me sit on the exam table. I'm grateful to get off my feet.

"Give him five time segment partitions," Quayex says, returning to his card game.

I get a call on my handheld. The ID says it's from Chestla, but I find myself staring into Eugene's squinty-eyed face. My heart collapses into ice. If she were able to, she'd have called herself, no? I force myself to breathe. "Is Chestla…"

"A totally kick-butt Babe?" Eugene nods vigorously. "You'd better believe it. Watch this."

He activates the phone's internal holofiles, which blocks him from view, but leaves audio contact. There's about a two-minute clip, the highlights of which are Chestla kicking the weapon out of sabotage-guy's hand, and her smacking him into unconsciousness using the handle end of a machete, knocking the gas mask off of his face. As he falls, the silver apparatus he's holding sprays a mist into the air. Ay, no. Chestla turns her face away, a hand over her mouth. She's seen the same holo I have, and even in this grainy capture, I see panic in her eyes. Claro está this may not be the weaponized version of Pure275 – or Pure275 at all — but what else would a chocoteur be spraying in a cacao grove?

I feel breathing on the back of my neck. I look up to find Mertex staring at the holo. "That may be the best choreographed fight I've ever seen."

"Shut up, mijo. That's real life." I focus on the handheld. "Eugene, she didn't breathe any of that stuff, right?"

"Maybe a little," he admits, as the clip ends and he comes back into view. "She's washing as much of it off as she can right now. But her lungs seem to be working OK so far."

"Gracias a Dios."

Eugene nods. "Yes, well, she's tasked me with uncovering the identity of this man." He points the camera at a groggy looking guy tied to a chair, obviously the same one who'd been fighting Chestla in the holo. He has a relatively large build, and a face I've never seen before. He coughs weakly.

"Lo siento, Eugene. I have no idea who this is. Nada."

He shrugs. "It was worth a shot. I guess I'll have to run his DNA through the computers. We have access to HGB's whole system down here."

"I work for HGB," the guy says weakly. "It's their contingency plan. You don't want to get caught looking at that on the network."

Doc comes up behind me. I can feel his breath on my hair, the air flowing past all those teeth he bloodied when he cleaned up after Private Chlaf. Chicken skin breaks out on all my limbs, despite how his voice sounds calm and logical. "What brings you back down here? I already told you you're going to die, and there's nothing I can do about it."

"You're dying?" Eugene asks, confused. Damn. Why'd he have to understand Zantite?

I swallow, only there's no saliva left. I hang up the phone. "I just thought you might have something for the anxiety, to help slow down my heartbeat. Or maybe something for the nausea."

He puts a hand on my shoulder. "Of course."

When he comes back, Doc drops four tablets into my palm, two round white ones and two square blue ones. "Take one of each now, and one tonight."

A chill goes through my stomach. "That's it? Eso es todo?"

He puts a gentle hand on my arm. "I'm afraid we're just delaying the inevitable here. I'll be honest. This is going to be a very painful way to die. If it gets too uncomfortable, I can sedate you until the end comes, or even just stop your heart."

My heart starts beating even faster. "I think I'll hold off on that for a while."

I text Tyson. *Is there any circumstance under which you'd give me the antivenin without me having to go with you?*

Almost immediately, Tyson replies, *Can't think of one.*

CHAPTER FOURTEEN

As Mertex escorts me back up, I call Brill on my sublingual. I'm on the edge of hysterical hyperventilation. *Tyson said I have nearly a week before his venom kills me, but Doc only gave me enough medicine for today and tonight. Doc's acting like he doesn't want to waste meds on a hopeless case. What am I going to do mañana?*

Brill exhales heavily. *Try to calm down, Babe. Getting upset will only make your condition worse. I'll bribe the guy, if it comes to that.*

That makes me smile. *Are you in the freezer again? Your voice sounds extraña.*

No. I'm in the galley, trying to be helpful. Urgh! I dropped another one. Let me let you go. I need both hands for this.

My handheld dings with a message.

Delicious mango skybound!!! I have your coordinates and I'm on my way. Keep lithe sparkly party, Bo.

Qué? This makes no sense. I pull up the history. Apparently, I sent Tyson a text politely asking him to come save me. There's only one way that could have happened. Jeska must have cloned the phone when it was in his pocket.

"Hey!"

"What?" Mertex asks. He has no idea about all the conversations I'm having as we walk.

I shake my handheld at him. "You think you can trust people!"

"No." He shakes his head. "I absolutely don't."

When we reach the galley, the guys have opened two large windows into the mess hall, and Plelix is passing out breakfast plates. Though most of the crowd is made up of lemon-skinned giants, there are quite a few non-Zantites out there, many more than Mertex had implied. Some of the tables are covered with boxes, but the rest are crowded, and this is just supposed to be one crew shift.

"Hey, major." One of the Zantites from the mess hall pokes his cabeza in through the window. Plelix leans forward. The other guy drops his voice and the two speak excitedly.

"Let's get started on the dishes." Varnex starts stacking plates that have come back in through the other window.

Jeska raises an eyebrow. "You never want to do dishes."

"Remember how engineering went planetside at the spaceport, su?" Varnex has switched to Krom. He seems to do that when he wants a private conversation with Jeska. "Somebody got me a gallon of joke soap. It makes scads of howlili, and when they pop they turn everything they touch orange." Varnex holds up the bottle.

Yeah, there are still Krom words I have to look up, but I'm going to guess that one means bubbles.

"Let's sneak it into everybody's bath soap bottles." Jeska takes the container and switches to Zantite. "Plelix, this is going to be better than the time you set Gorvex and Ferix's watches two hours ahead."

Varnex snorts. "Didn't they both swear to get us back for that?"

"They already did. Remember the glue in my desk?" Plelix slides the serving half of the window down. Once they've explained the practical joke potential to him, he turns to Mertex. "Want to help us see how splebadkz it is?"

"No." Mertex seems to be trying for condescending, but something's off in his voice.

"Jeska, un momento…" I shake my head. "Can I borrow you

for a moment?" I tug on the Krom's sleeve, addressing him in his language.

"Haza." He hands the soap bottle to Plelix. It's left an orange smudge on his palm.

I lower my voice. "Where's Brill?"

Jeska's eyes dip towards a matching tangerine shade. "You want to talk about him? With me?" He pauses and takes an impossibly long breath. "He went looking for you, if you must know. Right after you told him Doc only gave you a day's worth of medicine."

I get why Jeska's angry, but I didn't pass Brill in the hallway on the way back. A spike of worry edges past the antianxiety meds. "He's wandering around on this ship? What if somebody decides to eat him?"

"Relax, little one." Jeska smooths my hair again. I need comfort too badly right now to pull away from the oddly intimate touch. "He's got clearance to be here. Nobody's going to hurt him. More's the pity."

I squeak, "Jeska!"

"Sorry." He sits on top of the bread safe. "I don't really want to see him dead. Honest."

I lean in closer, trying to keep my voice from carrying all the way over to Mertex, who's watching us with interest. "It wasn't Brill I wanted to talk about anyway, chico. It's this." I hold out my handheld, showing him the text from Tyson. "What right did you have to clone my phone? Why would you call the one person who's bent on taking me back to Earth? Seriously, por qué?"

"I didn't call him, I texted." Jeska's half-smile doesn't match the storm clouds in his eyes, and I don't allow his lame joke to relieve any of the tension. He puts a hand on my arm. "Are you really stubborn enough to die over whatever you did? Ga. So Doc doesn't want to waste medicine. Let me translate that into reality for you, su. You may be alive for the next five or six days, but the damage to your organs is going to be irreversible after more like two, and that's if you're lying down resting, instead of bursting your heart over things like what just happened to Meredith Vasquez. Before you can escape Tyson, you have to let him help you."

If the chill in my thudding heart is tempered at all by the antianxiety meds, I can't feel it. "What just happened to Meredith?"

Jeska's pupils disappear as black takes over his irises. What's he got to be terrified of? Unless he's afraid for me. "Bo, maybe now's not the time—"

"Qué? What happened to Meredith?" My legs are shaking. I suddenly feel faint.

Jeska moves fast, taking me by the arms and somehow I'm the one sitting on the bread safe, and he's standing with a wrist against my forehead, checking for fever. My blood's on fire. So's my gut. He should be contento I haven't burst into flame.

"You need to breathe slowly and drink another glass of yewstral." Jeska tucks thick locks of my hair behind my ear. "I looked up Vasquez after you mentioned her to Tyson. If your charges are anywhere near as serious as hers…" Jeska stares at me. "I'll do what I can to get Tyson to let you go with Brill."

I grip the edge of the bread safe with both hands, feeling so dizzy that if I don't I might fall off. "That's not going to happen. Nunca. Tyson wants to arrest Brill too, if he can find something to charge him with. He knows Brill was there at the chocolate buy."

"Figures." Jeska opens the cabinet and reaches for a human scale glass.

"Tell me about Meredith."

He turns back, his empty hand clenching into a fist. The black irises shift toward a muddy russet. "Her trial lasted all of two hours. On Krom we would never... Such a public spectacle… The comments they posted… How can your people claim respect for sentient life?"

He has to be wrong. Meredith's trial isn't supposed to start until the day after tomorrow. I fumble through a search with the handheld, but my hands are shaking so bad I drop the device. Jeska picks it up, but he doesn't offer it back to me.

I hold out a hand. "Your people sold you. You think that's any better?"

Brill walks through the door. He sighs. "What do you want me to do, Babe? Buy him back? It doesn't work that way. Once somebody's bound to a Zantite ship, it's for life."

"It's true." Jeska unbuttons his cuff and pulls up his sleeve. He flips his palm upright and shows me a narrow scar running up his forearm, above a fainter ragged red line circling his wrist. "There's a tracking device fused into the bone, with a charge they can detonate from anywhere. I'd have to saw off my own arm before I left the ship, and even then I probably wouldn't escape."

I look from the evidence of such horrific invasion over to Brill. Mi vida. "How could you?"

He's studying Jeska's scars, and his face has gone un poco pale. "I'd rather not discuss it in present company."

I swallow hard, wondering when he *will* be willing to talk about it. "Tell Jeska to give me my phone."

Jeska hands the device to him instead of me. "She wants to see the holo of Vasquez."

Brill puts the handheld in his pocket. "Look, Babe, I don't think that's a good idea. Dr Tassiks explained to me that you shouldn't get upset right now. After I talked to him, I put through a few calls. I can get that antivenin from one of my resources. He can be here in two, three days, tops."

"Jeska explained Doc's reasoning también." I swallow back a sudden bout of nausea. "I don't have three days."

"Then we'll meet him midway. You haven't been impressed,

have you? I'll pay whatever Crosskiss wants to give up his claim to you."

"Did you just offer to buy me?" I say this louder than I meant to.

Plelix and Varnex both look up. Mertex smirks. The door swings open and a new Zantite walks in, blinking and looking up at the cciling. "Can I usc your sink? I think I'vc got something in my eye."

"Gorvex, I–" Jeska starts to say, but the Zantite shoulders past him, catching the stream from the sink and splashing his face.

This must be one of the victims of Plelix's watch prank. He grumbles, "What's with the bubbles? I'll get soap in my eye."

Varnex smiles, showing way too many quease-inducing teeth again. "We were just doing the breakfast dishes."

"At least breakfast is good since I got moved to this shift. You guys may be grukknegs, but you know how to cook."

Whatever a grukkneg is, none of the guys look offended.

Gorvex turns away from the sink. Half a dozen bubbles have popped against his skin, staining the yellow of his head with bright orange starbursts. "I think it's out now. Would you mind taking a look?"

"Sure." Plelix's jaw tenses as he works to keep a straight face. The gesture reminds me so strongly of Crosskiss's jaw just before he unhinged it that I flinch back against the wall, cold fear zinging through my chest. Ay. These overreactions are getting embarrassing, but I have absolutely no control over them.

The minute Gorvex leaves, Plelix and Varnex start giggling, which causes a complete disconnect in my brain. They sound like harmless schoolgirls.

"I wonder how long it will be," Varnex says mid-laugh, "before he looks in a mirror."

Mertex shakes his head. "You guys stink. I hate bullies."

There's a gran diferencia between being a bully and participating in a two-sided joke war. Why can't Mertex see that? Jeska stares at him until the Zantite takes the hint and walks back to the prep station, pouring some powder into a massive bowl.

"Did you just say you want to buy me?" I repeat. Since when did Brill have enough money to do that anyway?

"It's not like that." Brill takes my phone out of his pocket and flips it over in his hand. "Would you rather stay here?"

"You could have tried to do something *before* I got bitten, loco boy, considering everything I risked for you."

Jeska looks from me to the handheld, that mock chocolate bar. His eyes go wide and flick through violet to tangerine. "You didn't, Cray." Jeska takes a step towards Brill, into his zone of personal space. "Tell me you didn't take this naive child as paqunell so she would help you steal chocolate."

My face flushes with embarrassment. I've never heard the term before, but *qunell* is the Krom word for heart, and with that prefix, it means something like *preliminary heart* or *beginner's heart*. No sé if he means girlfriend or something degrading, but it's grammatically not related to the word for wife.

"She's hardly a child, Jess. She understands that one way or another, chocolate has to be shared before somebody decides to take it by force. We fell in love. I'd do anything for her."

"And in exchange, one way or another, she's going to die for you." Jeska punches Brill again, this time in the gut.

He doubles over, dropping my handheld onto the floor. Plelix and the other two Zantites turn toward the sounds of violence.

Brill holds up a hand. "It's OK. I deserved that one, too." He manages to straighten up. "But let's be fair, Jeska, cousin of mine, distant though that may be. If you'd been a competent translator back in the day, none of us would be here right now. Darcy wouldn't have felt like he needed to take so many chances trying to redeem your family name, and he wouldn't have pulled me into it. What I was trying to say earlier? Darcy isn't in prison. He's dead."

"Dead?" Jeska's eyes sink to a deep, disturbed red-toned rust. He leans back against the counter, like it's holding him up. "My baby brother?"

I still feel like I'm watching a telenovela, and I've turned it on in the middle of an episode.

Brill's eyes glitter with moisture, and his voice goes soft. "He escaped from the pre-trial detention center, but they shot him as he fled. He came to me covered in blood, asked me to hide him, to get him help, but it was too late. He died in my arms, and with his last breath he asked me to promise him I'd set everything right – that I'd redeem *your* mistake, su." *When Krom bleed like that...* I shudder. His eyes flush pink and he casts an embarrassed look at me. "I may have crossed a few lines I shouldn't have in my determination to keep that promise, but I never lied about what's at stake for your planet. Our history books record what has happened on a dozen worlds when similar mistakes were made. It's stomach-turning reading."

Jeska doesn't contradict him. If First Contact gets botched so often, then how do they feel justified in doing it? It's supposed to prevent conflict, no?

"Qué? What mistake?" I'm feeling weak, though I can't tell whether it's another bout of what the venom is doing to my internal organs, or from my sudden understanding that Brill's motives are so different than I'd guessed. He'd confessed that our relationship had started with him using me. Now I'm finding out why.

Jeska's hand goes to his side. "Do you know about the riot that happened in Iowa during Krom-Earth First Contact?"

I nod. Actually, there was more than one riot. The first happened the day the Krom landing party was uncovered and driven back onto their ship. Pero, there had been a rumor that someone had been left behind, or that another ship had landed, intent on destroying the Krom and thereby exposing us to even more hostile aliens. Humans had done horrible things to each other, trying to uncover hidden aliens or pod people – everything bad SF movies had taught them to fear. The Krom hunt that followed lasted for months. Jeska's sad eyes look like he is remembering it all.

"You were there?" That was fifty years ago. He'd have to have been in his twenties to have taken his Voyage of Discovery. He looks maybe thirty now, tops. Delayed Krom ageing just isn't fair.

Jeska lets his hand drop. "Humans are so close physically that we didn't expect to be detected. The captain told us to just throw on some opaque contact lenses and try not to talk too much. I was posing as a researcher at U of Iowa, to gain access to the Herbarium there, and the head of the department had such beautiful legs. Young guys get stupid around legs like that, and I was curious whether our species were compatible, so I asked her out, but the closer I tried to get, the more alien she found me. During the riot, she stabbed me with a pitchfork." He touches his side again. "It still hurts during damp weather. We had to leave before we finished the mission – and before I doublechecked all my translation work."

Brill told me he wanted to be another De Clieu. Shtesh. He never mentioned he knew the guy who had lost chocolate for Krom in the first place.

I'm tired of not knowing important information. I make my tottery way off the bread safe and take back my handheld. I finish my search for Meredith's name.

Jeska winces, then he looks at Brill like he'd like to hit him again. "Do you know what your boyfriend managed to bring back on his Voyage of Discovery? A small shrub that proved useful in treating gout. Not much to show for two years, is it?"

I glance over at Brill. He'd told me he'd never participated in a First Contact. I'd assumed that meant he'd skipped his

Voyage of Discovery. Which is silly, no? According to the Codex all young Krom men – and a lot of the young women – are expected to undertake such a journey.

"Babe? Are you that upset that I never found anything?"

"You've done enough here, Cray," Jeska says. "Why don't you get back on your ship while you still have time? Tyson's on his way to bring Bo the antivenin she needs to survive *your* mistake."

Brill shoots a questioning look at me. "He's coming here?"

I swallow, my throat dry at the thought of facing the scaled Galactic Inspector. "There may be a problem with that, chicos. When we were in the hallway, Crosskiss told somebody he won't slow down to let Tyson catch up. We're going full speed in the other direction. Pero, unless you can clear it with Crosskiss to get me off this ship right now, I'm not going to last long enough to go find either Tyson or your supplier."

Jeska rubs at the orange stain on his palm, but it isn't going anywhere, no more than I am. "So what's it going to be, Cray? You really going to negotiate her freedom with the general?"

Brill's eyes are a clear blue, like he hasn't a worry at all, pero his hand trembles. "Haza. Yeah. It can't be that hard to find him." He starts to walk out of the galley.

"Wait!" Plelix points with a spatula that needs washing.

"La, thank the Codex." Brill's posture relaxes.

Jeska rolls his eyes. "Oh, grow up, Brill. Then maybe you'll deserve a girl as loyal as Bo."

I blush, thinking about Kaliel. Ay. What do I know about being loyal?

Brill makes a face that doesn't look particularly grown-up. Then he pointedly turns away from Jeska. "What is it, Plelix?"

"I don't like to eavesdrop, but I couldn't help hearing what you guys were saying. It dovetails with some gossip that got passed to me third-hand."

No visible ears, yet Zantites must hear like bats. I try not to groan. I guess I didn't really expect to keep *any* of my secrets as a prisoner aboard an alien ship. "Qué? What did they say?"

He drops the spatula into the sink. "That the Galactic Police contacted Admiral Zooka, demanding we rendezvous with your toxic detective, but that Crosskiss insisted we pretend not to have received the order. The general's too worried about missing that last transport full of delegates." Plelix moves over to the small mountain of chocolate stacked against the wall and picks up a block in each hand. "I've got an idea that might not get us any closer to Tyson's ship, but should at least keep us from moving away. And it's certain to be leffergked as just part of the practical joke war."

"Increíble! That's great!" Hope soars in my heart. Plelix has been nothing but kind to me since I showed up in his galley. Despite the teeth hiding behind his spongy lips and his raw soldier's form, I move to hug him. My finger slips on the handheld and some preliminary music plays before the official Galactic Liaison Tribunal of Earth Logo starts its holographic spin.

"There's a catch." Plelix says un poco louder to be heard over the music. "Only one person here is small enough to fit inside the engine."

He means me. He should just say it. It's me. *Soy yo.*

"*Inside* the engine?" I squeak. "That sounds muy dangerous."

"It is." Plelix looks at me with sympathy, gives me the hug I needed, then steps back as the holo starts in earnest.

Meredith appears above my hand, two feet tall, wearing an orange jumpsuit, cuffed. Her eyes have lost their intelligence and luster. They must have sedated her, to get her into the courtroom. Her long dark hair swings in front of her face.

"Por favor," she says weakly. "My dog. Botas. Don't have him put down."

An unseen voice assures her the corgi is available for adoption for several more weeks at a shelter in Hawaii.

Then the cheerful narrator summarizes the trial, noting that the date was moved up so as not to interfere with the judge's anniversary weekend, then the scene changes to the judge himself reading the guilty verdict. The music turns ominous, and we are treated to a view of the guillotine, also two feet high.

"Eyahh!" I flinch and drop the phone. Oi! You can even see the bloodstains in the wood. The holo keeps playing there on the floor.

Brill comes up behind me and wraps his arms around my shoulders. "Come on, Babe. Don't watch this. It won't do any good."

I push away from him, still feeling feverish and sick, trying to will tears for Meredith into my terrified too-dry eyes. "She saved me once. This is the least I owe her."

She comes out onto the platform between two escorts, sharp in their military dress uniforms, sabers hanging at their hips. Not only has the tribunal staff cut her hair, they've styled it into an adorable pixie cut. She's got on the same smudged-look eyeliner mis hermanas keep trying to copy from the fashion magazines, and they've put her in a flattering, knee-length pale lilac dress, the same color Krom eyes get when they're feeling a bit mischievous. She's beautiful. I can't breathe.

A poll pops up next to her shoulder. The live audience has voted, and seventy percent would buy the dress for themselves or a significant other. As more people view the holo, a second set of numbers appears, fluctuating. The poll asks me to vote. Nauseated, I kneel down to decline. My leg still aches, but whatever Doc did brought the swelling down enough that the knee bends without too much pain.

The camera filming this holo is mounted on a tiny drone, and it circles Meredith, spiraling up from her Cinderella-like crystal heels and young legs, all the way to her face. Whatever they gave her must be wearing off, because she looks terrified.

A bar comes up, asking if I want to move to the shopping page to participate in the auction to buy her shoes – the actual pair she's wearing – or her diamond ring. I recognize that diamond. It's her wedding ring. No, no y no. My stomach feels even more leaden as I exit out of it.

When the two masked executioners bring forth the board, she runs for the edge of the stage. She gets maybe three steps before her escorts catch her, each one holding one of her arms as though taking her onto a dance floor, while one of the executioners steps in front of her with the board, the other moving behind her to get the bungees in place. The escorts step back as soon as her arms are strapped to her sides. She screams as the masked duo tip her forward, and the camera comes around to get a close-up of her face as her neck slides into place. The camera stays focused on her eyes, on her repeated, "No, por favor," right up until the blade comes down and her cabeza tumbles out of sight. Blood spurts the camera, and excited comments from viewers start scrolling up the right side of the field, but I can still see the raw flesh between her shoulders, the arms still secured tight to her sides. Only, in my mind, it's not her body anymore, but mine.

I turn away and Brill pulls me to my feet. I bury my face in his jacket, weeping. He wraps his arms around me, rubs my back. I can feel the rumbling of his chest when he says, "Stop looking at me like that, Jeska."

CHAPTER FIFTEEN

I've barely gotten myself back together – the weeping keeps threatening to start up again every time I remember those comments – when my handheld rings. The worst had been MechaMathGeek, who'd said *I can't stop watching this! I keep replaying it slowmo to study her eyes as the head comes off. It's totally going to be in my next manga. So cool!*

Kek.

I check the phone's display. It's Minerva. The impending tears disappear, replaced with dry fear. Frank had said he was going to meditate on the consequences of my possible *muerte* before he called me back. I step into the freezer to find privacy. I slide on a fresh coat of lipstick before I answer, activating a live holo of Frank and Mamá standing side by side on a beach. He's placed the phone on something. There's a green tint to the ocean behind them.

I blink in confusion. If he's going to kill her or something, why does she look so happy?

Mamá thrusts her hand at the camera. "Frank proposed!"

She lets out a squeal of delight, which I try to match but can't. My heart's too busy turning to ice. I paste a smile on my face. "Felicitaciones! Have you set a date?"

"We were hoping you'd be coming home soon, to help with the wedding planning." Frank's face betrays nada of the cold subtext to what he's saying. At the same time, he's living out some extraña fantasy about him and Mamá being together for real, like she'd marry the man who killed her first husband. Frank's eyes are full of meaning when he says, "We're toying with the idea of a secluded honeymoon sailing from here to Bermuda, but it'd be best for you to come give us your input."

My gaze flicks to Mamá. Her eyes look genuinely happy, not pinched stage-happy. She has no idea that Frank just threatened to lose her in the Bermuda Triangle if I don't cooperate. Nunca. She asks, "Bo, are you inside a freezer?"

"Sí, Mamá. I got my first catering gig, aboard an alien ship."

"Really, mija? That's wonderful." *Wonderful* has six syllables. "I cannot condone you sneaking out on your job – we actresses have to take our work seriously – but if you take lots of holo it will make a fun story for the feeds, and everyone will forgive you." She still doesn't know what I've done. That body bag flashes in my mind again, only this time it's not zipping shut over my face, because, just like Meredith, I'm not going to have a head, and I now have a vivid picture of what that looks like. Unless they toss your cabeza in there with you. I shudder. No, they're not just going to forgive me.

Frank raises a skeptical eyebrow. "So what do these aliens eat?"

"Whatever you make for them." It's a horrible joke, and I've earned the glare he shoots me. I wait for Mamá to finish laughing. "Mira, Mamá, I've got an idea for your wedding, but I want it to be a surprise. Can I speak to Frank un momento alone?"

"Sí, mija." She blows me a kiss and exits the camera's field. I love her so much my heart hurts. We've been fighting a lot, and I'd kind of lost focus how precious she is to me. Until now.

I wait until I hear her going into the other room. "What do you want, Frank?"

"Nothing new. Just with Meredith dead, I felt I ought to remind you to keep your focus on getting home. I was going to tell you to watch the holo and think about Kaliel, but now that I see you, you already don't look so good."

Sweat beads my brow, even inside the freezer. "That tends to happen when you're dying. I'm about to go risk what little life I have left to try and give Tyson time to catch up to this ship."

"And what ship is that?"

"You wouldn't believe me if I told you, viejo." I grab a bag of frozen vegetables and hold it against my forehead, cooling the fever enough to let me think. "How'd you get the date changed for Meredith's trial? And what about Kaliel? Is he going next? Or do you keep your promises?"

"You credit me with far too much power, Bo. I didn't even know about Meredith until after it happened. I couldn't have done anything to help her anyway." Frank brings his thumb and forefinger to the bridge of his nose and closes his eyes. He's got a headache, too. It's not much to have in common, but it does give me sympathy for him since I caused it. "As for Kaliel, I haven't managed to get the treason charge dropped, but I did sweet talk a friend of mine into pushing his trial back two months. Remember, that cancels out the reprieve I offered you."

"Entiendo." *I understand*. My chest goes cold again. That's what I told him I wanted. I can't hate him for not offering me my own life too, like I can't hate him for killing Papá when Papá was guilty of treason – though believe me, I've tried. Pero, Frank's helped me more than I would have expected.

"I'll keep working on getting Kaliel's charges reduced to something that won't require a shave, just as soon as you show me those beans being destroyed. If you do it live right now, I'll catch the recording on my end."

My mouth goes to cotton, and it feels like a gran ball of the fluffstuff's sinking into my stomach. "I can't."

"What?" Frank's eyes turn cold, the way I imagine they'd look against his sniper scope.

I flinch back, then feel silly. He's just a holo. "One of the crewmen on this ship took my bag. I don't think he knows what he has. Yet."

"Damnit, Bo. Are you trying to give me a heart attack?" He takes a deep breath. "OK. How about this? I'll give you ten hours to either surrender yourself and the beans to Tyson, or to send proof of the beans' destruction and your own death. Or some combination of that. Let's call it a reverse wedding present – both your mom and Kaliel get to live."

I wish I'd never answered this phone the first time. Frank wouldn't be able to leverage anything against me if I didn't know about the threat, no? I still haven't figured out how I'm going to get the beans back. My throat feels thick. "Por favor. That's not enough time."

"Look in a mirror, Bo. You're not going to live past that deadline without Tyson. I have to make sure you use every minute you do have left keeping Earth's future safe. And that's exactly how long I have until I have to report back to my superiors on the success of my mission, before they send in a couple of people to 'help' me."

"Are you in danger, too?" Por qué am I afraid for him? I shouldn't even care if he dies – but I really do.

"No." He gives me a wry smile. "But there could be collateral damage. Some of my colleagues are not careful, or discreet."

He makes it sound so simple, I almost want to laugh. Surely that's a sign that my brain is turning to soup. "Gracias, Frank."

His eyebrows come together in a puzzled v shape. "For what?"

"For letting me see Mamá happy one last time."

I have another call interrupting that one, so I switch over to Chestla. She looks troubled, unable to make eye contact, even over the holo. A pile of Hershey bar wrappers clutters the table behind her. Claro está. She wouldn't have been able to resist demolishing the chocolate I'd thought tasted like glue. "Have I failed you, Bo?"

Eugene must have told her what Doc said. "I'm not dead yet, mi amiga. There's still a potential antidote to what I've been poisoned with." And that makes her look like she's about to cry. Maybe she can tell I don't really believe that I'll get the antivenin. I say, "Oye! Look at me. Whatever happens, this is not your fault."

She rubs the back of her hand across her nose and sniffs loudly. "I can't… not again. I'm going to find a way to get to you."

I shake my head. "There's no time for that. And it's too dangerous." She winces. I sigh. "Mira. Focus on what you can do there. Then if I do die, maybe it won't be por nada."

Her slitted eyes finally make direct contact. Her posture straightens. "Of course, cesuda ma." I have no idea what that means, but I'm guessing *client*, or maybe *boss*? "The guy with the bug spray's name is Hector Valencia, and he wasn't lying when he said he works for HGB. He's been employed as an executive for nearly twenty years. But HGB has notes all over his file. They suspect him of sympathizing with a group led by CyberFighter321. Eugene and I cracked into some ultra-classified stuff looking for the contingency plan he was talking about. It doesn't exist."

I think about the guy's build – and the guy I'd seen in Meredith's holo. "Show me his hands, por favor."

"His hands?" Chestla sounds confused, but she goes into the other room and starts talking to the guy. She flips the camera around, zooming it in on first one of his bound hands then the other. And there's the scar.

"Chestla, that *is* Cyberfighter321."

Chestla blinks those slitted eyes. "There is nothing cybernetic about this man. He was easier to defeat than one of the robotic monkeys."

"The Cyber part probably just means nerd." I hesitate. "Let me talk to him."

She tilts the camera so that Hector's face fills the holofield.

He asks, "Who are you?"

"I am... I mean I was... an amiga of Meredith's." I guess that's true. "You were the one backing her, right? The one who gave her the jetpacks and the vapguns?"

He shrugs and struggles against his bonds for a few seconds. "Maybe. But we parted ways a long time ago. She wanted to stop another war from happening. She couldn't see that this tipping point is an opportunity."

"So you decided to kill one of the cacao plantations, to increase the conflict, no? To ensure war."

He smiles. "See? You get it. Why couldn't she?"

Tears bite at my eyes. "Shtesh! Were you even there? At her execution, did you even show up after what she tried to do for you?"

I'll forgive him if he says he didn't know the date had been moved up.

"Of course not." He looks genuinely confused, and I sigh in relief. Pero, then he says, "I didn't ask her to do anything. She broke into HGB on her own. And she made a good mess of it, too. I've been in this rainforest for days, giving HGB back their own poison." He coughs again. "Though that part may have backfired."

"I can't look at this kek anymore," I say.

Chestla points the camera back at herself. "What are we supposed to do with him now?"

I honestly don't know. I feel hollow inside. "If you turn him over to HGB or the police, he'll be in line for the teeter-totter. Pero, that will just make him a martyr, and then he gets what he wants." I keep hearing the noise from the holo, that *swoooosh* of a blade falling towards Meredith... "But if you let him go, he'll keep trying to start a war. I'm no diplomat, and I'm trying to escape a ride on that same board myself. I'm in no position to tell you what to do."

"I could just kill him here, and simplify matters." Chestla says that just as matter-of-factly as Frank would have. Which sends ice dancing down my spine and makes the hair stand up from the back of my neck all the way down my arms.

In the background, Hector says, "Oye!"

"No. Dios mío!" I run a hand across my eyes. "That wouldn't simplify anything."

"You're right," Chestla says. "Legally, it's not self-defense anymore."

"Just try not to do anything drastic." I sigh, my breath visible in the cold. "Not like I'm about to do. I'll call you back."

"But Bo…"

I hang up, and stare for a long moment at the sides of meat hanging in here. If I'm going into the engine, I have to do it now, before I lose my nerve.

When I exit the freezer Varnex hands me a black military-style pack, the shadow image of the one I really want.

"I'm ready." I sling the pack full of expensive chocolate bricks over my uninjured shoulder, then I pour myself the last of the yewstral. I need all the brainmelt delaying power I can get. Doc and Jeska both made it clear that the more exertion my heart undergoes, the shorter my remaining time will be.

Brill's eyes have gone deep gray. "You should be lying down resting."

"No y no. I don't want to think about lying still." Every time I do that, I picture Doc's serene face offering to stop my heart, and then I start wondering how he'd do it, and that's a spiraling cycle I don't want to head into. I hand Brill the rough drawing Varnex has made of the engine. "Besides, does it look like you'd fit through there? Why are you guys all so big?"

"I apologize thoroughly about the poor quality." Varnex holds up a vegetable peeler like it's a pen. "I had to sketch rapidly. We don't have a lot of time to get all this food done."

Mertex scowls at me. "Which is why you should be working until you drop, like you promised the general. And they're going to lose out on my work too. Don't think I'm letting you out of my sight."

I grab a frosting spreader and a meat fork and stuff them in my pack before I turn towards the door. "Then let's do this rápido."

Mertex hurries around me into the hallway, and Brill follows. He really is trying to look out for me, which is going a long way into working him back into my affections. I'm completely confused as to where our relationship stands right now.

Jeska puts a hand on my shoulder. He flashes me an encouraging grin, but his face quickly sobers. "Seriously, watch out for Murry. He's up to something."

"What is his problem, anyway? Did you guys do something cruel to him?"

Jeska moves his hand away. "Nothing more than we do to any other transfer. Short-sheeted his bed once, things like that. But he didn't like it, and he didn't fight back. So we stopped."

"So you never bullied him?"

"I've never bullied anybody." Jeska picks up his whisk, preparing to remake the ruined sauce. "Personally, I think Murry was born without a sense of humor."

Brill and Mertex are speaking in rapid Zantite in the hallway. They go silent as I approach.

"Qué?" I strike a pose, pretending I don't look terrible. "Are you chicos talking about me again?"

"In a way." Brill starts us walking towards the elevator. "Mertex says he gets the bounty on you in with his next pay packet, whether you leave the ship alive or not. I asked him what he's going to do with the money. Did you know there's a way to buy a promotion off this vessel, to an office job back on Zant?"

I catch a glimpse of myself in the elevator doors. Ay, my

face is starting to look puffy. I wonder if that's fluid buildup from my crashbanging organs. I shudder. "Would something like that work for Jeska?"

"The Krom is better off here." Mertex steps inside the elevator and we start for four, the level above the engine room. "At least when we make port, there's a chance he'll find company on his own scale."

Brill makes a noncommittal noise. His lips thin into an embarrassed line.

"What?" Mertex asks.

Brill taps at the elevator wall a couple of times with the heel of his boot. "I've known Jeska for a long time, and he's never been just looking for company. He wants a family, but that's not going to happen for him on Krom, and it's not going to happen on Zant. Once a man turns his back on all the values of his home, he doesn't belong anywhere."

Ay, vaya. *Wow.* So what does Brill think about me? I've broken one of my home planet's most serious laws – and yet, I don't feel I've abandoned what it means to be human. Pero, there's no going home. If I do survive, will he be there for me to cling to, to give me somewhere to belong? I can hardly make myself speak. "And that gives you the right to sell him?"

Brill frowns. The elevator dings. "Mira, Babe, it's different on Krom. Jeska's mother packed his bags, and the money went to pay for Darcy's lawyer. The Hayats were short on cash. Most of their funds were tied up in an investment."

So they'd sold the son they considered failtastic to try to save the other one. That's horrible. Mamá never gave up on me, no matter how many times Mario had shown himself more successful. Brill grew up in that culture, and it explains a lot.

As we make our way down the hall, the *slusssh* and *whisssh* of the engine echoes up from beneath our feet. People are working down there. I'm catching snatches of their conversation.

"I can't believe you write your mother."

"Oh, yeah? Well, if you wrote your mom, she might send care packages."

From somewhere else, "Look, I'm going up to the gym to lift. Meet me there when you can."

I look over at Mertex, confused. He points to a foot-wide grate in the floor that runs the length of this section of hallway. "Slot ventilation. It prevents fumes from the engine from choking those guys to death in an emergency. This hall isn't used for much except maintenance."

"This is it." Brill bends toward the floor and runs a finger along the edge of the Zantite-size access panel Varnex's drawing has labeled *Central Engine Access. Bo enters here. Watch for spinning pistons.*

It's thick black metal, framed by the plush carpet. It's heavy, but it comes up easily enough when we pull on it.

"Qué? What's a spinning piston?" I ask Mertex.

He just shrugs.

"Gracias for all the help," I say sarcastically as I climb into the gaping hole, clinging to the maintenance ladder.

"Bo? Babe?" Brill's still holding the panel. "Be careful, alright? I love you."

I don't answer. I still haven't decided if I'm ready to say I love him again. I activate my sublingual, calling his new number. *Keep talking to me.*

He puts the panel down. It's weird to hear his voice out loud and in mi cabeza at almost the same time. *I'm going to track your progress with the sketch.*

Gracias. This time it's sincere. I descend into a tall u-shaped chamber. There's all sorts of moving parts down here, especially on the far end of the flat wall where a nozzle is layering dark goo in a way that reminds me of a 3D printer. It's hard to see around a wide pole made up of segments that bisects the room, about five feet away from the ladder.

Brill leans over the hole, watching me climb. I'm starting to get used to the echo following a second after inside my head. "I want to make you happy. Feliz, right? I'll even sell my ship and find a job on whatever planet... Bo, watch out!"

I look away from the ladder. One of the pole segments has started to rotate. A bar radiating out from it supports a blunt, curved metal piece shaped like a foot-wide hammer – which swings toward my head. I suck in air, my limbs freezing in panic. Brill moves so fast, I can't really describe what's happening, only that I fall about eight feet to the floor, and he takes the brunt of the spinning piston right in the gut. It sweeps him from the ladder. He manages to flip over onto the top of it in the few seconds before it impacts the wall, where it crushes a circle of something into dust. The shattered black substance slides down a channel out of sight. Oi! If I'd been stuck to that thing, I'd have been smashed into two pieces. The drawing flutters down to the floor along with fragments of the matte black rock.

As the piston starts to withdraw, Brill leaps off. He lands awkwardly, then puts a hand over his abs. "That really hurt."

"I'm impressed. After the last time, I didn't expect you to save me." I visualize him sprinting off that dock while I lay bleeding. It's not so much that part that I'm emotirated about, more that he didn't even look for me afterwards.

"I'm trying to change, Babe. I've never had anybody to care about before, and after Krevia, when I thought it was too late, I realized I should have stepped between you and that bullet."

He easily could have. He moves so fast, he could have dashed over and grabbed Tyson's gun. Or he could have picked me up – even though my weight would have slowed him down, he probably could have gotten both of us away, if he hadn't been so terrified of Tyson. Maybe that's what he'd been intending to do, if I'd flitdashed the direction he'd been indicating instead of toward the pier, but we'll never know now.

He moves toward me. "I love you more than my own life. Please give me the time to prove that to you."

"Hopefully it won't come to that," I laugh, though his words really have touched me. Tears bite at my eyes. "Pero right now, the one thing I don't have is time."

He looks like he's gotten punched again. "Hanstral about Tyson. I never meant for you to get hurt." He hesitates. "When I first approached you on Larksis, I thought we'd have a few laughs, you'd give me some information, then you'd file me under near-misses like Stephen. By the time I realized I wanted to be with you, it was too late to tell the truth about why we met. I knew it would be over as soon as you found out."

"Oye." So he and Stephen had discussed me after all. "When I was locked in the cell on Tyson's ship, I decided it must have been all about the money. Pero it's not, no? Darcy must have been muy, muy important to you."

"I spent over a year trying to find a way to get to Earth, or to find someone willing to sell me black market cacao saplings, before I even heard your name. The frustration of getting nowhere..." He looks down at his boots. "You have to understand. For the kind of promise I'd made Darcy, I'd pledged my very life. All any Krom has is his honor and–"

A grinding noise comes from above. We both look up as the panel slides into place.

"Hest!" Brill blazebangs up to the top of the ladder, banging on the sealed exit. "Either Mertex is standing on it, or he glued it in place."

"You guys, don't go anywhere!" Mertex's voice comes through the ventilation grate, even as the distinctive *sripppp* of duct tape coming off a roll echoes down to us.

"Are you loco or just mean?" Even to myself, I sound tired. My throat aches, and my lungs feel like I've been running in the cold. Doc's right. This is going to be una muerte lenta y dolorosa, a *slow and painful death*. I've never heard that phrase used before outside of a telenovela cheesecast, but now I'm living it.

When I look back at the ladder, Brill's got a gun in his hand, his head tilted like he's listening to follow Mertex's movements.

"Brill!" The idea of the cowardly Zantite lying cold with a hole in him sends my heartbeat pounding in my ears again.

Brill takes one look at my face, and his eyes tint pink. He holsters the gun. "I know. What would be the point? We'd still be stuck down here."

Mertex's voice echoes through the grate. "I've just captured two ukkat personnel inside the engine. That's bound to be worth another bonus in my pay packet, which should give me what I need to buy the promotion. Bo, it might even put you in a position where your boyfriend could be impressed, though technically, I guess Jeska would have to be the one to sell him. If I can work it so that I get half the fee, that would cover the cost of decent quarters back home. It's not personal, you guys."

Brill comes back down the ladder. He whispers, "That's the kek who has your backpack?"

I nod. "Let's hope Mertex just thinks he's got a small fortune in Earth spices. You wouldn't really have shot him, would you?"

"Probably not. I don't take death lightly." He sees the unasked question, *have you ever killed a person*, shining in my eyes. He turns away, won't let me see his face. "You don't know what it's like, to be boarded alone in deep space, to know that the only thing on your ship that's not valuable is you. And still I almost couldn't do it, not until I was looking down a gun barrel, and they were talking about how to keep my blood off the upholstery. That was the first time. There have only been a couple of others." He breathes in almost forever, giving me time to absorb his words. "It's not the kind of thing I wanted you to know about me."

I knew he lived with danger. I never thought about the feo reality of it, how isolated that must feel. I want to comfort him; at the same time that iron-hard coldness I've just discovered makes me want to pull back. Mertex moves noisily away overhead.

I wind up just clasping my hands together in front of me, trying to ignore how sick I feel. "Brill, what are we going to do?"

"Call me mi vida. I've missed that."

Tears spring to my eyes. "I don't think we've made it back to that point yet. I'm not sure if we can. You're not the hero I thought you were."

He turns back to me, his eyes an intense gold. "At least let me try to be."

There's so much power and desire in his face that I take a step away, overwhelmed. I'm afraid he's going to misinterpret that, so I step rápidamente forward again and put a hand on his sleeve. "OK, mi héroe, how are we going to keep you from growing old on this ship while sharing a monster-sized bottle of iron supplements with Jeska?"

"I don't think Mertex can work it to get me impressed." Brill's eyes slowly fade from the gold, going purple with concentration, without a hint of gray. I guess he's not as frightened of being stuck here as I am. "But the general would be well within his rights to eat me."

"All because you jumped down here to save me, sí? One moment out of character could cost you your life." I'm teasing – sort of – but he looks at me seriously, the gold working its way back to the surface of his irises.

"It'd be worth giving up mine if I could find a way to save yours." He rubs a hand just under his ribcage, where a monster bruise is probably starting to form. He breaks into a sheepish grin. "We have a saying on Krom. No good deed goes unpunished."

"Cómico. We have that same saying on Earth." Despite what I just said, I have this loco urge to kiss him. He steps in closer, and I can see he's hoping to be kissed. He'll take it as me accepting him back as mi vida, not just a connection of warmth and danger and the moment. No sé if I'm ready for that, but he's right there, waiting, and we don't have much time.

Above our heads, there's a mechanical *swoosh*, and two of the pistons swing around together, shattering their black rocks. Something moves the massive slab up, so that all the circles are filled in. That pole has nine segments. The holes in the wall reveal nine circles. Oi! If that keeps up, in just a little while all nine pistons will swing through at once. Brill stares wide-eyed at the dust filtering down before being vacuumed away by a suction vent in the floor. "Maybe you can spot another way out while you're delivering that chocolate. I'm guessing if we'd had permission to come down, we'd have shut those hammers off first."

"Sí." I reactivate the sublingual, ready to hear his bubblechatter if there's a status update. "Stay with me, mi héroe."

I cross the room and push my way into the opening. Even I don't really fit. I have to take the backpack off and hold it in front of me while I hold my breath until the space widens out. I tell him what I'm doing as I follow the only possible path, until I reach the little pocket next to the coolant chamber. There's a ton of heat being sucked along the wall. I concentrate on not touching it as I inch toward the junction between the coolant tube and the main reactor. I can hear the voices again.

"It's better than being stuck cleaning toilets."

"I don't know. I always wanted to play kuggek in a band."

I use the frosting spreader to pry apart the seam in the wall, making sure I don't disrupt the reactor. I unwrap the bars of dark chocolate, stacking them against the wall, levering the edges into the seam. The chocolate's already softening. It won't be long before it melts.

I pause for a moment, leaning against the cooler wall. It wasn't that much exertion getting in here, but my legs are threatening to fall out from under me like I've just run for miles. My heart is beating like a frightened rabbit's, and I have a strange metallic taste in my mouth. Damn Tyson and his loco sense of justice.

"Hey!" somebody shouts. "Something's leaking out of the reactor! Shut it down! Engines at full stop, now!"

I smile and make my way back to Brill. I shut the sublingual off when I can see him again. "They turned the engine off."

Above us, four pistons swing in unison, dangerously close to Brill's head. I must have missed number three.

"They only turned the reactor off, Babe. This contraption's still running."

Brill can't possibly fit through any of the gaps in the equipment. No y no! I am not going to lose him, after I just found him again.

I snatch the sketch from him. There's another exit hatch on the other side of the tangle of electronics Varnex has labeled the control center, which is actually up on four, over part of the reactor. To take that route, I'm going to have to squeeze in with the bundles of wires and do a near-vertical climb.

Brill takes the drawing away from me. He's seen what I'm looking at. "Ga. Absolutely not. Your heart's not going to be able to take that."

"So I'm supposed to just hide in a crack and see whether you're quick enough to avoid being smashed to death? No y no. I at least have to try."

"Ga, you don't. I'm serious, Babe." Brill's irises are lost in darkness and worry. "I don't want you in more danger because of me. Not again."

He tries to hold onto me, but he doesn't fight me when I push him away.

"This is pan comido – bread to be eaten. Like a piece of

cake." I kiss him on the cheek, not quite the connection he was asking for, but enough for where we are right now. "Just keep talking to me, OK?"

He does, creating a soft stream of consciousness in mi cabeza as he tells me about what he's been doing since Krevia. I squeeze back through into the coolant area, where panicked crewmen are trying to decide whether to believe their gauges or their eyes, and whether or not to alert the general and evacuate. I hope none of them get chompcrushed over this. I follow the wires to a hole in the wall about two feet above my head. I reach up and grab onto the lip of the hole. I'm too sick to be walking around, let alone doing chin-ups, but I manage it and scramble inside. The effort overwhelms me. I tell Brill, *I gotta hang up por un segundo.*

Without waiting for a response, I sever the connection, barely managing to turn around in time to puke onto the floor below the opening, instead of on the slick metal in front of me. There's not much in my system, but it's still gross. Guácala! All my limbs are trembling, but I force myself to climb. I refuse to die alone in a dusty tunnel.

My sublingual rings and my chest goes cold with renewed fear. Has Crosskiss already made it back to Brill?

Sí? I answer urgently, but it's not Brill. It's Kayla.

When are you going to tell me what's going on, Bo?

Qué? What do you mean? I try to sound casual, but that's muy difícil when you're splayed out in a tunnel, pushing your way forward like a mole.

You told me in your last text that you were on Earth. I thought when I finally made it to Rio, you'd be here to show me the sights, but HGB wouldn't say anything about you, then they didn't want to let me leave.

Lo siento, Kayla. I left unexpectedly.

She sighs. *Are those mercials holonique or aren't they? Did you really tell the cameras Kaliel's a hero?*

The rawness of her anger resonating in my brain takes me aback. I need a moment to compose my thoughts before I answer. *He's not a monster, just a person who got caught in a hard situation. I can't pretend I don't hope he's found innocent. No y no.* I close my eyes, picturing Kaliel's face, the way his eyes had lit up when he'd spotted me coming back into the club where we had danced. *I kissed Kaliel. I know I shouldn't have, but I won't apologize for it.* Except to Brill, of course. Thinking back, I never did say I was sorry for abusing his heart. I can't die here, not without making that right. *Pero I didn't make any holos for HGB.*

Kayla's silent for so long I think she's hung up. *You can still be my best friend, as long as you don't expect me to forgive the flying dork.*

I'm feeling lightheaded, but when I open my eyes I can see the end of the tunnel. *You don't have to forgive him, but I hope you want justice done, chica. If I don't make it back, testify at his trial in my place, por favor. Tell them he had nada to do with what I did. They'll believe you, no? You have no reason to lie.*

She sucks air on her end of the connection. *You want me to defend him?*

I touch the edge of the tunnel, can almost see the flat floor in front of me. *Watching him die won't bring your abuelita back. Por favor, Kayla.*

Grant a dying girl's last wish.

I'll think about it. What did you do anyway?

I try to lift myself those last few inches onto the floor. I'm too weak. I lose my grip and slide back almost a foot. I hold onto the wire bundles, shivering. *It's muy complicated. Trust me, they'll know. I have to go.* My vision is trying to tunnel in. *Kayla? You've always been a good amiga. I love you like you were one of mi hermanas.*

Kayla laughs. *Don't be so serious, Bo. You sound like you're dying or something.*

I can't answer her around the sudden lump that fills my throat. I hang up before I start bawling. I am dying, but I can't let go yet. I'm too close to saving Brill from Crosskiss or from those crushing pistons, whichever'd get him first. I gather all my remaining energy into pulling myself up. Pain twinges deep in my chest. Either I pulled something, or I'm having a heart attack. I slither out onto the floor, trembling. I use the wall to make it to my feet. I push open the door and stumble back up the hall as that pain twinges again, even deeper. I fall to my knees and start pulling tape off the hatch. The pistons lift again with a ringing clang, almost in time with another twinge. I'm having a hard time breathing, let alone talking out loud. *Brill! Can you hear me?*

"Babe? Please hurry. That was eight." His voice is echoing through the panel, and also in my head.

My fingers feel swollen and slow, but I get the hatch open and Brill races up the ladder. He's almost reached the top when my vision starts going black at the edges, more insistently this time. I collapse, one hand reaching into the hole. I've held on as long as I could. Idiota Tyson was just too slow. I breathe out. I don't breathe back in.

CHAPTER SIXTEEN

I wake, coughing out stale air. Brill is leaning over me, both hands crossed in the center of my chest, which feels bruised. Ay, I hope nothing's broken in there. He's just shifting to blow air into my lungs, and not for the first time, judging by my lipstick smeared across his chin. Relief melts the slate in his eyes back to gold as he pulls me to him. "I told you your heart couldn't take that kind of abuse."

He's chiding and loving at the same time, and I still don't know how to feel. He's saved my life twice within the space of an hour, and still I can't melt into him the way I used to – pero I'm getting close. He picks me up, carrying me against his chest. "I'll get you down to Dr Tassiks. He'll have something that will help you hold on until Tyson gets here."

Does he not care anymore that Tyson will probably arrest him for his part in the chocotheft? Obviously, that's what he's been running from the whole time I couldn't find him. Whatever the penalty is for selling contraband, I'm sure it's not as high as what I'm facing for stealing it. "I thought you kept saying we didn't need Tyson."

He stands up awkwardly, without putting me down. "I'm a kek. You know that."

"Doc said he doesn't have anything else for me." I take a deep breath. Brill wants a chance to prove he's the guy I need. I'm going to trust him. "I have to get those cacao beans back,

280

por favor. If I don't send Frank proof that I've destroyed them, in eight and a half hours, he's going to kill Mamá."

Brill's arms stiffen around me. He closes his eyes, like he doesn't want me to see what's going on inside his head. I can feel his heartbeat, already jackrabbit by nature, speeding up. When he finally looks down, his eyes are sky blue. He hugs me closer, but I can feel a distance in him as he decides what's most important. He may still choose me and mi familia, but resent me for it later. I feel my heart pulling away from him again. He shouldn't even have to think whether a commodity is more important than a life.

Brill clears his throat. "We can't let that happen. Jess told me his quarters are up on nine."

I manage a smile, nestle my head against the leather of his jacket. "Plelix said they lay out the bunk assignments by division. So Mertex's room should be right down the hall, no?"

Brill carries me to the elevator. When the doors open, we come face to elbow with Crosskiss, who frowns, mouth widening in a way that sends chills all the way to my toes. I swear my heart tries to stop again. Mertex is standing behind him.

"What are you doing here?" Crosskiss eyes me in Brill's arms.

Brill gestures with his chin. "I apologize thoroughly. She went into cardiac arrest. I am trying to get her to go down to the doctor."

Crosskiss goes un poco pale. "We can't have her dying on us yet." I cringe at the *yet*. "She still needs to help in the kitchen."

"Perdón, pero your doctor says there is nothing else for me. I will return to the kitchen."

Crosskiss squints, studying me. "I'll talk to him."

"But, sir," Mertex protests. "About the thing I wanted to show you–"

"We're here to find out what happened to our engines,

corporal." Crosskiss looks out into the hallway. "And we seem to have the wrong floor."

We ride down a level with the two Zantites. I feel Brill's rapid heartbeat against my cheek in the uncomfortable silence. Once the door has closed behind them and we've started riding back up, Brill asks, "Am I the only one who finds it odd how concerned that guy was about your health, considering he tried to execute you a couple of hours ago?"

"You picked up on that too? He doesn't want Tyson coming aboard to get me either, pero, what use could I be to him?"

"I don't know. But I plan to find out." Brill insists on carrying me all the way to Mertex's room, which is easy to find, since the crew names are posted on a sign next to the door. He sets me down so that he can jimmy the lock. I totter into the room. It's generously sized, with two bunks and a door I'm guessing leads into a closet, plus a partially open one that reveals a sliver of a sink. Brill opens the closet door, steps inside. I hear him digging through Mertex's stuff.

I don't have the energy to follow him in there. No y no. I'm still holding onto the main door frame. The far wall has panels set into it, marking furniture that can be popped out as needed. There's the outline of a dresser in the middle, with the button for each drawer, and a smaller piece – maybe a table or a desk – flanking each side, close to the bunks. Attached to the foot of each bunk, there's a metal bin, likely a laundry hamper.

I collapse onto the bunk on the side of the room with the holographic movie posters plastered above it. There's something hard under the pillow, pero it doesn't look like more collectabilla. "Oye!" I pull out a golden box with a sheaf of grain and a loaf embossed on it. I hold it up. "The guys are looking for this, mi héroe. Mertex may not even know yet he's been pranked." Then a sickening thought hits me. "Pero what if he's the one who took it? How are we going to get this back where it belongs without him realizing we searched his room?"

"Hold onto it, Babe. I'll give it to Jeska privately. I doubt Mertex did it, though. Ga. He's just as likely to get executed as the others." Brill comes back into the main room, where he rifles through Mertex's clothes, then flips the toggle that trades Mertex's bureau drawers for those of his roommate. He even pops out the desk and goes through the drawer on it, though it is too shallow to hold a backpack.

"Babe, there's nothing here."

"De veras? Are you sure?" I'm about a breath away from tears, picturing Frank pushing Mamá overboard, almost hearing her scream as she hits the agua. I'm not thinking about how harsh an accusation it will sound when I add, "I know how much you want that sale."

He sucks in a breath. Brill won't look at me. "I'll tell you whose room you ought to be checking. Jeska's. Do you know what it would mean for him to secure cacao for the honor of Krom? They'd let him back into society."

"If he wasn't bound to this ship. It doesn't make sense." I shake my aching head. "Nada makes sense."

I close my eyes. I don't mean to fall asleep, even though I'm beyond slypered, but when I wake, Brill's sitting on the edge of the bunk, running his fingers through my hair, trying to hide the tears in his eyes. He's opened a bottle of yewstral – who knows where he got it – and he helps me drink about a quarter of the bubbly liquid. It's not as good as when it is cold, but it still tastes agradable.

"Brill." I need to get my apology out, but I can hardly look at him. His eyes dance from gray through violet to green. I reach out to touch his face, his cheek just starting to get stubbly in a way that's not yet noticeable. "I'm sorry. Ita hanstral. I shouldn't have kissed somebody else, no matter what."

His irises slowly go murky, ending in a gold so deep it's almost black, tinged with mahogany. "I shouldn't have overreacted." He turns his face away, leaving me puzzling over the meaning of what I've just glimpsed inside him.

"We need to get down to the galley." My lungs hurt when I breathe in, but otherwise I'm feeling a lot better.

"I suppose so." He seems reluctant to leave the bed, reluctant to let me stand. "Lo siento, too. I'm such a kek." He looks down at the floor, to where my backpack is resting against Mertex's desk. Eh? If he recovered it while I was sleeping, why does he look so sad? "I found it in the closet, but I didn't say anything." He gestures with his head toward the little door. "I thought that I could record proof of selling the beans, then contact Frank and save your mom. I wanted to, as you said, be the hero you need."

I sit up. "So you lied to me and then made me feel bad about calling you on it?"

He tilts his chin toward his chest. "I know. It was a bad plan. I wasn't treating you like an equal. Frank put it into your head that I'm a liar, and he's right. In my line of work, I have to be. But I've tried to be honest with you. I may have left out a lot of things since we've met, but I've told you exactly two lies: at the restaurant, when I was trying to spare your feelings, and just now, when I was trying to be the smartest guy in the room."

"What about when you said you'd never been involved in a first contact?"

Brill blinks, genuinely confused. After a second, his irises shift, as comprehension dawns. "Babe, it's not contact if the planet's uninhabited. We ran out of fuel and had to ditch on an asteroid that had broken off somewhere else. The only thing that had survived the low oxygen were those bushes."

I'm not sure what to think about that. I hold out a hand. "Give me the cacao. I still have time to save Mamá."

Brill looks at me, his eyes a deep mahogany. "They weren't in there, Babe. I tore this room apart. I even looked for holes in the mattresses." He could well have been quick enough to do all that and then put the room back together like it had never been touched. *And* get me yewstral. "I'm telling the truth. Suavet quellbada."

From a shortened form of *heart* plus the word for *promise*. So *heart promise*, meaning, *I vow.* He sounds sincere. And yet...

"How am I supposed to believe that after what you just said?" I push myself up off the bunk and totter towards the door.

He follows me, helps keep me steady as I make my way along the hall. "I don't know how I can prove I don't have the cacao. But you know me, Dabe. You have to realize that I'd never do anything to intentionally hurt you or your mother."

I want to believe that. And yes, while he's been insensitive, he has never been mean. Pero I can't help thinking about that bit I've read of the Codex, where it talks about doing the wrong thing for the right reasons. If that's his guide, how can he promise he's not lying? Claro está, I may be missing something. Jeska's Krom too, and as far as I can tell, *his* eyes have always honestly matched his feelings, even when it wasn't to his advantage.

When we get back to the galley, Brill holds the door open for me. He looks puzzled. "What is that noise?"

I shake mi cabeza as I step past him, listening to a steady banging coming from the other side of the window.

Plelix looks up from a pot where he's stirring chocolate cream. "Varnex is making a giant mold of Garfex. We're going to fill it with molten chocolate and flash freeze it."

"I've also added in his wife." Varnex's voice comes through the thin layer of metal. The rhythmic banging never stops.

The only Zantites I've heard of by name are movie stars. I try to remember that one, but can't. "Who's Garfex?"

Mertex scowls at me. "Don't say it like that. He is the most royal Zantite personage."

Jeska turns away from the oven and half-bows. "King Garfex the Great, His Holiness, the Supreme Ruler of the Eight Realms, Holder of the Trident of Awe."

"Wow," I say.

"Yeah," he replies. I count at least seventeen shades of sarcasm in that one syllable. "He's a self-proclaimed chocofan." Jeska steps in close and smiles at me. He blinks, and while they were closed his eyes have shifted from green to the light golden shade of a beam of sunlight. Dating on Krom must be extraño. Does Jeska even know he's developing feelings for me?

Brill notices though, even if his only outward sign is a sharp intake of breath. He shoots an equally sharp look at me.

I pretend I didn't see either the sunlight or the storm clouds, turning instead toward the closed window. "Varnex, can I come out and see your work, chico?"

"I'd be flattered."

I loop through the hallway to the cafeteria door. Brill's friends must have brought all those boxes and boxes of HGB dark directly in here for Varnex's project. There's more chocolate sitting on just one of the mess tables than came into the galley. A few crewmen are sitting at one of the other tables, drinking from mugs and eating pie, which has to have come from a small dessert buffet set out on a table against the wall.

To the right of the galley, there's a room-sized blast freezer. I approach the open door and examine the cavernous space. I've never seen anything like it. "Why is this thing so grande? So big, I mean."

Varnex, busy constructing his mold on a track system that leads inside the freezer, looks up from his work. "Sometimes, when we're low on supplies, we stop on one of the Class 082 registered planets, and the soldiers go hunt for target practice. With this baby, we can preserve all the game at once. It was also perfect that time we built a replica of Orlux's bunk out of ice cream. You should have seen him when he woke up in the middle of the night with it half melted." Varnex laughs, but it's a sad sound. He steps back and knocks over a flat spatula that measures roughly three feet across. The thing has a handle the size you'd find on a human shovel.

I pick up the spatula and lean it back against the wall. He's probably planning to run it around the inside rim of the mold, to pop any bubbles inside the chocolate. No one's eating this sculpture, so it doesn't have to be washed. "Orlux was a good friend, no?"

"He was from my hometown. We were in the same learning pod, so when I fetched up here both of us were relieved to see a familiar face. He'd gotten married, she had a vindictive ex, same old story." Varnex turns back to his work, banging savagely on the metal. "You know, I never heard Jeska call Orlux by his full name before. He used to call him Ollie."

It strikes me that the way Jeska uses all those nicknames must be some sort of rebellion – conscious or unconscious – of the culture that had abandoned him.

Pero, I doubt Varnex is in the mood to discuss it, and his project looks time-consuming, so I leave him to it. For a moment, I stand in the hallway between the galley and the mess hall, wondering if anyone back on Earth is missing Meredith Vasquez the way Varnex is missing Orlux. Other than Botas, of course, watching a cage door, waiting for someone who's never coming for him.

I go back to Varnex and I pull up holo from Meredith's feed to show him. It's not like I knew her all that well, not like she's the same thing   a near brother, or in my case sister to me, pero, it feels muy importante. I search for Botas by name and wind up clicking on a cast I haven't seen before. Meredith has three women with her, each of them holding a dog of a different breed, while Botas sleeps against Meredith's shoe. She's still wearing a wedding ring in this one, still looking young and unbroken by loss.

She giggles as one of the other dogs – a chihuahua by the look of it – leans over in its owner's grip to lick her hand.

"So today is the third anniversary of the day I rescued Botas from the pound, chicos, so I wanted to take this opportunity... OK, enough, tranquila."

The dog is trying to climb her shoulder to lick her face.

The owner pulls the dog back out of reach. "Lo siento."

She wipes her hand across her cheek. "Pero like, I just want to say go rescue a dog today. For me. And Botas. He hasn't always had it easy, you know. He got abandoned here, or maybe just lost, and by the time he wound up in the shelter he was sick and nearly starving at less than six months old. I'm going to show you some pictures, but fair warning, they are no apto para cardíacos." *Not for the faint of heart.*

The image shifts to a half-grown version of the corgi. He'd had mange or something, causing large scaly bald spots on his back. And he'd hardly been able to lift his head. And there was goo coming out of one of his eyes. Meredith had taken one look at that – and still hadn't hesitated to bring him home with her.

The holo switches back to the women and their pets, all healthy and squirming. Botas had survived and healed. Maybe he'd be able to do it again.

My handheld rings, and I shut off the holo to answer it. It's Chestla.

Without preamble, she asks, "Can I have Frank's contact information?"

"Por qué?"

She rolls her eyes. "So Hector's actually a very bad man. He said he was hungry, so Eugene tried to hand-feed him a chocolate bar. They got into a fight over it, and Hector smashed his chair, then tried to strangle Eugene with the ropes we'd used to bind him. Shy little Eugene! I barely pulled him off in time. I don't think Eugene's going to be able to talk for a while. Not that he ever does, anyway. But I trussed up Hector like an ekaqu, and left him by the gate, along with his spraying equipment. I want Frank to come get him before something eats him, and I want to explain my side of what happened."

"Sí. OK." I give her Minerva's number. "What about them being able to trace your phone?"

"That doesn't matter as long as they're not coming inside the wall. Besides, since when have I been able to not talk to people?"

Still. Chestla talking to Frank. En serio. Who would have thought?

When I return to the galley, Brill leans back against the counter, and one side of his leather jacket swings back. There's a box-shaped outline in the jacket's liner. Heat fills my chest and face, and a heavy sigh escapes me. He's lying after all.

I raise an eyebrow. "Are you going to tell me that's not what I think it is?"

"It's not, actually." He gives me a wry smile. Then he pulls out a paper-wrapped box, about the same size as the viability box, and hands it to me. "I've been meaning to give you this."

I open the paper. It's a bottle of perfume.

"It's the most expensive one I've found, made from rare flowers that only grow on a single island on a planet deep in the Betelgeusian system. It costs more per ounce than the mortgage on your mother's house. I brought it back from my ship as my apology for not being able to get you the antivenin."

My chest goes cold, and the anger that's been lurking beneath the surface since Krevia breaks through. Why did I think Brill understood anything except monetary value? Is he even capable of real love? He's the one who talked me into putting myself in danger. "Who cares if it's expensive? What good will this do me once I'm dead, loco boy? You want to make my corpse smell nice for the undertaker?"

Moisture glitters in Brill's eyes. "I take full responsibility for this situation. If you die, I'll make sure your family is taken care of. Send your sisters to college, whatever they need."

I narrow my eyes. "That sounds almost exactly like what HGB did for Mamá after they killed mi Papá."

His eyes turn the color of pain. "I'm sorry, Babe. I don't know what to do here. I've tried to understand your culture, your feelings, but I just can't." He bangs a fist backwards into the counter. "A Krom girl would have demanded a gift of atonement just for letting her down. You know. Before."

"Just say it, mi héroe. You left me for muerta." My hand trembles as I put my palm on his chest, against his heart. The fast beat, normal for a Krom, echoes steadily against my hand. I take his hand and put it against my ribcage and let him feel my heartbeat struggling to catch up to his.

He flinches. "Haza. I left you for dead. I talked you into fulfilling my promise, and I put you in danger, and if you die, it's entirely my fault. I'm truly sorry. What can I do to make things right?"

"Nada. If you think a gift like this will fix what's gone wrong between us, what's left to do, Brill?" I snap my teeth together in shock. I think I just broke up with mi héroe. In Portuguese, there's one word that's always resonated with me, one that doesn't translate well into English. *Saudade* is the feeling of longing for someone or something that you love and which is lost. Looking at Brill, who is staring at me in stunned silence, that feeling washes over me. I lean back against the wall.

He swallows visibly. "If that's what you want, I'll leave."

I look into Brill's eyes, the complex dark golden shade of love mixed with remorse. Tears bite at my eyes, but I force them back. "What I want is to stop being hurt. Every time I turn around I find out something else about you, something you didn't want me to know. Who are you, really?"

He starts to say something, then closes his mouth. His eyes have turned a pale gray I've never seen before. Finally, he tries to speak again. "I've shared more of myself with you than I have with anyone else in my entire life. I know my weaknesses are obvious. Half the time I don't live up to my own ideals. I'm sorry my life's not simple. I thought you realized that and were giving me the time to open up. I guess I don't know you either." He turns to Jeska and bows. "I know you probably don't believe this, but it was good seeing you again, Jess. I'll tell your mother that you're doing well."

Jeska stops chopping the chocolate and puts his knife down on the cutting board. He bows back at Brill, complete with that closed-fist salute. "Safe journey and true heart, my friend. As long as you carry my brother's memory with you, you remain a brother to me."

They both straighten up at the same time. Brill turns away without saying anything to the Zantite cooks, who are desperately pretending they haven't witnessed any of this.

He leaves. Which means he's got the cacao, that that's what he really wanted.

I want to run after him before that swinging door closes, but I don't. What would be the point? I just stand there and let a few estúpido tears fall.

Jeska moves closer and wipes them away with his thumb. "You OK?"

"I always wanted to teach him how to cook, pero he never let me." Though right now, what I really want is for Jeska to lean in and kiss my sadness away, the way I did for Kaliel a lifetime ago. I know on some level he'd like to, but it seems cheap to tell him I spotted that hint of sunlight in his gaze.

Jeska gives me a weary smile. "On Krom, upper-class guys don't cook. They either marry someone who's good in the kitchen or they hire a maid. Brill grew up without prospects or money, but his mother believed if she taught him refined manners, and his father helped him become a shrewd trader, everything he needed would come together. That's why he glommed onto Darcy. As hard as it is to say, my brother's encouragement was probably the worst thing that ever happened to your *leldada*." He's pulling the word *leldada* for boyfriend, from Universal standard, not at all like what he'd called me earlier – Brill's *paqunell*, his *beginner's heart*. Does that mean Jeska's realized that he either underestimated or misunderstood mine and Brill's relationship? Not that it matters now.

"Ex-boyfriend."

Jeska laughs. "That guy's still besotted with you, su. You could call him on that tongue phone of yours, and even after what you just did to him, he'd be back here in a heartbeat."

"Now por qué would I want to do that?" I try to make it a joke, but I'm still sort of crying. I wonder how Jeska spotted my sublingual. Overall, he's been hard to figure out. "You know Brill once caught the galley of his ship on fire trying to make toast? If he aspired to be Darcy, you come from the upper class, too, no? So how come you cook so well?"

"Whatever job I get stuck doing, I'm determined to do right. I knew nothing about food when I first walked into this galley, but I've watched seasons' worth of cooking holos and diced a ton of zarroxes. How does the Earth saying go? Sometimes old dogs learn new tricks."

"You realize you don't look much older than me?" I tap his lips with my finger, emphasizing my point by tracing down from there along the outline of his chiseled jaw.

He catches my hand and moves it away from his face. "Don't. It won't make you feel any better, and Brill won't be jealous. He'll just be hurt."

CHAPTER SEVENTEEN

Jeska closes his eyes, then turns his face away, hiding the color of his irises. "I need a break. If anyone needs me, I'll be in my room."

I try to keep prepping food, but I can't stop thinking about the clock counting down on Mamá's life. I need help, and there's only one person still aboard this ship I can ask.

"Plelix, I'll be right back, por favor." Before the Zantite can protest, I slip out into the hall. I make my way up to Jeska's room and knock. When he answers, he's holding a photo frame. The whites of his eyes are tinged red, like he's been crying.

He gives me a stern look. "Bo, I don't think this is a good idea. I thought I made myself clear downstairs."

"I'm not here about that." I can't help glancing at his crotch. Classy, Bo, real classy.

He steps back, letting me into the room. As he closes the door, I glimpse the image frozen inside the frame, of him and another dark-haired Krom.

"Is that Darcy?" My insides feel prickled with glass. I'm looking at a dead man.

"I can't believe he's gone." Jeska presses the button that brings his desk out from the wall and sits sideways in the attached chair. He gestures for me to sit on the nearby bunk. "He'd just turned thirty when I left. That's a tenth of his expected lifespan."

"Lo siento." Wait. I switch back to Krom. "I mean I'm sorry." I take the frame. Darcy was handsome, with a generous smile and unruly hair. It's hard to imagine such a vibrant life cut short – only there's Meredith. And Kaliel. And me. And ay, Noodles, if you really think about it. "Looking at Brill reminds you too much of him, no?"

"Brill reminds me of what Darcy thought of me." Jeska reaches across and scrolls through the pictures, most starring the same people, a dozen or so different Krom. He stops on one where Darcy and Brill stand outdoors wearing formal garb that has that cheap feel of school uniforms, each holding the bridle of an identical gray horse. Horses adapted beautifully to life on Krom. The guys are both smiling, and in the background someone has laid out a full-on hunt breakfast. "When I made my mistake, Darcy hadn't even been born. Can you imagine what it's like, having a brother who despises everything you stand for, belittles everything you sacrificed?"

"Actually, I can. Mi hermano… my brother Mario judges me harder than the media."

"I wouldn't worry much about what your planet's media thinks. The mockery they made of that woman's execution was worse than anything I've seen a Zantite do aboard this ship."

I bow my head, remembering Meredith hitting that button from across the room, allowing me to escape. She was too fabuloso to have ended life that way. "The public nature of the death is supposed to be a deterrent."

"I think we could both use a drink. Grab a couple of glasses from my bureau drawer." Jeska fishes inside the collar of his shirt and pulls out a golden chain threaded through a small silver key. He unlocks his desk and takes out a flat flask, then replaces the chain around his neck. I glimpse the corner of what looks very much like the seed viability box farther back in the drawer. He did take it. Hurt and disappointment courses through me, along with remorse for having accused Brill.

Jeska's watching for my reaction. Our eyes lock. His have gone a raisin-toned purple-black.

Finally, I look away. "Which drawer has the glasses, chico?"

"Second from the bottom."

I open the drawer to an extensive collection of shot glasses, the kind of collectabilia you get at tourist traps the galaxy over. I pick one at random. *Praxshion 5*, it proclaims, *the Paradise Moon*, above a picture of their moon princess dancing on a beach. These aren't confettiglass. Jeska should have wrapped them in tissue paper.

I lift another one. *University of Iowa*. I turn it in my hands, letting the prismaglass catch and refract the light. "This has me curious, chico. What made you pick a place so close to the town that claimed it would someday be the birthplace of the most famous fictional starship captain Earth has ever had? You were watching our castsignals, no? It was some sense of irony?"

"It was coincidence. We found an inconspicuous place to land a ship in the middle of a bunch of corn fields. But it played into a lot of humans' pre-existing fears. It was a mistake." Jeska grimaces. "Only the first mistake we made." He stares at that glass like it's showing moving pictures of the past. "I've never come across a culture like yours, one that had such a fascination with the idea of aliens, even before going interstellar. That's why your art in turn fascinates people across the galaxy."

"We had more than just fears."

"I know. I saw that sign at Riverside, you know. 'Future birthplace of James T Kirk.' The face of humanity's hopes and dreams of space travel, before all the mistakes that ruined it for you guys. I sat on that bench that's right by the sign, once, too, and took tourist-type pictures after I'd watched a few episodes of the show. Is it true the rioters burned that bench after we left?"

I curl my hand around the glass's cold surface. I don't want to talk about how we had indulged in darkness. "A mistake isn't a rejection of ideals. Brill implied something more serious happened to you on the way home from Earth."

Jeska gestures for me to hand him the shot glasses, which he fills with clear liquid. He gives me back the one with the moon princess before he upends his, then fills it again. "Do you know what mistake I made?"

I sip from my own glass. The liquid is pleasantly floral, but ay, so potent. "Sí, you brought back a coca plant instead of a cacao tree, but the plant died, so it shouldn't have been that grande of a deal."

"The plant didn't die on its own. I killed it. I know it's gross, but I poured pee on it every day until it shriveled. The captain caught me at it. I had willingly destroyed a lucrative commodity which could in theory be used for medicinal or military purposes, committing wevdaglarin while on an official Voyage of Discovery. Breaking the code of the Benevolent Ideals isn't the kind of thing you can go to prison over, but it does make you a social pariah, and it brings shame to your family." Jeska downs his second shot. "It was just dumb chance that I even realized what I'd collected. I'd been crosschecking the new commodities to make sure there weren't any duplicates, and once I realized the leaves didn't look anything like the ones in the Earth databases under *Theobroma cacao*, I had my mystery plant analyzed in the lab. It was going to be more addictive to Krom, and a lot of other peoples galaxy wide, than the early neural enhancers, and those cooked the brains of millions."

"Pero Brill once told me neural enhancers can completely change life for the families that can afford them for niños in the right stage of development. He sounded jealous he'd never gotten any." Claro está, no one will sell them to humans, at least not legally, until we disarm the weapons pointing out at the universe. We're stuck with things like the neural patch, which helps with recall and retention – especially when it comes to language – but won't make you any smarter, and doesn't give you anything you haven't already learned the hard way.

"Some of the drugs are spectacular." Jeska points with his empty shot glass. "But there's still a lot of black market stuff that will melt the cells right off your cerebellum. Darcy was too young to have ever met our Uncle Rebo, who burned his brain out on Lotvrek, back when it was still legal on Krom. He wound up in an asylum, and some of my earliest memories include visiting the room where he'd started drawing on the walls, masterful sketches of life inside an insane mind. Sometimes I wished Darcy had seen what that stuff had done to him, then maybe he and Brill wouldn't have gotten caught up trying to sell it."

I down the rest of my shot, glad the alcafuzz is blunting my emotions. "Are you telling me Brill's a drug dealer?"

"Not exactly. Darcy found ten cases of the stuff in Aunt Doreen's basement, and he was so determined to prove he wasn't like me, he'd have sold anything. I'd gotten yelennet haeko – *discovery footed...* the nearest Earth term I know is *gone walkabout*, though yelennet haeko implies more a sense of commercial purpose – for a while, to give him a little distance, and I'd just come back, which made it worse. Brill already had a network of trading contacts, so Darcy talked him into finding a broker, but something went wrong. When the Galactic Inspectors showed up, my little brother pushed Brill out of the ship before it left atmo and drew the pursuit to himself. Your boyfriend had to swim home." Jeska shakes his head at the two guys in the picture. "All that daring, all that pride, all that desire to be a hero. And where did it get either of them?"

"I told you, he's not mi hermoso anymore. You saw him walk out." My heart hurts again just at the thought.

"Well, you were cruel to him. What'd you expect him to do?" Jeska looks at me with irises purple in deep concentration. "It seems like you never really got to know any Krom customs or culture. Why is that?"

I shrug. I've been asking myself that all day. I'm afraid it's because I'm too self-absorbed. "We always wound up talking about history or art or food or Earth. Brill never seemed to get tired of listening to me talk about my planet and my people, but he always got really quiet when I asked about his. He talks about Gavin and Zarak and the rest of his friends like they're his family. Verdad, I thought he was an orphan."

"Hardly. His family's huge." Jeska shakes his head. "He probably never talked about home because he's ashamed of his place in it. Our society has an intricate class system. Brill's the only son in a family with four daughters, and he managed to arrange for one of them to marry Darcy, which was a scandal in itself, but made Darcy dearer to him than a brother. If either Brill or Darcy were to be able to claim a commodity as important as chocolate, then all the girls, including Darcy's widow, would get the kind of dowries that would keep them from having to take dangerous work in the ginadas. His father failed as a trader, so their standing was already extremely low." Jeska rubs a finger across one of his eyes. "I've known Brill since he was a toddler, and he really does believe that if he lives according to his code of honor, everything will work out for the best, but life's been hard on him. I think you are the only good thing he's ever had. Having you not trust him could damage him for a while."

I shake my head. "You still think I should give Brill another chance? Por qué? After you've punched him twice in one day."

"Wal." Jeska pours us each another shot. "One of the reasons he makes me so mad is that he's got so much potential. I can't help but blame him for what happened to Darcy, because as much as my brother wanted to do great things, he wouldn't put in the work to make them happen. If Brill hadn't given him the name of that broker, he never would have gotten it on his own. It's like… makatesalle." There is no translation for that word, and I don't understand the concept, even though

Brill's tried to explain it. I just comprender it is important to the Codex. Jeska continues, "I know it's not exactly a match for Earth logic, but I respect Brill for his work ethic and his loyalty to his friends, even more than I want to punch his face in."

I try to process this, try to see Brill as another Krom sees him, as a balance of beauty and flaws.

"It doesn't matter now whether I still want to be with him. I don't have much of a future with anybody." I drink my shot, wondering if this too is medicinal. I'm definitely tipsy, honestly more dripsy, in the process of crossing that line into drunk, but my lungs don't hurt so much. However, I don't even try to engañar myself that they aren't still weakening. I gesture towards Jeska's desk. "Brill was right about you, though. I told him there was no way you would have taken the cacao. I came up here to ask you for help because I assumed he left with the beans."

His eyes tint toward coral. "I couldn't help it. Murry is a kek. I left him the Squidrider bag, and I don't think he even realizes anything's missing." Jeska twirls the glass in his fingers. "I meant to give the viability box back to you, but the temptation got me. Do you know what would happen if I finally garnered chocolate for Krom? I might wind up with a prosthetic arm, but I could get my life back. I could find a girl who's into redeemed heroes, and have a couple of kids and..." he looks shyly up from half-lidded mint green eyes "... open a restaurant."

I put my shot glass down on the desk and take one of his hands in both of mine. I'm trembling from the venom, but I try to steady myself. "As much as I would love to see you happy, I have to destroy the beans." I squeeze his palm, then hold out my hand for the desk key.

He removes the chain from his neck and lets the key sway back and forth. Then he swings it high enough to loop upward. He catches it in his palm. "Ga, su. I'm not going to let you destroy your only bargaining chip. You and Brill and I need to have a little strategy session. Between the three of us, we may be able to get you out of here alive."

"Brill's gone, remember?" I look away. I speak careful Krom, making sure he understands. "If I don't provide proof those beans are gone too, my mother will be killed. There's not much time. She'll be dead before I am."

He stands up, putting the chain back around his neck, tucking the key away inside his shirt. He crosses his arms over his chest, over the key. "Really, you'd be better off if you let me sell them for you."

I feel the warmth drain from my face. "You wouldn't dare."

"Not without your consent, no. But if you sold the cacao, what good would all the threats be? It'd be out of your hands."

"No, please. Por favor. No." I sound like Meredith, begging for some control over a situation obscenely larger than myself.

"Brill's right, you know? This is all my fault." He gives me a half-smile. "When Krom makes first contact on an isolated world, the inhabitants usually don't even know we've taken anything. If I'd done it right, by the time you went interstellar you'd have been ordering hot chocolate at coffee bars on Maagon and not even wondering where either the coffee or the chocolate came from." He smooths my hair again, that soothing and infuriating sensation. "You're shaking. Do you want me to take you down for some more medicine?"

I close my eyes, not that that hides my anxiety or how sick I am. "No y no. I'll be OK. I've only got a few little hours left to convince you to help me save mi Mamá."

Jeska tilts my face so that I have to look up at him. His eyes are pale yellow. I think he's finally going to kiss me. Instead, he says, "You do realize that Tyson still might not get here in time? Brill could live a couple hundred more years without you. If you don't let him apologize, he's going to spend all that time believing you died hating him. I don't think that's true."

"You saw what happened down there, Jeska. He just left!"

My throat thickens again, so that the last word comes out strangled.

"I think you missed the most important part of that." He stands up. "He left without even mentioning the cacao."

My mouth slides open as I take in that goodbye in a new context. Jeska knew the cacao was safe up here in his desk. He had offered Brill that respectful bow because mi héroe had finally proven he cared more about me than about a commodity.

What I'd accused Brill of is enorme, and I'd had absolutely no proof. And like he'd said, a Krom's sense of honor is important to him. When he had promised me – actually vowed – he was telling me the truth and I hadn't believed him, no wonder he'd decided the relationship was over. I owe him a ginormous lo siento. I groan. I am tonta de remate, *stupid with overkill*, which literally means that if stupid was a soccer ball, mine wouldn't just trickle over the goal line – it'd slam hard into the back of the goal.

CHAPTER EIGHTEEN

When we get back down to the galley, Brill's there, standing next to Plelix, and my heart jolts. They are both chopping zarroxes. Their rough knife skills have me worried that one of them is going to lose a finger.

Brill looks up, his eyes an embarrassed pinkish-apricot. "They're not letting anybody leave until they figure out what went wrong with their engine, so it was either sulk in my ship or hang out with you guys, and you know me. I promise I won't bother you, Ba... Bo. I did bring back a few choice supplies." He points with his knife at a whole box filled with quizllens.

He knows they're my favorites. He has always been thoughtful like that. Pero, I made my choice, and I refuse to cry in front of him now. It doesn't help that I'm still just alcafuzzed enough not to have tight rein on my emotions. I don't think I've ever consumed this much alcohol in one day in my whole life.

Brill holds eye contact with Jeska for a moment. "May I have a word in private? There's something I turned in at the security desk's lost and found when I thought I was leaving that I think you might want." They walk together into the hall. Brill comes back alone.

A few minutes later, Jeska come back, face flushed, sucking in one long draught of air. If he'd been running at full Krom speed, he could have made it down there and back. He gestures Brill toward the pantry.

As soon as they've disappeared inside, the same loudspeaker that had announced the reward on mi cabeza squawks to life. "I am thoroughly sorry for the interruption. Attention all personnel who have been assigned for security, hospitality and catering for our special event. Please meet in the auditorium now for a short briefing."

"Well, that's us." Plelix places his knife down on his cutting board. "Bo, can you finish chopping this?"

"So you trust me with a knife now?"

Plelix opens his gigantic mouth, taken aback for un momento. He runs a hand across that scar on the side of his head. "I guess I do."

Jeska emerges from the pantry holding the bread starter box.

Plelix rushes over and grabs it from him. "It was in the pantry?"

"Something like that." Jeska's eyes go violet. The rest of them just look relieved.

Plelix puts the box on the counter. "I hope this briefing doesn't last too long. We need to get that stuff rising as soon as possible."

As the door closes behind the cooks, Brill brings out two bags of something that could be cake flour, given the cake-shaped logos on the front of them, along with a bag leaking brilliant purple crystals, labeled in Zantite as haraggaha sugar. He says, "I've tasted Zantite food before, and their desserts are weird. I've never seen one involving frosting. Yet, when I told Jess about the cake you were planning to make for your mom, he said that something like that might win you sympathy with Crosskiss. If you want to make it with the fruit I brought, he said this flour could work. What do you think about this sugar?"

"I'm sure it's fine." Tears are forming in my eyes again. I can't stop them. Damn Krom. Charming *and* sweet. "Pero you're going to help me, no? I'm finally going to teach you to cook, if it's the last thing I do."

His smile crumbles at my poor choice of words. "Right. We better get on this quickly, then."

Somebody's already got a couple bricks' worth of white chocolate – that creamy blend of cocoa butter, milk solids and sugar – melted and set aside for something. Qué pena! *Too bad for them.* I snag the bowl. I get Brill started dipping the quizllens, showing him how to get a straight line that shows off the contrast of the teal against the white. I keep looking up at him as he works. Do I have any right now to tell him I've realized that breaking up with him was a mistake?

I remember the first time I saw him, how hot he looked at that party, even though he'd been wearing an old T-shirt and jeans. I know. Mi first hermoso, the shallow soccer player, had been hot, too, and I'd promised myself I'd look deeper after that. There was something more to Brill, even that first night. He'd actually listened to what I had to say, thought about it, and gave honest opinions. I don't think that part was an act.

I think about what Chestla said, how her first love died never knowing she cared for him. My lungs hurt even worse now when I breathe, and trembling is starting to feel normal. I can't deny how much I love this flawed, beautiful guy. I don't want to die without him knowing that, and I'm running out of time to say it. But what if he doesn't feel the same way anymore? I should have known he wouldn't put Mamá in more danger. I hadn't even given him the benefit of the doubt, which you're supposed to do for people you love.

"Mi héroe?" I say hesitantly, not sure if even that pet name is too much.

He looks up. His eyes are sunlight again. "Babe?"

"Lo siento. I didn't accept your apology. I should have believed you."

Brill turns, still holding one of the fruits. It drips a line of white chocolate onto his jacket. "Aw, su." He pops the fruit into his mouth and grabs a towel. He wets it at the sink and starts dabbing at his jacket. "You don't have to say things like that just to be civil." There's still un poco white chocolate on his bottom lip.

I take the towel away. "I mean it. I still love you. Tesuaquenell, no? You carried off half my heart when you walked away."

Before I can lose my nerve, I kiss Brill for the first time since Krevia, tasting the sweetness of the chocolate that brought us together in the first place, hoping I'm not about to be rejected.

His lips sear mine as he kisses me back. He tangles his hands in my hair, and tears spring to my eyes. He's giving me himself again without reservation, despite the fears he's confessed about being hurt, even though I've failed him just as much as he failed me. The contact only lasts about a minute, but it bridges the rift between us.

When he pulls away, I study his face, uncertain, though the tipsy in me has me feeling hopeful. "Are we back together?"

He frowns. "I don't think so. Ga. You were right. You deserve somebody who's not going to hurt you, who understands what you need." He runs a hand through my hair, then lets it fall to his side. "I love you, Babe, but I'm not that guy."

My heart breaks, and it hurts deep inside. "But you're mi héroe. Isn't that enough?"

"I think it would be different if I was still your vida." His eyes are gold, in contrast to his words. "Don't think I'm abandoning you. I'll do my best – with all my might, as these guys say – to get you somewhere safe. And then I'll let you make a life. Without me holding you back."

"Mi vida–" I breathe.

"Don't. That hurts too much." He looks away, down at the floor. "This is hard enough. Jeska explained why I did what I did, but that doesn't excuse it. I knew it was over, back on Krevia, when you shoved me out of that booth. I've just been kidding myself that it wouldn't matter."

I cut my gaze to the pantry. They were only in there for, like, three minutes. "What else did he say?"

"I told him what's in my desk." Jeska comes back in from the hallway, pulling open a red bag. "Crossstitch said I'd better stay here to keep an eye on you. And he gave me these cookies as a reward."

"Isn't that odd?" Brill's still got my lipstick on his face. I gesture for him to wipe it off, which reminds me to put another coat of glossy pink-toned red on my own lips.

"Maybe." Jeska eyes the contents of the bag, pretending like he didn't notice what just happened. "Crossword said Murry got a pay bonus, and he didn't want me to feel like he's been playing favorites since I'm not Zantite."

"Then share. They're probably not as good as Bo's, but I love chocolate chip." Brill snags a cookie.

"Ay, wait. Something's still not adding up here. Don't eat that." I take the bag out of Jeska's hand. Oi! They're *Mrs Field's*. Suddenly feeling stone cold sober, I smack the cookie away from Brill.

"What'd you do that for?" He looks at the cookie, smashed in half on the floor.

"These were processed on Earth. You guys both need to be more careful about what you eat." I flip the bag over and peruse the print on the back. *May contain traces of peanuts, soy and tree nuts.* I point out the text with my finger. "Aren't you both deathly allergic to peanuts?"

Brill goes pale. "Wal. All Krom are."

Happily, I'm not. I fold the bag top closed, setting them aside for later. "I overheard Crosskiss on his handheld specifically asking someone to bring him this brand of cookies. Chocolate's expensive. Cookies exported from Earth are even more expensive. He doesn't seem like the kind of guy to give something like that to the kitchen help. Pero, with a little bit of research, you can find out that most cookie plants on Earth also process peanuts..."

"Are you saying Crosskiss was intentionally trying to kill us?" Brill brushes traces of the offending cookie off his fingers, looking horrified.

"Not you. No y no. He didn't even know you were on board at that point."

"This is ridiculous," Jeska laughs, but it's a nervous sound. "Why would someone as important as Crosshatch be worried about somebody like me?"

"No lo sé." Tension's still knotting my shoulders. That had been such a close call. "I might just be paranoid. He could have just been trying to be nice."

Jeska pokes at the smashed cookie with the toe of his boot. "I don't know which is harder to believe."

I put the Mrs Fields' on the counter and try to heft one of the bags of flour. Oye. I used to tote things like this around the kitchen at school all the time. Now, I barely get the bag off the floor before I have to let it drop. My heart's hammering from the exertion, and I can't seem to get my breathing under control. I try to keep it even enough to speak normally while looking into two pairs of worried Krom eyes. I crashbang miserably, leaving gaps in my words. "I'm sending Brill's phone the choctastic cake recipe. You guys get the ingredients measured and laid out in order while I find a whisk big enough to effectively combine the dry parts. Comprenden?"

Once my back is turned, and I'm rummaging through industrial sized utensils, I send Tyson a quick text. *How far out are you?*

By the time I get the recipe typed, Tyson has replied. *A couple of hours. I don't know how you got the ship stopped, but I'm pink dancetype bubbles about it.* Layla's Pride*'s slippy fast.*

"Grab me some shortening to grease the pans," Jeska tells Brill.

Brill goes back into the pantry. It sounds like he's talking to himself in there. When he comes back out, he isn't holding any food. Instead, he says, "Gavin confirmed the presence of a potential buyer. The guy's not Krom, but it is an alternative to destroying the beans, and does return the legacy for chocolate to Jeska's family, in at least a minor role."

Jeska puts a hand on my shoulder. "Don't worry about how this affects us as you make your decision. I was resigned to living out the rest of my life on this ship anyhow."

Brill nods. "All I want is to see you safe."

I believe him. Now. "Let's say I decide to sell. Which I'm not. Yet." I'm still not sure if that will stop Frank's order. "Who's the buyer?"

Brill holds up his phone. "Gavin's supposed to be sending a picture, but it hasn't come through yet. The guy's one of the ambassadors already on the guest list. I don't have his real name, but he said that we would know him by his feathered hat. Wait. I forgot." He goes back into the pantry.

Jeska takes the chain from around his neck. "Take this. Now that I know that, I don't want to give myself room to give into temptation."

Brill comes out of the pantry again, this time carrying a tub of vegetable fat. "It's not like you'd need a key to get into your own desk, Jess. It didn't trouble you at all getting into Mertex's room."

Jeska palms his key. "I've been working with Murry since he transferred to this ship. That was over two years ago, and this was the first time I've seen anything personal of his. Even after looking at everything he owns, I still haven't figured him out."

"Everybody wants something, chico." I let him pour the chain into my hand. My gaze wanders to Brill. "It's just a matter of figuring out what."

I want him. Only this time, it took me too long to figure it out.

Jeska starts pouring dark flour into a smaller bowl. "Open that, would you?" He points with his chin to the golden box. "But not too close to your face. It reeks."

Brill picks up the box and unstoppers the lid. A bitter yeasty smell reminiscent of month-old gym socks marinating in blue cheese fills the galley. I clap a hand over my nose and try not to gag. If I'm going to be muerta, I'd really prefer not to be tortured first.

Brill holds out the box. "Is this stuff supposed to be moving?"

The surface looks more like white cotton candy than it does any bread starter I've ever seen, almost like someone spread it with a thick layer of cobwebs. It undulates and swells, and just looking at it sends a crawling sensation across my skin. I stare in disgustination as the layer starts cracking apart, and dozens of tiny spiders scuttle out of it, some of them clambering onto Brill's hand. He yelps, and by the time the box hits the floor, he's crouched on the counter, frenetically wiping at his spider-laden arm with his other hand.

The spiders are scurrying away from the mess of starter and web, which is oozing onto the floor. Jeska picks up the box, which landed on its side. "A spider must have laid eggs in here last time we checked to make sure this stuff was still alive. We took on supplies from Earth around then. I think there's enough left to make at least a small loaf."

"But there were spiders in there, su." Brill's still checking his clothes, making sure there aren't any more spiders on him. He's making me feel all itchy.

"Don't tell anybody. Better Garfex eats a few shreds of web than he eats us." Jeska dumps what's left into his bowl, stirs it with the other ingredients and puts a towel over the top.

"But what about the spiders all over the kitchen?" Brill's still crouched next to the cutting boards. I want to laugh. I would feel embarrassed for him, but Krom are so mucho more – no sé what, just *more* – that this weakness makes him seem refreshingly human.

"Don't worry." Jeska pulls a hand-held vacuum from under the counter and starts suctioning up the spiders. After a minute or two, it looks like he's gotten all of them.

Brill's standing beside me, looking like he was never freaking out. I didn't even see him move. He points at the key still looped around my wrist. "Remind me sometime to tell you about when Darcy took his big brother's Argotyen Microharp. We followed Jess around the whole mansion watching him unlock every door and bolthole in the place."

"I think you've just told her," Jeska smiles, looking wistfully off into space, probably remembering little-kid Darcy. "Look, Brill, I'm sorry I hit you. It was just such a shock. Both times." He starts wiping the vegetable fat across the surface of the cake pans. "I've got a fresh bottle of yewstral hidden behind the scouring pads. Any takers?"

Brill looks conflicted, his eyes the deep, dark color of ancient fern leaves. He turns toward me. "If I drink yewstral with him that means he's giving up any claims to a grudge over me selling him. And I have to forgive him for hitting me. And for everything else."

In Krom, there's a color word for almost every shade of emotion, and that concept has bled into English in the form of our blended words. We had a few before first contact, things like cyborg and hangry, but nada like what's available now. I wish I had time to learn all the Krom color words, to comprender why there's a hint of fear and a bit of anticipation mixed into that particular shade.

I put a hand on his arm. "Let's get these cake layers in the oven first, por favor."

We combine the rest of the ingredients and pour the mixture into the prepared pans. Brill slides the layers into the ovens while I stand shakily, unable to lift the batter-filled rounds.

I've never felt so helpless. Nunca. Soon, I'm going to breathe out and not be able to breathe back in again. I've already done it once, and it was the most disturbing moment of my life. Next time, I'm probably not coming back.

I need to focus on something else. Jeska's washing up the dishes, and the noise is tremendous. Softly, I ask Brill, "How come whenever I asked about your familia you always changed the subject? I never knew you had all these... connections."

His eyes go the color of sand. He sighs. "I was trying not to hurt you. My folks – they absolutely do not want to meet you, and I didn't want you to think badly of them, because I love them, and I care what they think."

"Ay." I look away, down at the floor. "So you told them about me?"

In my peripheral vision, I can sense him nodding. "It didn't go well. They watch the news – have done for years." Which means, even if they're ready to get over me being an Earthling, they've seen enough feed to know about my checkered past. "After that, it just seemed easier for you to see them as a blank rather than hostile."

"So that's why you don't want me to go to Krom." I turn toward the cabinet where these Zantites keep the good stemware. "I think we all need that drink, no? I'll get the glasses."

Mertex comes in from the hallway. He must be here for the tray of egg-based appetizer pies going onto the cocktail buffet, pero he's got the oddest look on his face, a determined frown, mixed with an embarrassed green blush and wide, excited eyes. Alarm klaxons start sounding in my head.

I hold out one of the glasses. "Join us for a drink?"

"There's no time for that. Crosskiss asked me to take you to see Doc."

Cold fear spikes through me. What if Crosskiss has decided he wants my heartbeat stopped after all? No. Nunca. I'm supposed to still have more time.

"I'll take her." Brill puts an arm around my shoulders. His hand's trembling. "Later, if it's necessary. She's fine for now."

"Crosskiss asked me to do this personally." Mertex pulls me away from Brill's protection.

Brill's hand goes into his jacket. Before it comes out with his gun, I shake my head. "Por favor, mi héroe." If he kills Mertex, the ship's rules won't protect him anymore. "I'm coming back, right?" My voice sounds overly bright. Inside, I'm quaking.

"I think so." Mertex looks genuinely puzzled. "You still have to help cook."

Brill and Jeska both stand there, watching solemnly. Given the shade of their eyes, I'm surprised neither of them tackles Mertex on our way out.

Mertex pushes me to move faster, but that makes mi cabeza pound so much that after a few steps, I stop entirely. I'm dizzy, and I realize I'm not that far from having to go to Doc's anyway. To let him sedate me until I die. The sheer reality of that takes my breath away.

I rest my hands on my thighs and let my head hang forward. It's not posed, but it gives me the idea to play for sympathy. "Can I have at least some of my stuff back? I've got some pictures of home. Maybe you saw them?"

Mertex smirks at me. "I think I'll just hold onto it all for now. You'll be dead soon enough."

As in as soon as we get to Doc's? Or when the venom inevitably kills me? I try to hide my fear with bluster. "Gracias. You're a real humanitarian."

He gives me a tooth-baring frown. "That's not a proper Zantite word."

"You know what I mean. Besides, I was being sarcastic." I lean against the wall to rest, but find myself sliding down it to a sitting position.

He gets me into the elevator, where we ride in silence, him just looking at me with this half-pleased expression, me trying to get my breathing under control again. When we get out, he picks me up and carries me the rest of the way to Doc's office. Nobody's in the main room, so he sets me on the exam table and looks into the little subchamber. He says something, and

Doc comes out pulling off bloodied gloves. Egah. It's not Zantite blood, but rather from one of the many planets that specialize in arterial red. Doc washes his hands with citrus-scented soap then dries them before turning to us.

Mertex holds out a folded piece of paper with a gold sticker wrapped around the long open edge. "This is what Crosskiss ordered."

Doc takes it and cracks the seal. Why didn't the general send the order electronically? He must not want this traced back to him. Which is alarmante.

I raise an eyebrow at Mertex. "I bet you peeked."

"Of course I peeked. Better you than me."

Fear spikes through my chest.

Doc folds the paper again. "Are you quite certain? He's requesting the injection they give to soldiers going on guvvave missions."

Vave is part of the Zantite word for death. *Guvvave* can't be a good thing.

Mertex makes a flappy gesture toward me with both hands. "He kept her alive so she could help feed the dignitaries. She can't do that if she's complaining that she's about to have a heart attack every five minutes."

I let out an indignant noise. "I have not been complaining."

"Well, you were quite upset when you did have that one heart attack earlier."

"I nearly died, you loco kek." I jump up off the exam table. The room's gotten too quiet. I look around. "Oye, where's Doc?"

"I'm right here." He comes through the door from that little operating room, tapping a capped syringe filled with murky liquid swirled through with tiny flecks of gold.

"What's that?" I back up, bumping into Mertex. My heart, already nearing its limits, starts beating even faster.

"The soldiers like to call it the Invincible Heart. It imparts an incredible sense of wellbeing and vitality. You won't even realize you're sick, and the effects will last for several hours. Perhaps longer. Given your physiology, it's difficult to tell." Doc gestures with his chin, and Mertex lifts me back onto the exam table, then stands in front of me, arms crossed. There's no way I'm going to make it past him into the hall. Nada, nunca, not at all.

My mouth feels like I've swabbed it out with cotton balls. "And then what happens?"

Doc shrugs. "I don't know. If you had a trlkevv gland, the Aurum79 would overstimulate it, then collect inside it and shut it down, and then you'd die, but you don't have such a gland. You may be fine – at least until the venom already in your system kills you – or this injection might end your life immediately. I truly am sorry."

I flinch back. "Then don't make me take it!"

Doc looks sympathetic. "Crosskiss will kill you himself if you refuse his order. Otherwise, he would lose face in front of the corporal here, and me. Not that I matter much. My guess is that your body will metabolize the drug. Consider a few hours of simulated wellbeing a gift." He uncaps the hypodermic.

"You people are all loco." I flip in a backward somersault off the exam table, though my heart squeezes with the exertion, and my vision tries to narrow. There's nowhere to go except the operating room. I slip inside, squeezing my eyes shut as I try to hold the door closed with my body. There's no handle and no lock, so I don't stand a chance against two Zantites trying to push it open. I open my eyes. There's nowhere to hide, nada, not even under the operating table, which stands high on four slim arched legs. Doc's patient's face looks just as human as mine. I do a double-take. Oi! He's not a patient. The man's muerto. A plastic sheet covers the bottom half of him, but above it, his skin's been sliced open and pulled back, his ribs cracked apart. The chest cavity's empty, just sunken raw flesh.

Silent tears start streaming down my cheeks as I stare in horror, unable to keep my body from sliding with the door as it opens. Is this a reverse alien autopsy? Or worse, is Doc a vivisectionist?

Doc himself peeks around the door. He holds out an entreating hand, like I'm a rabid dog. "I realize this is unsettling, Bo. I'd hoped you wouldn't have to see him."

I let out a wordless sound. "Por qué did you kill him, if you're so worried about what I feel? What can human life even mean to someone like you?"

Doc shakes his ginormous head. He smiles, but stays careful not to show me any teeth. "I didn't kill him. He was given to me by pirates. They'd can-openered his ship and were planning to find a quiet spot to jettison him into space."

Brill's right. Being boarded must be terrifying, and then you end up, well, like this. I'm already so weak, I fall to my knees.

"Por qué would pirates bring you a dead guy?"

"In a roundabout way, it was because of your young man. That Brill is a rather charming fellow. You would not believe what he offered me if I could use my contacts – sadly I don't have any – to secure you a dose of antivenin. When I said I couldn't, he spread a wider net of possibilities, and some friends of a friend of a friend of his brought us this cold pilot. They proceeded to implore me to perform wholesale organ transplantation – because they know that to any physician life, be it Zanthe or human or otherwise, deserves respect."

Doc thinks my life is worth something. And yet, he's willing to give me an injection that might end it. I can't process how to feel about that. I nod toward the operating table. "You really did that because you're trying to save me?"

Doc peers into the guy's empty chest. "Trying is the operative word. This person's lungs were severely damaged by the depressurization caused when your would-be benefactors pried open his front door. You may be interested to know, the pirates were human."

"Mn," I squeak, trying not to imagine what Doc must think of my species, how *we* treat life.

His face remains serene. "I've been looking in the databases, and no one seems to have perfected synthetic human lungs – though there was supposedly promising research before your First Contact War. There are just hearts and kidneys. Someone showed up with a set of those, too."

I manage a smile. "Brill has a lot of friends."

"Apparently, so do you. I have the rest of the organs prepared, in case I can think of another solution, but please, don't get your hopes up." He looks down at his boots. "I'm not sure if it would have worked anyway, given my meager abilities and your unfamiliar anatomy."

I start crying in earnest, lost in my own shifting moral bounds. If a man can kill another man to take his ship, then turn around to answer a cry of distress, does that make him a monster or a héroe? A little bit of both? Is that what it means to be human? Or was Brill right, that héroes always strive to do the right thing, even if we sometimes make the wrong judgment calls? If I'm a héroe too, why does everything I do only leave death and complications in its wake?

I don't even realize that Doc has slipped the needle into a vein in my forearm until he pulls it back out.

"Mnph!" I squeak as he slaps a bright yellow adhesive bandage over the spot and pats my hand with such gentle care that I almost expect him to give me a lollipop. I don't feel any different.

Mertex shifts in the doorway. I look up at the sound of his clothes moving. He's just staring at me and Doc kneeling side by side in front of the operating table. I can't read his expression, but if I had to guess, that's respect shining in his eyes. His mouth slides open, half-grin, half-awestruck gape. "The Invincible Heart. How does it feel?"

I shoot him a look. "This stuff may not even work on me, mijo."

Doc helps me to my feet, blocking my view of the table. "Do me a favor, Corporal Makanoc, and cover the body. Her customs are different from ours. We should respect that."

Mertex starts to say something, then looks down at the bandage on my arm. "Of course."

"Wait." I move around Doc and look at the pilot's face. He was still young, maybe thirty, thirty-five at the most, with thick dark hair and a dimple in his chin. "What was his name?"

"Charles Sullivan." Doc nods at a flight jacket folded up on a shelf, which must have contained ID.

I point down at the pale hand resting atop the sheet. "That ring means he was married. If you can't send the body back for burial, I'm sure his wife would appreciate if you at least sent the jacket and the ring. Por favor."

"Why would you assume we would not return him?" His brow wrinkles. "If not to the planet, at least to an embassy."

I blink, confused. "Pero what about that permaplaqued heart?"

"This person's death was not a punishment, nor the result of a duel, so there's no reason to erase his remains. And his body is not past the point of preservation, so there's no need to incinerate anything to protect his family's sensibilities." Doc pats my shoulder. "Besides, we can't exactly send his courage home if you're using his heart."

I can't look at Charles any more. I tilt mi cabeza away, but out of the corner of my eye, I still see Mertex pulling up the sheet.

Mertex escorts me from Doc's office. He can't seem to take his eyes off that yellow bandage.

I push the uniform shirt back down to my wrist. "I think I actually am feeling a little better, no?"

"You'll tell me if it's amazing, right?" His grin shows a few too many teeth, and I take a step away, instinctual panic pounding through my veins. The wattage of that smile dims. "Sorry. I've just never known anybody who…" He lapses into silence, and we walk to the elevator. Once we're in the car, he asks, "If absolutely anything were possible right now, what would you like to do before you, you know, kick off?"

At first I'm sure he's just being cruel, but when I study his face, I believe he really wants to know. "If you're talking selfish wishes, I've got a ton of those. I could eat mi mamá's tortilla soup, go out dancing one last time, or swim in the ocean on Larksis 9 again and touch one of those fish that look like stingrays but transfer endorphins through your skin. If I was home, I'd want to hang out with my sisters and hug my nieces goodbye. But I can't do any of that because I've got to use whatever time I have left to keep other people from dying for my mistakes."

Mertex stares at me.

I have no idea what he's thinking. Finally, I break the eye contact. "What about you? What if you'd been poisoned, and there was a good chance you wouldn't see mañana? How would you spend your last twelve hours or so?"

"I'd have one of those last wish societies arrange a date between me and Minda Frou."

"The Zandywood star?"

"Don't use such an inappropriate, inexact Earth-centric translation." The elevator doors open and he steps out before me. He looks back, and his face softens. "But yes, her. I'd take her to a romantic restaurant and feed her off my fork, and when my time was up, I'd have her sing me to my sleep. You know the song, the one from *Wandering Wild*."

CHAPTER NINETEEN

"Go on in there." Mertex stops outside a door about twenty feet down the hall from the galley. "I have to pee."

This ship is crewed entirely with guys, so there's probably not a ladies' room. Yet, the constant bouts of fear have been wearing on my poor bladder. "I could stand to use the facilities myself, por favor."

"Not these you don't. Use the one up in Jeska's quarters. It'll probably look familiar."

Eeeeg. I don't think I want to know. "Ay! How am I supposed to get into his room?"

"The locks on the crew rooms aren't great. If you push down the handle but pull the door up and to your right, chances are it will pop open."

"En serio? I mean, seriously?"

He puts a hand on his chest. "You think I'd joke about the best way to get information on this ship?"

I laugh. "Aren't you afraid about me running off?"

He makes that hissing splatting sound. "My orders were just to make sure you made it downstairs, and that Doc carried out *his* order. Besides, there's not really anywhere for you to go." He disappears through the door. The hall is empty. I guess everyone else is still in that briefing, and it would be nice to clean up before facing Brill and Jeska again.

I make my way back to the elevator, trying to comprender

Zantite logic. Mertex is treating me like I've become his equal, just by taking an injection. The elevator opens on Jeska's floor. I knock on the door to his room. When neither he nor Varnex answers, I perform Mertex's little trick with the door, and just like he promised, it pops open. I look into the bathroom. These guys may have to share showers in that room down the hall, but at least they have private toilets. On one side there's a cylinder-shaped contraption that I'm hoping belongs to Varnex, and on the other there's a chromed-out device that resembles nothing so much as a hole in the floor with a shelf full of toilet paper above it.

I've primitive camped before, so it's not a problem, except that the thing keeps flushing the whole time I'm near it. Afterwards, I wash my hands with the same scented soap Doc had, which turns out to be an overstock Bath and Body Works product, with a fragrance based on Myer lemon and sea salt. We must really be close to Earth.

I take the key from around my neck. Before I can bring myself to open Jeska's desk, my handheld rings, requesting a full holo. It's Minerva.

I answer it, expecting to look Frank in the face, but it really is Minerva. "Do you like my new doll?"

I can hardly make out the image because she's holding the doll so close to the camera, it's blurry. "It's beautiful, mija. Is that why you called me?"

"Yes. Your mom gave it to me. She said it was from you, too, so I called to thank you."

I smile. "Of course it is. I'm so glad you like it." I can't help but like such a polite niña, even if she is connected to Frank.

"I like your mom a lot. She brought everybody presents, even Grandpa. He's playing with his right now. Want to see?"

I start to say that I'd prefer not to, but she's already running through the house shouting, "Grandpa! Grandpa!"

Frank looks up at the camera from a seat at Mamá's kitchen

table. Her abuelita's antique fruit bowl takes center stage, obscuring whatever he's holding. As Minerva rounds the table, Frank's present comes into view. He's got Mamá's knife sharpening steel in one hand and a squatly triangular dagger in the other. My heart goes cold. Oi! Why'd I have to see that?

From somewhere behind the camera, Minerva says, "Show Bo your present, Grandpa."

Frank smiles at her with what looks like genuine affection. "Why don't you put the handheld on the table, sweetie. Go play with Isabella while us grown-ups talk."

She complies, and suddenly Frank takes up the entire field.

"I take it you got a pequeño gift from Chestla, too, no?"

He nods. Which means Cyberfighter321 is muerto. And I'm still not sure how I feel about that. Frank says, "It will be in her favor, diplomatically speaking, if she's captured alive."

Not that he cares, one way or the other. "Did Mamá really buy you that knife?"

Frank holds up the short blade. "Is that irony? I never can tell what is and what isn't."

"I don't think it matters, viejo."

"She's got superb taste, your mother. This is a museum piece, an actual knight's thrusting dagger circa 1350. The original bearer would have favored this for bursting open links of chain mail, or prying his way through the weak spots in armor. This particular one was said to have belonged to–"

"That's fascinante, pero if it's such a valuable piece, why are you sharpening it?" I refuse to keep listening to him talking about people dying as a result of that blade.

"I think you know why, Bo. People still argue over whether daggers like this were originally used dull, counting on the weight behind them for penetration, but historical accuracy aside, I prefer a razor-sharp blade because it hurts less. Lavonda chose it, so I can't use anything else. I'm ruining the gorgeous patina now, because you're running out of time, and I hate

waiting until the last minute to prepare. Things can get sloppy."
He cringes, as though remembering something that's *gotten
sloppy* in the past. "I wish I could choose a different target – that
brother of yours, perhaps: he's been annoying to me for years
– but I am rarely allowed those kind of decisions."

It hurts to hear him talk that way, but somehow I'm not
feeling the same panic as before. It's just extraño to think about
Frank knowing Mario well enough to be frunoid. "Have you
been watching us all that time?"

Frank shrugs. "On and off. You're just one of my assignments.
But we never did figure out who your father was working for,
or whether your mother might have been a participant. We'd
pretty much given up. When you took up with a traveler of the
Spice Road, they called me back in."

So this Frank crisis only happened because I'm dating Brill? I
refuse to feel guilty about that. "Viejo, if you get proof of death,
then I want proof of life."

"What?" Frank looks confused.

"I want to see that Kaliel's OK, talk to him también. Know
what I'm giving myself up for, no?"

Frank growls. "That could take some doing. I don't have
time for distractions right now."

"So you're saying you couldn't do it?"

Frank laughs. "I see you still have your sense of humor.
Fine. I don't know if it will be in time, but I'll try to arrange it."

Not in time. Meaning he expects proof of my death before he
can manage to get me on the phone with Kaliel. I try not to
think about it. "Where's Mamá right now?"

"She's in the bath, preparing for our date tonight, which I
sincerely hope we get to have."

I still don't get this guy. "Is Minerva really your granddaughter
or is she some kind of miniature superspy? Because you don't
strike me as a grandfather. Lula…" My voice catches. "Lula was
a grandfather."

"My wife died in a car accident the same year you lost your father. I think that's what had me feeling so sentimental at his funeral." One of Frank's eyebrows goes up. "How are you looking better? You've got color in your cheeks, and your face isn't even sweating anymore. You didn't escape from Tyson again, did you?"

"No, Frank." I find myself smiling. I'm feeling better, too. The nausea's disappeared, and my heartbeat has normalized. "Have you ever heard of the Invincible Heart?"

His other eyebrow joins the first. "Are you on Zant?"

"Not exactly. Por favor, Frank, don't do anything rash. I'm muy close to recovering and destroying the cacao." I place the handheld on Jeska's desk and sit on his bunk.

The door pops open and Brill walks in. He sees me on the phone and looks relieved, but stays silent.

Frank splutters out a laugh. "Don't you do anything rash. Do you have any idea what you've shot yourself up with? The few humans who've tried that stuff have become, shall we say, unstable. Of course, the case files I've seen were for muscle-bound space jockeys who weren't exactly rule-followers in the first place, but it's addictive, and even though you don't have the same glands as a Zantite, it will build up in your liver with repeated doses until it kills you just as dead. It happened to every case."

"Stop trying to scare her, Frank." Brill sits on the mattress, far enough away that he's not touching me. "At least now we know that the dose you took isn't going to drop you into a grave. If a Krom took that stuff – well, the heart doesn't explode... exactly. It's one of the commodities even we wouldn't share. We'd catalogue it, given the chance, but..." He shudders. He turns his face towards me, his eyes still gray. "I'm sorry I couldn't get close enough to find out what was going on in there."

I should have known he'd follow me.

"Brill." Frank runs the dagger across the sharpening steel again. "I was hoping to talk to you."

"That's hard to believe, unless you've found a way to introduce my throat to that litoll knife of yours through the holo." He's looking appreciatively at the weapon.

I roll my eyes. "Don't get him started, Brill. It's a dagger, end of story."

Frank tests the needle-like tip of the blade with his finger. "That's a tempting idea, Cray, but not what I had in mind. I've had a word with a couple of HGB botanists, and there's something about those seeds you ought to know before you go trying to sell them. They've been engineered with a suicide gene. Plant them and you may get trees, but those trees will produce sterile seeds. All the viable plants without that gene grow at HGB headquarters in Maui."

I lean toward the holo. "If you're so sure that what we have is worthless, why are you still threatening to kill mi mamá over them?"

"My superiors believe in being sure, as do I." Frank places the dagger on the table. "I learned that from the movies. Did either of you ever see a golden oldie called *Jurassic Park*?"

"Que? You mean the whole life finds a way thing?" I think about that seed bank back in Rio. It looked like someone was collecting samples from any number of trees, most of them not from the authorized strain. I have to stop myself from grabbing Brill's arm to try to telegraph my excitement. What if I stole something that doesn't officially exist? Something not programmed to chococide?

"Frank," Brill says, "none of us can afford to sit here chatting about movies when we're running out of time to find your worthless seeds." He reaches out and hangs up the call. Then he shakes his cabeza at the empty spot where the holo had been. "This whole suicide gene is a bunch of hooey. What if something happened to Maui? One good coating of magma, and chocolate's gone for good." Brill's eyes tinge toward eggplant. "Jeska's a botanist, and Dr Tassiks has a state-of-the-art gene sequencing lab down there." When did Brill see that? I can't imagine where Doc's even hiding another lab. Brill flips my handheld over, so that it looks like an actual chocolate bar. "Between the two of them, they should be able to tell if that engineered gene actually exists."

"It doesn't matter." I open my hand, which has been clutching that tiny key so hard it has left an imprint in my palm. "I have to save mi mamá."

Brill closes his eyes, keeps them closed. "I still think selling is a better option, but I can't guarantee your mother's life."

"Por favor, mi—"

"Do what you have to do, but don't ask me to help." His voice is intense, his eyes unable to settle on a color. "Ga. Can't you see, Babe? It'd be exactly like what got Jeska kicked out of our society. If anyone found out, I'd become just as much of a pariah as he is."

I let his hand go, sudden frustrangeration bubbling up inside me. "Dios mío, Brill! So what if you lose face? We're talking about someone's life. You've got tons of amigos, and half of them aren't even Krom."

His eyes land on a murky gray, and for a moment I think he's going to bolt from the room. "But the Beneficent Ideals state that destroying a contested commodity will only foment continued conflict and could even start a war."

No, no y no! I move to the desk and unlock the drawer. I take out the viability box. He's wrong. I have to destroy this thing. I *want* to destroy it, after all the pain it has caused.

Jeska's got a whole matchbook collection in his desk, from almost as many places as he's got shot glasses. Put that together with the metal laundry bin, and I've got the perfect method of destruction. I cradle one of the matchbooks in my palm. "Haza. Don't help. But if you don't mind, could you at least hold the camera? Por favor. I promise, I won't tell Gavin."

Gavin is so caught up in the Krom way of doing things, the personification of what a "proper" Krom should be. Super strict vegetarian. Puts family above everything. Always looking for the profitable trade. And he and Brill are so close.

Brill's already got my handheld on his lap. He picks it up. Tears glitter in his eyes. "Lo siento, Babe." He wipes the tears away. "I don't care what Gavin thinks. But when those beans burn, that means that I've failed Darcy. There's no way anyone will let me get this close to claiming chocolate again."

"I know you miss him." I feel a pang of sympathy, and I really want to put my arms around Brill. When I had fallen in love with him, I had no clue Darcy even existed. I didn't understand him then at all, and I'm still not sure I do. But like he'd told Frank, you don't have to justify love. You also can't just turn it off.

I pull the empty laundry bin off the bunk and move it into the center of the room, then I grab all the spare toilet paper from the bathroom and pile it into the bin. I light a match and drop it in. "Listo? Are you getting this?"

Brill runs his thumb along the edge of the handheld. He's looking at it, not me. "Wal. I've double checked twice that we're recording. It would kill me if this were all for nothing."

I retrieve the viability box from the desk and point it at the camera. "Here you are, viejo. Mira. Take a good look so that you can verify that all the cacao beans are present and accounted for, por favor. I am going to open the box and dump them all into that flaming bin."

I pop open the first seal, careful to remain in full view of the camera.

There's a hissing noise from above my head, and a mechanized voice says, "Fire detected." I manage to get the seal closed again as a layer of foam cascades from dozens of nozzles set into the ceiling, putting out the toilet paper and covering the carpet, the bunks and both of us.

"Ergaww!" I splutter and drop the viability box as I race toward the bathroom to try to get this stinging stuff out of my eyes. Oi! I slip on the slick floor and have to grab onto the sink for balance, pero I get the tap turned on. I repeatedly splash agua into my face, almost instantly cooling the sting. I blink away excess moisture, and my vision clears. There's a pink and purple shimmer to the foam. As it washes away, the entire inside of the sink retains a layer of glitter flakes.

"Babe, are you OK?" It sounds like Brill's off the bunk, making his way toward me. He's probably also got a face full of foam.

As I turn toward him, now that I can see again, the main door pops open. Jeska's standing in the doorway, so much faster than any human could have gotten there. "What on Zant do you two keks think you're doing? The ship's computer just informed me that my bunk's on fire."

He's wading ankle deep through tiny glittery bubbles, but the foam quickly dissipates into a dry residue, which would be easy to clean away if it wasn't for the glitter. He looks from the bin, with its ashy toilet paper, to the viability box lying upside down on the floor only a couple of feet away. Then he looks at mi héroe, who is still trying to wipe the residue off his face. "What are you trying to do, Brill, get Bo killed?"

He punches Brill, square in the middle of the chest. This time Brill punches him back, lower in the stomach. When he's recovered enough to speak, Brill says, "I didn't deserve that one."

Jeska points a finger in Brill's face. "You know as well as I do what happens to Bo if she goes back to Earth without a bargaining chip."

"And you were the one who told her to do whatever she wants with her property. She knows what's going to happen, too, and she still wants to save her mamá." He says mamá with a Spanish accent. I really am starting to rub off on him.

Jeska's eyes flick toward an angry brown. "Su–"

"Enough!" I find myself jumping between them, pushing them apart before they can start hitting each other again. They both stare at me, shocked.

Jeska puts a hand on his chest where maybe I shoved him harder than I'd intended. "Shtesh. What happened to you?"

Brill's irises have gone black, and I think that this time, maybe, he's scared of me. "Dr Tassiks gave her a rage drug at General Crosskiss's request. Perhaps we should speak more softly until she learns how to control it."

I start to get indignant at the implication that I've got no self-control, but as Brill's words sink in, I realize he's right. "Lo siento, chicos. I didn't even realize the Invincible Heart had started working."

Jeska smiles. It looks genuine. "Not your fault." His eyes go purple and his smile broadens out into a straight line. "They give that particular cocktail to guys who've volunteered for suicide missions. Any idea what Crosskiss is planning to make you do?"

I shake my head. "That's bad, no?"

"One problem at a time," Jeska sighs. "You two should have at least waited until we'd finished the conversation Murry interrupted. There's got to be another way, one that doesn't involve selling out what each of you believes in."

Brill looks down at the viability box, so close to my would-be fire, and shame flames into his eyes. "I'm not guilty of wevdaglarin. I didn't try to stop her, but all I did was hold her camera."

Jeska picks up the viability box. "That's between you and your conscience. I'm the last person who'd level a charge against you."

Shame creeps into me, too, also magnified by the drug. I'd been so focused on Mamá, I never considered that Brill's values mean just as much to him as mine do to me, that crashbanging in his quest to save Darcy's honor might break him. The disappointed look Jeska gives me only reinforces that thought. Ay. I flip my hair back, which just specks glitter onto my face again. I paste on a smile. "Now you chicos can put your skills together and help me find another way to destroy those beans before Frank decides to put his dagger through mi mamá's heart."

"Let's think for a second." Jeska tries to brush away some of the glitter covering his bunk, pero he only succeeds in stirring it around. "What else could we do from here to rescue someone on Earth?"

I say, "Lo siento about the glitter. Why would Zantites even put that stuff in fire extinguishers?"

"They don't." Jeska's eyes go violet for a moment, despite the seriousness of the situation. "V and I are the latest victims of the practical joke war. You may have noticed the doors to the crew rooms don't lock effectively."

"I could call some of my friends." Brill sounds muffled because he's got the agua running in the sink, trying to wash glitter out of his hair. "See if anybody knows somebody on Earth right now who's close enough to perform an extraction."

I hesitate, a sudden image of Sullivan's stilled face, his soft eyelashes nearly brushing his chalky cheeks, filling mi cabeza as stark evidence of some of Brill's network of friends' other handiwork. I don't want anything to do with that kind of people. And yet, Brill's promised me that his closest friends aren't like that – that he's not like that. And sí, Gavin's a dork, and Zarak can't seem to remember my name, but neither of them seem cruel. I can't fix this on my own, and Brill deeply needs to help me, to cancel out his guilt for the fact that I'm dying.

"Sí. Por favor. And I'll try calling my brother, and a couple of *my* old amigas." I picture Mario's skeptical look the last time

I'd been at his house. It will take a bit of doing to convince him Frank is dangerous, but I have to at least try. I'll have to tell him what I've done, but what good is the Invincible Heart if I'm still afraid to be honest with mi own hermano? "He needs to get over there pronto and start to fill the house with people." Still, I can't be completely honest. I can't tell mi hermano that Frank killed Papá. Knowing Mario, he might try for revenge and get himself killed too. "The hardest part for your amigos will be convincing Mamá she needs to walk out on an engagement party that's going to look like Frank's idea. We're going to need a cake." I suck in a breath. "Ay, no. My cake layers! They must be burning to a crisp by now."

"I took them out before I came up here." Jeska sits down on his bunk, despite the glitter. "Don't worry. They're cooling on the counter. They're perfect."

"Just like you, Babe." Trust Brill, even having broken up with me, to be just cheesy enough to make me laugh. He's still trying to brush sparkles off his jacket.

"This can't be your first experience with glitter, right?" I shake my head. "I can't believe you grew up with four sisters."

He makes a face. "Why do you think I spent so much time at Jeska's house?"

CHAPTER TWENTY

Jeska investigates the contents of the boxes full of booze. With an approving little smile, he pulls out several bottles then grabs the más grande ice bucket I've ever seen.

Plelix pulls a swirled-green glass bowl from the crowded bottom shelf of a two-tiered rolling cart and washes dust off it.

My handheld rings. It's Frank, and my heart drops. "Now what, viejo?"

"So I couldn't get you an actual call, but this is the security feed from his cell." Frank pops it up, and there's Kaliel, sitting at a desk, reading a paper book. Which makes sense, if they took all his electronics. He doesn't look hurt, just bored. And tension deep in my stomach releases.

I take a deep, clear breath, and feel bad for rudely referring to Frank as *old man*. "Gracias, Frank. I mean that."

"Don't spend too long watching this, Bo." Frank disconnects before I can draw him into conversation, but he leaves me tapped into the feed.

A guard comes into view at the corner of the cell. "Visitor."

Kaliel looks startled. "Is it that lawyer again?"

The guard leers. "It's a girl. Nice legs, too."

Now Kaliel looks disgusted. But he follows the guard – and the feed follows him – down the hall, to a small room where there are two chairs and a coffee table. The guard waits at the door.

Kaliel looks startled again, and when the camera gets close enough, the girl turns out to be Kayla. She's wearing that slouchy, green knit brimmed hat she always favors, because she hates her unruly curly hair. Heat bites at the back of my eyes. I'm just so proud of her for being there.

Kaliel gestures at the table. "You chose the room without the partitions, Miss Baker?"

I didn't realize he even knew who she was.

"I'm not afraid of you." Kayla's got her phone in her hands, fiddling with the screen, even though it's off, a sure sign that she's nervous. "Bo asked me to come. She seemed to think it will help me find closure."

Kaliel nods. "I can see that." He manages a sad smile, which is incredibly sexy, despite the circumstances. "Does that mean you'll be coming to my execution, too? It'd be nice to at least have a familiar face out in the audience."

Her eyes go wide. The fiddling stops. "Even someone who hates you?"

"Even so. If my death brings you peace, by all means watch." He looks down at the floor. "My parents have already said they're not coming, so I'm going out on that stage alone."

"You say that like the sentence has already been passed."

"It might as well have been."

My heart squeezes. His reprieve has to be enough, even though he may never know what I gave up for him.

Kayla tilts her head. "Bo seems to think there's some reason for you to have hope."

Kaliel smiles, and it's more real than the last time. "If I live, will that ruin your sense of closure?"

Kayla studies him for a long time. "Now that I've met you, I don't know anymore. You were this huge specter in my nightmares, but you're shorter in person. I still think it would be justice. But I'd have to be completely heartless to actually want to watch you die."

He tilts his head. "You could always close your eyes."

She laughs. "This feels like Bo's set us up on some kind of demented first date. I don't even know what to talk about."

"Please. Talk about anything you want, or they'll make me go back to my cell." He sighs. "That sounded desperate. Look, I'm guessing that whole seeing me as a person thing is Bo's point." Kaliel sits down. "So what do you want to know?"

Kayla arches an eyebrow at him. "They just announced your trial's been pushed back two months."

"So my lawyer says. I don't get it." He puts a hand on the arm of her chair. "I can't tell you why."

Kayla shakes her head. "I don't care about the why. I want to know – what are you going to do with the time?"

"Finish as many of the books on my TBR list as I can." He shrugs. "What else can I do from in here?"

Kayla smiles. "I read a lot myself. Maybe I can get hard copies of a few of my favorites."

Jeska leans toward the holofield. "What are you watching?"

I look up at him. "Proof that my best amiga is more awesome than I thought."

Jeska motions to the stacked cocktail glasses on the top shelf of the cart. They're a variety of sizes, to accommodate the different guests. "Most of those haven't been used in a long time. Would you mind giving them a polish?"

"Sí. Sure." After one last look at Kaliel's handsome face, I close the connection.

I start wiping out dozens of glasses. After a few minutes, I realize I've cleaned the same glass three times. I can't help it – most of my brain's busy flashing through moments with Kaliel. I wish Frank hadn't brought him to mind – even though I'd been the one who asked. I sidle over to Brill. "What if Frank talks them into canceling Kaliel's reprieve? If our plan works, he's going to be mad that we've outsmarted him, and that may be the only way he can get back at me."

"Even if he could do that – and it'd be hard for him to call in a whole set of favors to recall favors he's already called – your precious pilot's still got a couple of days. That's long enough for whatever's going to happen up here to play all the way out."

My precious pilot. Brill's still jealous.

My muscles feel tight, like overwound springs. I need to move. I need release. Out in that hallway, it sounds like they're kicking up for a doozy fiesta, the delegates laughing, grunting, gibbering, burbling as they pass our door. Plelix taps a button inside the edge of the outgoing serving window, and the whole thing becomes a screen. He taps the up arrow at the edge of the screen to get it to the right channel. After a long moment, the arrow disappears.

We all gather around the image to watch the delegates peering at the little holographic namecards, settling at their assigned tables. Mertex winds up standing at my right elbow. He smells like mothballs. It even overpowers the unpleasant odor of the ceremonial bread baking in one of the ovens.

I wrinkle my nose and try to edge away. "Guácala! Was your dress uniform in storage?"

He pulls a string of plastic-covered spheres out from under his shirt collar. "A lot of us wear moth necklaces during missions that aren't likely to go well. The smell tends to deter summary execution, especially if you crack one of the beads open and smear it on your face."

"Cowards wear them," Plelix mutters, but Mertex acts like he didn't hear. Plelix's frown looks fierce, and his biceps bulge as his hands clench into fists at his sides. "He's saying he has no confidence in my command. Those 'moth balls,'" he says the relevant words in hard-edged English, "don't even contain the Earth chemicals that make them poisonous, just wax and fragrance."

Jeska laughs. Mertex glares at the Krom. Not wanting to wind up in the middle of that, I keep my eyes on the screen.

The conference ballroom has been transformed into a *mundo maravilloso* of white tulle and crystal. Tall silver vases with live plants cascading out of them stand at intervals against the walls. There's a hunormous display of chocolate bars near the tables set up for the buffet. Only about a dozen of the ambassadors are Zantite. One guy has stubby tusks protruding from the corners of his mouth. And I'm pretty sure that the lady with her back to me isn't wearing a complicated gossamer cloak. Those are wings. Two thirds of the people in that room are wearing feathered hats or headdresses. I shoot Brill a look. I'll know his buyer by the feathered hat, eh?

He shrugs and makes a *don't blame me* gesture with his hands.

I get a message from Kayla. *I thought a lot about what you said, so I stuck around to meet Kaliel.*

It feels *extraño* to tell her I watched part of that interaction. I type back all the things I couldn't ask Kaliel through that one-way holo. *Did they really push back his trial? How is he holding up? Did he keep his promise to lay off the beer?*

Her reply comes almost immediately. *One question at a time. You were right. Kaliel's not what I thought. I can see why you kissed him.*

I glance over at Brill and feel heat come into my cheeks at this reminder of my betrayal, my contribution to our relationship meltdown. *I've got no claims on the flying dork, KayKay. Kiss him yourself if you want to. Only, would you mind not bringing him up next time you see Brill?*

Claro está, the next time they're likely to be in the same room is at my funeral.

"You see the guy just coming in the door?" Mertex points, and his arm comes uncomfortably close to brushing mine.

I nod. "Sí. He'd be hard to miss."

Not that the guy's tall – he's short for a Zantite. Pero, he's wearing a thin crown and an orange tunic over beige trousers, a combination that makes him look like a large, moving piece of fruit. A jeweled cloth-of-gold cape is drawn up in swirls about his shoulders. The cape's bottom just brushes the floor as he moves.

"That's King Garfex." Mertex shifts slightly, and his arm does touch mine. We both jerk away. "The woman that just put her hand on his shoulder is Queen Layla."

She's much taller than the king. Light seems to gather to her bald head, which is adorned by a jeweled circlet. A sapphire four times the size of my thumbnail dangles onto her forehead. Her silver and white dress covers her from her neck to her ankles, yet something about the way she stands makes it seem quite revealing. It's like they put together the décor in the ballroom just for her. Maybe they did.

It's probably the way the Invincible Heart keeps intensifying everything, but it's like I'm six again, and Layla's Cinderella. "Vaya! They sure know how to enter a room."

"They do at that." Varnex pushes himself between Mertex and me. I can't decide if he's doing it for my sake, or if he just wants a better view. He's still got splatters of chocolate on his sleeves from filling the mold for the sculpture, which he left to settle before freezing. Varnex smiles down at me. I grin back, not even caring that he's showing his teeth again. Is that because of how much I have come to like these guys, or just the drug? No lo sé. He chatters on. "They're supposed to represent the highest Zantite virtues, but a lot of people just don't like the royal couple."

"No? Why not?" I watch Garfex and Layla move through the crowd, shaking hands, laughing at jokes. They're surrounded by half a dozen similarly dressed courtiers. "They seem nice enough. He reminds me un poco of my Abuelo Jorge."

"The king's rule is absolute, and sometimes the laws he makes are arbitrary." Varnex makes a slashing motion across his throat. "If he decides he doesn't like you…"

Mertex rolls his eyes. "Don't listen to him. It's nothing like that."

"It is so. Sometimes." Varnex pushes his lower teeth out in a double-rowed Zantite pout.

One of Garfex's attendants drops a golden cup, which spills fizzing blue liquid on the king's boot. Garfex says something. The attendant shakes his head. Garfex lashes out and bites off the guy's arm.

I gasp, trying to make my brain process that that really just happened, while my stomach flips over without questioning it. The guy looks down in dismay, his face creasing with pain as he wraps his own cloak around the injury and swiftly leaves the camera's range.

The need in my muscles intensifies, demanding to run, though I can't decide if my legs are telling me to flee for the docking bay or to dash into that room and save the injured Zantite. Neither makes logical sense, so I try to quiet the trembling in my calves without anyone noticing.

"Don't worry. He's not going to bleed to death. When we get injured, it heals over fast. There are more prosthetics on this ship than you'd guess." Varnex switches back to his previous train of thought like nothing's happened. "A lot of people are disappointed that there isn't a royal heir. Some say Layla refuses to have a child because she's concerned about her figure."

I'm still trying to process what happened with the guy who got his arm bit off. I mean, en serio? Hoping for a safer subject, I ask, "So who's the lady with the wings?"

Varnex peers at the screen, blinking. "Who?"

Mertex snorts. "She's talking about Admiral Alabaster. Don't let him hear you called him a lady."

"Eh?" I take a closer look. No y no. Still looks like a woman to me, what with the curly long white-blond hair and the swively outward-pointed hips. The admiral half-turns towards the camera, looking down his long, curved nose at someone who's just called his name. You could almost call that nose a proboscis, pero he's got a mouth too, complete with a white-blond handlebar mustache.

"Come on, you guys." Plelix taps the counter. "We've still got a lot to do."

Kayla's sent me a text, with an attached MegaGalactica holo. Feeling slightly guilty, I move into the freezer to take a quick look. She's said, *Look Bo! I'm all over the feeds.*

In the holo, two reporters, one a Myska like Tyson, the other a tentacled blob with a ginormous head are sitting at a desk, speaking crisp Universal. The Myska says, "It may be too little too late, and people are already calling te feed a hoax, or a media spin attempt, claiming te guard in question was bribed by Johansson's lawyers. What do you tink Feddoink?"

Feddoink replies, "It doesn't matter whether it's real or not, Blizzard. I don't think Earth's courts will be swayed by an act of kindness committed by a prisoner who knows he's being filmed. It may not be a game-changer for the pilot, but it certainly is a legendary bit of holo. What do you think, folks?"

The image switches to the prison, where Kaliel and Kayla are still talking, but this is a different camera. They're in the background. The focus is on the guard standing in the doorway. Something happens to the lights – the holo slows down here, giving us representative frames along with the subtitle *lights flashing at a frequency known to cause seizures in susceptible Earthlings.* The guard groans, then pukes, then starts to twitch.

From off camera, a voice says, "It worked! Let's get out of here!"

From doorways at the far side of the room – apparently the areas with the partitions – six people, three in prison orange, three in street clothes, emerge and step over the seizing guard.

"Come on Johannsen," one of them calls back. "Escape the shave."

The voices are not matching up with the screen-shotted video. Pero, a few of the stills show Kaliel running. I suck in a breath. Ay, he said he'd never do that.

Kaliel's rush towards the door stops at the light switch. He drops the room into shadow, but the camera's emitting a spotlight bright enough to show grainy figures, moving in real time. Kaliel kneels by the guard, who hit his cabeza on the bottom corner of the door frame when he went down. "Give me your sweater. His scalp's bleeding bad."

Kayla's still standing in the middle of the room, a hand over her mouth. The guard starts seizing again.

"Kayla!" Kaliel's trying to get the guard turned onto his side.

She takes off the cap-sleeved cardigan and moves to help him turn the flailing man over. "Why didn't you go with them?"

"Because I don't want to be a fugitive for the rest of my life. Because I don't want to die at the end of some bounty hunter's gun barrel." The guard stops seizing. Kaliel sticks two fingers into his mouth, clearing it of saliva and sick. Then he balls up the sweater and presses it against the guy's head. He moves Kayla's hands to hold it in place. The audio catches a groan. Kaliel looks down with compassion, then hardens his gaze as he looks back at Kayla. "I want to see the end with honor."

Kayla's eyes are huge, her lips parted as she watches him rip the sleeve off his own jumpsuit and use it to wipe the guard's face. "You know, I really don't think I could watch your shave after all."

The commentators are back. Feddolnk says, "Of course, the other prisoners were captured. But if they were already scheduled for a shave, it doesn't matter. As the Zantites say, they can only execute you once."

The commentators are laughing. I cut the holo off. It's not funny. No. And it's damn cold in here. So I join the others and try to find a way to actually be helpful.

Jeska picks up three different sized shot glasses, which he uses to deftly fill the bottom of the cocktail glasses with three different types of alcohol. Brill adds ice and a fizzy mixer to take up the extra space. He also fills stemmed wine glasses with Pandozale – trust him to bring the best – and places them in a ring around the squat Zantite-sized cocktails on the first tray. Plelix takes that tray out, and they continue the process.

Jeska hefts the third tray, filled with mostly smaller glasses, balancing it easily on one palm, gesturing at me with the other hand. "I'll carry, you serve, and we can leave Brill back here playing bartender. Follow my cues. We need to placate these people in order of importance."

"Bueno." I turn to follow him.

Brill tugs at my sleeve and whispers, "Don't forget to look for Gavin's buyer."

When we enter the ballroom, Plelix is already standing in front of the stage where Garfex has set up court. One of the courtiers takes a cocktail from his tray. The guy who lost the arm returns, standing off to the side with a fresh cloak swirled strategically to hide the injury. He's holding a spray bottle which he spritzes onto the King's cabeza to reduce shine, then he ducks back against the wall, out of Garfex's line of sight.

"Don't say anything to Alabaster if you can help it." Jeska moves us toward the Admiral, who is in animated conversation with a green-faced being that looks like a humanoid-ish booger with a round face and hard, beaky lips. That mouth reminds me of Noodles, which reminds me of Larksis and Chestla and everything I left behind. A completely different form of *saudade* washes over me, this one filled with homesickness and swaying palms.

Beak-guy blinks oversized eyes, brushing long lashes made of something more like fiber optics than hair against his cheeks, and I shiver, momentarily picturing the dead pilot lying butchered in Doc's office.

His clothing is fashioned from shells that shimmer like mother of pearl. The body of his jacket is carved from a single shell, the swirled tip creating a slight hump on his back. The joins in the garments and the gloves covering his slender hands are made of stiff golden cloth, as is his crown. All that beauty brings to mind Meredith, in the glory of her last moments of life.

Muerte y muerte y muerte. I can't shake the sudden feeling that this guy's going to die. I want to warn him. But that's estúpido, no?

"Greetings and salutations. How is everything tonight, admiral?" Jeska's question sounds innocent enough, but the admiral tenses his shoulders so much that his wings flutter out.

He twists the strands of his mustache with one hand before answering. "Fine."

Jeska attempts an awkward curtsey while holding the tray out in front of him, which would be hilarious if he didn't look so nervous. The way the admiral's legs bend, I can see why a curtsey might come more readily in his culture than a bow. Jeska's rendition, however, is just awful. "I'm so glad you are enjoying this event."

I curtsey too. This guy doesn't look muy dangerous – he might weigh all of seventy pounds – but a bead of sweat rolls down Jeska's cheek.

"Might I say, admiral," Jeska says, "your mustache is looking thicker and more youthful than ever."

Alabaster twirls the handlebar again. "Thank you. We were briefly allied with the group from Ellum 5 that had established the colony at Farder. The spas there were quite enjoyable. The loss of the bread made from the fountain of youth plant has saddened me greatly. But the people. That was the greatest tragedy."

"I am thoroughly sorry for your loss," I say softly.

Alabaster sniffs as he takes a glass from my hand, the sound amplified through his fantástica nose. "I am still suffering greatly for my ally. And then I boarded this ship, where I have been insulted of course."

"Of course." Jeska leans forward sympathetically. "In what way?"

I look at the shell guy, who's pointedly not listening to the conversation.

Alabaster says, "First by being kept waiting to dock my ship and then almost continually since I have arrived. The final straw was being seated at this table."

Jeska makes a sympathetic, "Mmmmmmhhh," noise.

I must look confused because Alabaster smiles straight at me. "You must understand that there has been an ancient conflict between my people and the people of Lord Zfffrrrt here for centuries." He twitches a shoulder in the direction of the shell guy. "I have not continued the conflict this day because I promised my wife I wouldn't kill anybody on this trip. So while I might otherwise vent my anger at this insult, I would not break such a promise to one so dear to me."

Zfffrrrt says something softly in his near-buzzing language. He shakes his head when I offer him a drink.

Jeska translates. "He said, 'We have been having a rather pleasant conversation, actually.'"

We move on around the table. As I pass back towards Alabaster, he grabs my arm. Ay! His hand pinches, but doesn't really hurt. I freeze.

Alabaster lets out a breath that puffs up his mustache. "Young miss, my sense of honor demands I inform you that you have been insulted too."

Instinct says to pull away from him, but his ridged fingers might cut me. I choose my words in Universal Standard carefully. "What do you mean?"

He blinks up at me. "Are you not of Earth?"

"I am."

"Then perhaps you should ask yourself the purpose of this conference." With that, he releases me and glares venomously at Lord Zfffrrrt. "Pleasant conversation? Next time, say intriguing or brilliant."

As soon as I'm reasonably sure we're out of earshot, I whisper to Jeska, "OK, that was weird, chico. What *is* this conference about?"

"I don't know. I wasn't invited to the briefing, remember?"

I cut a glance at Crosskiss sitting over near the king's court. He's laughing at something the delegate with the tusks has just said, but he notices me watching. His brown eyes go predator cold, sending a shiver down my spine. I'd usually flee for the galley in the face of such hostility, but something in my brain – or perhaps something that came out of Doc's needle – angerzents it. No lo sé what's in the glare I give back, pero Crosskiss's face takes on the barest hint of green, and he looks down at the table.

Ay, no! I don't want to be on the wrong side of Crosskiss's need to feel he has the upper hand. And now he's going to be watching me more closely. I still need to get more information on what's going on here. I nudge Jeska. "Take me over toward that display, por favor."

We work our way in the direction of the mountain of chocolate bars. The drinks run out before we get there, but Jeska trades trays with Varnex. I can still feel Crosskiss watching me. I do my best to put Jeska between me and his line of sight, and I turn my hip toward the wall when I draw out my handheld. I never thought I'd be happy Mamá bought me this kiddie phone, but it looks enough like a chocolate bar that I can nestle it into the real things. I set the holo to record constantly, then pick up the last glass of Pandozale from the tray and offer it to the nearest delegate, a Zantite female who has an unfortunate tendency to talk with her hands. Before she notices me, she finishes up a story about some restaurant where the fish entrée was "this big."

She flings her hand at the glass, which shatters, spraying

the ultra-expensive wine all over me and the delegate next to her. The confettiglass sparkles harmlessly to the floor, but the delegate stands, wiping Pandozale off his tie, which is made of an iridescent waterproof material. His white shirt and jacket are ruined.

"Hey! You did that on purpose." He's not looking at the flighty Zantite. He's looking at me.

"I assure you it was an accident." I try to remember the Zantite words for a formal lo siento. "I apologize thoroughly, sir."

"Sir?" The delegate turns. "Don't you mean madam?"

Jeska winces. He drops his tray and rushes to step between me and the angry delegate. He bows, hands in fists at his side. "Our deepest regrets are yours forever, Madam Empress."

I look over at Crosskiss, and he's smiling, like he's just won something litoll. Despite the IH, my stomach turns leaden as my chest fills with ice. The king tore the arm off one of his own courtiers for spilling a cup on his shoes. What will he do with a stowaway who just insulted a foreign dignitary?

I glance at the king. He makes a come-here gesture at Crosskiss, who then approaches the stage. They exchange a few words, then Crosskiss looks over at me. I'd swear he's ready to blow me a beso. Damn. That can't be good.

Crosskiss moves to the side, and the one-armed courtier steps forward. "The king will retire from the party for a few moments to resolve this breach of conduct privately. He apologizes thoroughly for the interruption."

Crosskiss is already moving toward me. I glance at Jeska, who looks horror-struck.

I put my hand on his arm, trying to sound upbeat. "Come on, diplomat. Help me talk my way out of this one."

Jeska's eyes have gone onyx. He addresses Crosskiss. "I apologize thoroughly, sir, but I humbly request to accompany this female into the interrogation room. I fully understand that I may as a result share in her fate. I have no complaints."

Crosskiss looks back at Garfex, who downs his glass of Pandozale. "What difference does it make?"

To Jeska, I'm sure it makes a lot of difference. And his muerte will be on my conscience. When Crosskiss puts a hand on my shoulder, I push it away. "I can walk by myself!"

Where did the strength to do that come from?

Crosskiss looks surprised, too. He whispers, "You are taking well to the Invincible Heart." Then he gives Garfex an odd look. I still haven't figured out his game here. Why hype me up for a suicide mission, then march me out to be executed?

Jeska walks out in front as we make our way down the empty hall. He obviously knows where we're going, but he doesn't seem to be in any hurry to get there.

"Pick up the pace, corporal," Crosskiss orders.

"Garfex won't be ready to receive us for a while." Jeska looks back at me, not the general. There's sympathy mixed with affection in his amber eyes. "There's no need to rush."

"Are you being insubordinate as well, Hayat? Don't you care that you have at least a chance to survive after being so impulsively gallant? I understand this tiny person is considered attractive for your respective species, but you won't be spending any private time with her once she's dead."

Jeska turns away, pero I catch his eyes changing toward brown. "That has nothing to do with it, sir. She already has a boyfriend."

Por qué can't Jeska get it through his head that Brill's given up any claim on me? It's annoying that he thinks he knows something we don't.

"Ah, yes," Crosskiss says. "The pirate who won't go back to his ship."

We pass the door leading back into the galley. Brill's still in there. I'd almost forgotten about his ship. If we can manage to make it past the guards, we could rendezvous with Tyson somewhere on his intercept course. We'd be giving up the cacao, verdadero, but it's not like I'm going to get a chance to destroy it anyway if Garfex chompcrushes me.

I reverse direction and fake my way back past Crosskiss, ducking through the galley door, slamming it shut behind me. Brill looks up, so startled he drops the bottle in his hand. Moving blur fast, he catches it again before it hits the floor. "Babe?"

I barrel past him, grabbing his hand. If we can get into the mess hall, we can escape. Varnex told me that door on the far side of the blast freezer leads down to the trash and recycling chutes. If we take the recycling one, we should wind up inside the docking bay. "Help me get off this ship!"

I pry at the service window, and Brill's hand is next to mine, helping me work the latch. "La, I've been waiting for you to say that. I promise I won't kill any guards. I think I can override the lockdown mechanisms and–"

"Halt, stowaway!" Crosskiss opens the door, not moving hurriedly. There's a vapgun in his hand. I freeze, though there's more angerzentment bubbling inside me than fear.

Brill's gun is in his hand, so fast I didn't even see him move. "Who do you think will be able to fire first, su?"

Crosskiss hesitates. I slide the window up. Brill pushes me, and we tumble through to where Mertex is wiping down tables and clearing away the debris from the crew's lunch. The mold of the royal couple still rests outside the prepped blast freezer. I inhale the velvety decadence of liquid chocolate as I race toward that little door on the far side, nearly overwhelming my heightened senses. Ay, I brush against the filled mold, but I'm far too light to tip it over.

"Stop them, Corporal Makanoc!" Crosskiss shouts.

I cut a glance at Mertex. Despite the new respect he'd shown me in the hallway, he doesn't hesitate to follow his commander's order, advancing menacingly toward us.

Brill skids to a halt. "Bo!"

I stop, too. Before I even see him move, the key fob to his ship comes flying into my hands, and he's drawn his gun again. "I love you, Babe!"

He wants me to take his ship, the closest thing he has to a home, and run. My legs want to flitdash, but I can't do it. I can't leave him. No y no. I can't breathe either.

Mertex makes that car-shattering siren-like wail again. He rushes Brill, who fires. Mertex goes silent as the smell of moth balls intensifies in the air, but he doesn't even slow down. I doubt one of those plastic beads could have stopped a bullet, pero who knows what was in his shirt pocket. He grabs the barrel of the gun and twists it back around towards mi héroe. It goes off again. My heart freezes. No. Y no. I scream.

It takes a heartbeat before I realize there's a hole in the wall separating the mess hall from the storage spaces beyond it, not in Brill's head.

Brill ducks, wrenching the gun away from Mertex. He turns to look at me, his eyes pure onyx. He looks disappointed that I haven't moved, and that, more than anything else, hurts my heart. He tries to dash towards me, pero Mertex grabs him around the middle, one hand on each side. Eso es imposible. My chest tingles, and my brain feels all swimmy, like it's loaded holonique. How did Mertex catch a Krom? Cómo? He must have anticipated how Brill would dodge, making mi héroe run into him. Mertex lifts Brill off the ground.

"Oye! Stop!" Nobody's listening to me, least of all Mertex.

Brill tries to fight him, kicking backward at his shins, but he hasn't got the angle or the leverage. He gets the gun pointed down and shoots Mertex in the foot. Rather than let him go, Mertex lets out this extraño hiss and throws him upside down into the mold, gun and all. Brill's calves and feet stick up out of the viscous liquid, but they tense, jerking once before he stops struggling and starts to sink more evenly. I gasp. Ay, nooooooooo! He must have hit his head.

"Brill!" I rush forward as Mertex limps over and presses the button on the freezer. The mold starts rolling along the track, heading inside. Icy cold dread blazebangs through my stomach, moments later replaced by caliente anger. I pick up the oversized spatula still leaning against the wall and wave it menacingly at Mertex. "Mira, tonto idiota! You turn that off!"

He takes a step back. "That'd be kind of hard, Bo, with you swatting at me like that."

"Then get out of my way!" The stuff that Doc shot into my veins has been building me up to a boiling heat, and the thought that Mertex could so casually dispatch Brill after that moment of connection Murry and I had shared in the hallway bubbles me over. I can't even form words, just noise, as I rush at him with the flat end of the spatula swinging like a scythe. Mertex dodges out of the way, but I catch the edge of his arm, drawing thick blue blood. I don't even care. He scrambles under one of the dining tables.

I punch the red button and the door to the blast freezer stops halfway down.

Mertex comes back out, holds his hands up, takes a cautious step towards me. "Bo, you can't save–"

The hell I can't.

"You still want to know what the Invincible Heart feels like?" I charge at Mertex, the spatula straight out in front of me, intent on incapacitating him, though to be honest, the IH has unleashed the part of me that wants him muerto for hurting Brill. A solid blow may well cut him in half, and we both know it. His eyes go wide, and he backpedals. The fear in his face touches something inside me, something muy human. I flick the spatula up at the last moment, so that I hit him with the full flat surface. He stumbles over a chair and lands on his back on one of the tables.

"That's convenient if he dies and you have to eat him." Crosskiss's voice comes from right behind me. He'd been there the whole time, holding his vapgun on Jeska. Maybe the Zantite rules about duels had kept him from interfering in the fight, maybe he'd just wanted to see how the IH had changed me.

I turn to face him, pero before I can swing my weapon around, he's grabbed me and pinned my arms to my sides. I glance over at the blast freezer. At Brill. At everything I care about, slipping away. If Brill's not dead yet, every second counts.

Crosskiss's right hand presses painfully hard on my left forearm until I drop the spatula.

"Mmmmmmhhp." I kick him. He flips me around so that I'm facing away from him as his arms constrict my chest. I can feel his massive heartbeat against my back, slower and steadier than mine. I bite his upper arm through his uniform shirt, pero I don't even break skin, and he just squeezes me harder until I stop. Then he lets up enough for me to draw in a lungful of air.

Mertex isn't moving. I may have killed him after all. I'm not sure how I'll feel about that, after the drug has worn off. Right now, I'm only panicked over mi héroe. I struggle against Crosskiss's grip, desperate to get to Brill, pero I'm not going anywhere.

Jeska goes to Mertex and checks for a pulse. "He's alive, sir."

As if to confirm this, Mertex lets out a groan and sits up. "Wow, Bo. The Invincible Heart completely transformed you. That is so awesome."

Heat rises into my nose, at the back of my eyes. How can I feel relieved he's alive after what he just did? But I do.

Jeska moves closer to Crosskiss. "Please, sir, show mercy. Bo has just proven how brave she is and–" Crosskiss backhands him so hard that Jeska's neck snaps sideways. Oi! I'm afraid it's broken, but Jeska steps away and seems to recover. There's a hand-shaped orange mark across his cheek.

I take advantage of Crosskiss's distraction and the release of half his grip to wrench myself away from him and rush over to the blast freezer. I get it started on reverse, the door lifting, the chocolate mold starting to trundle forward.

"Ay, yes! Por favor, Brill." It still might not be too late. Brill's book lungs might have saved him, as long as his unconscious body hasn't breathed in chocolate. I watched him go for twenty minutes without breathing once, when he was trying to be stealthy, and he's been underwater at the beach for a lot longer than that.

Mertex gets off the table and pushes me out of the way of the button. He reverses the direction and simply stands where I can't get back to the controls.

"What did you do that for, mijo?" Tears spring into the corners of my eyes, heating my nose and chest. Weaponless, I start beating at his abdomen and arms, whatever I can reach.

He doesn't try to stop me, just moves his hands down to protect his crotch. He winces whenever I land a decent blow. There's pity in his eyes. "I do apologize, Bo, but looking weak in front of the general is hazardous to my health."

Jeska touches a hand to the side of his face, which is starting to swell. His eyes have gone garnet-toned, like happiness turned inside out.

The lights dim as the blast freezer pulls an amazing amount of power.

No. No, no, no, no.

I gasp and my head jerks back, as the horror fills my chest with ice, and my vision tunnels in. I can't let myself faint, not here, even though my legs are turning to rubber. Everything feels slow and disjointed, like in a nightmare. I stop punching and just rest my balled up fists against Mertex's chest. I'm out of time. Brill's dying, and I can't stop it.

The freezer dings, the sound almost like the oven timer I had back at the dorm. And it's done. Irrevocable. I fall to my knees, wrapping my arms around myself. The key fob, only half in my pocket, falls to the floor. "Nooooo!"

Hot tears burn at my eyes, and I let them fall, dripping spots of raw grief onto my borrowed pants. I don't care that the Zantites are watching. My hands are shaking, even braced against my body, and I'm hiccoughing back snot into a throat that feels thick and raw.

My brain's rejecting the reality of the situation, my tingling skin trying to put me anywhere but here. How can he just be gone? I stare in slowmo at that closed freezer door. Mi héroe's last words were *I love you*, and I didn't even get to say it back.

"I knew Earthlings were weak," Crosskiss says. "Look at you, reduced to nothing."

I'm still trembling pero the tears disappear in the wake of the Invincible Heart. "You're a monster."

In a way, I'm talking to myself, too. I'm the one who's supposed to die here, not Brill. I shouldn't have asked him to help me escape. He loved me enough to give his life for me. Now what am I supposed to do without him? It's like I've swallowed a lead weight, and now it's sinking into my stomach. The tears are burning hot at the back of my eyes again. I blink them away. My legs are still so shaky, I don't even try to stand.

"A monster?" Crosskiss peers down at me. "Isn't that what Earthlings think of my entire species?"

"Not all of you." I look at Mertex's sad eyes. He may not be a monster, pero he's not going to help me either.

"Mertex, we're short two servers in the ballroom." Crosskiss steps toward me, the vapgun in his hand again. "Get new drinks in there immediately."

"Yes, sir, general sir." Mertex flees the mess hall.

I can't outrun the blast of a vapgun, and without Brill I've got nowhere to go. There's no way I can get through Crosskiss's guards and onto Brill's ship on my own. It's flattering that Brill even thought I could. I bow mi cabeza and wait for the vapgun blast that will surely end my life, too. Pero, that blast never comes.

"Come on, Bo. It's time to see Garfex." Crosskiss pulls me to my feet.

I'm still shaky, still on the verge of tears, but I manage to stay upright. "Why don't you just kill me right here?" The Invincible Heart must be blunting my fear. "I understood what you said to Jeska. I'm not walking back out of there, no?"

Crosskiss's breathing comes faster, blowing my hair against my neck, drawing up bumpy piel de gallina again. "If the king prepares for an execution, there is going to be an execution. I'd rather it not be me."

Pero, didn't this guy decide not to eat me because I'm toxic? And didn't he have Doc shoot me up with something that would kill a Zantite, especially one who decided to snack on my liver? Jeska's sharp intake of breath suggests that he's just figured out the same thing. Crosskiss plans to use me as a weapon, to assassinate Garfex. But por qué? The shakiness fades as I snap my focus onto this revelation.

Crosskiss pushes me toward Jeska. "Here, loverboy. She doesn't have a boyfriend anymore. Get her cleaned up. Use the sink in the galley. I don't want either of you out of my sight."

"I am truly sorry for your loss." Jeska hugs me close and smooths my hair, which does nada to calm my muscles, which want movement, release, revenge.

"He died trying to save me, Jess." I find myself using Brill's nickname for him. I guess Brill rubbed off on me too. Damn Krom.

Jeska looks surprised. Was he not talking about Brill? Was he referring to my own impending death? He holds up a hand. "There's a chance—"

"Move it, Hayat. Don't make me tell you again, or I will execute you where you stand, no matter what pretty words you told the king." Crosskiss vaporizes my oversized spatula, then turns the weapon on Jeska.

A chance of what? Escape? I wish Jeska had a sublingual so

he could finish telling me about it.

I stare at that freezer door, tasting loss with these exaggerated emotions, as we exit the mess hall. I keep looking back, until we reach the galley. How can Brill really be gone?

My sublingual rings. It's Mario. I answer it, trying not to let on to Crosskiss that I'm bubblechattering with the outside. *How's the fiesta planning going, hermano?*

Shhhhhhh! I'm on a handheld. His command hisses through my brain. He whispers, *Not that great. Two guys just showed up, and Frank introduced them both as his best man. One of Brill's friends walked in, and they recognized him. Frank's got him in the garden shed. Guests are starting to arrive, and I'm climbing up into the treehouse with Isabella's binoculars to see what's going on. Can you ask Brill what I should do?*

Nada! Don't do anything!

Jeska helps me over to the sink, though the way my body feels all taut and restless, I'm tempted to fling him away. He turns on the tap. "It's too bad that you don't look sick anymore. Maybe we could paint measles on you with that joke soap."

I splash agua on my face. "It wouldn't look realistic. Then Garfex wouldn't believe you, no matter what you say."

"What I'm thinking is so far-fetched that I hardly believe me." Jeska hands me a dishrag. "Wash your neck and arms and then put on as much of that perfume Brill gave you as you can stand."

Crosskiss clears his throat. "No perfume."

How did he hear that?

Who's Garfex? Mario asks. *And what did Brill say?*

He's not here. Heat flashes in my nose again. That's as close as I can manage to saying he's dead – and that he took his phone into the freezer with him. Tears blur my eyes. I don't know the details of his plan, except that it was supposed to involve half a dozen guys, not just one. *Pero you're a history profesor, not a héroe. Don't do anything that could leave your girls without a papá.*

I won't, Pequeña. Frank's got the guy on his knees and... Dios mío! He killed him, Bo. I've got to get back into the house before they realize I saw that. He hangs up.

"Oye!" Damn Brill. How could he die when I need him like this? I throw the dishrag onto the counter. It skids into the unfrosted layers of my chocolate cake. The frosting's right there in the bowl. If I don't do any fancy edging, I could have the whole thing put together in five minutes.

My mission's a failure and Brill is dead, but it would be nice to complete *something* before I join him.

"General, sir." I hope Crosskiss doesn't take the *sir* as sarcastic. I'm sure my pronunciation's not so great in Zantite. "I'd like to take the king a gift."

I point at the cake.

"Why?" Crosskiss blinks a couple of times.

"Because I was going to graduate from culinary school, and that's not going to happen, and because the last thing I was supposed to do before I left was to present a cake like this one at a dinner in honor of my mother, and I didn't get to do that either. You've already taken the life of my love. At least give me this."

He considers this. For a moment, I think I see something non-monstrous in his eyes.

"Hurry, then." Crosskiss's vapgun never wavers from its aim at Jeska's cabeza as Jeska and I each grab a spatula and spread the rich, fudgy frosting over the layers. We alternate placing the white-chocolate-dipped quizllens on top. That brings a bittersweet smile, as I remember watching Brill dip them, tasting chocolate on his lips afterwards. He was a really good kisser.

Jeska picks up the platter, supporting it easily from underneath. I would have had to use two levbots or a sturdy cart to transport a cake that size. He whispers, "I hope you've got a plan."

"Not really." The frustration of not being able to run full

speed at the general and kick him in the chest is gnawing me out of my skin. I grab a stack of plates and some forks and a blunt knife. "Pero everyone says Garfex adores chocolate. It can't hurt, no?"

"I'll carry those." Crosskiss holds his hand out for the flatware. It's not like I could reach high enough to jab his eye out with one of them or anything, though the idea is appealing, and no sé whether to credit that to the Invincible Heart or to my own.

We continue our interrupted walk down the hallway, Jeska moving slowly out front, me watching his well-formed shoulders and feeling shamefully disloyal for admiring the view as we move farther away from Brill's lifeless body.

Jeska stops in front of an unlabeled door. I open it for him and find myself stepping inside a gran room with a smooth gray floor that slopes toward the center, where there's a drain. On the right, an oversized octagonal boxing ring with a circle of folding chairs around it takes up most of the space, and to the left a long table with metal rings along the center extends halfway down the length of the wall. A second row of rings set into the floor under the table already have shackles threaded through them, multiple pairs in various sizes. The table only has chairs on the far side. We'll be facing the center of the room, looking towards that raised platform with nada on it except a single thickly padded wing chair. I look back to the drain, and my heart squeezes. How much blood, in how many shades, from how many different species, has been washed down it?

I glance behind me to Crosskiss's vapgun. Has the Invincible Heart made me strong enough to take it from him? He catches me looking and raises one of those practically non-existent eyebrows.

"Don't even think about it, stowaway." He uses the gun barrel to wave us over toward the table. Jeska places the cake down, then moves around to the far side. From the side without chairs, Crosskiss leans down and shackles him in place. Then he points to a seat two away from the Krom. I sit, though everything inside me demands fight or flight. Crosskiss clamps a shackle around one of my ankles, pero the cuff is too grande and he's having trouble getting it tight. "Watch it!" he says as he moves around to my side of the table to get a better grip. As he leans down, I grab for the gun.

He's at an awkward angle, so I manage to wrench it backwards out of his hand. It feels hunormous in mine. I fire at the ring securing Jeska's feet to the floor. It's a chancy move, given how vapguns behave, but the ring and the chain and one of the cuffs disappear, and he seems to still have both his feet.

I swing the gun back around at Crosskiss, bare inches from his face. He hits me, his fist impacting my chest like a tree trunk. I fire convulsively, but the blast only vaporizes a row of insignia off his uniform. He takes the gun away from me as I struggle to breathe. The shackle closes tight around my ankle.

Whatever that chance Jeska had mentioned was, it is gone now.

Garfex comes in from a door behind the big chair. He's taken off the cloak, and the tunic he's wearing is black. Fantástico. He doesn't want to get his good clothes dirty. "What's going on in here?"

"Nothing, Your Holiness." Crosskiss straightens up. He glares at me, daring me to contradict him.

I glare back, unable to talk.

"Let's get this over with. I'm needed back soon for the referendum review." He drops into the wing chair, swinging one leg over the side arm and curving the other under him. Three courtiers follow him in, standing in a row behind his seat. The guy who lost an arm down the gullet of his king is here to help carry out our executions, one sleeve of his tunic hanging empty at his side. Is that irony or no? As Frank would say, I can't tell. Garfex stretches, like it has been a long day for him, too. "One of you's a stowaway and the other caused an interspecies incident. Have either of you any complaints?"

I speak through dry lips. "Actually, Your Highness, sir, both of those were me. Jeska is merely here to provide proof of my fate to my family."

I hear Jeska's sharp intake of air, but he doesn't say anything.

"Fine." Garfex waves a hand. "Have *you* any complaints?"

My hand goes to my sternum, which is bruising as we speak. "Yes, several. But first I have a request. Share this cake with me."

Garfex blinks like maybe he's not sure he heard me right. "Your last request is for me to eat cake?"

The word *last* should be feartastic. I credit the Invincible Heart that I remain calm.

"Mira, I was supposed to be a chef…" I shake my head. He's not going to care about that. "Please. Allow me a few moments to pretend that my life is still headed in a civilized direction, and to talk to you. It's really good cake. Have you ever had a quizllen fruit?"

Jeska moves around the table and picks up the knife, cutting into the dense chocolate layers. "Respectfully, Your Holiness, quizllens are native to Larksis 9, home of one of the best cooking schools in the galaxy. The fruits are exquisite on their own, but just imagine them enrobed in chocolate."

The way the king's eyes widen, his amor por chocolate is not exaggerated.

"Well, I guess it wouldn't hurt. You speak Zantite strangely, young girl, but at least it's not painful to listen to for such a short amount of time." Garfex comes down from the platform, grabs one of the folding chairs from the boxing ring and sits down opposite me. Jeska cuts him a thick piece of cake, piling several extra quizllens onto the side of the plate.

Then he cuts three more pieces, handing one to me and offering another to Crosskiss, who looks like he'd like to refuse. I don't blame the guy – he's got poison on his mind and he's taking food from someone he tried to kill with a chocolate chip cookie – but protocol gets the better of him, and he takes the plate. Jeska wolfs down half of his slice, probably to prove to everyone that it's not poisoned.

Garfex picks up his fork and studies Jeska, likely waiting to see if he keels over. Pero, he addresses me. "You said you have several complaints. Do you deny the charges leveled against you?"

With my blood pounding through me, demanding action, it's the hardest thing in the worlds to sit here calmly, as though we're taking tea. Careful not to slip into Spanish, I say, "No. I'm not a diplomat, and while I intended no offense, I made a mistake." I plunge my fork into the back of the cake, where the choctastic frosting's the thickest and there's the near-crunch of a perfectly cooked outer edge. "I more wish to complain about you trying to put a colony in our solar system. That's illegal, is it not?"

Garfex gives Crosskiss a sharp look.

A green blush breaks out over the bridge of the general's nose. "This only proves stowaways must be executed without mercy before they bring intelligence back to their home planets."

I take a bite of cake, determined to enjoy it, if it is the last thing I do. Which it may well be. If it is, Jeska had better be quick getting proof of death to Frank. And that Krom better be willing to destroy those beans.

"Claiming a planet is only illegal if the solar system's primary inhabitant has filed official plans or colonization efforts are already underway. There's no sign of habitation or construction on that rock we were looking at." Garfex taps the table. "What else do you have to complain about?"

I hold up my plate. "You have been trading with pirates to get chocolate, and since your vessels have been in the area, the rogues have started killing transport crews. I know you're not directly responsible for these deaths, but you're certainly not helping the problem."

"And what else?" Garfex finally takes a bite of his cake.

"That's it."

He looks surprised, like I've missed the más grande objection I should be making.

Crosskiss says, "She didn't hear the speeches." Like that explains it.

"This cake is amazing." Garfex shovels in several more torktuls, then pops a quizllen into his mouth. He looks over at Crosskiss, then blinks a couple of times. "Have you changed rank? There was more insignia on your uniform when you first greeted me, and I know *I* didn't demote you."

Crosskiss's cheeks take on a hint of green. He cuts his gaze over at me, warning me not to say anything. "There was an accident. I will have it replaced."

"No matter." Garfex points with his fork. "Call for the queen. She has to taste this."

"I'm glad you like it." I feel a blush rising in my cheeks as I watch Crosskiss speak into his communicator. It shouldn't matter, no? Not what the man who is about to murder me thinks. But I take pride in my work, and his enjoyment seems sincere. I cling to this single moment, my one happy thought since Brill's death.

Jeska's eyes have gone a clear, bright yellow as he's been watching me interact with Garfex. "You should know, Your Holiness, sir, that Bo is a second-generation celebrity cook. Her people value her so much she has been named the Princess of Chocolate."

He's laying on the exaggeration a bit thick, pero I don't interrupt.

Garfex looks at me appraisingly. "Be that as it may, neither that status nor these objections make any difference to the outcome of your case. You are speaking of proper Zantite military tactics. If your people object, they can declare war." Garfex holds up a quizllen fruit. "But we should be making cake like this with the chocolate we have been paying those pirates for. I will grant you a stay of execution long enough for you to meet my wife and help her write down the recipe for this delightful confection."

"You are most kind." I don't point out that confections are candy, not cakes. After all, he's using a Zantite word, and I may well have the meaning wrong. I should be panicking right now. This must be whatever allows those guvvave warriors to face death head on, no pun intended.

"But sir," Crosskiss protests, "this criminal nearly killed a member of the crew with a kitchen utensil." He leaves out the part about me taking his gun.

Layla comes in the main door, surrounded by several courtiers. She puts a hand on her hip. "Surely you aren't adding multiple executions so soon before dinner. Garfie, you know even one spoils your appetite."

Garfex laughs. "The wife's usually right, and if the rest of the food tonight is half as good as this cake... honestly, you're not that appetizing." He grins at me, showing every one of his nine billion teeth. "Make that a stay of execution until after the ball that starts after dinner. If you can figure out by then what your other objection should have been, I'll dance with you."

CHAPTER TWENTY-ONE

As soon as the king and the courtiers have left, Crosskiss drops his plate onto the table. He's eaten everything but the frosting, which stands up like the outline of a phantom piece of cake. He takes out his vapgun again, holding it against his hip, at the ready in case we do something else unpredictable. He gestures Jeska into the seat next to me. "I don't like this game Garfex is playing with you, stowaway. It isn't fair to ask you to spend your few remaining hours fretting over clues that won't change anything."

"As opposed to working my fingers off in the kitchen? No y no. If you care so much, you'd have just let me and Brill leave."

Crosskiss's frown deepens, and he goes a shade towards chartreuse. "You volunteered for that."

I try to stand, yanking at the chain still securing my ankle to the table. "Qué? Was that the other objection I was supposed to make? That you had no right to kill a guy authorized to be on your ship? Or was it simply that I object to being eaten?"

Crosskiss looks amused. "Not even close."

I slap my hands on the table. "Then why don't you tell me?" The Invincible Heart is making this confinement almost unbearable. I want to go over there and shake that smug idiota until he talks.

"Because I, unlike Garfex, don't underestimate your ability to get information off this ship before you die. I think it's better if you don't know." He nods at my chair. "You two wait here. I'll be right back."

I flop down in my chair, crossing my arms over my chest. The door closes behind Crosskiss. I try calling Mario, but he doesn't pick up. Neither does Chestla. Or Mamá. I can't help fear the worst, though Frank's deadline hasn't yet passed.

Jeska puts a hand on my arm. "That was close. I didn't think either of us was going to leave this room."

"Sí." And though I'm relieved, my chest still aches, and not just from the bruise. Brill hadn't found a way to stay his own execution. I don't know his family, don't even know who to tell what happened to him. I'll have to get the information from Jeska.

Oye. That makes it real. Brill's dead. A profound wave of grief washes over me, and I curl forward, ignoring the desire to move, to act. Nothing I do will bring him back. Jeska rubs my back until a bit of the tension leaves my shoulders. I sit up straighter, and he smooths my hair again, the gesture so familiar now, so comforting, and at the end of it, he turns my face toward his. He wants to kiss me. It would be so easy to let him, but I've already been disloyal enough when I'd kissed Kaliel. That had truly hurt Brill, and I don't think there's room for anyone else in my heart right now, not until I get over the pain of losing mi héroe.

I turn my face away. "I thought he said this ship didn't have a brig."

Jeska sounds sad. "You really do love that kek, don't you?"

I don't say anything. I don't have to.

"I wish that I had met you first." Jeska kisses my forehead and runs a hand along my cheek, and I want to melt against him. I really do. But I do have self-control, no matter what Brill said. Jeska's voice turns businesslike. "This isn't a holding area. It's for official duels and interrogations. Confining people in here would be considered cruel and unusual punishment."

"As opposed to eating them."

Jeska's staring at that drain, and I wonder if he's imagining how his own life is likely to end if he stays here long enough. "Zantite logic is different. Most of them would consider the reprieve Garfex just gave you cruel, leaving you alive knowing you're soon going to die."

He says it so bluntly. *Soon going to die.* I, on the other hand, struggle to speak around the heartbreak thickening my throat. "I still don't comprender why they had to kill Brill. They'd already captured me."

Jeska picks up a fork off the table and starts bending it. "That one's harder to explain. It has a bit to do with finishing what you start. If Brill survives, Mertex won't be permitted to try again, unless Brill challenges him to a duel. Most Zantites don't commit violence without a reason. Even Crosswired only tried to kill me with those cookies because, aside from Murry, I was the only one who knew I'd warned him not to eat you. And we all know Murry wouldn't dare try to warn Garfex. It doesn't make any sense unless righting whatever grudge he's got against the king is worth dying for, because afterwards, it will be obvious what he's done. Doc would figure it out, if no one else, and then Layla would have to personally execute—"

"What do you mean if Brill survives? Jeska, he's dead."

"Maybe not." Jeska's eyes are still garnet. He kneels beside me and sticks one of the bent fork tines into the lock at my left ankle. "Krom bone marrow produces iololla, chemically similar to Earth's glycerol, which you guys use to keep frozen biological samples from degrading. It's like natural antifreeze. Varnex didn't want that chocolate sculpture brittle, so I told him to set the freezer on a relatively mild setting. There's a reasonable chance Brill's vital tissue hasn't frozen through."

"Qué? Then what are we still doing here?"

"I don't know." Jeska stands and gestures down at my feet. The shackles lie open on the floor. "We should hurry."

"Sí. Vamos! Naramoosh!" A thrill goes through my heart as I race across the room. Mi héroe may still be alive. Jeska really should have led with that instead of wasting vital seconds comforting me, but even in an emergency, Krom always seem to find time for logic – and for romance.

I open the door to the hallway, coming face to face with Crosskiss, who's talking on his handheld. "No, it was a practical joke. We're under way again, top speed to… I'll call you back." He looks down at my unshackled ankles, frowning in disapproval. I frown right back.

Crosskiss sighs. He backs out of the doorway and makes a sweeping gesture that I should go on past. "I was just going to tell you that His Holiness has requested one of your recipes be added to the menu for tonight, something representative of Earth."

"No hay problema!" I'm practically running down that hallway.

"Why are you two in such a hurry?" Crosskiss calls after us.

"We need to get back to the galley." Jeska's urgent tone gets me moving even faster.

I glance back at Crosskiss, who's headed for the elevator. Ay, whatever clue I'm missing must be important, but I can puzzle on it after we free Brill's body – with or without him in it – from the mold. Jeska stops in front of a strange symbol embossed in the wall. He puts his hand flat against it, and a large panel below starts to retract.

"Eh? Now you want a Vend-a-Coffee?" I'm trying for a joke, but my voice comes out all stressed. I need to keep running, or I'm going to climb that wall.

"Actually, coffee's not a bad idea. Go on into the galley and fill a thermos with as much as you think he'll be able to stand, and send out the guys to help me with the mold." Jeska pulls a canvas bag from inside the panel. "These are emergency medical supplies. Here's hoping we need them."

I know what he's trying to do. In case he's wrong, and Brill's heart is frozen solid, he wants me busy so I don't have to see the inevitable death agony on mi héroe's face – and so that I can still feel like I'm doing something to help.

"Gracias, Jess." I kiss him on the cheek, then I race into the galley.

Plelix and Varnex look up with relief. Mertex knocks over a jar of something squiggly and white, he's so shocked to see me.

"Where's Jeska?" Varnex asks, putting his knife down on his cutting board. He's looking at the empty hallway behind me, fear in his eyes.

I glance at Mertex. "Brill got pushed into the chocolate mold and frozen. Jeska thinks he might still be alive, so he's trying to help."

"By Garfex! I should have been more careful." Varnex runs out of the galley, Plelix close at his heels. Moments later, their voices echo through the closed serving windows.

Mertex wipes the spilled squiggles into a dishtowel and throws them in the trash. "How come you didn't tell them how it happened?"

"How come you didn't tell them he was in there?" I open a cabinet. Jeska said there were thermoses in here somewhere. "You're not proud of it, even if you were following orders, no?" I sigh. "Mira, I'm supposed to be getting coffee on the off chance you didn't manage to kill someone I love. A little help finding the thermoses, por favor?"

"Jeska really thinks he's alive?" Mertex reaches over my head to a shelf in a cabinet I couldn't have gotten into without the stepladder and hands down a black thermos. When I nod, he swallows visibly. "Is Brill the kind of person who would ask for vengeance under our laws? If the courts were to consider that order unjust, he'd have the right to have me executed for following it."

Now I'm beginning to understand the finish-what-you-start

logic. After all, dead men have no complaints – nunca. "Brill was never the sort to hold a grudge."

Was. Oi! I just referred to him in the past tense. Hands shaking, I fill the thermos with coffee. A few specks of glitter wind up floating on the dark surface. I fish them out with a spoon.

My sublingual rings again. I set the spoon in the sink and answer it.

Bo? It's Chestla, calling me back.

I sniffle a little, realize there are tears streaming down my face. *Hola mi amiga.*

Bo, are you crying?

I force the tears to stop, wiping at the corners of my eyes with my thumbs. I'm not up to talking about it. *De nada. Qué pasa? What's up?*

I've been going nuts, sitting here with Eugene being absolutely silent. And you know me. I clean when I'm nervous. I found an entire hidden underground level to this lab.

Vaya! Wait. She doesn't know that word. *Wow!* I don't sound entirely enthusiastic in either language. I should be more intrigued, I know, but I'm more focused on Brill.

Don't jump up and down because it's so cool.

Lo siento. There's just a lot going on here.

I just thought you'd want to know it looks like they were testing all kinds of stuff down here during the early days of HGB. We found cases of this green liquid, and Eugene's going to analyze it. But there's more recent stuff too. I tried your handheld, because I wanted to show you some of it.

I wipe at my eyes again. *I don't have it on me right now. Just describe what you see.*

OK. She hesitates. *There's a stack of cardboard boxes stamped with big red x'es on the side, marked To Be Destroyed. Each box is filled with bars of HGB dark. Eugene's analyzing one now. He's already found significant amounts of Pure275, but who knows what else is in there. And there's copies of paper packing slips, dated this year. It looks like four of these boxes got shipped somewhere, but the sender's handwriting is so bad, I can't tell where. The most readable part looks like Catanista or Capanida. It's definitely not Canada.*

I drop the spoon with a clatter into the sink. *Dios mío!*

Chestla's finally got my attention. Jane Smith was right. Chocolate laced with Pure *had* been in that warehouse. Only before Jane could get to it, they had moved the stuff, to a location no one would connect to the Yucatan. I imagine one of those bricks of HGB dark in Papá's hand, him in his fireman's gear looking so dashing as he got ready to tell the world about one of HGB's secrets. I gasp. If she was telling the truth about that... and one of the members of her group had gone missing... is it possible Papá had been working undercover for the Global Court? Meredith might have known how to contact Jane Smith, but she'd taken that information to her grave.

Should I tell Frank? Chestla asks.

No! But no lo sé, maybe he could help put all this together. *Mira, I already told him sort of by accident that that messed-up chocolate exists, and he was muy curious about it. It could make him motivated enough to come in there with you.* I can't focus right now, can't think. Brill may or may not be alive, and I'm still expected to try to fix everything else. *Do what you think is best, or just wait. I have something I have to do, then I'll get back with you.*

OK. Her voice is small. *You take care of yourself, Do.*

You too. I hang up on her.

Mertex and I make our way around to the mess hall door just as the other three guys flip the mold over onto the floor. That tight feeling's winding me up again, giving me an urge to run over there and rip the metal encasing Brill away all by myself. I can't do that. I have to wait, though I think I'll go loco in the next few seconds, wavering between grief and hope, fighting everything the Invincible Heart keeps telling my body to do.

Varnex taps the mold all over with a rubber mallet, then he, Jeska and Plelix each take an edge and pull it up off the chocolate. The sculpture forms a perfect likeness of the royal couple, lounging with an array of chocolates and gift-wrapped packages, except that Brill's cabeza tilts at an angle across where Layla's face should have been, and one of his hands appears to be emerging from Garfex's throat. His cheeks are bruised purple, pero his lips have gone pale, with just an undertone of icy blue. Dios mío, no por favor. Mercifully, his eyes are closed.

I clutch the thermos to my chest. He's dead, after all.

"V, get him out of there." Jeska gestures frantically. "We've got to get him warmed up."

I cross the cafeteria and put a hand on Jeska's arm. "Jess, he's not breathing."

Jeska looks at me like I'm a kek. "Of course not." He breaks some of the thinner pieces of chocolate away from Brill's neck and wiggles two fingers in close to Brill's skin. "But he has a pulse. It's slow but steady. He's in shock." Jeska tugs on Brill's eyelids, revealing rusty orange unconsciousness, which looks completely different from when I've seen them a similar color from anger. It's like looking through a clear marble to get to the burnt ocher shade.

"He looks dead to me," Varnex says. Pero, V doesn't hesitate to start chiseling Brill out of the sculpture. "But you're the expert on being Krom."

Jeska wipes chocolate from Brill's nose and mouth, so that he *can* breathe, if he's able. "I also had to take wilderness survival training before my Voyage of Discovery. I just never imagined the first time I had to use it would be indoors."

Brill's not going to be in any condition for coffee any time soon.

I turn back to Jeska. "What can I do, por favor?"

"Look through the medical bag for a heat wrap." Jeska carefully removes as much of the chocolate as he can from around Brill's face.

I find the heat wrap and open the package. It must have been vacuum sealed, because it expands until the folded mass is larger than the medical supply bag it came out of. I lay it out on the floor according to the instructions on the package, and it seems to keep getting bigger. Inside the folds, there's a garment that looks like a cross between a lifejacket and a onesie, with the thickest pads at the armpits and the groin. It's sized for a Zantite. A tab at the shoulder says something that translates roughly as *Break Once Occupied*. "Now what?"

Jeska points with a hand darkened by smeared chocolate. "The double-door at the back of the blast freezer leads through to the area where we process game. Brill's skin is a little more fragile than a Zantite's, so grab a couple of hides from that stack to put between the inner vest and his clothes before we activate the gel."

"Qué?" My chest prickles with cold as I eye the freezer door.

"Nothing's going to happen to accidentally turn it on." Jeska looks over at Mertex. "Right, Murry?"

"Right," Mertex repeats. "I promise."

I step inside the freezer chamber, striding quickly between the tracks, throwing open the back door. I'm in a sterile white room that, despite the cutting tools along one wall, the ominous person-sized sink in the middle of the room and the equally ominous drain in the floor, has been transformed into a crafting area. The stack of tanned hides sits next to a taller stack of stretching forms, and there's a whole crate of antlers that have been prepared for carving – and a few half-carved projects that have been returned to the basket. Someone has made dozens of bone crochet hooks in various sizes and placed them upright in a vase that says:

...And beneath the starlit skies, the wandering sailor mends his nets and makes his clothes. – Durquay / Please only take one hook of any given size. – Orlux

Ay, Orlux, reduced to a heart and a pair of boots.

By the time I find two soft long-haired hides, Varnex has finished chipping Brill out of the sculpture. He and Plelix get mi héroe centered in the heat wrap. I swaddle him in the hides, soft fur side in. As we're getting him into the heat gel contraption, I ask Varnex, "Did Private Chlaf…" I realize I don't know the Zantite word for crochet.

I ask Jeska in Krom, and he translates it as, "jakkag," to which both Plelix and Varnex nod in understanding.

"Most of the crew do." Varnex looks so sad I regret asking the question. "Crossedleads encourages it–"

"Nope," Jeska interrupts. "Can't use that one. We agreed no changing the Cross part this week."

Varnex rolls his eyes and helps tuck the extra cloth behind Brill's back. "Crossfire encourages it because it connects us to our seafaring roots. He holds periodic competitions, and he always wins, not because he's the general, but because he really is that good. Orlux would always come in second, which surprised everybody, because otherwise he was a total klutz. I think his sweet ways with those hooks were why Crosskiss," he emphasizes his correct pronunciation of the name, "overlooked so many of his infractions."

"I'm sorry, V." Jeska breaks the tab on the heat gel then pulls the edges of the wrap over Brill, like mi héroe's a burrito with his cabeza on the flattish pillow sticking out of the top. "That kid never should have been impressed."

I kneel beside Brill, placing my hand on his cheek, which feels like ice.

"Ay, no, mi hermoso," I whisper. I think of all the pet names I called him as our relationship deepened. He'd earned them all. "Mi idiota. Mi litoll. Mi amor. Mi vida. Mi héroe. Don't give up. Por favor. Just don't."

The Invincible Heart has me pacing the room, burning energy, wasting precious time. I keep coming back to Brill, touching his face or hands, adjusting the wrap. After what seems like forever, but is probably closer to half an hour, he starts to shiver, which means the heat wrap is working, pero he's still not breathing. Chocolate starts dripping out of the top of the wrap, making a puddle around his head. Jeska's staring at Brill as though willing him to live. Funny how just a few hours ago, Jess'd socked this same guy in the face.

"Is he going to be OK?" I ask.

Jeska's pearl gray eyes say he's still worried. "As long as he doesn't go into cardiac arrest from the temperature change." There's the fragility of Krom cardiovascular systems again. At least Jess is being honest with me about Brill's odds.

Varnex and Plelix have gone back to check on whatever's cooking in the galley. Jeska sits at a chair at the same table I'd upended Mertex onto.

Brill's skin gradually feels warmer under my hand. Ay, yes. I rub the sides of his face, gently trying to add some of my body heat to his. Mertex kneels down opposite me. I lean protectively over Brill. "Don't you dare touch him, mijo! Jeska told me if at first you fail, you don't get to try again."

Mertex moves back, looking un poco scared. "I just want to see him breathe. This is the coolest thing ever. It's like that scene from *Everlasting Love*, where they all think Minda's character's dead, only she's taken a drug that makes her just seem dead—"

Jeska waves a dismissive hand at him. "That whole film's a knock-off of *Romeo and Juliet*." Then Jess looks to me. "Except, since Zandywood can't end in tragedy, they live."

Mertex shoots Jeska a look so comic and yet fierce that some of the tension goes out of my heart. In a world that allows for the existence of Mertex, Brill has to live.

"So this is cooler than when I kicked your butt all hopped up on the Invincible Heart?" I picture Chestla's sad eyes as she told me she wished she'd had time to teach me to defend myself. "I have a friend stuck on Earth right now who would pay money to see a holo of that fight. The girl you saw kick that guy's gas mask off, remember?"

Mertex laughs. "Maybe not cooler, but at least equally cool. I mean, look at him."

Plelix and Varnex come back with a mop and a pressure sprayer. They upend the mold and start tossing the broken chocolate pieces into it. Brill's cheeks still look discolored from the trauma of being frozen, but underneath that, he's starting to regain color.

I put a hand on his forehead. "Jess, he's stopped shivering. His skin feels like normal temperature. When's he going to start breathing again?"

"As soon as he regains consciousness, or his body decides it is running out of oxygen. Go ahead and unwrap him, so he won't overheat."

It takes some doing to get him out of the heat vest, and pieces of the fur from the animal skins stick to the melted chocolate on his skin and clothes.

"Let me clean him up a bit." Varnex brings the pressure sprayer over and starts removing the caked-on layer of chocolate from Brill's clothes. He turns the pressure down to almost nil and washes mi héroe's face off un poco more carefully.

As the agua hits his forehead, Brill sucks in air, and his eyes shift from ochre to violet. They waver toward gray when he sees Mertex kneeling over him. He slowly turns them blue and smiles like he's not freaked out. "La, su, do I have a headache. What happened?"

Jeska holds out a hand to help him sit up. "Somebody tried to freeze you."

"Just look at this jacket." Brill takes off the black leather and holds it out. He seems to be recovering muy rápidamente. "That's the second one ruined in a month. Do you guys know how expensive these things are?"

My heart aches again, this time with happiness.

"Come on," Jeska says. "I'll loan you some clothes and then I'll get Doc to take a look at you. I know you don't want a uniform, but I've got a couple of T-shirts. Sorry, but I don't do leather."

What I hope he means is, *let's get away from Mertex so I can get you up to speed on what's been happening.*

I put my hand on Brill's cheek. "Don't you go die on me again."

He looks a little uncomfortable at my touch, but his eyes light with sunlight. "Babe, I wouldn't do that to you."

"I brought you some coffee." I look down at the heat wrap, now soaked with chocolate and agua. "I guess you don't need it, though."

"Actually, coffee sounds perfect." He gives me a quick kiss on the cheek, careful not to smear chocolate all over me. "I still feel chilled inside."

I retrieve the thermos, holding it against my chest. How do I even tell him one of his friends got shot back on Earth? "Mi vida?"

His eyes go wide, and I hear him suck in air.

My own heart gives a startled jolt. I didn't even think when I'd said it. Pero, I won't take it back. Mi vida, the most important person in the galaxy to me, my very life. He has to realize he's earned that name now. But will he accept it? Or is he still determined to sacrifice his happiness along with mine? I watch his irises shift like kaleidoscopes, thinking.

"Babe?"

My heart lifts with joy.

"Simón!" Literally that's a name, but it more or less means, *Oh, yeah!*

I hand him the coffee, cup his face in both my hands and kiss him, right there in front of everyone. He kisses me back, though he's still trembling from the shock his body's been through. This time the chocolate smearing our lips is dark and bitter, touched with sadness, but stronger and more delicious for it. I lose myself in the heat of the beso. Shared hearts indeed.

When we finally break the kiss, there's silence in the room. Jeska's staring at the floor. Mertex looks like he's about to applaud. The other two cooks are acting like they didn't see anything out of the ordinary. Brill and I step apart, and Varnex hands me a towel to wipe off the smeared chocolate.

And while there's a spark of happiness in me, it doesn't override all the other worries.

"What's wrong, Babe?" Brill always could tell when my emotions shift, even though I don't have telltale eyes. "Did I do something?"

"No, mi vida. Nunca." I tell him, bluntly, about his friend's death and Mario's predicament, then I ask, "Can you find out what happened?"

He takes his phone out of his pocket and pushes the menu button. Miraculously, the screen lights up. He talks to somebody, his eyes going darker and darker gray. When he hangs up, he smiles encouragingly at me, despite those eyes. "They're both still alive, and the plan is a go. Frank's friends only recognized one of the three guys who went in to scope out the situation, and mi amigo never broke from insisting that he was just there trying to get a message to me, since I'd gone communication dark. The rest of the team is just waiting for Mario to get your mamá into the backyard."

"I don't know how to thank you for doing this."

"You don't have to, Babe. I kinda love your mamá too." He puts a chocolate smeared hand on mine. "I'll get Jess to bring the box down to Doc's, in case you need a backup plan."

Chestla calls my sublingual, and as soon as I answer it I realize I forgot to call her back. Ay, no. I really am a kek too. Brill and I make a perfect pair, no? I try to apologize, but she interrupts.

I would love to keep digging for information, but I've been landlocked too long, and I've eaten Eugene's entire store of salt. This isn't an urgent problem – yet. But I need ocean water within the next day or so, or my blood pressure's going to drop too low for me to be of any use. If I don't get a plan of action soon, I will have to try to leave this rainforest on my own.

I feel a jolt of panic. *Ay, no! I will try to come up with something soon.*

Don't forget about me. Chestla hesitates. *Please.*

Before I can think of anything comforting to add, she hangs up, just as Brill's handheld rings. Shtesh! Everybody else's problems keep piling down on us. It's un poco overwhelming.

He pops up a holo of Kayla – an angry Kayla with her arms crossed over her chest. She's in a hotel room with a bed covered in a shabby striped comforter behind her.

She whips off her hat, still clutching it in one hand, and her hair goes wild around her face. "What the heck, Brill?"

He doesn't look surprised. "Did you watch it?"

"For about a second."

"What are you two talking about, chicos?" I ask.

Kayla catches sight of me in the background and shifts towards me. "Spiderlungs sent me a holo of another ship being blown up. Which is just cruel."

I wince. She's been through so much. Ay-ay-ay. What was he thinking?

"No, it's not cruel." Brill shifts the phone so I'm out of Kayla's view and she has to focus on him. "Look, I saw that holo of you helping Kaliel save that guard. It's obvious you want to give the guy a chance. You need context. You already hate me, so this coming *from* me should make it easier. HGB shows their pilots all the recovered feeds, even when they aren't public. Just remember, Kaliel saw this too, about a week before his accident."

"Accident!" Kayla squeaks.

"Just watch the holo."

Kayla's face is going pink, and I'm pretty sure she's going to hang up. But then she puffs air through her lips. "Fine."

The image fills Brill's holofield too. It's eerily familiar, grainy black box footage from an HGB vessel identifying itself as the *White Mousse*. The cameras face outward, shifting through varying directions and magnifications, until a vessel comes into view. It's solid black, would be invisible except for the star behind it outlining it starkly, humped and swept back, like a turtle crossed with a boomerang.

The pilot, labeled Yvette Glasgow in the subtitles, says, "Please identify yourself and change course."

The camera loses the ship as the *White Mousse* fishtails left.

"She's trying to get the vessel out of her radar blind," Brill says. "She wouldn't have seen it at all except for the star."

Pero the ship's back, almost immediately, following in the same spot.

"Look, dude." Yvette sounds scared, but angry too. "That was your third warning. Please don't make me fire on you."

There's no response, but the ship seems closer, then disappears as it moves out of the star's silhouette. The quality of Yvette's voice changes, and she's talking directly to the black box. "I've never fired on a live target before." She hesitates. "What if their com system's just down and they're foundering? I'm going to attempt one more communication."

There's a flash from the blackness, as the spacejacker ship ejects a projectile, then the crackle of electricity as the *Mousse* loses artificial gravity followed by the crackcrunch of something shattering and screaming in areas the cameras can't reach. Then Yvette's body comes floating past, super zoomed in. Oi!

My chest feels empty and iced over. She never even fired back.

I can hear Kayla crying in the background of the chatter of the pirates looting the disabled ship. After a while, she kills the holo, which puts her back in the field.

Her eyes are red, and she glares at Brill. "You're right. It is easy to hate you, looking at us with that superior smug Krom expression, judging us for hurting ourselves."

Brill shrugs. "As long as it helps you be a little more objective about Kaliel. But I'm not trying to look smug." He wipes a hand across his chin, swiping at a bit of chocolate residue that must be irritating him. He only winds up smearing it.

Kayla blinks at him. "What happened to you?"

I lose the thread of their conversation, because I'm struck by how similar Yvette's spacejacking was to Kaliel's report about the SeniorLeisure ship. "How did you get this footage, mi vida?"

Brill looks down at his phone. "My friends tend to keep an eye on Galactic events, and pirate attacks are getting more frequent. Someone who knows Gavin sent that out the day after it happened."

"You had it the whole time?" I didn't mean for that to sound like an accusation.

Brill looks startled. "I didn't think it mattered. HGB already has this feed. If they'd wanted to use it to defend Kaliel, they'd have done it. And honestly, I don't know whether it helps or hurts his case."

I shake my head. "The situations were so similar, it almost looks like it was choreographed that way."

Kayla gasps. "Are you suggesting it wasn't an accident? That my grandparents were... what? Collateral damage for something?"

I feel heat building in my face. "No sé what I'm saying. It was just an impression."

Kayla hangs up.

"Honest?" Brill says. "Part of the reason I didn't show you that feed is because I didn't want you thinking better of Kaliel. But that's not really fair, is it?"

"None of this is fair. To any of us. Nunca." Least of all Chestla, who I've abandoned in the rainforest. "Before you go, can I borrow your phone?"

I contact Chestla using Brill's handheld. She said she's cracked into HGB's computer system, and I keep having this nagging thought about Kaliel.

Chestla's face is fierce, her teeth bared when she answers the phone. I almost hang up. I swallow before I speak. "Are you OK?"

"I'm doing better than the sentries who just tried to stop me from crossing the fence." She's whispering. I can see the HGB facility behind her. "But I don't know how much farther I'm going to get. There's, like, a million of these guys arriving in helicopters."

I thought she was going to wait for me to call her back before trying to escape on her own. She must be losing confidence in me as her cesuda ma.

"You're probably better off inside the wall. They can't fly choppers through the bionet."

She groans. "After all the trouble I just went through to get out?"

"Chestla, those sentries." Ay, I can't even bring myself to ask it.

"They're all still breathing. Don't worry, Bo. I understand the diplomatic implications if I kill an Earthling. But my duty is to you. How am I supposed to protect you if I can't even get off this planet?" She starts walking back towards the wall, her cheerful personality already recovering. "So why'd you call? Do you have a plan to get me out of here? Maybe into town? I am ready to lick me some tortilla chips."

"Not yet. Lo siento, chica. I hate to ask this, but if you're going back inside anyway, can you see if HGB has any other footage of Kaliel's accident? I have a feeling that they're hiding something. Or if not them, somebody is."

"I can take a look. What exactly am I looking for?"

I share my theory, and Brill's eyes get wider as I speak. Pero, Chestla's grinning now that I've given her a mission, a way to still help the cause, so to speak. There's shouting in the background, and Chestla looks over her shoulder. "I gotta go."

"Me too," Brill says as he takes his phone back. He turns and follows Jcska out of the mess hall.

I turn to the three Zantite cooks. "Crosskiss told me Garfex now expects to sample a dish representative of Earth. I don't know about all of Earth, but Mamá Lavonda's signature dish is pork with annatto and ancho chilies. We have a number of options to replace the pork, and I had both those spices in my bag. Mertex, do you think you might be good enough to share?"

Mertex blushes green. "I ought to return your bag anyway." He gives the other cooks a stern look. "But I get it back when she dies."

CHAPTER TWENTY-TWO

Normally, Mamá's pork dish marinates overnight and cooks for three hours, but we cut that down to an hour and a half total using a vacuum sealer and a massive pressure cooker. As I set the timer, I try not to think about how my life's been compressed in the same way. I'll be dead in a matter of hours, days at the most – only, I don't feel sick. No y no. I feel stronger, more energized, more assertively *me* than ever before.

I've got to keep moving, so that I won't go loco waiting to hear that Mamá's safe. I take the tray of cookies the guys made for the break into the ballroom. The delegates are up out of their chairs, stretching, chatting, and in at least one case, napping. I set the cookies on the buffet table then make my way over to the display of chocolate bars, with its *Please Do Not Take* sign.

I slip my handheld off the display, verifying it's the phone, not a snack, before I slide it into my pocket.

"Miss Benitez." The voice, close to the back of my ear, makes me jump.

"Yes?" I turn, expecting to see a guard who thinks I stole one of the bars. Rather, it's one of the courtiers. He puts his hands on his knees so that he can balance while bending down to my level. He's smiling but only showing hints of teeth, maybe part of his diplomatic training.

"His Majesty mentioned your name to Minda Frou, and

she would like to meet you. Would you accompany me to her suite, please?"

I'm confused. What is a Zandywood star doing aboard this ship? I guess she's one of the delegates? I smile back at the courtier. I don't dare say no. "I'd be delighted."

Minda's got a reputation for being wild, so as we walk toward the elevator I dab on some of Brill's perfume as an execution deterrent. Though, ay, it might not work. This stuff smells amazing – light and floral and crisp, like biting into an Asian pear. I hadn't even opened the bottle before, so I'm just now realizing that Brill chose something perfect for me, not a cloying old lady scent like I imagine when I think expensive fragrances. My face feels hot, and at first I think the fever's returning, but it's just hitting me how little I understood about his sense of honor when I rejected this gift.

When we enter Minda's suite, she's lounging in a chair with an oversized seat cushion long enough for her to stretch out her legs. She's wearing a turban-like head adornment and a fluttery dressing gown over a tight black outfit. A half dozen Zantltes sit on other pieces of furniture, chatting drunkenly. Minda gestures with a glass of clear liquid as she points out something from one of her films to a humanoid couple staring rapturously at the household.

Minda catches sight of me and a big grin breaks over her face stretching her mouth to show the heavily serrated ripping edges on her teeth. I think that marks her as being from their southernmost continent. Maybe I'm getting used to Zantltes, maybe I'm just still under the influence of the Invincible Heart, but she's muy bonita. "Bo, you came! That's my friend Nona over there, and I don't know the rest of these people – except for the Carters here. They're from Earth."

The blonde, curvaceous Mrs Carter coos, curling her arm through the crook of her husband's elbow. "Who would have ever imagined me and my poopsie in space?"

Qué? Is she for real? I think the guy knows his wife sounds like Vapid Barbie. He pats her hand and gives her a patronizing smile. Then he looks over at me. "I know what you're thinking. We're the last people who belong at this kind of party. The missus and I entered the big HGB contest to win a week with Minda, and she just happened to be coming here."

"Which reminds me." Minda picks up a book off the side table and hands it to me. "HGB sent me a couple of things as a thank you for participating. I understand that you are to be executed after the ball tonight, and I am thoroughly sorry for your family's loss. Do you think you might autograph this before you go?"

The ice that flashes through my chest at the word *executed* is getting familiar, pero I still haven't accepted that it's really going to happen.

I turn the book over in my hands. Out here, fifteen billion miles from home, and Mamá's still right there, beaming that smile of hers right off the cover. It would be *The M.O.M. Cooking Guide: 365 Bodacious Dinners*, the one with the swimsuit photo of me and mis hermanos on page fifty-two. The girls are still showing up regularly in her newest books. Despite everything, picturing Isabella, the more sensitive of the two, all grown up and looking back on these embarrassing keepsakes makes me smile. "Sí. I mean, sure."

She gives me a pen and I sign my name. My hand shakes, pero not from venom or fever. I'm worried that Isabella and Sophia could wind up growing up without any more of these books. Idiota Frank.

As I'm handing the book back to Minda, my handheld rings in my pocket. My stomach heavy with anxiety, I silence it. Please, please, Frank, have a little patience with me. Don't get carried away and hurt anybody just because I'm terrified to offend a high-strung Zantite. Minda smiles again as she examines what I've written – *Have a Bodacious Life!* – then she nods towards the phone I'm sliding back into my pocket. Somehow, there's a speck of glitter on her cheek now, though I haven't touched her.

"Go ahead and answer your call. If you need privacy, try the bathroom. I guarantee you, it's soundproof."

I don't want to know how she knows that. Nunca. I pick up the call. It's not Frank. It's Mario. There's a ton of noise coming from behind him, a Benitez fiesta de familia in full swing. "Hermana, I need you to give Mamá a hint about the surprise you've got planned. She doesn't want to go see it."

He's talking about the extraction crew Brill has put in place to take her to an undisclosed, safe location from an undisclosed location in her backyard. She's not safe yet.

My legs suddenly weak, I sit on the edge of the oversized bathtub with its rack of bubble bath options. I drop my voice. "Mario, if she won't go, you'll have to drug her. Take one of her sleeping pills and dissolve it in a glass of punch. I'll have the surprise moved to her bedroom. You'd better leave with them, OK?"

Mamá takes the phone. "Mija! Muchas gracias por the cake. You know how much I like polka dots, and to think that you found someone on such short notice to shape it like a Gucci handbag."

Ay, right. I just hope she doesn't scrape the frosting down to where it recently said *Congratulations Rita!* Rita will be celebrating first place in the *Color Me Happy* cosmetics line's regional sales competition cakeless because I convinced my old friend Sandra that I needed her edible art more urgently. "I just want you to be happy, Mamá. Listen, about Frank–"

"I know. You changed your mind about him, and you have worked together with both him and Little Mario to make this fiesta happen. That makes me so happy, all those bits of mi familia coming back together. I was just telling Frank how your brother named you. I sent him to go get that frame with all your baby pictures stored in it."

"What are you talking about named me, Mamá?"

"Hold on. Here comes Frank now. I will make this call holo." She presses a few buttons, which beep in my ear. I pull the handheld away from my face and watch as Frank appears in the holo on one side of her and Mario on the other. Mario looks nervous, with his arms crossed, fingers of one hand tapping rhythmically against his other elbow. Frank's wearing a tight-lipped smile. I don't see any sign of the dagger – yet.

Mamá puts a hand on her fiancé's arm. The words bubble out of her like she's told this story a million times. So why have I never heard it? "Frank, I had Bodacious when Mario was four. She did not look like an Isabella, the family name Big Mario's abuelita wanted for his first-born daughter, and we had been fighting over whether or not to change it. When Little Mario finally got a look at the baby, my mijo says, 'That's one bodacious babe, Mamá!' It was so funny it broke the tension, and we were all laughing, my perfect little familia, and it wound up on her birth certificate."

I wonder if Frank feels guilty for ruining that perfection by killing mi papá eight years ago. There's no sign of it on his face – or any sign of the fact that he left someone dead in Mamá's garden shed an hour ago.

Mario's staring at the pattern of the carpet, obviously embarrassed. He looks over at Frank. "Bodacious means bold and audacious. It's one of the original blended words, back before hangry, way before emotirated." There's no way he could have *not* become a history

professor. He turns away, returning a moment later to trade Mamá a cut-glass cup for the phone.

I hear him laughing as he trails through the party. "OK. It's done."

"Thanks, mi hermano. And Mario? You know I love you, don't you?"

He stammers something back about us needing to get together sometime. The odds of me surviving long enough for that to happen are slim, but there's enough closure here for me to find peace.

I hang up the phone and send a quick text to Brill asking him to update the plan. He replies with, *As you wish*. Cheesy, but we both loved that holo when it was re-released on Larksis. It touches my heart for real. We're back together. He loves me. Tesuaquenell – he has half of my heart – and now I know I still have half of his.

He adds, *Still down in Dr Tassiks's lab*.

I've got another message waiting, but the knob rattles insistently. A female Zantite squeezes past me when I'm still only halfway out the door. Minda pats the foot of her chair, gesturing for me to sit by her. I cross the room and sink onto the plush cushion. Minda points toward the Carters. "These two have seen every one of my holos."

"We've been having a bit of a holocade." Mr Carter pats his wife's knee again. "We both agree that *Wandering Wild* is her best ever. Do you want to watch it with us while we wait for dinner? There's worse ways to spend your last day."

I'm shocked these humans *aren't* shocked about my impending execution, but they're Zandyfans, so Zantite culture must seem natural to them. I love a good dramatic story, and Mertex had included a song from *Wandering Wild* as part of his last requests. The holo probably is as good as they claim. If I didn't still have to dispose of those beans to appease Frank, I'd be tempted to lean back against the arm of the chair and let my last hours tick away.

Pero, I can't. But what if denying Minda makes her mad? Those serrated teeth are close. I swallow hard. "Please don't be insulted, but I still have things to do."

"Of course, darling." Minda sweeps her hand towards the door. "Thank you thoroughly for the autograph."

As I head down the hallway, I check that message. It's from Chestla. *This hasn't been easy, but we've been sorting through all the data from SeniorLeisure. It looks like the court has been focusing on recordings from Kaliel's ship, but check this out. It's from a passenger's family vlog. PS I'm getting thirsty for salt, cesuda ma. Ideas?*

I open the holo. It's pretty standard Galactourist stuff. The old guy's taking a selfie, with his wife, in front of a holo of the ocean that has the SeniorLeisure logo floating above the waves, each letter shooting off one at a time as fireworks then burning back in. The ship name shows up below it: the *CaptureVista*. He turns, panning the camera across the lobby. Then he walks up the hall, towards the bridge, until he reaches the point where a large red sign says *No Passengers Allowed Past This Point*. He stops, but films as much of the forbidden space as he can. And as he swings the camera past a row of holoportraits, there's a pequeña red box that just looks out of place with the decor. With blinking dots and wires on it. In case I missed it, Chestla's enhanced the holo. And zoomed in on it. And circled it with neon virtual paint in hot pink with a caption in her bubbly handwriting that says, *Communication jammer*. With a heart for the dot above the *j*.

I reach the elevator and punch the button for the first deck, staring at this unexpected evidence. Someone blocked the communications array of the SeniorLeisure vessel, so that it couldn't respond to Kaliel's request for identification. On purpose.

And then it hits me: *CaptureVista*. Chestla had said the packing slip she'd found had read *Catanista* or *Capanida*. What if that tainted chocolate had been bound for this SeniorLeisure ship? And someone else was desperate to stop it from being delivered? Oi, no? It's not enough for proof, and I still have no idea who the players are here, but I text Chestla my theory.

The elevator arrives, and I start playing back the holo of the Conference speeches. Given the split-second camera placement, I'd managed to capture a reasonable chunk of the room. I forward through people chatting and eating cookies and waiting for the formal event to start up again. When Garfex sweeps back into the room, his cabeza misses the holo's capture area, but it's still definitely him talking.

"Thank you all thoroughly again for allowing us to step in at the last moment to host this delegation. As one of the galaxy's most famous chocolate addicts, I have a vested interest in the outcome." There's a smattering of laughter, which he allows to die down. "I just tasted the most delectable chocolate cake, made from an Earth recipe which my wife now has in her possession. I wish you all could have sampled it. It may well have swayed your decision. But there isn't time for that. Are there any closing comments before we vote?"

Admiral Alabaster stands. "I also wish there was more time to consider this issue, but we must act decisively. The humans are pointing guns deeper and deeper into space. Their pilots are so nervous they're firing on passenger vessels. I may be the only one here who thinks of chocolate as a secondary letekka, but this situation is a prokeskvave ready to blow open. If we can't isolate them from the rest of the galaxy, we must disarm them."

I whimper softly. Is he saying what I think he's saying? That my muy grande objection should have been to the fact that they're voting to invade Earth? En serio?

Pero, that can't be right. The elevator door opens, but when I don't get out, it closes again. I can't look away from the holo.

After Alabaster sits, Crosskiss stands. "I agree with the admiral. Breaking the monopoly on chocolate isn't the only letekka. We aren't intent on destroying the planet, just forcing it to interact with the galaxy on fairer terms. We could learn so much more about how to do that if Earth would just open its borders. During the *Layla's Pride* drekk, we've already determined the military weak points. I'm more interested in the things we could only learn about secondhand. For instance, I would like to taste what their culture calls shaved ice – particularly the more colorful versions from Thailand and Korea. I would also like to visit the Eiffel Tower in Paris to see if that city really does have a strange power to inspire love."

A delegate whose face is almost entirely obscured by his tangled hair stands next. "I question looking for value in humanity, judging by those people Minda Frou brought with her. On their home planet, these Earthlings wantonly kill each other – and you should see what they view for entertainment. It's a broken and debased race."

The discussion continues for a while, then one at a time they stand and vote to form a committee to decide how to best forcibly open Earth's borders.

The elevator door opens again. A Zantite crew member wants to board. He steps back to let me out before he gets in. As I pass him, he says, "I hope it gets better."

"I do too." Pero, I don't see how that's going to happen. Nada, nunca, you know the rest. I stagger like a sleepwalker down the hall toward Doc's office, anger and fear and frustration pingponging around inside my heart, the drug in my system making me want to smash something.

When I walk in, Brill's sitting on the exam table, pouring the last of the coffee from the thermos into its cup. His T-shirt says *I Ate the Whole Thing* with the picture of a ten-scoop ice cream sundae underneath. He hates logos on his clothes, pero he must not have had much choice. I guess Jeska collects souvenir Ts, too. When he sees me, Brill puts the cup down beside him on the table. "Babe? Oh no, did the drug wear off?"

He jumps down off the table and I lurch into his arms. The soft fabric feels nice against my cheek, and I cling to him.

Jeska comes out from the operating room, studying a complicated holographic datagraph. His eyes have gone mauve. "The suicide gene does exist, but it was present in only two of the samples. That's the good news. Bad news, Bo was right about the modification that turns these things to mush if you try to clone them."

I suck in a noisy breath. Jeska's analyzing the beans, when Brill had clearly understood I'd asked him not to. Por qué nunca! That's presumptuous of both of them. Even if they are trying to help. Brill looks at me nervously, but I smile, so he knows this research into chococide is not a dealbreaker for our fragile reunion.

Jeska looks up. "Bo? You OK?"

"Oh dear." Doc moves around Jeska and puts his hands at the spot where my neck and my jaw come together, examining my lymph nodes. "I had hoped this wouldn't occur quite so soon."

I push his hands away. "Would you stop it? I still have plenty of your supersoldier drug running around inside me. I just had a shock, no? I found out all those delegates out there voted *yes* to invade Earth."

Well, Doc obviously didn't know. His hands fall slowly to his sides and his mouth gapes open. "I'm thoroughly sorry for your loss."

"Sí, well, there's nothing either one of us can do." I turn back to Brill and bury my face in his shirt again. It's so comforting being wrapped inside his arms. I just want to stay there until the end. It's a better way to spend my last hours than watching some estúpido holo. "I officially give up."

"You can't do that." Brill lifts my chin so that I have to look up at him again. "You're more important now than ever, and not just to me. If you break the monopoly on cacao, the stuffed shirts out there will lose interest in Earth far before they can get organized enough to invade."

"Pero, how can they even do that? I thought we had protections through the Galactic Courts. Anticolonization laws, laws against breeching borders and murdering citizens. Earth was given details on all of that when we went interstellar."

Jeska shakes his head. "That kind of stuff protects against individual criminals, and rogue civilizations. But an official declaration of war is different. They'd file that *with* the Galactic Court, stating reasons for the grievance. They still can't claim land on your home world, and they can't take your people. But if they win the war, they can do just about anything else."

"Ayyyyyyy." I've decided once and for all to destroy the beans, to save mi familia. Now they're saying I can't, because I need them to save my world. Oi! It's an impossible choice. "Pero they kept saying chocolate was only a secondary letekka," whatever that is, "that Earth's unpredictable violence makes it a danger to the galaxy."

"And you believed that?" Jeska's violet eyes are laughing at me. His gaze shifts to Brill. "I told you she was naive."

"Could we have a minute alone?" Brill asks.

Jeska and Doc go back into the operating room.

I lean my face against Brill's chest, mumbling into his T-shirt. I miss him smelling like leather. "Tell me we're going to make it through this, now that we're back together."

His chest rumbles against my ear as he laughs. "I was so shocked to hear you call me mi vida again, even more shocked you meant it. We both know Jess has feelings for you, and I know how the story's supposed to go. It's like when Juan Carlos dies so Marta can have true love with Raul without feeling guilty."

Is he talking about *El Amor Duele*, the telenovela known in English as *Love Hurts*? The one I've been afraid to tell him I'm addicted to, because I don't want him to think I'm shallow? The one I've missed the last four or five episodes of, leading up to the finale? Dios mío! "Juan Carlos dies?"

Brill looks startled. "You watch *El Amor Duele*?"

"Sí. It's from my culture. What excuse do you have?"

He shrugs, not the least embarrassed. In fact, his eyes are powder blue. "It seemed like a fun way to learn Spanish."

I smile. Pero there's still that spoiler about my favorite character. "How did Juan Carlos die?"

The smile falls from Brill's lips, though his eyes are still blue. "He sacrifices himself to save Marta and Raul from the gang who think they stole all that drug money. There's no other way the story arc could have worked. At least they gave him a noble death. I'd have been OK with something like that."

Something like dying in a pool of chocolate, trying to help me escape. Had his hunormous character transformation really come from watching a soap opera? Or had he finally gotten the courage to live up to his own ideals?

"Pero, you didn't die." I take both his hands in mine. "I'm grateful to Jeska for that. He's the only one who believed you might still be alive in that freezer."

"My point exactly. It's like he's hard-wired to do the right thing." He shakes his head, though his eyes show admiration rather than scorn. "Whereas I'm always going to have to struggle not to put my own self-interest first. Not that I would have let him die just so I could have you for myself if the situation had been reversed, but I would have thought about it for a good minute."

"I'm OK with that, because you get to the right place in the end." Letting his hands go, I hug Brill as hard as I can. "Jeska's a great guy, but I don't love him. *Te amo*."

He pushes me away, tilts my face up so I'm looking into his now-gray eyes. "Is it me you're in love with, or just what you wish I was? I really will sell my ship if that's what you want, but—"

"Don't even think about selling it. Nunca. I'm not asking you to change who you are, not now that I've started to comprender what that is." I put a hand on his cheek, feeling small inside in the face of what I've done to him, repeatedly, since the day we met. "I'm sorry I discounted that before. I don't know why you forgave me for treating you like your values didn't matter."

"Because you're hot." His eyes dance toward violet. "Kidding. I don't always understand you either, but I promise to try."

I hesitate, but there is still one thing I'd like to understand. "Can I ask you something?"

"Anything, Babe."

"You told Frank that to get your eyes to change to a color you aren't really feeling, you need a memory strong enough to be more important than the present. When you're scared, pero you force your irises to blue, what are you thinking about?"

He hesitates and looks down at the floor, inhaling an impossibly long breath. Finally, he looks me straight on. "Do you remember the night on Larksis when you tried to teach me how to samba? You were so patient, and at the same time, that little dress you were wearing was so hot."

"You remember my clothes?"

"Sí. How could I forget that white dress, with those tiny black polka dots and red double cherries printed all over it? I wasn't in love with you then, not yet. But we went and sat on the hood of that kalltet rentacar, and you actually cared which stars pointed toward Krom. It made me feel important in a way nobody ever had before – not because you needed anything from me, not because you were trying to get me to live up to any particular expectations. It was the best night of my life."

"Mine too." The words come out as a whisper because as he was talking, his irises shifted to that clearsky blue. It didn't look forced, wasn't a lie. I'm part of one of his happiest memories.

CHAPTER TWENTY-THREE

Chestla's ill. You wouldn't be able to tell if she was human, but there's just something lacking about her presence and energy that's obvious even through the holo. She's still smiling, but her face looks tired and un poco feral. "It wasn't a random piece of space junk Kaliel ran into. A cloaked ship fired that fuel cell at the *Nibs*. This is from one of the hall security cameras, still sending gritcast to the central box even as it got blown off the *CaptureVista*."

She pops up a holo. Just as she said, the feed's spinning, dizzying inside the confined field. But she slows it down, and on one of the revolutions, there's a black arced ship caught in silhouette against the light of the explosion, just for a few frames. It looks just like the spacejacker craft that had murdered Yvette.

"It has to be the same ship," Brill and I say at the same time.

"You think?" Chestla asks sarcastically, killing the holo.

"This is probably enough to get Kaliel out of the teeter-totter line," I say. "You did amazing work. Muchas gracias."

"Great." She's not summoning her usual enthusiasm.

"We still don't know who we can trust with this," Brill points out.

"Cierto," I sigh. "Someone had to have ordered this set-up, someone powerful."

"Chestla, can you send me a copy of that holo?" Brill asks.

"I hate to complain," Chestla says. Clearly she's doing something to send the file to Brill. "But have you thought about how you're going to get me down to the sea?"

Brill looks up at me. There's still a smear of chocolate on the side of his face, right next to his ear. "What emergency resource can she go to for salt?"

I wipe the chocolate off him with my thumb. He smiles, and his eyes go a shade toward gold. I'm feeling a bit like sunlight myself, but when I think on Chestla's predicament, my heart sinks. Oye. "Salt's one of the rarest things in the rainforest. I've even seen butterflies clustering around turtles to drink sodium from their tears."

Chestla says, "I'm a bit too big for that to work."

Brill's eyes are tinting toward aquamarine. "That's a beautiful image, though. If Earth ever opens its borders, I'd like to see that with you."

Yep, definite sunlight in my heart.

"You guys!" Chestla scrunches up her nose. "I'm sorry, but all this romance is making me feel like you're not focusing on my problem."

"Lo siento," I tell Chestla. "Rio's at least close to the ocean, so elements like salt blow inland with the breeze and fall in the rain. Maybe you can find a cave somewhere that has collected solidified runoff."

Chestla shakes her head. "There's nothing like that inside the wall. Eugene and I have been over the map."

"What about salted caramel? There may be some in the archive of chocolate bars in that facility." Brill's seriously grasping at straws. It looks like he's only half paying attention, as he sends a message out on his phone.

"Really, mi vida?"

Brill's quiet for a moment, his eyes shading back and forth between purple and gray. "I already called in my favors to get your mom out of the line of fire. You may have to bargain with Frank."

"What else can I give him? I've already promised him the cacao beans, and he's got three different claims on my life." I'm not afraid of death anymore. Still, even the Invincible Heart doesn't make what's going to happen to me feel like justice.

"You've got holo of the biggest threat in Earth's history. Surely that's worth something."

I study the closed door, where Jeska and Doc are reviewing that holo on the grande-sized field in the operating room. "Shouldn't I just give him the file? Or send it to somebody who could do something about it? It hardly seems right to barter Earth's future."

"Don't worry. He won't keep it to himself." Brill takes my hand in one of his and squeezes reassuringly. "And this way, your friend gets to live."

"Yes, I'd like that." Chestla looks nervous. "While you guys do make an adorable couple, you realize my life is on the line here, right?"

My handheld rings, and Brill moves to switch over the call. I can still feel the warmth after he pulls his palm away from mine. "It's Minerva."

I take the phone from him. "It's Frank. What do I say?"

"Whatever it takes." Brill puts a hand on my arm. "You got this."

Frank's face is flushed crimson in the holo. He's outside, in Mamá's backyard, with the sun going down behind him. "Where in the hell is your mother?"

Ay, yes! Brill's team must have gotten her out. "Hola, Frank. I can honestly say I have no idea. I'm not even on the same planet as you guys." I try to hide my smile, but judging by the increasing anger etching frown lines across the assassin's face, I'm not doing a very good job. "Don't tell me you're not secretly relieved she got away."

"On a selfish, personal level, maybe I am. But one person's

life is not worth sacrificing the future of our entire planet – no matter who that person is." His eyes go soft for a moment, but when he looks back up, they're cold again. "Now I'm going to have to meet with my superiors to find something else that will persuade you to destroy those beans. I assure you you're not going to like it." Frank raises an eyebrow. "Are you getting sicker? That's a medical office."

"Don't worry about me. Look, Frank, can I trust you?"

He blinks, and the frown takes on a different quality. "You know I'm a weapon. I follow orders. I'm not about to betray those orders to help you, and I won't keep your secrets."

"Pero do you keep your word?"

"You're worried about Kaliel." His phone dips and I catch sight of the dagger in his other hand. "His trial's been moved, just like I promised. I'll send you a copy of the paperwork."

"What if I could prove somebody set him up?" I study Frank's face, wishing he had telltale Krom eyes. Is Frank the kind of man who would bury that information along with Kaliel's body? Or would his twisted code of honor compel him to see justice done?

Frank looks at me, as intently as if we really were mere feet away from each other. "Then I would suggest you get your butt back here and present whatever you have to the court. Or send it to someone you really trust."

"Gracias por the advice," I sigh. He's just made it clear that I *can't* trust him, not with Kaliel's life, especially not if I die. "I still have a favor to ask you. You remember Chestla? The one who nearly made you pee your pants at that gate?"

"She'd be hard to forget. She will not stop calling me."

I laugh, despite the tension. "I need you to get her offplanet. I can trade holo I took of alien diplomats discussing a sensitive Earth-related situation."

"Not going to happen." He points to his own chest with the tip of the dagger. "Weapon. Obeys orders. What part of that suggests I'd commit treason?"

I think about what Chestla actually said. She just needs salt. "How about this, viejo? I'll send you an encrypted file." I glance over at Brill, who has to encrypt it. He gives me a thumbs up. "And I'll have Brill give you a set of coordinates somewhere deep in the rainforest. You send me a holo of a drone delivering a fifty-pound bag of salt to those coordinates, and then leaving the area, and I'll send you the encryption code."

"Why salt?"

I lean forward. After feeling helpless throughout all of this, any bit of control is bound to bring me a sliver of joy. "I finally know something about alien biology that you don't."

Frank rolls his eyes. "Do you seriously want to test my patience right now?"

"No. Lo siento. The salt. Chestla needs it to survive. And you need this information."

He's wavering. I can tell from the way his lips have gone all scrunched. "So what prevents me from staking out these coordinates and capturing her when she arrives?"

"After you view my holo, I think you'll agree that Earth needs all the amigos it can get, and killing a citizen of Evevron won't help. I may die today, but Brill won't, and I swear he will tell her people personally if she disappears."

"I'm interested." Frank points the dagger at his phone. "I'll do my best to make it happen, Bo, but this information better be worth it. And you still owe me a holo of those cacao beans in return."

I try not to let my expression waver. "I'm going to make that happen, too." I'm just planning to send him holo of a monopoly-smashing chocolate buy rather than of the beans' destruction. I'm no longer conflicted, now that Mamá's safe. "Look me in the eye and promise me you won't poison that salt."

Frank smiles, the expression warming his face for the first time all day. "Poison's not my style."

The operating room door opens, but Jeska waits in the doorway until I finish my call. Then he says, "You guys have got to see this. Gavin's buyer's made contact."

"Speaking of Gavin." Brill's phone is ringing, and when he answers we're all treated to a two-foot-tall version of Brill's best friend. The size does nothing to mute the smugness of Gavin's frown. It looks like he's at a tradepost or a refueling depot. Which means he probably isn't far from where we are now.

"You don't even want to go looking for that ship." Gavin crosses his arms over his chest.

I give Brill a questioning look.

Brill says, "He's talking about the black ship that took a shot at Kaliel."

"You know who they are?" I ask.

Gavin nods. "It's a distinctive ship. Those guys are serious mercenaries, but with a reputation for discretion. Even if you could capture them, they'd die before telling you who their clients are. And I prefer my best friend alive, thank you very much. Sometimes life's little mysteries are better left unsolved."

And I'd thought this would fall so neatly together. "So they're not working for HGB?"

"I doubt it." There's noise, mingled voices, and Gavin holds up a hand to someone out of range of the camera. "Some old friends have offered to buy me a drink. I've got to go."

"So do we," Brill says. "Safe journey."

"Oh," Gavin adds. "Tell Kayla thank you for the book list. I'm really enjoying number forty-seven."

I guess Brill must have forwarded him Kayla's list after all. Has he en serio gotten through half of it? How fast do these guys read?

Doc's householo, which has been placed so that he can see it during surgery, has frozen on the face of a guy whose orange complexion makes him look un poco like an oompa loompa.

The guy's wearing a rather spectacular feathered headdress in red, peach and yellow. The feathers cascade out of the holo's capture area. Doc leans on the table that had so recently held Sullivan's body. I wonder where the dead pilot's gone off to – him and his precious healthy organs. I wonder, without shuddering gracias to the Invincible Heart, if I'll be joining him there, soon. After all, I'm nearing the expected expiration of the drug's effects.

My handheld notifies me I've got a text from Tyson. *I am at the coordinates where Brill reported your ship stalled but the empty sadness expanse puzzles me. Where are you?*

Is everyone talking to Tyson? I give Brill my handheld. "It's for you."

I watch him input, *Have resumed previous course. Expect to rendezvous with the transport containing the remaining delegates within the next couple of hours. Trajectory detailed below.*

"How do you know that?" I can't help but ask.

"He's just that good." Jeska starts the holo moving again. "Now, here's your buyer." In the image, the orange guy picks up my phone and points it at a handwritten note he's hiding in the palm of his other hand. The action is smooth, almost like he's a stage magician – believable given the get-up he's wearing, which looks like someone crossed a tuxedo with a sari. En serio. I can't believe I'd missed this when I watched the holo through the first time. Jeska backs the image up to the note, then freezes it and zooms in on the writing, which is in English.

Suite 412, %4030 ZTS, very much! want to buy, come alone;

The guy may have a limited vocabulary and no understanding of English punctuation, but his message is clear. Well, mostly. "What's 4,030?"

Doc says, "We measure time in a forty-six segment day with forty partitions to each segment. ZTS stands for Zantite Time Standard."

My phone is still set to Larksissian Daysaving. "What time is it now?"

Doc consults his computer. "38-32."

Jeska turns off the holo. "You've got about two hours."

My phone dings with a text from Frank. *Can you please remind Kayla that they're recording every word she says to Kaliel? She alluded to some video footage that she shouldn't have access to, and that's going to make it harder for me to keep my promises. But given this, and your earlier thoughts, I suspect Kaliel will be fine after our business is concluded.*

There's a bumpclip attached. In it, Kayla's back in the same chair in the visitor's room, saying, "I do take comfort from that. To know that you had your reasons. I just... I miss my grandmother so much." There are sudden tears in her eyes.

Kaliel puts a hand on her shoulder. "I know how you feel. I lost my grandfather on my Dad's side when I was fifteen. We were really close. He used to take me ice fishing on the Torne river in Abisko, and we'd talk about life."

"Sucks, doesn't it." She puts her hand over his, which I did not see coming.

He freezes. "Kayla, I'm getting really mixed messages here."

"Maybe because I'm having really mixed feelings." She doesn't move her hand. "What you did was horrible, and it's going to impact me for the rest of my life. But who you are? You're funny, and humble – and you have that adorable smile. How do I reconcile that?"

"I don't know. But even if you did, it wouldn't be fair of me to expect–"

She leans over and kisses him, stopping his words with her mouth. I feel a quick pang of jealousy. After all, she's my friend, and it hadn't been that long since my own lips had been on Kaliel's. But who am I to deny them both the comfort they need? I suddenly feel voyeuristic watching this, and I look away, about to turn it off, pero Kayla says, "I feel guilty now, like I'm somehow betraying Bo."

Kaliel squeezes Kayla's hand. "She was never mine."

And that's where Frank's cut the clip, right where it's enough to break my heart. And yet, it's what I needed. Proof that even when I'm gone – which will be soon – those I leave behind will be OK.

CHAPTER TWENTY-FOUR

"We're not letting you go in there by yourself." Jeska holds out the seed viability box together with the folded printout of the genetic choconalysis.

I take it, studying the beans in the dim green glow that marks each one as still viable despite the abuse I have put them through. "I know you think I'm naive, but do I look completely kalltet?"

"Not at all, Babe." Brill takes my free hand.

"Why do I recognize this room number?" Jeska taps at the holo as though it's solid.

I find it familiar too. "It's just down the hall from Minda's suite."

"Wal. There's only one hall of suites for visiting dignitaries. But that's not what's ringing the bell." Jeska snaps his fingers. "That's the number V wanted me to remember because it's the last room Lyex managed to get the joke soap into. We dared him, but we didn't think he'd really do it."

"You met Lyex," Doc says, miming a circle around his face. "He's the near-adolescent with the unfortunate acne problem."

Jeska nods his agreement with this assessment. "So now V has to sneak up there and get all the soap back out before any ambassadors go to their rooms to take a shower, and the kid winds up being executed over it."

Ay, no. I groan, picturing Minda's oversized tub. "Or worse, a bubble bath."

"Focus, people." Brill holds up a small silver contraption with a short needle sticking out of it. "My gun cracked in the blast freezer, and the only weapon Dr Tassiks here will let me have is this dart thing. We're walking into a dangerous situation practically unarmed."

"There's every chance that Oompa Loompa is honorable," Jeska points out. "Still, if that gun's in one piece I'd like to hold onto it. Nobody has to know it doesn't work."

"That guy's not an Oompa Loompa." The way Brill says the name, it's obvious he's never heard it before. "He's a Svegarian,"

Jeska looks at me, and we both start laughing.

"What?" Brill looks a little hurt.

"Nada, mi vida, just, in all your research on chocolate, you never ran across Earth's most famous movie starring it. Oompa Loompas handle the chocolate in *Charlie and the Chocolate Factory*. They're orange."

"Well, if that's all." Brill kisses me, just a quick brush of lips on lips. "We'll just have to watch it together later."

He's still assuming there will *be* a later.

We head out into the hallway. Brill keeps close by my side. Jeska walks behind us with the gun butt strategically visible in his belt. My handheld dings. I silence it, but the message chain from Kayla has popped up. I don't want Brill to see what I said about him, so I tilt the phone away. Kayla's typed, *Do all men who think they're about to die kiss so intensely? It's too bad he's guilty. Kaliel's so much hotter with his brains attached.*

I pull my hand out of Brill's so I can type. I tilt my face away too, trying to hide the sudden blush I know is staining my cheeks. I am so stupid. I need to get the evidence that will clear Kaliel into the hands of someone he can trust, no? And Frank had sent me that holo to tell me exactly who. I hadn't expected the viejo to help me, not after what he's said, so I'd missed it.

Actually, Kaliel's been set up. Check out the proof.

"Babe, this is hardly the time to be sending messages."

"This one's important, just in case we don't make it back." I attach all the files Chestla had sent and forward it on to Kayla.

The door to 412 stands ajar. Eh? Brill and Jeska exchange a look, their eyes fading to identical shades of deep gray.

"It shouldn't have been you," Brill tells me softly.

"Qué?" I'm confused.

"You were the first human I'd ever met. I believed what everyone said, that humans were half-literate, greedy beings. When I found out you weren't like that, I should have let you go, found somebody who deserved to wind up here. I'm sorry."

"Mi vida—"

Brill shakes his head. He swallows visibly before he pushes on the door. It swings silently open.

"You must be the thief." The man sitting in the suite's big chair crosses his legs and leans back. He's humanoid and deeply tanned, pero not orange. Instead of a feathered hat, he's sporting a brown leather jacket and green button-up shirt with a beige T peeking out from underneath. With his short-cropped dark hair and warm brown eyes, he looks human. The longer I stare at him, the more I'm convinced he *is* human.

I hesitate. "You're not the guy who left me that note."

Beside me, Brill pulls the weird little gun. "Babe, I know this guy. Remember how there are OK pirates and bad pirates? This guy's one of the really bad ones."

The bathroom door rattles, catching everyone's attention. There could be a dozen backup pirates in there.

"That note told her to come alone, Cray. If you could just listen for once in your life, nobody would have had to get hurt."

"Brill? What do I do?" I wish he had a sublingual.

The pirate holds out a hand. "Come on, doll, hand over the magic beans. Uncle Jack wants to climb a beanstalk."

I freeze, remembering the name of the friend of a friend who got me into Lula's shop. "Un momento. Is this the same Jack?"

I'm tilting my head, trying to see if Jeska's drawn the broken gun without actually turning to look, when I pick up crosstalk on the sublingual. I take a step toward Pirate Jack, trying to make the signal clearer.

"The same as what?" Jack's smile scrunches up his nose. *Two of them are armed. Wait for my signal to sweep in and take them out.* His jaw twitches.

I stall, trying to hear a response. "The same as Brill's contact in Rio."

"No, Babe, this guy's probably never met Lula."

I suck in a breath. "Then you must be the one who brought the dead pilot."

Jack looks confused. "Why would I do that?"

"He's also not the kind of guy who would go out of his way to save a life." Brill's eyes have gone a deep, angry whiskey tone. "What *are* you doing here, Jack? I thought I recognized your voice on that holocall. I've known Gavin a long time. He wouldn't have set me up."

And I wouldn't have expected Gavin to have any human amigos – especially not the likes of these guys. Maybe old friends had been just a euphemism... and possibly, *going for a drink* hadn't been all that voluntary.

"No, he didn't mean for us to overhear him setting up this buy. But he does talk too loud. We had to keep him from warning you. I was afraid he was going to find a way to tip you off when he answered your call for information, but I guess people with attachments back home are easier to control. Don't worry. I'm sure somebody will find him before he starves to death."

I wince. Gavin's got a family. I met them once, his wife and two little boys who don't deserve to grow up like I did, without a Papá.

"Brill," I say slowly, "he's got backup coming in from somewhere."

Brill looks at Jeska, then back at Jack. He fires the dart gun twice into Jack's chest.

Jack's bubblechatter sounds woozy. *I've been tranqued. Get in here now.*

The closet door bursts open and three pirates carrying vapguns pour out of it. Brill manages to dart one of them, pero that just makes the other two angry.

"Give us the beans," the stockier one demands, "and we let you live."

"Like anybody believes that." Brill edges in front of me, shielding me from the most immediate danger.

The moment draws out into a silent stalemate. They don't know which one of us has the beans, so they don't dare vaporize anybody.

Behind us, the door pops open, drawing everyone's attention. Varnex is standing in the hall, slackjawed. "I just came for the soap."

Brill fires, but his gun's out of darts. I lunge at the stocky pirate while his attention is still on mi vida. I pry the vapgun out of his hands. In the struggle, the gun goes off, and a brand new hole zapblasted through the wall reveals the bathroom, where the terrified Oompa Loompa has drawn back from the door wearing nada but a towel around his waist. He's got a communicator in his hand. He says in soft Zantite, "Don't shoot. Only call I because the water wouldn't turn off, and somehow locked I the door."

Behind him, a tub full of orange bubbles cascades over the edge, sending agua streaming across the floor.

Jeska throws his useless gun at the other pirate, pegging the guy between the eyes. With a groan, the guy falls like a sack of tarpos.

The guy whose weapon I took, now the only conscious pirate, grabs me around the throat. I hit him with the vapgun. The gun's energy canister breaks open, splattering him with thick blue goo that looks a lot like Zantite blood. Almost immediately, I smell burning flesh. He screams and lets me go, bolting into the bathroom, desperate to get the stuff off. Nausea creeps up my throat. Oi! I'm human, and he's human and we just did that to each other. We really are a barbaric species.

We wait until the screaming has stopped, and he's done flailing around in the tub. As he makes a desperate dash for the door, Varnex grabs him.

Varnex looks down at his orange-stained prisoner, hissing sympathetically at the deep burn on the guy's shoulder. "I know what you're thinking, but I'm not going to eat you." Varnex goes for a good-natured smile, but he's showing those rows of gleaming teeth again. The guy squeaks in terror, then faints. Varnex looks at me. "I've got to stop doing that."

Brill looks at Jeska. "You're the expert on diplomacy. I gotta see what I can do to help Gavin." He pulls out his phone. But the answering phone rings in Jack's pocket. Cold lead fills my stomach as Brill's eyes shade towards ash. If Gavin really is trapped somewhere, his greatest danger is dehydration and stress to his cardiovascular system. It's possible he's already dead. Brill calls someone else. "Hey Zarak, I need you to get the word out–"

"I know where he is!" the guy in Varnex's grip blurts, having recovered from his faint. He swallows visibly. "If you just let me go–"

"I gotta call you back." Brill advances on the guy. "Where?"

"If you just–"

"My best friend's life is not a bargaining chip. If you don't tell me where he is, I'll just let Varnex here eat you after all."

"What?" Varnex looks startled. His mouth drops open in surprise, and a wet spot appears on the pirate's pants.

"OK, OK." The guy swallows again. "We stuffed Gavin into a hidden cargo hold on his own ship and set it adrift. If you call your other friend back, I can give him the coordinates."

The viability box weighs heavily in my pocket. I'm right back to having to destroy the beans before Frank tracks down Mamá, or gets assigned a new target. Brill's busy handing off his phone, so I turn to Jeska. "That Oompa Loompa's not going to buy anything from us now. Nada, nunca, no way."

"We have to get what's left of these guys back on their ship before we can worry about that." Jeska peers through the open door into the suite. "I don't know how we're going to explain away the hole in the wall, or the ambassador in the fetal position in a puddle of orange bubbles."

"Why don't we just bring them to security?" Varnex shakes the guy he's holding, who looks ready to puke.

Jeska puts a hand on Varnex's arm, stilling the motion. The pirate gives him a grateful half-smile. Jeska shakes his head. "An incident like this involving humans, right now, on this ship, is bound to move up the timetable for the invasion."

"What invasion?" Varnex peers down at the pirate, as though he might be able to explain it, but the terrified captive doesn't even look like he knows how to speak much Krom. Varnex was at the briefing. I guess they didn't go into it.

I jut out my chin. "Your people are going to invade Earth."

"Well, don't look at me." He sets the pirate on his feet. "I still want us to be friends."

Two suites down and across the hall, a door opens. Minda Frou peeks out. "What on Zant is going on out there?"

"Minda!" I have this loco idea. "I have a huge favor to ask you."

Minda steps all the way out of her suite. "For one so brave in the face of certain death? How could I refuse."

Jeska, Brill and I briefly explain what happened, and the ramifications. When she hears the words *invasion of Earth*, Minda looks back at her suite. She quietly closes the door. "No need to alarm the Carters. They really are very nice people, once you get to know them, but I can't help but wonder if the tour organizers had me bring them here as an example of how unbalanced Earthlings can be. They want to cosplay as characters from *Beginning to Love You* for tonight's ball."

I can't picture any scenario under which that goes well. "Please don't let them, por favor."

"Of course not, not now. But I doubt that is the favor you wanted to ask."

"Could you play off what just happened here as a publicity stunt for your next holo? Say it's something to do with pirates, and then when it doesn't happen, that the studio canceled it."

"Absolutely not."

My heart sinks, even though Minda's smiling.

"The studio would never dare cancel a Minda production. If I declare I'm doing a holo about space pirates, somebody damn well better bring me a script!"

Sí, Minda rocks.

"We can get these guys out of here." Jeska picks up the abandoned vapgun. "Along with their weapons, but there's an ambassador in there who's going to need convincing."

"Just leave him to me." Minda steps over Jack as she enters the suite.

"Don't touch the orange bubbles," Varnex calls. "They stain."

"Good thing for the guy lying in them then that he's already orange," Brill says as he picks up the remaining vapgun. He passes it over to me. Varnex tucks one unconscious pirate under each arm, while Jeska and Brill lift Jack together. I've got the gun, which leaves me guarding the guy I hurt, not that he has any reason not to play nice, since we've just promised to release him on his boss's ship. The only tense moment comes when we all squeeze into the elevator, and he tries to dash back out, but Varnex grabs him by the collar without dropping his unconscious cargo.

When we get down to the docking bay, which is on the other side of the ship from where I'd originally entered, we find Lyex manning a kiosk in front of the bioscanner. Past the device, a baker's dozen of armed guards fan out, one about every six feet across the widening entrance to the bays.

Lyex eyes my vapgun, and I immediately hand it over to him. "I'd like to turn this in to the lost and found, no?"

Brill lifts Jack's shoulders, showing off the pirate's unconscious face. "These guys partied a bit too much. We need to get them back on the *Shimmering Pearl* and out of here before they cause a scene."

"Wait, mi vida. Did you just say that a pirate named Jack belongs on the *Pearl*? En serio?"

Brill shrugs, awkward given the way he's holding Jack. "What can I say, Babe? He may be a horrible person, but he's a fan of classic Earth literature. *Mutiny on the Bounty*, *Treasure Island*, all of those."

"There was no book for *Pirates of the Caribbean*." Jeska puts Jack's feet down, leaving the guy sloping awkwardly until Brill lowers his end, too. "They've made twenty-seven sequels to a movie based on an amusement park ride. And there's another one coming out next year."

"Why are you so obsessed with Earth culture?" the conscious pirate asks. He obviously speaks more Zantite than Krom. He may even have understood what we told Minda.

I notice Brill running his hand along the cuff of Jack's jacket, admiring the buttery leather. I guess he's still missing his own.

Jeska doesn't go into his history with my planet. "It's a hobby. I've been stuck on this ship for a long time, and I can't crochet to save my life."

The pirate looks at me. "Jakkag?"

I'm not sure whether he didn't comprender the word, or if he's confused as to why crochet would be an important part of life aboard a military vessel. Either way, I answer him in English. "Crochet started in most cultures as a way of mending fishing nets and making clothes. These guys turned it competitive."

I gesture to Jack, who lets out a snore. "Why the *Shimmering Pearl*?" I emphasize the *shimmering* part.

"Because, well, look at it." The pirate waves his hand toward a spherical ship parked not far away. Its iridescent silvery paint job gleams like mother of pearl.

"Guys?" Lyex leans forward over the counter. He's obviously been waiting for a break in the conversation. "They figured out what happened to the engine was just a bad practical joke, so I can let you take everyone through who has clearance to leave, but she can't go." He points at me. "Crosskiss had to execute Orlux because of her, so he's not likely to react with mercy if we let her escape."

My breath catches. Lyex blames me for Orlux's death. It hadn't even occurred to me that might be my fault too, but I can see that, in a muy roundabout way, it is. I glance at Varnex. Does he hold me responsible for the loss of his amigo, too?

Varnex shakes his head. "Don't blame yourself, Bo. These events are bigger than any one of us." His arms are constrained by the pair of unconscious pirates, but he still manages to gesture with his hands at our small ring of humans, Krom and Zantites.

"I'm thoroughly sorry for your loss," I tell Lyex. "I'll wait right here, no?"

Jeska and Brill pick up Jack and head toward the pirate ship. Without warning, the strength goes out of my legs and I have to grab on to the counter to keep from falling over. Dios mio! My grip falters and I wind up on my knees, my heart racing, my blood no longer singing with strength. The Invincible Heart has abandoned me all at once.

"Take Jack's shoulders," Brill shouts to the pirate, who does. Brill races to my side. "Babe, are you OK?"

"Not so much. I think it may be time to go to Doc's." We both know that means either a desperate attempt at surgery, or an injection that will let me sleep through the rest of this ordeal.

My handheld informs me I've got an incoming message. It's the holo of Frank's drone delivering the salt to Chestla. Gracias, Frank. I watch a few seconds of it, think I catch a glimpse of her freckled face peeking from between two trees, pero my heart's racing too much for me to be sure. She's shadowpopped before I can get a second look.

I send the encryption code, and then I collapse, my knees sliding out from under me, pain twinging deep in my chest. Brill catches me before my face hits the floor. I'm still not afraid. Perhaps the Invincible Heart has at least left me courage. "Promise me, Brill, you'll save Chestla and Kaliel. Ay, I can't have any more deaths on my conscience."

He rolls me over and lays me gently on the floor so that I'm looking up into his face. "Promise, Babe."

I've done what I can. It will have to be enough. My insides feel on fire again, with the same intensity as right after Tyson first bit me. I close my eyes and surrender my consciousness in the face of the pain.

I dream of fire again. This time, I'm safe behind the barrier. Mi Papá lifts something from the midst of the flames, only instead of a child, he throws mountains of chocolate bars out a window to safety. Brill shows up, and he shatters the barrier with a single shot from his broken gun. I pull Papá out of the flames, while Brill sets off a sprinkler system that shoots out streams of pink and purple glitter. *We put out el fuego,* I tell Papá, *I managed to save you.* He kisses me on the forehead. Tears glisten in his eyes as he shakes his head. *No, mija. You have forgotten the earthquakes.* The building starts to shake, then the floor cracks open, and all three of us fall through several floors to one filled with burning ice. When I look over, my father's been flash frozen, and unlike Brill, he's not coming back.

CHAPTER TWENTY-FIVE

"Bo? Babe? Don't leave me." Brill's got me in his arms, shaking me. That nightmare seemed to go on forever. How long was I unconscious? Brill's wearing a brown leather jacket and off-white T. Qué? The only thing that makes sense is that Jeska took Jack's clothes for mi vida, which makes me rethink a lot of what I'd assumed about the ship-bound Krom. But when did Brill change?

I groan. "Why aren't we at the Doc's?" I should be sedated by now. I hadn't expected to wake up, not ever again.

"Shtesh." Brill's mouth has formed a determined line. "Please don't ask me to take you somewhere so final. Por favor."

I manage a small smile that turns into a grimace as pain twinges in my chest. Apparently, even Doc had overestimated how long my death would take. "Tyson's not going to make it." My words hurt Brill. I can see that in his face, even without looking at his eyes, and that hurts me, even more than the thought of dying here. I manage to clasp my uncoordinated hand in his. "I don't want to leave you, mi vida, but I can't stop this. You always knew we'd be playing out this scene someday. I was never going to be yours forever."

"I don't care, as long as it's not today. Sometimes we Krom can literally die of a broken heart, even if we're young. You wait. Tyson's coming."

"That won't happen to you. No y no. Your self-preservation

instinct's too strong." I laugh, but my burning lungs turn it into a cough. "I really do love you, Brill. Promise me you'll remember that for the rest of your unfairly, insanely long life. That's not asking too much, no? To be remembered?"

"I thought I was the one with all the cheesy lines." Brill kisses me with such fever that I think I'm going to ignite. I wish I had the strength to kiss back the way this moment deserves. When Brill finally pulls away, there are tears in his eyes. I can't take his grief. I'm not even dead yet, but I see coffinwood in the deep mahogany of his irises.

Jeska comes back through the scanner. "I don't mean to interrupt, but he's here."

He? Could he mean… Hope flares in my heart even before Tyson looms over Jeska. I'm still chilled by the Galactacop's fer-de-lance appearance, but I've never been so glad to see anybody in my entire life, nunca. I drop Brill's hand and push him out of the way. "How did you get enough speed to catch this ship?"

Tyson doesn't say anything, just unzips his jacket and pulls out an oversized hypodermic filled with pink liquid.

The silence is unnerving. "Say something, por favor. Tell me it's not too late. Tell me the damage isn't so much that I'm going to die anyway."

Tyson shrugs his rock-hard shoulders. "We should know witin a couple of hours. I understand tat you've been doing everyting possible to make your condition darkness sandcastle-melting star-disintegration." He rips open my borrowed uniform shirt, baring my bra. Then he pulls the cap off the hypodermic and places his cool hand flat on my chest, moving it slightly until he finds what he's looking for. "Tat is your heart, right?"

I nod, too terrified to speak. Moisture's forming in my eyes. I blink it away, stare into the golden depths of his eyes and see compassion.

"Tis is going to hurt cactus fainttype scream. Don't move

until I take te needle out." He moves his hand and plunges the needle into my chest, that pink liquid filling my heart then gushing through my body as he depresses the mechanism. My entire being catches fire. He withdraws the hypodermic then holds me down as the muscles in my forearms and calves contract uncontrollably.

"Ayyyyy!" Inside, I'm panicking. I've never lost control of my body before. The way I've clenched my teeth, I'm doing good not to have bitten through my tongue. I want to cry or scream, but instead I black out and dream of nothing at all. Nada.

When I come to, I'm lying on Doc's exam table. Everything still hurts, but I no longer feel like I'm on fire. I've got on a new shirt. I try moving my limbs. I seem to have regained control of them. Bueno, no?

Brill's not here. Oy! Why isn't he here? "Mi vida?"

My voice rasps out in a whisper."I tout we'd lost you!" Tyson engulfs me in a reptilian embrace, pulling me up off the table. I don't think he even heard me asking for Brill. Either that, or I don't want to know where mi vida is. I hesitate to ask again. I'm used to hugs from mi amigos, but they're nothing this rough or heartfelt. Even Brill's hugs pale in comparison to Tyson's. Even though I can't breathe so well, it's kind of nice. He lets me go, then ruffles my hair. "I've never had anybody run before, not full of venom. You're eiter high hurdle brave or high hurdle stupid."

"Stupid," Doc says, closing his book. "But then again, most people are who try to play the hero. In this case, though, she's going to live. There's been some damage to her cardiovascular system, but if she's careful, she should be able to lead a normal life. Well, except for the addiction to the Invincible Heart." He shakes his head. "I've been doing some research. At least on Earth, she won't be able to get another dose."

I'm shaky, but I manage to stay upright by leaning back against the table. I make eye contact with Tyson. "Por favor. Don't take me back to Earth. I won't last long enough to *want* another dose, no? Why go through all this trouble saving me just so they can kill me publicly?"

"I had to save you because I brought you harm. Now, when I die, they will still say of me, 'His scales gleam in innocence.'" He makes a fist in front of his face.

I manage a smile at his bluster. My head's feeling a lot better. "What about the Krom kid?"

He pats mi cabeza with his ginormous hand. "I did penance for tat one, and for a few other things. My people have personal names, used only by family and close friends, tat we give ourselves when we reach te age of majority. Mine's Yalegusuri. It means penitent warrior."

"Qué? What did you do?" It must have been something bad for him to have taken that name.

Tyson ignores my question. "We've imposed on you enough, Doc." He holds out a hand to me. "Come on, Bo, it's time to go home."

I shrink back against the table. "No, por favor." My words echo Meredith's, just before that blade came slicing down. When I realize it, my heart freezes up again, and I can't form coherent sounds. I finally blurt, "Can I at least say goodbye to everyone in the galley?"

"We really could use her help." Jeska's leaning against the door frame. He can't have been standing there long. "Plelix sent me down to see if she'd be up to coming back. They're going to start serving dinner to the delegates in half an hour."

I know it's a stall, that this isn't going to end well for me no matter what I do, pero I'll savor any remaining moments of near-freedom I can get. "Let me finish what I started por favor. I promise I won't try to run, and when dinner's over, I won't beg for more time. You know I have to go with you before

Garfex gets around to executing me, no?" A horrifying thought strikes me, speeding up my recently normalized heart. "Will the guards even let me off this ship?"

"Tey have to release you to te autority you were fleeing when you stowed away."

"What happened to Brill?" I have no doubt – nada – that either Tyson arrested him, or he's left again. Both possibilities hurt my heart.

Tyson shrugs. "We had a nice talk about how he just happened to be at te scene of a major crime, where unbeknownst to him, his girlfriend was planning to sell stolen property. He seemed quite shocked, green-black eyes and everyting. So what am I going to charge him wit? He paid te fine for all tose parking tickets on te spot, and has already been judged over everyting else I know he's done." I wonder what all that is, but I'm not going to ask. Tyson tilts his head. "Unless you have someting you'd like to say? About how he forced you to commit teft? It could save your life."

I shake my head. He doesn't en serio think I'll betray mi vida, does he? "Stealing chocolate was my idea." Which is true. Brill may have talked about it, but I'm the one that decided to do it. "And if I know one Krom, is it any surprise I know others?" Which is technically not a lie, either. I just know Gavin and Zarak, not whoever those business guys were who wanted to buy the chocolate. I point at Jeska as an example.

Jeska shrugs. His iris color doesn't shift. "She knows at least three."

Tyson blinks. "I figured as much." He doesn't believe me. That doesn't matter.

Brill comes into the room, and Tyson gives him a sharp look.

"What?" Brill's drying off his face with a paper towel. His hair is wet again, like he's doused his whole head to try to wash away the evidence that he's been crying. He still hasn't gotten rid of all the glitter. "Babe, you're awake."

Tyson scrunches up his face, which is strangely flexible. "I was hoping to go before he came back. Now I'm never going to get you two parted. Fine. Stay for dinner. I'm empty food no-party blank myself. But when it's over, remember you said you won't beg."

"Sí, fairy godmother. I know I'm going to turn into a pumpkin."

Tyson looks perplexed, but Jeska snorts out a laugh. "You're the weirdest Cinderella I ever saw, su."

"Because I really don't want to go to the ball?"

"Something like that." Jeska's eyes are violet. He's laughing again, inside.

Brill doesn't seem to get the joke, but that doesn't matter. He kisses my forehead and whispers. "Don't give up, Babe. We'll think of something."

He hugs me close, prolonging the embrace until Tyson clears his throat impatiently.

CHAPTER TWENTY-SIX

As soon as we're back in the galley, nada has changed, even though I'm no longer dying. The final stages of cooking se ponen a la sexta marcha, basically *kick into sixth gear*. Jeska starts grating cheese onto the center of each of dozens of small plates. Brill helps me fill an industrial-sized mixer with cream from some unidentified Zantite mammal to go on top of the mousse chilling in the massive refrigerator. The other three guys are still chopping and stirring.

Crosskiss flings open the door and marches into the galley. "Now that everyone's here, I'm about to start my remarks officially welcoming the delegates to enjoy the recreation facilities and mess hall aboard the *Layla's Pride*. Will you be ready to start serving right after?"

"Yes, sir." Plelix gives that squiggly salute again, but he looks troubled or confused.

Crosskiss picks up on this. "Is something wrong, major?"

"No, of course not, sir." When Crosskiss raises a skeptical eyebrow, he admits, "It's just that some of your rank marks seem to be missing from your uniform."

Crosskiss glares at me, and my heart starts pounding as I remember what it felt like having his teeth scrape my back. I try to picture him with crochet hooks in his hands, but it doesn't make him any less feartastic. Finally, he turns back to Plelix. "Don't worry about that. I'll have it replaced after I address the delegates." Crosskiss eyes Brill. It's the first time he's seen mi vida since he came back from the frozen. "Shouldn't you be going back to your ship?"

Brill holds up the empty carton. "I'm helping."

"He's good in the kitchen, sir." Jeska looks serious, despite the hint of violet in his irises. "Respectfully, all us Krom are great cooks."

Hmmmm… Jeska's a good liar too.

Crosskiss, who apparently knows nada about the cultures of his subordinates, nods towards Jeska's rapidly growing line of cheese-laden plates. "So what do you have here?"

Jeska doesn't stop grating. "I'm adding final touches to fried cheesy skezer-grain polenta topped with a quick sopupousa sauce, sir."

Crosskiss taps the edge of one plate. "Why didn't you finish off this one?"

"Sir, you'll notice that the edging on that plate is green, while all the other plates have blue. The briefing made Plelix aware of Lord Zfffrrrt's dietary needs, so all his food will be served separately. The green plate contains plain unsalted polenta fried in plant-based oil instead of lard. I topped it with unseasoned, unsalted sopupousa puree."

Crosskiss picks up the plate and examines it. "Very well. Remember, everything must go perfectly. Your king's portions should be larger than the others, and he gets the scorched crust from the bottom of the lopfk and anything else that might appear special."

I hope Plelix made a lopfk, because I have no idea what that is.

Crosskiss turns towards me. "Admiral Alabaster has expressed an interest in seeing more of humanity, so I wish you to serve his table personally."

He puts the plate back on the counter and sniffs the air. "What is that foul smell?"

"That would be the ceremonial loaf, sir." Plelix takes a towel off the baked bread, and the foot-stink odor gets stronger. It's a pathetic poco loaf, but it's there, hopefully enough to save all our lives.

Crosskiss looks like he's trying not to gag. "Don't serve that. Garfex will just make me eat it." He leaves the galley quickly.

Tyson picks up a plate of polenta. "I swear on my heart, Bo, if you make me chase you again, I'll be knife shining want to go for re dead in dead in alive,"

I smile. Now that he saved my life, I kinda love the way he talks. "Where's the honor in that?"

Brill gives me a quizzical look. Is he remembering what he said a lifetime ago about honor, re-evaluating if I do understand Krom now? Or if I still don't get it, because we all know, if I get the chance, despite what I just said, I'll run? Pero, this time, he'll come with me.

"You know what I mean." Tyson glares at me, and those golden eyes freeze me to my spot. The almost uncontrollable need to pee reminds me again of how much I miss Chestla.

I place a serving tray on the counter and start stacking it with plates of polenta, Lord Zfffrrrt's first. "Don't worry. I'm half a semester away from being a certified chef, and for all I know this might be the only time I'll ever get to work in a professional kitchen."

My stomach grumbles. I should be able to keep food down now. I reach for a serving of polenta, breaking off a sauce-soaked edge and popping it into my mouth. The polenta's crisp, the cheese melty, and Jeska's coaxed an amazing amount of flavor out of canned sopupousas.

"Wow," I say, reverently. "Safea." Which is Krom for delicioso.

Jeska's eyes turn a soft blue. "You like it?"

I nod, too busy chewing to speak. I swallow. "It's almost like mi mamá's recipe."

"It is your mom's recipe, modified just a bit." Jeska picks up two more plates and adds them to the tray. "I guess we'd better get out there."

We all make our way down the hall to the ballroom and serve. Tyson trails along behind us, just being menacing. Claro. Jeska helps me again, while Brill assists Plelix, and Mertex and Varnex get partnered up on the far side of the room.

We start with Zfffrrrt. He says something in his buzzing language.

"He is thanking you for taking the extra effort to see to his needs," Admiral Alabaster says softly in Zantite.

"Please tell him that it is no trouble."

Jeska doesn't interrupt the conversation, just moves on around the table, holding the tray one-handed, serving with the other. Out of the corner of my eye, I catch sight of Tyson trying to stare disapprovingly at me while at the same time licking sauce from the plate with his reptilian tongue. He stops Plelix and takes another serving. Ay-ay-ay. I can't help but laugh.

Alabaster relays my message to his new-found ally, then smiles up at me. "Were you able to retrieve your phone from the display?"

My cheeks go hot, the laughter evaporating on my lips. I thought I had been so subtle. If I've offended him, I'm so muerta. "Sí, I did. And you didn't catch me at that part."

This time, *he* laughs. "Did *you* catch my good side in the feed?"

I say nada, just focus on keeping my hands from trembling.

"Don't look so frightened. It is natural that you want to know what is going to happen to your people, warn them if you can. I won't tell on you." Alabaster looks away from me, across the room, to where a new table has been set up for Minda Frou and her human guests. "That resolution was only the opening sakkag towards an invasion of Earth. The right representative would have a number of opportunities to change people's minds about the planet's worth well before that actually happens."

Does he mean me? No. He couldn't. Could he?

Lord Zfffrrrt opens his mouth to say something, but white foam bubbles burst forth from between his lips.

"Eeeeygah!" I cringe back in horror as the pupils of his eyes roll back, and he collapses to the floor, twitching uncontrollably. I scream as my brain starts to insist this is really happening. Alabaster unfurls his wings and flies across the table, hovering over the fallen royal. I move to try to help, but it's too late. The green guy's been poisoned. It's dissolving him from the inside out. He's stopped moving and starts deflating as the goo coming out of his mouth goes pink with blood and tissue.

Alabaster looks up at me, a question in his eyes, thankfully, instead of a direct accusation.

I take a step backwards, my heart hammering, my throat trying to close up. "I didn't... I wouldn't... I'm not a killer."

"Well, somebody sure is." Alabaster lands, facing me. His hands go to his swively hips, and I catch a glimpse of a knife handle hidden in a fold of his clothes. I am about to die after all.

Then I have a panicked thought. What if I gave Zffrrrt the wrong plate? I glance at the table and my shoulders un-tense. I point at the plate. "Mira. The rim is green. The rest are blue. I was told to give him the green one. I didn't plate it."

"Then who did?"

My breath catches. Oi, I've just implicated the galley crew. I shake my head. "I don't know. I'm thoroughly sorry."

Garfex stands up from his throne, peering from his platform out over the table. "What's going on over there?"

Admiral Alabaster draws a knife from each hip. "I demand immediate retribution for the death of my ally. I promised my wife I wouldn't kill anyone here today, so I leave it to the royal personage to do what must be done. Otherwise, I would start with this child, and work my way through your entire galley staff until the culprit confessed."

"What's that?" The delegate with the tusks picks something off Zfffrrrt's plate. "Is it a poison capsule?"

Tyson comes over and takes a look. "No, tat's a button."

Jeska leans in, hands clasped behind his back, careful not to touch the evidence. He must have put his tray down somewhere. "It looks like the ones on a general's uniform shirt pocket." When Tyson looks at him funny, Jeska adds, "When I first came aboard this ship, I worked in the laundry. After about three months, there was an opening in the kitchen, so I transferred."

I wonder who got chompcrushed to make that possible. Ay!

Crosskiss looks down. Indeed, his shirt pocket, if it ever had a button, lacks one now. He looks flustered for a moment, then he says, "I inspected the kitchen. It must have fallen off while I was looking over the food."

"Was Lord Zfffrrrt's portion plated by then?" Alabaster points to Plelix for an answer.

"I think it was. I'm pretty sure it was." Plelix looks around for confirmation. "Jeska?"

"It was. I plated all the polenta myself."

Alabaster's wings flutter out. "Then general, you have some explaining to do. Ambassador Grong just pulled that button out from under the food. It sounds more like you accidentally ripped it off getting a handful of salt out of your pocket to put at the bottom of the portion so my new ally would not notice. Turn that pocket inside out."

Crosskiss's cabeza has gone teal, but he does as requested and salt crystals tumble from the fabric.

"What is the meaning of this?" Garfex bangs his fist against his armrest. Crosskiss says nada.

"I believe I know, Your Holiness, sir, though this is going to sound a bit insane. I did not speak up before because I doubted you would believe me." Jeska closes his eyes for a long moment, as if afraid speaking up now might result in his own instant execution.

Garfex looks confused. "Well then, spit it out. There will be no judgment against you for stating your honest opinion."

"I believe that General Crosskiss poisoned Lord Zfffrrrt to force the execution of the girl who served the food to him to be pushed up, before she could die of other causes, which unbeknownst to him, have been mitigated."

Vaya. He sounds like a lawyer being played back at double speed.

"You're right, corporal." Now Garfex looks irritated. "That does sound insane. What difference would that make?"

"A great deal to you, Your Holiness, sir. When Crosskiss brought you Bo for interrogation, he knew she was suffering from a Myska bite. He had her injected with the Invincible Heart, not only to keep you from realizing she was filled with venom, but also to make her even more toxic to you." Jeska's eyes have gone that terrified pupil-obscuring black. "I warned him personally of her condition, when he was preparing to execute her after she was first found aboard."

"He intentionally tried to poison me?"

"Of course I did." Crosskiss breaks free of Tyson's grip "You married my mother then totally ignored me. Since you have no heir, our Noble law allows the queen's child to inherit. I want the throne."

Garfex looks at Layla. "You have a child?"

"You mean you didn't know?" Crosskiss goes green to the top of his head. He looks questioningly at Layla.

She blushes. "Garfie, Alex Crosskiss is my son, from my first marriage. When you asked me to marry you, I knew it wouldn't do for the king to join himself to someone who already had an heir. Alex was only three years old, so my family decided to have my sister's best friend adopt him. He was never supposed to know me, but I couldn't just let my little one go. I was like an aunt crossed with a fairy godmother. I'm afraid I spoiled him a little."

Garfex raises an eyebrow at her.

"OK, a lot." She bares her teeth. "And on his eighteenth birthday, I told him who he was."

Garfex laughs. "I wouldn't have cared. Look, Crosskiss, if that's all you want, I adopt you. If Layla ever gives me an heir, I'll probably eat you. If not, you can have the throne as long as I die of natural causes. That gives you a powerful incentive to be loyal to me. Being a prince means I'm inclined to pardon you for the unlawful murder of Lord Zfffrrrt. Bring forth the galley crew and the stowaway. They were responsible for ensuring the safety of everything produced in their kitchen. They should have checked that plate before serving it. I'm going to need some help here, so call in all the officers."

Zantite guards melt out of the tall vases, which must have been holograms. They grab us and pull us into a group at the left of Garfex's throne. I glance over at Tyson, but he's not jumping to my defense. Qué? He said they can't keep me here, unless I've broken another law. I guess allowing someone to be poisoned is on their books.

They've grabbed Brill, too, though they aren't moving him towards our group, just keeping him from rushing to join us. Plelix is both kitchen help and officer. No one moves to restrain him. He looks sadly at Jeska and Varnex. Is he really expected to help eat his friends? Is he really going to do it? Is he going to help them eat *me*?

My heart's pounding again. Plelix makes eye contact with me and I realize that he's been so kind to me, I'd forgotten what he is. Eh? How many executions has he had to participate in? I wonder if he ever ate anyone when he was a civilian, but now we're standing on opposite sides of Garfex's throne. Unless he's the one they assign to rip mi cabeza off, I'll never get to ask.

Garfex looks at each of us in turn. "You all have failed in your duty to care for the health of everyone eating your food. Furthermore one of you is a stowaway. Have you any complaints?"

Two of the guards push me forward until I'm standing close enough to Garfex to see up his nose. Ay, I guess stowaway is the greater crime.

"No!" Brill shouts. One of the guys holding him claps a hand over his mouth. My heartbeat feels like it could match mi vida's, and I hear it echoed in my ears.

I look to Jeska. Surely the diplomat will have something to say in our defense.

"Tyson," Jeska says quietly. "She needs proof of death to protect people back home. You need to be taking holo of all of this."

Tyson's eyes go wide, and he looks at me strangely. I nod.

Instead of taking out his tablet, Tyson steps closer and addresses Garfex. "But sir, even if my venom has been neutralized, she's still swimming with te Invincible Heart. Te side effects don't seem to be taking hold of her, but tey could be just as closed sleep bitten melting to you as tc symptoms Crosskiss gave it to her to cover"

Coming forward to the edge of the platform, Garfex leans toward me, his mouth gaping, his jaw still hinged in place. Claro está. I'm not grande enough for him to have to dislocate it to bite me in half. I struggle backwards against the two guards, but they keep my arms pinned solidly at my sides. I close my eyes, not wanting to see death coming.

My heart's about to pound its way out of my chest. My entire face gets wet with Zantite slobber, and goosebumps race along my limbs as I wait for the teeth to close in. Pero, they don't. I open my eyes to a close-up of Garfex's bluish tongue as he licks my face again. Pauf! I manage to squeeze them shut before he makes contact.

"She doesn't taste poisoned. My tongue would be tingling. Her body's had time to metabolize the Invincible Heart." He sticks his tongue out again to show us it's fine. I thought I'd gotten all the glitter off me, but a few flecks are stuck to his bumpy Zantite taste buds. It's custurbing.

I wipe my mouth on my shirt before I speak. "That only works for mushrooms and herbs." I cast a pleading look at the Galactacop. "Tyson! Por favor."

Tyson's face has contorted into more of a lopsided oval than a diamond as he's sucked his mouth inside itself. Now he's got his tablet out, typing something. "We're on a Zantite ship, Bo. He's well witin his rights to perform all tese executions."

"So you're just going to let him eat me? How's that justice?"

Tyson's tongue flicks out to lick his lips. "Give me a second. I'm looking someting up."

"It's no good," Brill says softly. One of the Zantites holding him looks like he's deciding whether to clamp his free hand over Brill's mouth again. "You're never going to get a Galactic Inspector to understand the difference between the spirit of the law and the letter of the law."

Shooting him a glare, Tyson steps between me and Garfex, holding up the tablet. "You can't have tis one. Tere's a prior claim tat outranks yours. She has to stand trial before te Galactic Court for crimes committed on Eart."

"Get out of my way, Inspector. I will not have my royal will challenged." I glimpse Garfex's face over Tyson's head. He doesn't look angry, merely matter-of-fact, and that makes him all the more chilling.

Tyson lengthens his spine, matching heights with the king. "You have no autority over an officer of Galactic Law. Lay a lip on my prisoner, and I will defend her venom pain melt deat-type. If you want her back after she has served whatever sentence is handed down, you may file a petition with te Galactic Court."

"That takes months, and you know a mere stowaway is not worth that much trouble. Just get her off my ship!"

Fantástica! For once I mean it.

The guards release me, and Tyson pulls me out of the way, starts to move me out of the room.

"Tyson," I whisper. "Stop. I can't just leave the others here."

"Tere's noting else we can do." He gestures for Brill to come with us. The guards release Brill, but mi vida hesitates, looking at the remaining prisoners. I love him for that.

Garfex points at Jeska. "Bring me the Krom. I understand the high iron content makes them delicious."

"Pero Jeska's got explosives in his arm," I protest.

"A Zantite knows better tan to eat tat part." Tyson tugs harder toward the door.

"Wait!" I pull my arm out of Tyson's grip – well, he lets me – and Garfex's attention turns back toward me. I swallow, my mouth suddenly dry. Ay! Too bad we drank all the yewstral.

I turn toward Alabaster and drop into a curtsey that brings me almost to the floor. I try to sound as formal and diplomat-like as I can, like the princesa-in-exile character on *Ay de mi Corazón*, which translates as *Woe is My Heart*. "Pardon my boldness, and be assured I mean no offense, but would your honor be appeased if, of all the peoples represented here, your planet was allowed to buy viable cacao beans?"

Brill's eyes go gold as he fumbles his phone out of his pocket and starts holoing me.

"Perhaps. What are your terms?"

"It is not me you may choose to bargain with, sir, but the Krom about to be executed. I gave him the cacao."

Brill lets out a startled noise, but when I look at him, he nods. He understands what it means to Jeska to get credit for this, and it fulfils his own need to clear Darcy's family name.

Alabaster curtseys. "That sounds like a rather exorbitant gift."

"Jeska is also a dear friend." As well as a hot Krom who's looking at me with sunlit affection in his eyes. I feel myself blushing. If we make it through this, I vow never to spend time alone with him. Nunca. Brill deserves my loyalty. And I'd like to live long enough to prove I'm capable of that. I have an idea that could save me, as well as the guys. "Which is why I must entreat the king. If Admiral Alabaster's honor is satisfied by the terms Corporal Hayat presents, and if I agree to go to Zant for two months to teach the royal chefs how to make all the recipes in *M.O.M. Takes the Cake*, will you spare his life, along with the lives of Major Sa and Varnex – many apologies, I never got his rank or formal name – and release them from this ship?"

"What about Mertex?" Brill asks.

Mertex was the one who nearly killed mi vida, but the Zantite does look rather pathetic with his arms pinned behind him. One of the courtiers just removed his mothball necklace. All he ever wanted was to get off this ship – well, that and a date with Minda Frou.

I smile at mi vida's generosity. "And Corporal Makanoc."

Garfex brings both hands to his chin, massaging his jaw, mulling over the proposal.

Minda Frou stands. "If Bodacious Babe Benitez comes to Zant, I'll waive my fees to film a cooking show with her, and I'll take her on a publicity tour of all the Major Fourteen."

Fourteen what? Cities? Restaurants? It doesn't matter. As much as I hate the paparazzi, I'd rather serve my time in the limelight than lose any of these guys. I nod. "Sí. Agreed."

"That one too." Minda's pointing at Mertex, of all people. "I think he'd make a cute sous chef for the female viewers."

I don't get it, but what do I know about what makes a cute Zantite?

Mertex blushes, and his mouth drops open, revealing all his feartastic teeth, but he doesn't look dangerous. He looks like a five year-old niño who just opened the best present ever.

"Fine. Whatever Minda wants, Minda gets." Garfex looks over at the actress in question, and there's affection in his huge brown eyes. Either he's a fan, or maybe there was once something between them. Either way, Layla doesn't seem bothered by her husband's show of afecto to this other woman. "If..." Garfex stops and clears his throat. "If Admiral Alabaster is satisfied. The last thing I need right now is to go to war with the Nilka." He starts to leave the throne, then sits back down. "And if someone gets me more cake. I skipped dessert preparing for these non-executions."

While Jeska and Admiral Alabaster talk quietly, Brill and I sit together at a small table. He's got one of my hands in his, like he's afraid to let me go, even for un segundo. We're both hoping that if this works, I'll be too valuable in front of the cameras to wind up on the teeter totter. That alone is worth the trip to Zant.

"You know," I tell him, "I like the brown leather on you better than the black."

"I do too." Brill straightens the open zipper. "Jack's got good taste, if nothing else. And his second did tell me where Gavin was with enough time for me to put in a rescue call."

"How is Gav?" I shake my head. "Nope. Nunca. That just sounds wrong."

Brill laughs. "He's sleeping off a monster headache, but he's going to be fine. He tried to send us a distress call, but we missed it."

"Qué?"

"Number forty-seven on Kayla's reading list was *Kidnapped* by Robert Louis Stevenson."

"So he didn't read all those books?"

Brill blinks. "Forty-seven books in less than two months? Krom move fast, but that doesn't mean we can read at that rate."

I feel my shoulders unknot more than I thought they would. I guess in the background of it all, I had been worried about Gavin, even if I wouldn't let myself admit it. "Pero now that he's safe, does that mean I can mess with him about being bested by a bunch of human pirates?" The look Brill gives me makes me laugh. "Too soon, maybe?"

We lapse into silence.

Brill's eyes take on a sudden tint of lavender.

I point my fork at him. "What's so funny?"

"I was just thinking about how upset you got when I wanted to buy you your freedom, and now, you just basically bought those guys."

"That's different…" I start to say, but is it, really? I laugh. "You're right. But isn't that what makes us perfect for each other?"

"Hey," Mertex says, "you guys have got to see this." At least it's a break from him saying thank you like the last dozen times. I think he's decided that Brill is litoll for saving his life, and he's been about one step away from asking for his autograph. We follow him into the hallway, where the furniture from the entire sleeping cabin of Brill's ship has been reassembled. In the center of the set-up, somebody's put the chocolate fountain, flowing with HGB dark, surrounded with fruit and marshmallows and cake bits. Mertex cuts his gaze over at Brill, looking nervously for his reaction.

Brill busts out laughing. "By the Codex, Mertex, did you have something to do with this?"

"A little. Plelix asked me to help. He called it one last practical joke for the road." Mertex blushes green. "The guys said you wouldn't be mad. Jeska said you'd expect it."

I put a hand on Mertex's arm. "I think you're finally developing a sense of humor. That's muy fabuloso."

He blinks. "Is muy fabuloso a good thing?"

"Yes." Brill shakes his cabeza at the old ratty comforter on his bunk. "Just make sure all this gets put back in my ship. Including that." He points at the chocolate fountain.

Tyson rushes into the hallway, notices us all standing there and visibly relaxes. He needn't have worried. I can't flitdash now. Not after making a promise that will save lives instead of threatening them. Almost as if Frank's heard my thoughts, my handheld rings. Ay, no. What else is he going to threaten me with?

"So I take it you're coming home," Frank says without preamble.

"It looks like it, right?" Though I'm still terrified of what's going to happen when I get there.

"It looks like you're going to be the face of chocolate after all. The feeds just blew up with clips of that holo you sent, and apparently the Bodacious Babe who's willing to go to Zant to save Earth has become something of an instant folk hero. Check the polls."

I blink, confused. I'd assumed that information would be kept top secret. "How'd that happen?"

"I may have leaked it to some FeedCasters I know." Frank pauses. "That should keep you safe for a while."

I sigh into the phone. "I know I've bought myself some time, but what happens after I get back from Zant? I don't know how this works. Am I going to find you in my room one night with a silencer on your gun?"

"If I was planning that, why would I have leaked those feeds?" Now *he* sounds confused. "For what it's worth, I'm proud of you, Bo."

"I'm proud of you too, Babe," Brill says as I hang up the call. We go back into the ballroom.

Jeska approaches our table. He pulls me to my feet and hugs me close. His chest is solid and warm. Definitely not spending any time alone with this guy. "You've not only saved my life, you've given it back to me. Who says you're not a born diplomat?"

He releases me from the hug, and I take a step backward.

I'm sure my blush is as neon as Krom eyes when they lie. "So I take it the negotiations went well, chico?"

"I even managed to retain eight of the beans, to attempt to start a cacao plantation on Krom. Assuming we will split the profit three ways, I'd like to use a large chunk registering cacao as an official commodity, and seeing if I can't make a go out of getting the beans to grow."

Brill stands and puts an arm around my shoulders. "That's great, Jess."

I take Brill's hand, but also address Jeska. "What about the restaurant you wanted to open?"

"A novelty like a cacao grove is bound to draw in tourists. Who may want to visit an on-site café." He shrugs. "I don't know. Just an idea. Right now, I'm a bit overwhelmed with having a future."

One of the guards approaches. "If you could please come with us, Corporal Hayat." The guy grins. "I mean Mr Hayat, Jeska. We're supposed to accompany you and Alabaster to your quarters to ensure the safe exchange of your beans. Then you can join Plelix and the others down at Doc's office to get the charge cylinder removed from your tracker." In a lower voice he adds, "You lucky spwevet."

As Jeska walks out of the room surrounded by the four guards and Admiral Alabaster, Brill catches my eye. "Promise me you won't go to his room to help him pack."

"Never, mi vida." I kiss him. When our lips part, I ask, "So are you coming with me to Zant?"

"You know I'm always up for an adventure." Brill rests his hand on my cheek. "Besides, su, I've never been there."

"After she gets te rest of her legal problems sorted out." Tyson puts a hand on my shoulder. "Come on, Bo, it's time to go."

I turn to Brill. "Are you going to follow us?"

Garfex clears his throat and moves to block our path. "You're not leaving just yet, are you? We haven't had our dance. I want to hear your other objection."

I swallow, trying to find enough spit in my mouth to talk. How can he sound so civil when half an hour ago, he was trying to chompcrush me? The same guards who recently restrained us are now rearranging the furniture, moving tables to the sides of the room to open the dance floor in the middle. A live band starts setting up in the area formerly occupied by Garfex's throne.

"Lo siento, I don't know any Zantite dances."

"Don't worry. I lead excellently."

I look to Tyson. "Didn't you say I turned into a pumpkin at the end of dinner?"

"I still do not understand tat reference, but circumstances being what tey are, I would not begrudge His Majesty a dance in exchange for his cooperation."

Queen Layla walks up and grabs Tyson's hand. "In that case, I claim you for the first nogkvek."

He's not laughing now.

I only come halfway up Garfex's chest, which makes dancing awkward, but considering that, he does lead well. After we have been dancing long enough for me to catch the rhythm of the music, he tilts his head down. I manage not to flinch, though I can feel his breath as he speaks. "Tell me, Bo. What should have been your objection?"

I try to ignore his teeth being so near to my face. "Ay, I object to you invading my planet. It may have issues, but I've met a number of your subjects, and your planet has issues too, no?"

Garfex sweeps me into a dramatic dip, which gives me a terrifying close-up of his smile. "That is one objection I will take under consideration." He straightens me up. "Oh dear, the song is ending already. It looks as though your young man would like to dance with you. Seeing you together makes me glad I didn't eat you. Congratulations on your brilliant diplomacy."

"Gracias. I mean, thank you."

He spins me out of his arms and into Brill's. Brill catches me. He leads me out onto the floor with a surety I've never felt from him when we danced before.

"Mi vida, you've been holding out on me."

He twirls me, and when I come back close against his chest, he says, "After I saw that holo of you and that – after I saw you dancing, I realized what it meant to you, and I may have taken a couple of lessons. Although, if you think that's dorky, then it definitely didn't happen."

"Earlier, when you said you felt like you needed to give me a gift." I look up into his eyes. "You didn't realize that you'd already done it."

"I don't know, Babe. I like the perfume on you. It makes you just that much more bodacious."

EPILOGUE
Six Weeks Later – Rio de Janeiro, Benítez Home

Brill and Mario are sitting together on the couch at Mario's house, watching soccer. Brill's really making an effort to bond with mi familia. He's even wearing a Brazil National Team jersey. It's not just show. He's become a real fan of soccer. Mamá and Mario's wife are in the backyard with the girls practicing their dance moves, and I've come inside to fix everyone a snack. Today's been one of my good days, the withdrawal from the Invincible Heart almost not noticeable, except as a tiny tremor in my hands. HGB managed to keep my drug addiction out of the feeds, so few people know what I've been through these past weeks. Mario and Mamá don't even know, and they're right here.

I've just dropped a plate of nachos and meatballs on the table for the guys when the doorbell rings. I answer it to find Frank standing there, both hands behind his back. My chest goes cold. He promised he wasn't going to kill me. I can't breathe. Dios mío! I thought he kept his promises.

When Brill sees him, mi vida dashes over and pushes me back behind the door, out of the line of fire. He's moving so fast, it takes me a second to process what just happened.

Mario stands up. "What are you doing here?"

Frank holds out the largest bouquet of gerbera daisies I've ever seen. "I want to apologize to your mother."

I suck in a shocked breath. But the tension in my chest uncoils. I move around Brill, who rests a hand on my shoulder.

"Frisk him for weapons, Babe, before you let him in."

I scrunch up my nose. "Eww… you do it, mi vida."

"I'll do it myself." Frank hands me the flowers, takes two guns and a knife off his person and places them on the coffee table. I study the weapons, wondering just how this man killed my father, what final words Papá said at the end. I don't think I'm going to ask him. Not now, nada nunca. I don't think I want to know.

Mario's jaw drops open. Frank takes one of Mario's hands in both of his for a hearty handshake, traditional sign of peace. "You have to believe that when it came right down to it, I wouldn't have been able to hurt your mother. She'd become so much more than just an assignment at that point."

I snort out a laugh. "Try convincing Mamá of that, no? She's been burning holographic holes in all the pictures of you two, to blank out your face."

Frank blushes. "I suppose I deserve that. I had hoped you would have left for Zant by now, instead of being here to poison her against me."

"Poison's not exactly my style either, viejo." I drop my voice low, so Mario won't hear. "You tell her the truth about mi papá and apologize for that too, or I'm going to tell her myself the minute you leave."

Frank nods. "That sounds reasonable. Do you think she'll forgive me?"

There's much hope in his face.

I gasp. "You're still in love with her." He has to realize that chances are slim that Mamá will want to be with the man who murdered Papá, but she's Mamá Lavonda, un poco larger than life and all heart. It's possible she'll eventually forgive him… if he grovels. If he earns it. He did help save my life, when it came right down to it.

A dog barks from outside the half-open door. A corgi bounds into the room and sploots onto the floor at Frank's feet. It proceeds to lick at the back of his shoe.

"Is that...?"

"Botas. Yes." He smiles down at the dog. "I just couldn't bear the thought of someone adopting him as an execution souvenir. He deserves better than that."

"But does he deserve you?" I ask.

Frank shrugs. "I've always been good with dogs."

Brill resumes his spot on the couch. He's half watching the game when he says, "Kaliel and Kayla are coming with us to Zant."

Even without testimony of the mercenaries, there had been enough evidence to get Kaliel exonerated – though his publicity rating is still crashbombed, in part because the Global Court sealed the evidence about the tainted chocolate. The chocolate is still there, though, stuck in the rainforest with Chestla. We'll probably never know who sent it, or who wanted that SeniorLeisure ship blown up. But like Gavin said, some mysteries are safer unsolved.

"And your friend Chestla?" Frank's frowning, maybe at the memory of being frozen inside her predatory gaze. "What are you doing about her?"

I raise an eyebrow at Frank, not sure how much is safe to say. "What makes you think she's even still on this planet?"

Frank frowns. "Because I got a phone call from her embassy. Someone..." he eyes Brill, "gave them my name."

Brill makes a shruggy gesture that means *what?* pero then he says, "Chestla would like to continue her research in the rainforest. But I doubt your HGB will give her a visitor's permit to poke around in their secrets, will they?"

Frank laughs. "The borders have only opened a crack. You of all people should know how hard those passes are to get. Chestla can't stay there indefinitely. But this embassy thing complicates my options."

I put a hand on Brill's shoulder, trying not to think what options Frank has left. I need the support. The IH residue shakes get worse when I'm stressed. I change the subject. "Pero, like, V messaged me that General Crosskiss got a visitor's permit. Apparently, after what Crosswalk said about shaved ice, they're eager to let him try one from whatever country he wants."

"You're doing the whole nickname thing again. Have you been talking to Jeska?" Brill's eyes tell me he's still un poco jealous.

"Not individually, mi vida. He just sends out weekly blasts about how the plantation on Krom is doing. I'm surprised you don't get them. You're on the list, no?"

"Just because I get them doesn't mean I read them."

"According to V, Jeska's quite the eligible bachelor now in your hometown. I just hope he finds a girl he can start a family with, not someone who's just after his moment of fame." I squeeze Brill's shoulder, belatedly realizing how much that sounded like I wasn't really talking about Jeska. But either Brill doesn't notice, or he lets it go. For now.

Mamá comes in, an empty pitcher in her hand. "Bo, the girls want more lemonade." She hesitates when she sees Frank, and he moves over to talk to her. She slaps him across the face, which is actually a good sign, from his point of view. If she was truly done with him, she'd have stalked back outside. But when he gets honest, it's going to get feo.

My handheld registers a holocall. It's from Chestla. I look over at Frank, then duck into the hall, where Frank and Mamá can't see me from the kitchen.

Chestla's down in the underground lab again. Before she can speak, I hold a finger to my lips. "Frank's here, chica, so speak softly."

Her eyes go wide. "Do you need an escape plan? There's this one kick I can teach you over–"

"Tranquila!" I'm whispering pretty loudly. "He comes in peace. I think. Qué pasa?"

"You need to get down here and see this vial of green liquid we found. The chemical comp test came back weird."

"You could send us the stats on that over the phone, no?"

Chestla sighs. "I know. But I am going absolutely cjingdeka without people to talk to. Eugene's all about analyzing this stuff right now. I don't think he even realizes there's a girl in his lab." She holds up a remote. "Besides, I've been cobbling together a couple of hours' worth of holo of that black ship. It could make for some pretty interesting viewing."

It sounds like she's proposing a girl's night – in a secret lab in a forbidden rainforest. To look for mercenary spacejacker pirates. "I told you, Brill promised Gavin we would leave that ship alone."

Chestla rolls her eyes. "How long have you known me, Bo?"

"Three years."

"And in all that time, have you ever seen me give up on a puzzle?"

I think back. Whether it was the weekly campus word search, or the faculty-vs-students scavenger hunt, she'd always finished unraveling things, even if she didn't come in first. "No y no," I say sadly. "Nunca. Pero, it's going to be impossible for us to get back into the rainforest. Just like we haven't been able to smuggle you out, no?"

"Tell Brill it's about the green liquid, and I'm sure he will find a way to get you guys in here. That stuff's super weird."

"I'm not going to lie to him, chica."

"Then just lead with that."

I lean around the corner and sneak a look at Mario. We've been getting along so much better lately, partly because I keep thinking about how Jeska never got a chance to make up with Darcy. I don't have the heart to tell mi hermano he may well need a revised edition of his bestselling book.

Brill comes around the corner. He raises an eyebrow at Chestla. "Everything OK here?"

"Tell him, Bo," Chestla says.

I hang up the handheld. I wrap my arms around Brill and whisper, "I hear you're always ready for an adventure, mi vida."

ACKNOWLEDGMENTS

First off, thanks to Jake for reading this manuscript so many times, and reassuring me you loved it more every time. You know most of the jokes in here, I wrote for you.

Thanks Cassie, Monica and Tessa (in alphabetical order – you girls know I could never choose between you) for listening to my rants and fiction-related crises – and being there whenever one of my characters dies. Even when you don't understand. You guys are the best non-writer friends a writer could have. There are pieces of all of us in these characters, but the best parts of Bo come from you three.

Thanks Mom and Dad, for taking me to that first writer's group so long ago, and never giving up the belief that eventually, with enough persistence, you'd be holding one of my books in your hands. Finally, here you go.

Thanks to my lovely agent, Jennie Goloboy, for believing in me, and to Angry Robot's Mike Underwood for taking a chance on this quirky little book.

In fact, thanks to the whole cyber-hearted Robot crew – especially Phil Jourdan, who encouraged me to just tell this story as it needed to be told. And Paul Simpson, copyeditor extraordinaire, who made sure nobody knows that I don't know the difference between *hoard* and *horde* – oh, wait.

I can't forget Sue Burke, the Spanish translator who fixed my shaky Spanish grammar, and my friend Jasmine, who double-checked my use of Mexican Spanish. After all these careful eyes, any remaining errors are my own.

As they say, it takes a community to raise a writer. So many people have been kind and encouraging to me over the years, it would take a chapter instead of just a page to thank them all. So thank you, all. I do want to mention the Denton Writers' Critique Group, who helped me shape the opening pages of this book. Also the members of the Saturday Night Write Discussion Group, who have been some of my biggest cheerleaders.

And thank you, dear reader, for choosing the Chocoverse to spend your time in. I hope you enjoyed it. See you soon for Book 2 – *Pure Chocolate*.

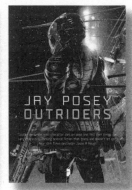
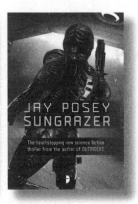

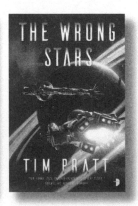

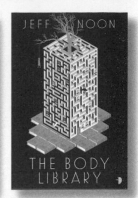

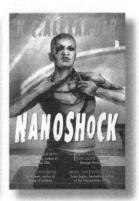
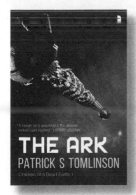
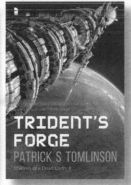

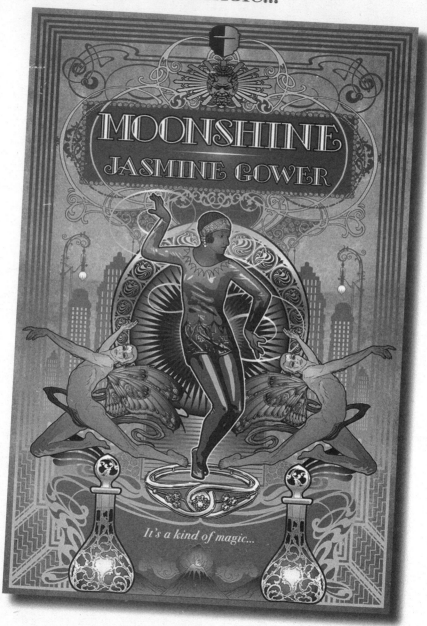

MOONSHINE
JASMINE GOWER

It's a kind of magic...